Alan White is the author of several best-selling novels, including *Death Finds the Day* (filmed as *A Long Day's Dying*), *Fathom, Crash Landing* and a series of suspense novels. *Ravenswyke* is set in his native Yorkshire. He travels widely, spending part of each year in England and part on the island of Crete.

Also by Alan White

The Long Day's Dying
The Long Drop
Crash Landing
Fathom
The Long Fuse
The Long Hand of Death
The Long Silence
The Long Summer

Alan White

Ravenswyke

A MAYFLOWER BOOK

GRANADA
London Toronto Sydney New York

Published by Granada Publishing Limited in 1981

ISBN 0 583 13231 6

First published in Great Britain by
Hutchinson & Co. (Publishers) Ltd 1980
Copyright © Alan White 1980

Granada Publishing Limited
Frogmore, St Albans, Herts AL2 2NF
and
3 Upper James Street, London W1R 4BP
866 United Nations Plaza, New York, NY 10017, USA
117 York Street, Sydney, NSW 2000, Australia
100 Skyway Avenue, Rexdale, Ontario, M9W 3A6, Canada
PO Box 84165, Greenside, 2034 Johannesburg, South Africa
61 Beach Road, Auckland, New Zealand

Reproduced, printed and bound in Great Britain by
Cox & Wyman Ltd, Reading
Set in Intertype Times

Granada ®
Granada Publishing ®

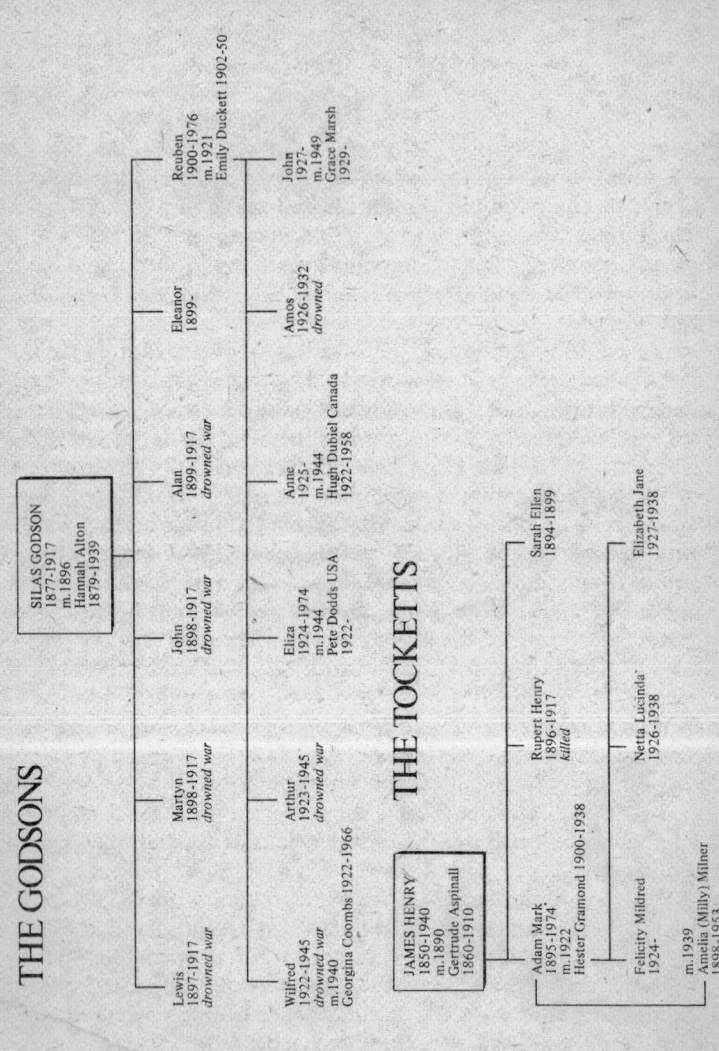

THE GODSONS

SILAS GODSON
1877-1917
m.1896
Hannah Alton
1879-1939

Lewis
1897-1917
drowned war

Martyn
1898-1917
drowned war

Wilfred
1922-1945
drowned war
m.1940
Georgina Coombs 1922-1966

John
1898-1917
drowned war

Alan
1899-1917
drowned war

Eleanor
1899-

Reuben
1900-1976
m.1921
Emily Duckett 1902-50

Arthur
1923-1945
drowned war

Eliza
1924-1974
m.1944
Pete Dodds USA
1922-

Anne
1925-
m.1944
Hugh Dubiel Canada
1922-1958

Amos
1926-1932
drowned

John
1927-
m.1949
Grace Marsh
1929-

THE TOCKETTS

JAMES HENRY
1850-1940
m.1890
Gertrude Aspinall
1860-1910

Adam Mark
1895-1974
m.1922
Hester Gramond 1900-1938

Rupert Henry
1896-1917
killed

Sarah Ellen
1894-1899

m.1939
Amelia (Milly) Milner
1898-1953

Felicity Mildred
1924-

Netta Lucinda
1926-1938

Elizabeth Jane
1927-1938

PART ONE

Reuben Godson sat at the stern of the coble, the handle of the tiller clasped firm in his hand, the lugsail already up and pulling. The coble surged along with ripples sounding under the bow in the gurgle he had come to know and love so well, crouching in the bows, watching his dad and his brothers handling the *Hope of Ravenswyke*.

When he left the mooring, gulls had flown overhead from their nests on the rooftops of Ravenswyke, cawking at him as if chiding him for being late. It was already half-past six in the morning; the sea was lead-green with no separation between the horizon of the ocean and the sky above. A light offshore wind filled the canvas of the sail spread wide, and the bow dipped under its force; he looked back over his shoulder and saw the Pitt brothers struggling with their coble, the *Jolly Lads*, easing it slowly down the tallowed planks of the slip to the horse team waiting on the scaurs below. Nellie was holding the bridle of Champion, the leading horse.

Reuben'd have the laugh on 'em when they came back on the tide. 'It'll blow up, mark my words,' Sam Pitt said when they dragged the *Jolly Lads* out of the water the previous evening. Reuben laughed and left the *Hope* out on its mooring all night. And then paid for his bravery and foolhardiness by spending half the night at his bedroom window watching the weather.

'If your dad was about he'd tan your hide for that,' Sam Pitt had said. 'You've no call to go risking your dad's boat when he's away to war!'

Sam's use of the word 'war' had caused him to rub the twisted leg that kept him out of the Green Howards; it was a well-known secret he'd walked across the moors to Pickering to enlist but, with his left leg bowed where it had mended badly after three multiple fractures when the first *Jolly Lads* had been wrecked off Ness Point, not even a recruiting sergeant desperate for men would give him the King's shilling.

7

Reuben chuckled as he saw them struggle to pull the coble and its sled straight on the scaurs at the bottom of the slip, the three draught-horses patiently waiting for the hook to be dropped in the ring of the trace. Steam rose from their nostrils in the cold morning air. Champion pawed restlessly at the black slate of the scaurs. It didn't matter, did it, who was first away; it wasn't a race, as Silas Godson, Reuben's dad, had so often said. But always, as the Godson brothers Lewis and Martyn, John and Alan, with Reuben and his sister Eleanor holding the heads of the horses, had striven to be away, the thought of being beaten into the water by the Pitt brothers or the Naseby family had been like a red rag to a bull. And, to tell the truth, there'd often been a twinkle in Silas's eyes as they'd bent to the oars, the first away. 'It's not a race, lads,' he'd repeat, but you could see the pleasure and fatherly pride in that twinkle and know that once again the Godsons of Ravenswyke had led the way.

Now that Silas and the brothers were all away fighting the war that was certain, so they said, to end all wars, Reuben was more than ever determined that, though he was too young to fight, he was old enough to keep the *Hope* where it belonged, out in front, first to take the waves and water, last to come back to beach, with the biggest catch. Because that was the way it had always been. In Ravenswyke the Godsons counted for something. First out, last in, with the most: that counted for something. Reuben's father Silas, his father before him, his grandfather, in an unbroken line that went back to the fifteenth century and beyond – the line was recorded only to 1420 when the cottage in Old Quaytown had been built and the first name had been carved into the ship's timber that ran the length of the main room. The names of all the heads of the Godson family followed down the ages, an endless and unbroken line. Reuben had no hope his name would ever be carved there; with four older brothers he'd never take over the Godson cottage or the *Hope*. When his time came to marry and settle down to family life, no doubt another extension would be built up the hill, and there he'd take his bride just as the younger sons had always done. Now the cottage had three bedrooms all on different levels, climbing up the steep cliff-side, and the private lavatory with running water was something not many Old Quaytown families could boast.

Lewis, the eldest son, was twenty and courting; when Silas

passed on, Lewis would come back from the funeral with the woodcarver and his name would go up on the beam. He and his wife would move into the front bedroom overlooking the street, and Hannah, Silas's wife, would move into the backs, as always happened. That was the natural order of things, the traditional way, and Reuben felt a glow of pride at the knowledge that, aged sixteen in this year of grace 1916, he was the only male left at home to keep these traditions alive.

Morning light glinted off the windows of Old Quaytown, turning the stone to the early-morning amber Reuben so loved. Smoke was already wisping strongly from the roofs of the houses and the boat-building shed near the mouth of the Cut, rising slowly, spreading out to sea as if pushing the cobles before it. Reuben tightened the lugsail sheet as he headed the coble south by south-east ten degrees off the point known as the Cliff, where the turrets of Tockett House broke the skyline. No smoke coming out of any of their chimneys, he thought, and mentally added, 'Lie-abed lot!' To stay in bed in the mornings was a mark of decadence, of riches ill-used!

The wind was freshening as the horizon cleared and the top of the sea began to roll. A squadron of gulls took off from the point below the cliffs, and when Reuben followed their flight he saw spray churning the surface of the water about a quarter of a mile out. He checked the line curled round the inside of the wickerwork basket. Eleanor had baited and laid it well; when he dropped the weighted end, the line would run while he flicked the hooks one-handed, faster than the eye could follow, off the basket's rim.

The air had taken on the colour of green bottle glass; in five hours, give or take an hour, the storm Sam had predicted last evening would arrive. There'd be no question of leaving the coble on its mooring tonight; it'd be a hard pull across the scaurs and back up the slip, with not many hands left in Ravenswyke to help. Not like the pre-war days when every coble would be seized by twenty hands and voices would shout advice as shoulders heaved, arms braced. Above all there would be the smell of the sweating horses and the tang of weed, waves and salt-crusted tackle.

The Pitt family were heading due east and Reuben smiled to himself. Sam had always been a stubborn deep fisherman, keeping his eyes on the horizon, often missing the signs closer inshore. They'd hoisted the lugsail on the *Jolly Lads* and that awkward-looking triangle on the improvised mizzen-mast; they'd need to strike that before they could start lining. But Sam would never be told; he thought of himself as a rigger, a man with a unique know-ledge of boats and sails. Damn it, sometimes the *Jolly Lads* went off looking like a Christmas tree! Reuben watched it screwing across the waves, the mizzen pulling the stern sideways, the for'ard lug righting it again. It was like fat Annie when she tried dancing, and her bosom and hips swung in different directions. Funny devil, old Sam Pitt; a stubborn cuss who thought he knew it all and wouldn't listen to any of the younger ones. That mizzen was holding him back, not shoving him forward. Reuben could imagine the lads had already asked Sam to strike it, but he knew they wouldn't get him to change his mind.

The *Hope* was forging along, sitting comfortably on the heaving waves, holding a straight line with effortless ease. Reuben looked around it, still not comfortable with his great responsibility. For months there had been warnings against fishing. U-boats were active in the North Sea, especially off this stretch of coast where they could lie on sandy patches. Whitby and Scarborough had been shelled from the sea, and mines laid. The inshore trawlers had proved suitable for mine-lifting and many had already been sunk in that dangerous work, Joe Higham from Old Quaytown, and Roger Smailes from Newquay Town already among the victims. Well, Reuben had a surprise or two waiting if anyone came near *his* boat!

The Germans had sunk the *Florence Nightingale* and the *Edith Cavell*, the twenty-one-tonner that had been named after a British nurse, the matron of a clinic in Belgium. They'd even executed her for helping British soldiers to escape. The *Hope of Ravenswyke* was certainly no twenty-one-tonner, but Reuben had a few tricks up his sleeve, if and when they came.

The rising wind had blown away the last traces of sea-fret and the hills above Ravenswyke were clearly defined in the cold November morning light, the fields stripped of wheat in scarred slashes against the autumnal green of the watered grass. Sheep would do well this winter if the weather stayed as mild as it had been since the end of the summer. As Reuben's eye made his inventory of the bay, his hands checked the lie of the line in the basket, testing the baited hooks on which the livelihood of his family depended. Yes, Eleanor *had* done a good job; the gobs of mussel were stuck firm around the barbs. He hardened the lugsail and headed the boat into the wind and waves. With the lugsail hard and tightened, the boat slowed. He slipped a tie over the tiller, checked to make sure the boat was holding into the wind along the south-south-east line. The *Hope* was a well-balanced boat and took each wave squarely and firm, yawing neither to right nor left. Reuben smiled, tapped the tiller taut against its tie, and the tiller sprang back to centre again, holding firm.

Now it was time to fish. Reuben licked his lips, tasting their saltiness, in anticipation of it. Though the procedures were the same, each time the same thrill of anticipation ran through him. He crouched to the side of the basket, which he'd dragged into the gunwale. He picked up the weight and cast it in the smooth motion Silas had shown him so many times, taking a couple of fathoms of line along a short smooth arc that cleared the boat. He watched the weight plop into the water and already his finger was in the bend of the first hook around the rim of the basket, flicking it out of the straw. The hook lifted clean and was pulled out of the boat over the gunwale, clearing the wood by half an inch. The first time Reuben had tried it, the hooks had flown high into the air, many falling short on their pinched arc, jamming into the boat's edge. Silas had laughed and freed each one with a deft flick. But he hadn't laughed when one had stuck in his hand and ripped out a chunk of flesh that could have been replaced by a broad bean.

Reuben's finger had already found and flicked the second hook, then the third, allowing the line to fall down through the water without pause and without snags, snaking from the basket in one smooth run.

As he worked, he checked his position, lining the edge of the Batts with the corner of a distant field. As he had expected, the *Hope* was drifting neatly on one straight course; this was the tricky time, for if the direction varied the line could wrap itself round the tiller, even the rudder below; the hooks would snag, the bait would be stripped, and he'd waste hours getting the mess sorted out.

The wind had freshened considerably and the waves were now breasting three and four feet, canting the boat with each swell, lifting the bow and snapping it down again. The *Hope* rode well – not like the *Jolly Lads* with that bloody mizzen, Reuben thought.

Twenty hooks over, twenty fathoms of line, and thirty more to go on this run. Reuben's hands were cold but he was used to that. At least his feet were warm in his dad's leather boots with three pairs of socks. And his back warm under the three guernseys his brothers wouldn't be needing until they returned home from the war. But, damn, his hands *were* cold, and sea spray stung the cut on the back of his knuckle where a hook had ripped him the previous day. He lifted his knuckle and sucked it, using one hand only to locate each hook and flip it just as the hissing line tensed to yark it off the coil.

Forty fathoms down. Forty hooks, and only ten to go.

He checked the line where it hung from the side of the basket, making certain it was fastened to the centre post. He could still hear the curses, feel the shame, when he dropped the fifty fathoms of new line that time, with the fifty new hooks, because he'd forgotten to tie back the end. The entire line disappeared, lost without hope of recovery. 'Good mind to send thee down to look for it,' Silas had growled. They'd tried dredging the bottom but then, to confound matters further, had snagged the line and had had to cut it away with two dredging hooks before they'd given up. Reuben could still feel the shock of Silas's hand smashing without mercy across his face, splintering one of his teeth. He could still suck the broken edge of that tooth and remember.

You'd have thought that would have taught him, but no lesson is ever learned right the first time and, when Reuben had thrown over the kedge anchor without checking first that the end was fast on the bowpost, Silas had almost exploded. He hadn't waited for them to get back inshore; he'd dragged Reuben amidships, had made him pull down his trousers exposing his backside to the biting sea air and had leathered him unmercifully until the skin was broken and Reuben had lain, blubbering his eyes out in the scuppers. That had taught him – it was the last time he'd forgotten to secure the end of a line. He could still feel the weight of that salt-encrusted leather belt on his arse.

Fifty fathoms out and down and the line holding firm. He checked the angle of drift, the tied tiller and the strangled sail holding the *Hope* steady into the wind. As ever he felt impatient to start hauling the line immediately, but how many times had Silas told him 'Let it ride, let it ride'? Of course, some of 'em would put a float on the end of the line, go away and lay another before coming back to haul in the first. But Silas had taught him to have confidence. 'If the spot is right where you've shot your line, there's no need of leaving it and trying somewhere else.'

With the line down they'd squat in the boat, take out the snap, smoke a cigarette they'd hand-rolled, or, in Lewis's case, light the pipe he'd taken to puffing. There wouldn't be much talk – fishermen don't go in for much of that – no matter how much Reuben would try to provoke them into yarning to him. He'd walk round the boat checking the lines, unable to leave the rigging alone.

'Have thee done, then?' his father would say eventually, with that lovely twinkle in his eye. 'Because if thee've done, we can start yarking it in.'

That would be the signal for them to start the haul.

Reuben, the youngest on board, grabbed the line by the post and started the long haul in. Fifty fathoms of well-hooked line is a long haul, too long for a lad in his teens, but in a sense the yarn twisting through his fingers became a talisman on which he counted the years of his manhood. Even from the start, however, it was a point of honour with the Godsons that, when you started a haul, you carried it on despite the arm ache, the long pull, the agony of your hands, until the first fish was over the gunwale and inboard. It could be five fathoms, ten, even twenty, with your arms being pulled fair out of their sockets as you braced your foot against the leeboard and hauled, praying the next bloody hook over the side would be the one carrying your fish. At first you'd be praying for the big one. 'Let me pull in a cod, a bloody great three-foot cod,' you'd say. 'Or a haddock, by Christ.' Reuben's biggest, off the Batts, had gone forty-one inches, and for a week he'd been the hero of Ravenswyke.

But, as you pulled and pulled, heaving and hauling that sodding heavy line, the size of the fish you wanted would gradually shrink until, in the end, you'd be more than happy with a mackerel sprat, a tiddler!

Reuben checked the lashing of the helm. No brothers to help him this morning no matter how long the line, however many fish on it adding to its weight and drag in the slow drift. He started the haul with a foot braced against the leeboard; each haul must be exactly the same length if the line were to relay itself neatly in the basket as he brought it in. Some people hauled in the line anyhow – then had to mess about unravelling it. That had never been the Godson way or, give 'em credit, the way of the *Jolly Lads*. 'In the boat, in the basket!' had always been Silas's motto. It took skill and precision to haul in a line with the *Hope* bucketing about as it now was, with a veering wind thrumming in the tightened lugsail threatening a turnabout that could, in extreme weather, flip the boat over.

Five fathoms in and coiled. The bait had been eaten and that was a good sign. Where there's small fish to steal the bait, Reuben thought, there'll be bigger buggers further down waiting to cannibalize them. It's the law of the sea. Ten fathoms in came the first bite. He thrilled when he saw the silver flash in the water and knew the next heave would bring one inboard.

Aye, with his brothers aboard, it'd have meant the end of hauling for Reuben, though not the end of work of course.

Could be a cod, a codling, a sole worth something, a haddock, even a halibut. They'd caught halibut off Ravenswyke. They regularly caught salmon escaping from the mouth of the Wyke by the Ravenswyke Cut. The familiar shiver of anticipation ran through him. Now his hands didn't feel cold, and he'd lost the bite of the cut on his knuckle. His whole being was centred on that silver flash below as he changed hands, holding the line with his left, braced firm, reached down with his right for the mallet and hung it from the rope looped around his waist.

Right hand forward on the line keeping the same measured distance and then with a slow heave, smooth pull – 'not a jerk, dammit!' as Silas used to roar – he brought the fish inboard. Nice one. Good for a first. It'd go twenty pounds. Very nice.

Line held down, left hand keeps it taut; two turns round the post to secure it as his right hand reached instinctively for the mallet and stroked firmly, knowing where to hit. The fish stopped its flopping, twitched once, and lay still. Reuben let the mallet hang, picked up the fish and spun it into the centre of the basket so that the line coiled, stripped the line from the holding post, and carried on with the haul.

If the brothers had been there it would have been Reuben's job to use the mallet while John or Alan, whoever wasn't hauling, would have been bending over the basket, taking the fish off the hook, throwing them to Martyn, who'd be gutting them, tossing the guts quickly over the stern, where the gulls would already be wheeling and cawking in hungry anticipation.

Most fishermen didn't bother to gut the fish they caught, but that was never the Godson way, until the lads went to war and Reuben was left on his own to haul in the line.

No gulls followed Reuben, as if they knew he didn't have time to make breakfast for them.

He hauled in a disappointing total of three fish, all codling. Two went fifteen pounds each and the other twenty. He untied the end of the line from the post, lifted it with the basket and stowed it forward still carrying its catch of fish.

Three bloody codling, eh? He was glad Silas wasn't there to see it. 'Shot your line in the bloody wrong place, haven't you?' he'd say. Well, where was the right bloody place? Could Sam Pitt be right after all?

He sat in the stern of the boat, thinking, eating his sandwich, his 'door-stopper' of bread and dripping. Eleanor had spread a bit of the jelly from the meat on it under the dripping, and sprinkled it with salt the way he liked it. Not that there was much meat about these days.

He looked out over the gunwales, staring at the swelling sea, willing it to talk to him the way it talked to his dad. The fish were down there somewhere, shoaling in a small area where the food was right, the temperature was right, the water movement was right.

He let off the lugsail sheet and turned the tiller five degrees. The wind caught the sail and dragged the bows over, turning the *Hope* beam on to the wind. He felt the hull shudder beneath him as it overcame its inertia and started to pull across the ocean, heeling under the force of the wind. He brought the tiller amidships, felt it comfort his hand as he stared out over the water.

'Feel it,' Silas always said, and then would add, twinkling, 'Ask yourself where *you* would be if you were a fish?'

Reuben sat there, trying to relax, trying to 'feel it'. He took out his bottle of cold tea and ate another 'door-stopper', as the *Hope* rode smoothly along the course he'd set without consciously working out where he was going. He put his foot up on the post, and rested his back against the stern transom rail, cradling the tiller under his arm. After the hauling his whole body felt warm. The wind blew across his brow, drying the sweat. He could see the reflections of the sun behind him every time a wave swelled; birds hovered over Ravenswyke and smoke curled from the cottages.

15

And slowly peace came on him, and he began to feel it, the peace and contentment of his world, the world of the Godsons of Ravenswyke.

The wind had increased its force and white horses already rode the crests of the waves half a mile offshore. Reuben stared at the horizon of land, instinctively remembering the sailors' saying, 'When Tockett Top puts on its black cap, sailor come home'. He estimated that the black cloud floating slowly off the moor top would take a couple of hours yet to cap Tockett Top; time to shoot one more basket and haul it in quickly before he ran for home, with the wind astern. Three of the Ravenswyke cobles had come out, one by one; inshore trawlers from Whitby and Scarborough lay in a line a mile off. Reuben stared out over the ocean, his nostrils sniffing the salt spray. Silas always said he could smell fish, and it seemed as if he truly could. But was that fish Reuben could smell or the impending storm? Half a mile north-east he saw a sudden turbulence on the water but it could have been a piece of sea kale rent from the bottom by waves. Now the wind had started to veer to the north and he'd kept pace with it, re-setting the lugsail, which had filled taut on the starboard. The *Hope* was surging further out into the ocean. The *Jolly Lads* was about ten points off his bow to port, but far enough away that he wouldn't be breaking the unspoken code of the sea by fishing the ground they had chosen to occupy.

Twenty minutes later he pointed the *Hope* up into the wind. The turbulence had disappeared beneath the surface, but some instinct, possibly some influence from his father, something positive and almost tangible, told him to shoot the line here. It hissed as it left the basket, the hooks coming out clean and well baited. When the fifty fathoms were down he sat in the stern, glancing over his shoulder to check Tockett Top. God, the black cap was moving fast off the moor top, much faster than he had calculated. The wind now had a keen bite to it. He rubbed his chapped hands together, debating whether to have another swig of the tea. If it'd been hot, he'd have taken a swallow but he didn't fancy it cold. He looked over the bow to the *Jolly Lads* and asked himself 'What the hell's he up to?' The Pitt boat had suddenly gone about, the lugsail and the mizzen smacking round with a slapping crack he could hear even above the keening of the wind. One of the Pitt boys, he couldn't identify which, was standing on the stern seat and appeared to be hanging on to the mizzen-mast. The mizzen-sail and the lug were both streamed out wide, and the *Jolly Lads* was running wild before the wind. As Reuben watched, the lug gybed all the way from starboard to port smashing one of the boys across his shoulder.

'Bloody hell, he's over!' Reuben said, and started instantly to haul in his line, knowing immediately from the weight of it that he'd a good catch. As he hauled he looked over his shoulder. The Pitt lad had been knocked over the gunwale but seemed to have caught a rope and to be hanging on. One of the brothers was hauling him back in; two more were in the stern wrestling with the mizzen. Reuben could guess what had happened; one of the stays holding the mizzen must have parted when the boat swung about and now they'd be struggling to get some kind of jury-line rigged on to it. Or at last, seeing sense, take the bloody mast and sail down out of the way. The sail must somehow have caught its halyard or the lads would have had it down already.

'That's what comes of being such a mean cantankerous sod,' Reuben shouted, knowing they couldn't hear him. Sam Pitt was notorious for never cutting a line except when he had to, even picking up bits of line other people had discarded and splicing them together. The *Jolly Lads* was a ludicrous boat to look at, its sails patched out of all recognition, its lines a tangled mass of splices, its hull held together by nails and varnish. Over the years, without ever realizing it, Sam had made the Pitt family a laughing stock.

Reuben hauled in his line as rapidly as possible, though still coiling it. The mallet was busy in his hand. Halfway down the line he'd already taken ten codling, each between fifteen and twenty pounds, and then he came to a sole, big, fat, succulent, juicy.

As he worked he watched the *Jolly Lads* out of the corner of his eye; the mizzen, still holding its sail, was canted forward at a hopeless angle. 'Cut your bloody line, you stingy old bastard,' Reuben shouted, but the wind carried his voice away. He could see the Pitt family struggling in the stern, and inevitably the wind, grown in force and gusting, did the job for them. The taut starboard halyard parted; Reuben saw the end of the cord flick like a whiplash across the face of one of the Pitt boys, and a sudden spurt of red as he fell back into the scuppers. The mizzen crashed

17

forward, caught the lugsail at its centre, and ripped it from top to bottom. The lugsail sheet was torn from the hands of the helmsman and the boom of the lugsail snapped forward against the starboard mainstay. The stern of the *Jolly Lads* swung over, bringing the boat beam on to the wind.

Reuben quickly pulled in the last hook and the weight, malleted the last fish, a sole, and dropped it into the basket. He stowed the basket by the mast foot and lashed it down, then he raced back and untied the tiller, heading the *Hope* towards the *Jolly Lads*. Once again he glanced over his shoulder and now he groaned – Tockett Top had already 'donned' its black cap and that, for some, could mean a sentence of death. The wind had changed its howl to a shriek of angry defiance; the waves lashed up under the gunwales of the *Jolly Lads*, canting it like a bobbing cork towards Reuben, the remains of the lugsail caught among the stays and whipping like ghost sheets, the boat already shipping water with each mad tumble to starboard.

Sam and his sons were fighting to get the welter of sails, sheets, spars, warps, stays and halyards under control, still, or so it looked to Reuben, trying to disentangle them rather than slash them away.

'He must be stark staring raving bloody mad,' Reuben said out loud, unable to believe his eyes as the *Hope* raced towards the *Jolly Lads*. He'd adjusted his direction to come up astern of the stricken vessel. Now the wind was gusting badly and whitecaps foamed on wave tops running eight, nine, ten feet high. The *Hope* held to its line, its nose rising above each wave crest, then yawing sickenly into the pit on the other side. Reuben went forward, quickly checked his mainstays, then raced back to head the boat up into the next wave. His mind assessed the position of the *Jolly Lads*, wondering which way he could go to help them. If he went downwind, the *Jolly Lads*, with all its rigging flying, would bear down on him. If he went upwind he'd miss anybody who might be washed overboard.

The *Jolly Lads*, half-filled with water, was wallowing like a pig in a midden as each wave punched up under the starboard gunwale, lifting the boat effortlessly and tossing it twenty or more feet. If it carried on as it was now, the *Jolly Lads* would be smashed on to the rocks below Tockett, the traditional graveyard of Ravenswyke sailors who ignored the 'black cap' warning.

Reuben made his decision and took the *Hope* upwind of the *Jolly Lads*. He uncoiled his best inch-and-a-half line and made one end fast round the centre post. The other end he fastened to the large yellow buoy they used for lobster-pot marking. Alf Pitt was clinging to the mast with blood pouring down his face where the rope's end had lashed him. He saw what Reuben was doing and clung to the starboard side with a boat hook in his hands. Reuben dropped the buoy over the side and paid out the line slowly, letting it slip through his fingers as the sea took it and floated it towards the other boat. Alf grabbed the line as soon as it came near enough and, without bothering to untie the buoy, he clambered forward despite the pounding waves which lashed him and made the line fast round the *Jolly Lads*' forepost. The line stretched between the two boats tight as a banjo string as Reuben pushed the tiller hard to bring the *Hope* fifteen degrees abeam of the wind, where it would have better pulling power, using the wind's own force to pull the bows of the *Jolly Lads* around. Reuben felt the *Hope* straining to move forward and knew that, at best, all he could hope to do so long as he had that dead weight on the end of the line was to hold his own, acting as an anchor, stopping the *Jolly Lads* from being pounded back on to the rocks. Once the bow of the *Jolly Lads* had come round, the boat rode straight. With so much water already inside, it had no hope of cresting the wave tops and the sea lashed over it each time.

Terrie Pitt came first across the line, hand over hand through the pounding sea, more often submerged than not. It took all Reuben's strength to hold the tiller to keep them on that beam direction. His sail groaned under the force of the wind and the mast seemed to bend. Reuben had no fear of his rigging; he thanked God for Silas's inviolable rule that the boat would never go out without every piece of equipment in perfect condition. Terrie scrambled over the side and lay, half-drowned, in the bottom of the boat, his heavy fisherman's clothing sodden about him. Now Alf had climbed on to the towline, his hands and legs wrapped around it as he drew himself along it inch by inch, with each sag and snap alternately drenching him and flying him on a trapeze up into the air, at one moment submerged beneath a wave fighting for breath, at the next hanging precariously over a twenty-foot trough. As he neared the boat Reuben kicked Terrie back into life and he grabbed his brother's guernsey and dragged him

19

aboard the *Hope*. Unlike Terrie, Alf used what little breath was left to him to curse. 'You bloody old bastard,' he yelled, waving his fist. He whirled to Reuben. 'I'll kill him, I'll bloody well kill him! That's the last bloody time he gets me to sea. Fuckin' mizzen-mast!' He whirled back again, shaking his fist high in the air. 'I'll ram that mizzen-mast all the way up your arse!' he yelled.

Reuben had no time to listen; he was working out how long he could hold the *Jolly Lads*' bow on to the waves. Certainly, if she turned athwart now, there was no way he could prevent her from going full circle, turning turtle, and then smashing herself inexorably on the jagged face of Tockett.

Even with the traditional high stern of a fishing coble, the *Jolly Lads* couldn't hope to run back into Ravenswkye with all that water aboard. They'd be swamped for sure. Silas would have known what to do! Silas would have worked something out by now! Reuben looked back over the stern at Tockett Top. They had precious little time left if he was to save the *Jolly Lads and* bring the *Hope* back into harbour.

His suspicions were confirmed when he took his line from the cliff edge to the high fields beyond. He wasn't moving forward, or even holding. He was drifting backwards under the pull of the *Jolly Lads*. At best, all he could hope to do with the present lash-up would be to keep the *Jolly Lads* bows out.

In other words, to make sure she crashed against the rocks stern on, taking the *Hope* with her!

'Can you hear me, Sam?' he shouted.

Sam was still messing about with his lines. 'Yes, I can hear you,' he shouted back. 'Just keep us headed the way we are while I get this lot sorted. Then I'll set to and bail her out!'

Alf stood up, dancing on the deck of the *Hope* with anger. 'You bloody stingy old maniac,' he yelled, 'cut the fucking lot and let's get out of here. Can't you see, you stubborn old mule, that you're risking all us lives, and the boats too, all for a bit of old clothes-line!'

'I'll have it free in just a minute!' Sam said, but that was the last straw for Alf. He reached into the box at the foot of the mast where he knew he'd find the gutting knives. His eyes blazed with anger as he brandished the knife in the air. 'Listen to me!' he said. 'Now you either cut the lines free, you chop 'em at this minute,

20

or I'll slash the tow. And then you can go to hell! And take that clapped-out bathtub with you!'

Reuben could see Alf meant it. He slackened the lugsail sheet and now, with the sail not holding so much of the wind's force, the two boats began to slip backwards faster. Their present line would put them aground under Tockett Top. What could he do? Abandon Sam Pitt, or risk losing the *Hope*? And how could he stand to face Silas, if he survived the rocks, to tell him he'd lost the *Hope* trying to talk sense into Sam Pitt?

Something was needed to enable them to sail northwards. There had to be some way of reducing the drag of the *Jolly Lads*. He shouted to Terrie. 'Get forward, Terrie,' he said, 'and bring us that line out of the locker. Tell your dad,' he said to Alf, 'that we're going to send him another line to fasten round his stern-post. If we can lash the *Jolly Lads* to the *Hope* along our lee side, we should be able to sail the two together.'

Alf had taken the rope's end and had tied it round his waist.

'What the hell are you doing?' Reuben asked, bewildered.

Alf smiled at him, but his lips, curling back to reveal his top teeth, gave him the expression of a wolf. 'I'm not going to *send* him another line. I'm going to take it to him. And I'm taking this bugger with me,' he added, brandishing the gutting knife. Before Reuben could argue with him, he'd climbed over the side on to the rope. The force of the waves shot him along the rope like a monkey up a ladder. As he climbed over the gunwale of the *Jolly Lads* they all heard him. 'Right, you bugger,' he said. 'Any inter-ference from you and I'll cut your throat!'

Sam cowered back. 'How can you talk to your dad like that?' he asked, but Alf didn't reply. He went into the rigging like a madman, slashing everything in sight. The tattered lugsail fell in a heap in the bottom of the boat, the mast was unstepped and came crashing down, narrowly missing Sam's head. Alf used a couple of pieces of the cut rope to make the mast fast in the bottom of the coble, protruding out over the bows. He swung to the stern past his father, who winced and cowered back again. He made the second line round the sternpost and then drew on it, while Terrie drew on the bow line, until the *Jolly Lads* was held by the two ropes parallel with the *Hope*, in the lee. They drew the ropes tighter and slowly the two boats came together.

Reuben hardened the lugsail sheet, and felt a sudden thrill as the *Hope*, bearing its unwieldy burden, began to sail itself forward.

The lugsail held the wind and the *Hope* began to crab, forwards and sideways, taking the *Jolly Lads* with it. Alf squatted in the stern of his boat and used his own rudder to supplement Reuben's. Only when the lighthouse and the mast on the ship-building yard were lined up did Reuben ease off the lugsail a fraction so that the two boats, without forward impulsion, drifted slowly down the line he had found, moving into the relatively calmer waters below the houses of Old Quaytown in Ravenswyke Bay.

Now the wind was howling with what seemed to be frustrated fury, but the cliffs were lifting it above their heads; the waves, meeting their own reflections, swirled into flattened spume robbed of all power. Once they were safely in the bay, Alf cast off the two lines. 'You'd better get 'em in quick,' he said, 'or this old bugger'll pinch 'em!' He picked up one of the oars and threw it at his father. 'Clap your bloody hands round that,' he said, 'and take us in, before I make you swim for it!'

There was one last frantic moment as Sam, sitting ludicrously waist deep in water, held his oar steady while Alf brought them round from the stern. The waves tried, just one last desperate time, to get under the gunwales and tip them. The water in the boat sloshed up over Sam's head and drenched him. Waist-heavy and sluggish, the *Jolly Lads* came round, stern on to the slip where Bill Craig was waiting, standing thigh deep in the water with the hook in his hand. He tossed it the last yard to Alf, who clipped it to the sternpost. The horses took the strain, and the boat was dragged ignominiously backwards up the slip, water sloshing out of it, a sodden mongrel saved from the turbulent greedy gulp of the hungry ocean.

Reuben stood off until he saw them safe, then dropped his sail, furled it neatly around the boom, and used his oars to put himself stern on. The last flick of the waves, the tide, the draught-horses and willing hands did the rest.

When the *Hope* was high and dry on the slip and his baskets stacked by the wall of the pub, Reuben walked across to the *Jolly Lads*. Sam was still messing about with the bits of rope that had nearly cost all of them their lives. Alf and Terrie were standing to the side, drinking from two mugs of hot tea Mrs Pitt had brought down for them. Half a dozen people stood around, watching. Alf offered his pot of tea to Reuben, who shook his head. He knew

Eleanor would be on her way and didn't like to take his tea until the *Hope*'s work was done. Alf looked past him at his father, then spat on the stones at their feet. 'Right,' he said, 'that's our lot, Reuben! Terrie and me, we're off to the bloody army!'

Terrie looked into Reuben's face. The smaller, quieter of the brothers, he'd always been the shy one. Eleanor arrived with Reuben's tea and he warmed his hands on the mug, looking at Terrie and at Eleanor. She'd heard what Alf had said. When Terrie spoke he looked at Reuben, still, but his words were for Eleanor.

'That's enough,' he said. 'The old lad will kill us if we stay. Us reckon we'd be safer in the Green Howards. And the war won't last for ever.'

Reuben looked at Eleanor and saw her biting her knuckle. 'Well, we shall all miss you, every one of us,' he said. 'But I can't say as I'd blame you! The old place, and the folks in it, I reckon, will be waiting when you get back.'

Alf put his arm round Reuben's shoulder. 'For a young lad,' he said, 'you're not bad with your dad's boat! Not bad at all! Reckon you saved all of us lives, if truth were known. If you were old enough, I'd take you into the pub and buy you a glass of summat!'

For once in his life, Reuben was pleased to be able to duck the invitation to have one in the Raven Hotel, as the pub at the bottom of the bank was called. For years he'd stood with the rest of the Ravenswyke lads outside the lower saloon bar door whenever there'd been a chance, sniffing the atmosphere of beer and tobacco, the mystery of the adult world of men, every time the door opened and closed. One day, he knew, he'd be in there with the rest of them, a half-pint of beer in his hand, a cigarette in his mouth. More than the drink and the smoke, he wanted to be with the fishermen, listening to their free talk of the sea, recounting the adventures, reliving the tragedies that seemed to be coming thicker and faster in this second year of the war.

But, this evening, he had something in mind other than the lower saloon bar of the Raven.

He walked rapidly up Cliff Street, turned left into the backs. Eleanor was looking after the fish for him; he'd seen Fearon, the fish buyer, hurrying down the steep Bank Street and didn't want to be delayed by him. Anyway, Eleanor, a year older than Reuben, was sharper when it came to haggling – she knew how to get round Fearon for another penny or two, especially since the *Jolly Lads* had come in empty.

His mother had made the bowl ready for him on the stool in front of the fire. When she saw him come in, she tipped half the kettle of hot water into it. He sat down and she bent in front of him and took off his boots. At first it had embarrassed him to see his mam bend down like that but Eleanor had talked to him. 'She used to do it for Dad,' Eleanor had said. 'She misses not having him around, so let her do it for you!'

He stripped his clothes off, stretched himself in front of the coal fire, feeling its warmth go into his naked body. His mother busied herself about the kitchen-cum-living-room that had always been the centre of his life. In this room, the family had always come together. They'd always sat together, talked, eaten their meals together. He looked round the walls marking all the little things in their lives. The brass ornaments on the mantelpiece in which Mam kept the money she saved from the housekeeping. The horses in harness pulling the sledge with the coble on it, all made of pot by that chap in Whitby who killed himself. The picture of Grandad on the wall with its brown-mottled cream-paper surround. Dad's chair covered in real leather! Mam's with moquette, not that she ever sat in it. Though they all called it Mam's chair, it had always been used by the oldest son in the room at the time. Now, of course, it 'belonged' to Reuben, and anybody sitting in it when he came in would automatically move to get up. Mam had put his clothes on it, his thick trousers with his underpants already inside them and, threaded through his braces, his vest and shirt that had been remade from one of Silas's.

He washed quickly, rubbing the carbolic soap into his skin, standing on the towel in front of the fire to sluice himself. Halfway through, his mother came and poured the rest of the hot water into the bowl.

'Spoiling me, are you?' he asked, joking, but then was sorry he'd spoken.

'It's only the one of you,' Hannah said, 'so make the best of it while they're away. You'll be taking your turn soon enough, when your brothers come back.'

He looked at her face, noticing the deep lines that the war and

24

the absence of her 'menfolk' had brought to her. In the last two years, it seemed to Reuben, she had grown noticeably older. She was tall and inclined to be a bit skinnier than most of the Ravenswyke women. Her hair, he now saw with a shock, was completely grey. Some instinct deep inside him made him long to put his arms round her shoulder, to give her a hug, maybe even a kiss on her cheek to show her he understood what a worrying time they were going through, to reassure her they were in it together. But he knew such a thing would never do!

'Yes,' he said, 'I'd better. They'll all be back soon enough!'

He dressed quickly, feeling the warmth in his vest and shirt, which Hannah had held for a few minutes opened in front of the fire to 'air'. He saw that Eleanor had blacked his boots for him and had even shined them a bit along the toecap.

Then he sat down and Hannah brought him his bowl of steaming hot potato soup. She'd even left a bit of the pig's foot in it. 'By heck, you are spoiling me,' he said. 'You'll be giving me eggs and bacon next!'

'Get it down you, lad,' she said. 'You're doing man's work, you need man's food in your belly!'

He glanced at the clock on the sideboard. Ten-past twelve. Hannah sat at the corner of the table watching him eat, watching him dip his bread into the hot liquid. 'Fewster let me have a bit of shoulder of lamb this morning,' she said. 'I thought we might have it tomorrow for our dinner.'

Despite the meat shortage, somehow she always managed to provide something for the Sunday dinner. 'I was thinking of going out again tomorrow,' he said.

'On a Sunday, Reuben? Whatever will folks think?'

'I don't care! If it hadn't been for that fool Sam Pitt, I'd have shot another basket today. The way they were coming . . .'

'How did you do, then?'

'We shall make a bob out of it. But if I could have shot again . . .'

She put her hand on his knee, a rare gesture for her. 'We mustn't be greedy, Reuben,' she said.

'That Sam Pitt . . . I could kill him!'

'Nay, don't say that. Don't ever say that. . . .'

'Him and his bits of rope. . . .'

She touched his knee again and leaned towards him, crouched

25

on the stool catercorners from him. Hannah never sat square at the table – that wasn't her way. She was like a hen pecking here and there, always ready to skitter off to the other side of the room to the table beside the fire oven where she did most of her cooking, to go to fetch another helping, another morsel. 'You've got to understand, Reuben, it wasn't always like it is now. The Good Lord knows we don't have much now, but I've seen your dad and Sam Pitt come back with every basket filled, and lucky to make two shillings out of the Fearons. There was a time you couldn't thoil the money to buy a bit of new line. It was either new rope, or a new pair of boots, or something to put on the table as a change from fish-head soup. And no choice in the matter. Remember that; Sam Pitt and your dad came up in the hard school – they didn't have it easy, like you do today!'

Reuben sucked his cut knuckle and laughed with the irony of her remark. 'If I have it easy,' he said, 'then nobody's ever told me!' It was her turn to laugh.

'Thanks for a nice dinner,' he said in a well-worn ritual, 'and please may I leave the table?'

'You're getting a bit old to be asking that, now,' she said. 'Where are you off to this afternoon?'

He winked at her. 'That'd be telling, wouldn't it,' he said.

He put on his tweed jacket and his raincoat. His cap was on the peg and he took it and held it in his hand. No Godson ever got up from the table without a please and thank-you, and no Godson ever wore his cap in the house.

'Well, behave yourself, and mind your manners!'

He turned at the door and looked back into the room. She hadn't moved but was gazing after him, watching him go. 'Our Eleanor will be back in a minute,' he said.

'I reckon. . . .'

'Terrie's going into the army.'

'It's time. . . .'

'Well, I'll be off then. . . .'

'I'll have your tea waiting for you. . . .'

'I'll not be late. . . .'

'Better not be. I'm baking some scones.'

He went quickly back across the room, bent down, and pecked her cheek. 'He'll have written, Mam,' he said, 'but you know what the post it like.'

'Yes, I know. . . .'

This time as he left the house he didn't look back. No Godson woman ever let her men see her cry.

He walked rapidly up the street away from the landing, turned the corner at the far end by the butcher's, and went along Bridge Street to climb the steep bank that led out of Old Quaytown. Despite the one-in-four rise he took the slope in long strides without pausing, nodding curtly to the folk he passed on his way. Dinnertime Saturday and the weekend had started. He didn't care to waste a moment of it in idle talk. Anyway, he knew what they'd all say. 'Heard from your dad? Where is he now? Ought never to have gone away!' And so on. His dad needn't have gone away – he could have stayed in Ravenswyke, could have sailed the *Hope* on mine-sweeping. They were crying out for men who could handle boats to drag the German mines out of the water. The lads working out of Scarborough had already dragged over fifty out, but it had cost lives. The *Condor*, with Bob Heritage and his crew of eight, had gone in May, the *Sapphire* in March. Somehow, Reuben was glad Silas hadn't stayed, but had gone to fight with the Green Howards.

But, by heck, he wished they could get a letter!

The Duckett house was at the top of the bank. Very grand. Amelia Duckett, they said, had paid £300 in cash for it after her husband had died and she'd sold up his boat, his 'down-bank' family house, his boat shares. And, they said, he'd left her nicely fixed with the Prudential. Reuben went round the back, past the lavatory in the yard, and knocked on the back door. He could hear footsteps and then the door was flung open. They were sitting round the kitchen table. 'Come in, Reuben,' Arthur Duckett said. 'You're early. I'm still having my dinner!'

Reuben went in diffidently, and said hello to Mrs Duckett and Arthur's sister Emily. They were eating corned beef and boiled potatoes, he noticed. Without saying anything, Mrs Duckett reached out to the kitchen dresser, got a plate, and put it by the empty chair. 'No, thank you, Mrs Duckett,' Reuben said 'I've had my dinner back at home.'

She reached into the tureen in the middle of the table, spooned out a heap of potatoes, took a slice of corned beef off the centre plate, and laid it on the potatoes. 'Get it down you,' she said. 'You're a growing lad!'

He didn't need to be told twice, though he felt uncomfortable. Damn it, she'd laid the cloth for Saturday dinner, a clean white one.

Emily looked across the table at him and smiled. He was too busy holding his knife and fork the right way to smile back, concentrating on cutting the corned beef and not dropping it off his fork.

'Come on, then, get a move on, Reuben,' Arthur said. Reuben realized with a shock that his friend had finished, and was impatient to go. He gobbled the rest of the potato down, felt a portion of it slide down his chin and drop on to the plate. He was mortified.

'Give him time to eat his dinner, Arthur,' Mrs Duckett said kindly. 'Take your time, lad, take your time. Food does you no good if you rush it down!'

Reuben had the last bit of potato on his fork, which he was holding like a shovel, when he saw the way Emily was holding her fork. the other way round, balancing a bit of the corned beef *and* potato on it. He reversed his fork, and the potato dropped off it, into his lap. 'Oh heck!' he said, picking it up with his hand and putting it back on the plate. 'Thank you for a good dinner,' he gabbled, 'and please may I leave the table?'

'You've got nice manners, Reuben,' Mrs Duckett said. 'You could teach our Arthur a thing or too!'

Arthur and Emily both went through the ritual, and got up. 'Leave the washing up,' Mrs Duckett said to Emily. 'I'll do it later. I'll just sit for a minute and finish my tea.'

Reuben looked at Arthur, and squinted inquiringly towards Emily as he put on his raincoat. 'She asked if she could come!' Arthur said with disgust.

Emily's eyes were pleading at Reuben. 'Can I?' she asked.

He shrugged his shoulders. 'Nowt to do with me, is it?' he said.

She took her coat from the hook behind the kitchen door and put it on. 'Right, then, I'll come,' she said.

Arthur was disgusted with Reuben. 'I thought you were a mate of mine,' he hissed as they followed the girl outside.

Emily was fifteen, going on sixteen, a head shorter than Reuben. He and Arthur had been pals a long time, and Emily had always been around. Their fathers, in an odd way, had been friends, despite the differences between them. Tom Duckett had always

28

been a cautious man, saving every penny he made from his fishing coble, using it to buy boat shares. 'It's all right for you!' Silas would say, joking. 'You've only got the two kids to feed!' No one, however, had been prepared for the amount Tom had left when he'd died of pleurisy after a soaking he'd got one night and ignored. He'd found the right wife in Amelia; she'd always invested part of her housekeeping money, pennies at a time, in an insurance policy with the Prudential, sold by the Friday night door-to-door collector who owned the Ravenswyke 'round'. Gradually, over the years, she'd increased the amount of the weekly payment, a halfpenny at a time, so that when Tom died there was enough to give him a good burial, with a ham tea. Ravenswyke had no better term of approval for a wife – she buried him with ham!

When Arthur left school at fourteen she'd continued her carefulness by getting him a job in the post office in Whitby. He was made for life, with a guaranteed pension at the end, so long as he kept his nose clean.

Reuben felt Arthur's hand on his arm holding him back so that Emily could draw a few yards ahead. When he was sure she couldn't hear them, he bent his head to whisper to Reuben. 'I've made up my mind,' he said. 'I'm chucking it! Don't say anything to Emily – she'll tell Mam.'

'What're you going to do then?' Reuben asked. Chucking a job in the post office? Mrs Duckett would have a blue fit!

'Will you take me in the *Hope*? I want to come out with you. Fishing. If there was two of us . . .'

'But you know nothing about it!' Reuben said. A lot of people got the idea it was an easy job. Lots of folk came out from York and places like that on the charabancs, found their way down into the Cut, and asked the fishermen to take them out for a trip round the bay and a 'bit of fishing'. Naseby had done it once. Charged the man and his missis sixpence for it, too. The woman had been sick all the way and the man had fallen overboard. It was a hard-earned sixpence – Naseby had had to spend an hour swabbing out the boat while the fishermen pulled his leg unmercifully. For weeks after that, whenever they'd help launch him, they'd wrinkle their noses and laugh. 'You were damned lucky she didn't shit herself!' they'd say.

'You could learn me!' Arthur said. 'Look, I've got a bit put by.

29

Nearly five pounds! You wouldn't need to pay me nothing until I'd learned. I could give my mam her fifteen bob a week and tell her I was getting wages off you!'

'You've got five *pounds*!' Reuben said incredulously, but then broke off. Emily had looked back and had seen they were lagging behind. She'd stopped to wait for them.

'What are you two whispering about?' she asked. 'Telling mucky jokes, I'll bet!'

'Mucky jokes? What do you know about that?' Arthur asked, horrified. 'If that's the way you're going to talk, you can go on back home!'

'You're not my dad!' she said. 'Anyway, Reuben said I could come! Didn't you, Reuben?'

'I suppose I did,' he admitted, his sense of fairness getting the better of his feelings of loyalty to Arthur. Anyway, he wanted to end the conversation Arthur had started. He wanted time to think. Being friends with Arthur was one thing, but bringing him into the *Hope* . . . There'd always been a *Hope of Ravenswyke*, and it had always been sailed exclusively by Godsons. Bringing Arthur in would be the same as admitting that he, Reuben, couldn't handle it on his own.

But how could he explain that to Arthur?

'Bloody hell!' Arthur said, recognizing the betrayal. He turned and started walking rapidly along the footpath that would lead eventually to Whitby, their target for the afternoon.

'Come on,' Reuben said to Emily, grabbing her hand without thinking, leading her on to the path in pursuit of Arthur. He didn't let go of her hand until they got to the stile at the far cater-corner. When they arrived, Arthur was already a quarter of a mile ahead, by the cliff edge.

Emily sat on the stile. 'Let me get my breath back,' she said. 'Where were you going, anyway?'

'Into Whitby. Where we always go on a Saturday afternoon.'

'Looking at the girls . . .?'

'What do you mean?' he said. 'We look at the boats, don't we?'

Now she was close to him, he saw for the first time that she had hazel-coloured eyes, neither green nor brown. Like the sea gets, sometimes, he thought, on a clear summer's day when there's little wind.

And then he reminded himself – apart from the black cap on

30

Tockett Top, that sea colour was the best indication a fisherman had of a storm to come. She reached out and took his hand in hers again. 'Are you *my* friend, Reuben? As well as Arthur's?'

' 'Course I am!' He couldn't understand what she was getting at, of course he was her friend. Hadn't he once thumped Terrie Pitt in the schoolyard when Terrie was pulling her hair that time?

'You've never given us a kiss!' she said, her eyes smiling at him, taunting him. 'Phil Naseby's given us a kiss.'

He tried to shrug his shoulders, but couldn't. Bloody hell. Phil Naseby, eh? Rotten bugger! 'Well, you know what the Nasebys are,' he said, sneering. 'That lot over in Newquay Town. Betty Naseby could hardly get in the door of the chapel for the size of her belly. I've heard tell they paid Tolly ten guineas to marry her. Here, you've not been doing owt else, have you?'

She laughed. 'That'd be telling, wouldn't it?' she said, still taunting him.

The storm that had threatened in the late morning, with its increasing winds lashing the wave tops, finally broke in earnest, with a crack of thunder that rolled across the moor to spend itself out at sea. Reuben felt the first dash of icy water in his face as the rain, coming from nowhere, scurried across the fields in thick sliding sheets that filled the air with choking spray.

Within seconds his raincoat and, he saw, Emily's tweed coat were soaked. 'Come on,' he said, 'back home. We'll never make Whitby.'

The field path was slippery beneath their feet, the spongy grass slicked by water. Always deft and nimble on the heaving planks of a boat, he floundered about here on land, sprawling full length a couple of times before they reached the far hedgerow. Emily ran easily beside him, her face streaming with water but her eyes gleaming with the sheer excitement of it. Overhead the thunder sounded and shafts of lightning cracked viciously from the sea to strike the moor top behind them. Reuben had been out at sea in storms like this – there you could accept them as being part of the life; here on land it seemed somehow obscene to be as wet as if he'd gone overboard. Even his boots had filled with water and his feet squelched in them. He looked about him in vain to find a sheltered spot where they could sit out the worst of it, but there was no byre, no barn, not even a thick hedge. When they went through the gate on to the path by the station he found she was laughing, turning her head up to the rain, catching the drops in her mouth. 'Isn't it *lovely*?' she shouted, her voice faint against the thrum of the wind.

'It's horrible!' he said.

She linked her arm in his. 'Don't be a spoilsport, Reuben,' she said. 'We're going to get wet, no two ways about it, so let's enjoy ourselves.' She linked her sopping arm in his and drew him down the road through the deserted streets. Nobody in his right mind would stay out in weather like that! As they walked along with their arms linked, he began to think that perhaps, after all, it wasn't so bad. He was wet through but it wasn't the first time and it was something infinitely comforting to have that thin arm linked in his, to feel warm inside no matter how cold outside he may be, to feel protective.

When they arrived home Amelia Duckett opened the door for them. 'Come on in, the pair of you,' she said, 'and get off them wet things.'

'I can go on down home,' Reuben protested, but without vigour.

'Aye, and have your mam chasing me for letting you catch your death of cold? I've put Mr Duckett's dressing gown by the fire in the front room. Take them wet things off and we'll see about drying them for you. You can stop and have your tea. . . .'

'I can't do that, Mrs Duckett. Mam's making scones. . . .'

'Then you'll have to have them for your supper. You're not going out again in this, and that's final. I suppose our Arthur went on ahead?'

'Yes. He should have been somewhere by High Batts Farm when it broke.'

'Then they'll take him in. Now get away with you into the front room.'

Five minutes later he was sitting at the end of the sofa by the blazing fire, a pot of hot tea in his hand and his clothes steaming on the wooden clothes horse by the fireside, when Emily came in.

'Are you decent?' she asked.

' 'Course I am!'

She sat on the sofa next to him, sipping her tea from a china cup. She was wearing a soft green woollen dress he didn't remember having seen before, with a white lace collar and lace around the cuffs of the long sleeves.

'Looks like Sunday,' he said.

32

'Go on with you. I made it myself!'

He was glowing with the warmth of the tea and the fire, and the presence of this new girl beside him, this girl he'd known all his life but never really looked at before. Her eyes still sparkled as they had in the fields and she seemed to look at him in a new way, as if constantly asking him a question he knew he couldn't answer.

'If you wanted . . .' he said, looking away from her face and those questioning eyes into the flames of the fire, '*if* you wanted . . . I could be . . . *your* friend as well as Arthur's. But, I warn you, there'd have to be no more mucking about with Phil Naseby.'

He turned to her. 'No more, you understand?'

She nodded, not trusting herself to speak. Then she leaned forward and put her lips on his; the angle was all wrong and they touched only in the corners; he turned his head so that his mouth went along hers but then their noses got in the way. Both of them heard the door rattle as Amelia opened it.

'How's the fire doing?' she asked, and then stared hard at them. 'Not misbehaving yourselves, are you, while my back's turned?'

'No, Mrs Duckett, honest,' Reuben said. 'We're not misbehaving ourselves!'

Ravenswyke is a small village set in the cliffs of the Yorkshire coast, between Scarborough and Whitby, emotionally and geographically divided into quite separate parts by the Ravenswyke Cut, as it is known, where the river Wyke runs into the sea. Once upon a time, the fishing boats of Ravenswyke sailed out of the mooring afforded by the entrance to the Cut; they spent a lot of the year tied to moorings in the Cut itself, safe, except in the heaviest weather, from the winds and the tides. Over the centuries, however, the Cut gradually silted up with mud and stones washed down the river by the force of water running off the moors that surround the village, and boats were forced to use the slipway which ran beside the northern edge of the Cut past the Raven Hotel into Old Quaytown.

On the southern side of the Cut at the start of Newquay Town the Tocketts 300 years ago had built a boatyard, with its own launching slip and dry dock. No fishing boat had ever moored into Newquay Town, not even in the worst storm.

The folk of Ravenswyke were separated by that Cut in ways

that could not be listed – only felt. Old Quaytown was the home of the fishermen, who had arrived in the fifteenth century to start building their cottages into the cliffs. They'd carved out alleyways so steep and so narrow you couldn't call them streets or roads, and no vehicle ever negotiated them. Every one of these narrow, twisting alleyways was named after the family that first went to live there. When the lanes were finally dignified by plates screwed to the walls of houses, and lit by gaslight, these names remained. The way to the Godson house became Godson Lane. There was a Pitt Lane and a Duckett Lane – though the Ducketts no longer lived there. Sometimes a lane led to two houses or more grouped around a square, and these became known by historical events. You could find Preacher's Square, where, it was reputed, John Wesley had once brought his fiery message of independence. Gasworks Square and Revenuers Close were self-explanatory, as was Smugglers' Alley, but you'd have to dig in your forebear's memory to decipher Annie Longleg Street. Annie Long earned the right to a street of her own when she defied the Fearon family, who'd always been the fish wholesalers and retailers, when she suspected they were cheating her out of her rightful due for her husband's catch. She loaded the two biggest fish on her back, and set off across the moors the sixteen miles to Pickering, to sell direct and do the thieving Fearons, as she called them, out of their profit. She sold the fish remarkably well, legend says, and set off for home across the moors. On the way, a freak snowstorm blew up, and when it thawed the body of Annie Long was found huddled in a sheep wicken, frozen to death, her purse still clasped in her hands.

From that day forward, no Fearon ever walked Annie Longleg Street, nor ever would. As soon as Newquay Town was ready, the Fearons moved out of their cottage and bought one of the new houses the Tocketts had built to rent to the workers they would bring to their new boatyard.

These workers were recruited almost wholly from outside Ravenswyke – foreigners brought in from Whitby, from Scarborough and Teesside, who quickly found they wouldn't be served in the two pubs of Old Quaytown, in Fewster the butcher's, in Marlow the greengrocer's. Tockett saw this and quickly had the sense to build a pub, the New Arms, and to open shops that sold everything.

Newquay Town had its North and South Street, its East and West Road. The streets were wide and paved, and the houses all back-to-back, sharing lavatories. They were built of brick, with slate roofs, and all had numbers fixed on the doors, which the Tockett family painted every ten years the same colour of green. If you worked for Tockett, you were given a house. If your man left Tockett to find his fortune elsewhere, or if he died, you moved out and on. The rent man came around on Saturday morning and gave only one week's grace before evicting non-paying tenants.

The story of Ravenswyke contains all those legends with which history enlivens its pages. There are tales of smugglers who brought, not cognac from France, but the infinitely more rewarding tea from Holland; of women who gave birth to Siamese twins who lived to be ten years old; of the drunken Silas Gilchrist, forebear of the doctor, who said, 'May God's lightning strike me if I ever take a drink again!' He did, and it did! Or so they say. Most of the legends, however, have to do with the sea, the cliffs, the boats and the men who sail them. There are stories of codfish fifteen feet long, two-headed lobsters, a man catching a thousand pounds' weight of salmon in one day when the Cut was streaming with the waters of the Raven. There are yarns about sailors being washed overboard by a freak wave, and being brought back inboard by the following one, and, of course, the inevitable mermaid, said to be seen off the cliffs a couple of miles north of Ravenswyke. These yarns spin out many a long evening in the cottages, as fathers instinctively inculcate sons with love-hatred for that mighty ocean that has been friend and foe, master and servant, benefactor and malefactor, to every one of them.

Ravenswyke in 1916, however, was a village already beginning its death throes, though none who lived there could know that except, perhaps, James Henry Tockett. His family went as far back as Ravenswyke itself. The Tocketts had started as farmers, sheep-herders some said, with Viking ancestry. Over the centuries they'd prospered as frugal, cautious yeomen, living within sight of the sea but recognizing how precarious would be any living derived from actually sailing on it. They'd left others to brave the winds and water and had established themselves as middlemen and suppliers, putting their profits to work by buying land holdings, acreage that few wanted on the moors and the cliffs overlooking that tumultuous and unpredictable sea. By the eighteenth century, the Tockett family owned all the land to the south of the Cut for fifteen or more miles, and had so enlarged the Manor House as to make it unrecognizable; it resembled a cliff-top fortress. They participated, by buying shares, in the building of boats in Whitby, not committing themselves, as the Turnbulls, for example, had done, to actually building the vessels with all the inherent financial danger, or to sailing them on the ocean, with all the risks to human life, but taking sixty-fourth shares after the boats had been built, letting others do the running and taking their profits.

Building their own boatyard and houses for the workers who would be employed there had been, in James Henry's opinion, a Tockett folly, a foolish whim on the part of one of his ancestors with a naïve philanthropic inclination that fortunately few of the Tocketts shared. Over the years, the Yard had given employment to many of the people who had come to live in Ravenswyke and liked to think of themselves, in the second and third generations, as native sons. But the amount of energy and time that had gone into the running of the Yard, into coping with the problems these people brought with them, had been far out of proportion to the actual money earned. Why, he could make ten times that amount by using the Tockett money the way money should be used, in the City of London. There a man's money worked *for* him, and with the natural prudence built into any Yorkshireman, and an eye for an opportunity, the Tocketts had prospered beyond anything his shipyard ancestor could have expected.

As the amount of money earned increased, year by year, as more and more London firms and the Exchange had invited the Tocketts to participate in joint ventures, so had the local investments slowly turned sour. Until the start of the war the Yard right here on the Tockett doorstep in Ravenswyke, in a manner of speaking, had been losing money hand over fist. The houses were now so dilapidated they'd need to spend thousands to cure the leaky roofs, to install the plumbing that folk were now demanding. Aye, *demanding*, James Henry reminded himself; what would his father and grandfather have thought of that! The potash mines, which were supposed to spew out the equivalent of gold, had caused more trouble than enough, with an average of four to five men killed a year, and many men dying early through (that socialist doctor was trying to say) lung infections caused by the potash itself (though, as yet, he hadn't been able to prove it).

James Henry Tockett sat by the fire, ruminating on all these things, in a reflective mood that Saturday afternoon in 1916. The firelight gleamed on the dark mahogany panelwork of the room, the heavy red plush curtaining, the chintz- and leather-covered chairs. It was a room in which a man could be isolated from the realities of life outside the house, down the bank in the village itself. But it was also a bridgehead from which the Tocketts had constantly launched their assault on the forces of ignorance and avarice that opposed them from time to time. Here a man could be emperor and king, hold undisputed sway over his dominion. James Henry crossed to the window of what he liked to call his 'study', with the fire warming his back even at that distance. Tockett always liked a roaring fire in the grate on a Saturday afternoon, when he came from dinner, drank a glass of brandy, settled down with his week's accounts, and alternately read and snoozed until teatime. Nobody ever disturbed 'the Master' on a Saturday afternoon.

This afternoon, he'd just been nodding off in his leather chair when the thunder started, with the lightning that seemed to crackle at every pane of glass in the leaded windows.

The centre window, however, was not leaded and from it he could see across to the horizon of the ocean, with much of Ravenswyke to his left. *His* Ravenswyke, indisputably his by right of line of descent. There wasn't a man in that village he couldn't buy or sell, he told himself. There wasn't a man down there who didn't owe his continuing comfort and prosperity to the Tocketts of whom he, James Henry, aged sixty-six, was the head!

Then why, God, oh why, did he and all the Tocketts before him since the sixteenth century have to face the scourge of what everyone called the 'Tockett Curse'?

He turned from the window, went back to his chair by the fire, and seated himself heavily. His papers, on the mahogany table that stood by his right hand, were ignored. He took up his glass of brandy and swirled it round in its balloon before sipping it, looking at the fire through the thin crystal glass, seeing the flames dance. Acting on a sudden impulse, he reached out and grasped the bell-pull.

Agatha, sitting in the downstairs kitchen with her after-dinner cup of tea, heard the bell tinkle and looked up at the box. Now who could be wanting her at this time of a Saturday afternoon? She recognized the window with its jangling flap, and got to her feet at once. Nobody kept the Master waiting.

He was sitting in his chair when she knocked and entered the study. For a few moments it seemed as if he hadn't seen her. She gave a low cough and he came out of his reverie. 'Mr Rupert left yet?' he asked.

'No, Mr James. He's not leaving until half-past four.'

'Then be so good as to ask him if he can spare me a few minutes, there's a good girl!'

The 'good girl' was three years older than James Henry himself, but that was the way he had always addressed her.

'It's getting dark in here, Mr James,' she said. 'Shall I light the lamp for you?' Agatha couldn't get used to the new ways; they'd had electricity in Tockett House for some time now, but she still behaved as if the bulbs had to be cleaned, the filaments to be trimmed. She'd taken her courage in her hands when the men had come in to do the wiring and had spoken to the Master. 'Would it be all right with you, Mr James, if I didn't have the wires in my room? I'd be afraid at nights that I was going to get a shock if it all leaked out.'

He'd laughed. 'It's not like gas that goes down a pipe, Agatha. There's nothing in the wires to leak out.'

But she'd known that couldn't be; how else would the light come in the bulbs?

'No, I don't want the light on just yet,' he said.

He sat with his chin in his hand when she had left to convey his message. The blackness of the cap of clouds had passed over the house top, and now he could barely see across the room, could hardly make out the engravings and paintings of the Tocketts that lined its walls between the bookcases – with so many of them showing the faces of young people. Young people and old people, few in the middle years.

He bent forward, seized the long brass-handled poker from its stand, and stirred the coals; the marble of the fireplace and the mantelpiece above it gleamed with reflected light. The heavy brass hearth-surround shone with its polished knobs at each corner. He moved his slippered feet in the pile of the Wilton carpet that had been specially woven for him, as if contact with its luxurious permanence might dispel the debilitating pall of impermanence that lay like a black hand on his heart and mind.

When the door opened, Rupert came in without speaking, without interrupting his father's reverie. He stood behind the second fireside chair, waiting to be told to sit. At twenty he was a good-looking young man, with that air of confidence that comes from a successful, exclusive family line. His blond hair was parted in the middle and curled a little behind his ears. His face was unusually long for a Tockett, the skin drawn tight across the bones of his temples. He had the Tockett dark, luminous eyes and carried himself erect.

'You don't need to go back,' his father said without looking up at him.

'I want to, Father,' he said in his quiet voice.

'You could stop at home, if you'd a mind. . . .'

'I know, Father. But I'd like to go back!'

'You could live in London. . . !'

'I'd like to stay with my regiment.'

'That means France, then?'

'Yes, Father.'

'Will you be with your brother, Mark Adam?'

'Yes, we'll be together. He'll need me to look after him.'

James looked up at his son, his mouth crinkled in a wry smile. 'Sit down, lad,' he said gruffly. 'Thank God you've a sense of humour.'

'I've always had the feeling I'd need it one day, Father,' Rupert said as he seated himself.

James shook his head from side to side. 'I've done you wrong, lad,' he said. 'You ought never to have been born. But when Sarah died like that, I thought that happen it was all over, that we'd managed to beat the curse. The first-born has always *lived*, the later ones have died! When Sarah died of it, her a first-born, and when Mark Adam stayed healthy, I thought that was the end of it.'

'Don't reproach yourself, Father,' Rupert said softly. God, how many times had he had the same thought. Leukaemia had always been contracted by the second and subsequent children. The first-born had always been immune. His sister, Sarah Ellen, born in 1896, had lived to be three years old before she'd died of it. Mark Adam, the second-born, James's heir, should have had it but didn't. And that had given James Henry and his wife Gertrude

39

the hope – false it had now turned out to be – that the Tockett Curse had run its course and was ended.

'I do reproach myself, lad. Till my dying day!'

'You talked with Dr Gilchrist, then?'

'Yes. He's heard from London. There can be no doubt about it.'

How does a man tell his own son he has only a short time to live, especially when he believes himself at fault for ever having brought that son into the world? One thing is certain: you say what you have to in the manner to which you were born. And, if you're a Yorkshireman, *and* a Tockett, you come straight out with it, without beating around the bush. 'I'm afraid, lad, he's given you a year, two at the most.'

Rupert Henry looked at his father with an infinite compassion in his eyes. Dear God, he knew how the old man was feeling. But what could he offer to ease his pain? He came across and knelt by the chair, with his hand on his father's knee. 'It's been a good life, Father,' he said. 'You've taken great care I've lacked for nothing. I'm ready to go out of it, when I have to. But you mustn't reproach yourself. I've had twenty good years, the best anybody could have wished for. Now I want to go back to France with the regiment. I'd like to see this war out – it can't last for much longer.'

'You'll come back, lad?' James Henry asked anxiously, his hand on his young son's hair. So soft, real Tockett hair, so smooth. He reached down and clumsily hugged the lad to him. 'You'll not do anything daft, will you, lad? Promise me that!'

'No, Father, I'll not do anything daft!'

He could smell the tobacco and tweed of his father's jacket, the brandy he'd drunk, smells he had not experienced for many years. The Tocketts had never gone in for sentimentality – a handshake, with a folded five-pound note in it, had been the nearest his father had ever come to intimacy.

He stood up and straightened his jacket. 'I'll be away then, Father,' he said. 'I still have a bit of packing to finish before I leave.'

'Willy's taking you in the car?'

'If he can get it started.' The bull-nosed Morris phaeton was always giving Willy trouble with its magneto, or so he said. He still couldn't get used to advancing the ignition and the mixture to start the car, having spent all his life flicking the tip of a whip over carriage horses' heads and clicking his tongue to get them moving.

James Henry remained seated when his son left the room. Gilchrist had said no more than six months, but he hadn't had the heart to pass that on. He sighed deeply, pulled the cord on the lamp that hung above his table and chair, then reached for the papers. Bingham's Yard in Whitby was building, asking him to take sixty-fourth shares, but he didn't know. He'd do a sight better, if the truth were known, to pull his money out of Ravenswyke and take it down to London. Then there was the matter of his own yard, in the Ravenswyke Cut. Of course it was doing well right now, in spite of the war, except that they couldn't find enough labour. Dammit, they'd even had to set women on to do some of the finishing and what could that lead to? A lot of the women were not like their husbands – they didn't realize where the Friday penny came from and were giving a lot of backchat. He'd told Alf, and all the other foremen, not to take any of it. He put the Yard papers aside and picked up the folder with the figures for the potash mine. Another gloomy story. Two seams, two, had run out that week, and two young lads killed when the roof caved in on them. They'd get compensation, of course, but every time another one was killed it increased the arguments for putting in extra shorings. Folks didn't realize that the safety precautions they were asking for could mean the difference between economic working, and closing the pit down so that the entire workforce of 200 would lose their jobs.

His eye was caught by a reflection off the mantelpiece and he stood up and took down the silver-framed picture that lad over in Danby had painted. A perfect miniature. Gertrude's face looked out at him, calm and serene. The miniature had been painted a bare month before she'd passed away in 1910. 'I wish you were still here, lass,' he said. 'You'd be a bit of comfort now, that's for sure.'

He took the gold hunter from his waistcoat pocket. Soon be time for the lad to be leaving. He went and stood again by the window. The study was at the side of the house, on the front corner. He saw the phaeton standing by the doors of what had been the stable before the world had gone motor-car mad. He watched as the slim upright figure of his son came out of the house. His trunk was already strapped to the rack at the back of the car. He got inside. Willy fiddled with the levers beneath the wide wooden steering wheel, then jumped out, grabbed the starting handle, and gave it a vigorous turn. Miracle upon miracles, the engine fired first time.

James Henry watched Willy get back inside the car, his leggings gleaming in the dark afternoon gloaming, the peak of his cap shining. As the car started, James Henry's eyes met those of his son, gazing at his window through the side window of the phaeton. 'Goodbye, lad,' he said softly. Neither of them waved – that wasn't the Tockett way.

When Agatha brought in James Henry's tea at five o'clock, she found him dozing still by the fireside, the papers neatly stacked on the table beside him, the lamp switched off. She put his tray on the small walnut-topped butler's tray, let down the legs, and set it beside him. He didn't stir. She stood there for a moment looking at his face, relaxed in slumber. She could see the sadness that lay on him, the deep lines of sorrow that seemed to have been carved into his features. Poor old lad, she thought. Everything and nothing. He'd got all the brass in the world, yet he couldn't use a penny of it to keep his own lad alive for one minute longer. Though Agatha had never wanted to get married, she'd been nurse and nanny to so many young people she could guess how a parent must feel at such a moment. What, after all, is money for, if not to give the ones who follow a good start in life? All men and women work for that one aim, to make life better for the bairns.

James Henry had been a good master; he was as tight as a drumstick with the brass, but he'd always been *fair*, and you couldn't say that about many of the better-off Yorkshire folk, the ship-owners, the big farmers, the fish merchants. As a class of people, Agatha despised them all. Except James Henry, her own master, and her affection for him was something she'd never be able to put into words. She laid her hand on his shoulder and he stirred slowly.

'I've brought your tea, Mr James,' she said.

He struggled awake, rubbed his eyes and fished in his waistcoat pocket for his hunter, the only timepiece he trusted. God knows there were enough clocks about the place, but he only believed the time that old family heirloom showed him. 'You've let me lie overlong,' he said. That's what he always said these days. As he grew older, she knew, he became more and more impatient with himself and his tiring body. He still had all his own teeth and never wore glasses, but, though he wouldn't admit it to himself, she knew it took him just that bit longer these days to get about from the potash mine to the shipyard to the insurance brokerage business. Aye, and he rarely attended the Masters' meetings these days, or the Philosophical Society. But he still went to chapel.

'Then you'd better drink your tea and quick about it,' she said, with a dash of the feigned asperity she used in her verbal dealings with him. 'There's quite a number of folk waiting to see you!'

The custom had started with James Henry's father. Any Tockett employee who fancied he had a grievance could come up to the house on a Saturday afternoon, after the Master had finished his tea. It was an informal meeting; nothing said in those private sessions was ever referred to outside the Master's study. When his father had died and James Henry had taken over the running of the businesses, he'd kept the Saturday meetings going. 'It's a pressure valve,' his father had always said, 'like you get on a steam boiler. If anybody's running a full head of steam about some grievance or other, whether the fault is ours or theirs, it's a useful way of letting the pressure off a bit.' Now that women were coming to the Saturday meeting, however, James Henry had needed to institute one small change. It was now understood he'd see only five people, one at a time. No committees, no vociferous pressure groups – just five individuals, one at a time.

The first, tonight, was John Fothergill. Not a member of the branch of the family that was doing so well in Whitby and New-castle – one of the poor relations whose father had settled in Ravenswyke thirty years ago as a fisherman, and had been washed overboard in winter when he'd ignored the storm warnings. James Henry had been expecting John Fothergill to turn up to one of the meetings, as soon as he could swallow his pride. Fothergill had walked off the job in the Yard, nearly a year ago, protesting the danger and inadequacy of the scaffolding erected round an unfinished hull. He hadn't worked since; James Henry had seen to that! 'Aye, John, sit yourself down, and tell me what I can do for you,' James Henry said. It was his standard opening. 'But first tell me, how is your missis, and how are all your children? It'll be seven now, won't it?'

'Eight, Mr James, by the time she's finished. She's having another!'

James Henry knew damned well Annie Fothergill was expecting again; he'd been confident that, when John realized he'd have eight mouths to feed, he'd be back again, looking for his job.

'Right, John, what can I do for you?'

John was squatting on the edge of the chair, his cap in his hand, his tweed jacket wet with the rain, his thinning hair slicked down across his forehead. James Henry looked at the man's thin cheeks, tanned by wind and weather. You didn't see many white faces around Ravenswyke. 'I reckon you know why I'm here, Mr James,' John said. 'Winter's coming on, and with eight mouths to feed I need to be back at work instead of ligging abed.'

'Haven't you got a job then, John? I heard tell you'd applied to Bingham's. Man with your skill, I thought you'd have been suited there.'

'I was suited, Mr James, until it came to the reference. Then, somehow Jack Friendly seemed to lose interest.'

'I expect they didn't have any safe work for you, John. I know how you like to have the *safe* work. 'Course, when it's piecework and you have a Master who's being fair and paying a bit more on the piece-rate than anybody else, you might need to take a risk or two sometimes. But a father of eight can't be expected to think that way, can he?'

'That piecework is a young man's game, Mr James. Always was. When your father was alive, it was an acknowledged fact that you could come off piecework when you married and had a few bairns!'

'Yes, my father was a wonderful man, John. I'm happy you reminded me of him. Such a pity he lost money in the Yard, hand over fist, with his funny ideas. If he'd still have been alive today, there's not a man in Ravenswyke would have had a job. The Yard would have been closed long ago, bankrupt, and you'd all have had to go to Teesside for your wages. Still, we've managed to hold on to it, and I reckon we will a bit longer!' James Henry reached into his waistcoat pocket. 'There's a couple of shillings for you, John. With your missis expecting, you'll need to buy a few extras for her, I expect.'

He put the money on the table top and John looked at it, his eyes dull. 'You've got hold of the wrong end of the stick, Mr

44

James,' he said bleakly. 'I didn't come up here asking for charity. I came asking if I could go see the timekeeper Monday morning.'

James Henry looked, and he thought. His eyes held the eyes of this man opposite him, the man who had rebelled, who had committed the unpardonable error of walking off the job in a Tockett yard. Few men do that and survive. 'Learned your lesson, have you, John?' he asked, his voice quiet.

'Yes, Mr James, I'm eating humble pie, aren't I?'

'Yes, lad, I reckon you are. Go and see the timekeeper Monday morning. It won't be your old job back – I can't have folk thinking you've bested me – but it won't be piecework, neither!'

John got up and fumbled with his cap, eyeing the two shillings lying on the table. 'Take the money, lad,' James Henry said, 'and buy your Annie a chicken. They say Fewster's got some nice chickens in – I'm having one for my own supper tonight.'

The next two were easy to deal with. Sam Storm's lad had consumption, it had been confirmed, and had been taken to Killingbeck, outside Leeds. Sam and his missis wanted to go and visit him. Would James Henry advance the fare, and take it out of Sam's wages?

'Nay, lad, I'll do better than that,' James Henry said, the thought of his meeting with Dr Gilchrist still fresh in his mind. 'I'll give you the money to take all the family down there!' He took a pound and two shillings out of his pocket. 'That'll get you all on the bus, and give you a bit of summat to take with you for the lad.'

'You're a wonderful man, Mr James, and God bless your heart,' Sam said.

Could Bill Clewson fence in that bit of land where he was trying to run a few chickens? 'Certainly not, Bill. That's Tockett land, and I'll not have any of it occupied!'

'But, Mr James, that used to be common land!'

'Check the Domesday Book, Bill, before you come telling me what *used to be*! And while you're about it, take your chickens off it. I'll not have folk taking a helping hand and wanting to snatch an arm. I let you start your chickens on that bit of land when you were off sick for so long. But now you want to fence it in and make a small-holding. So you'd better find somewhere else for your poultry!'

James Henry knew he had 'a bit of bother' when the fourth

person came in. Margaret Milner, known to everybody as Meg, was dressed in a black coat over a black dress, with black stockings and shoes, and a black scarf draped around her head. And the cheeky minx had sewn some kind of fur collar round her coat that looked like dyed rabbit skin. 'Well, now, Meg, this is a pleasure!'

'Not for me, it isn't, Mr James.'

'Well, now, you've come voluntary, haven't you?'

'I've come here, Mr James, because there's nowhere else to go.'

'Then you'd better make yourself comfortable, and sit down, and tell me what it's all about.'

'You know, likely enough, what it's about!'

'Do I?'

'My lass, Elsie! Working for Agatha! You haven't changed, Mr James, in the last – how long has it been? – thirty years!'

'Is it as long as that, Meg? Ah, you were a pretty young lass in those days. Very fresh, what you might call unspoiled.'

Even after thirty years, he could remember her. She hadn't been dressed in black in those days, with a fur collar around her neck. She'd worn a green-and-white-striped dress – he could remember it still – with a high neckline and a cameo brooch on a velvet band around her throat. He could still see the way she'd walked about the house, remember her large breasts seeming fit to burst the buttons on that dress, and the generous full swell of her bottom when she walked along the corridor. Even thinking about it now, at his age, gave him a stirring between his legs.

'Unspoiled I was, Mr James, until you got me doing all those dirty things! And now, it would seem, you've got my Elsie doing the same things all over again. At your age!'

Elsie's breasts were every bit as large as her mother's. Her bottom was just as firm, just as rounded. She moaned in just the same sort of way when he fondled her. And was just as happy when he gave her the three shillings.

'You can prove what you're saying, Meg? I mean, happen you've got witnesses and all?'

'Witnesses? Here in Tockett House? I've got the word of my lass, who's never spoken a false one in her life,' Meg said, mustering all the indignation she could manage. Strange, he thought, how the ones who are basically immoral can make the most shout on a moral matter – if you can call sexual gratification a moral

46

matter. All very well for the Bible to say: thou shalt not fornicate, thou shalt not com nit adultery, thou shalt not covet thy neighbour's wife. But the Bible said nothing about playing with a girl, between her breasts, stroking the cheeks of her bottom, rubbing between her legs until she could stand it no longer and asked you – no, sometimes pleaded with you as Meg herself had done all those years ago – to put it in her. 'Stick it in me, Mr James,' she'd pleaded with tears in her eyes, reaching for the hot hard bulge in his trousers. But he'd never so much as unfastened a button.

'Meg,' he said tenderly, surprised that he could still be tender. 'Your lass is going on twenty-two. She's a right to her own mind. She'd have been married by now if her young man hadn't run out on her, when he learned he was by no means the first to sample her favours. You've got a nice little business going, Meg, in and out of your back door late at night. Good regular income with very few overheads and no capital investment except a new mattress every so often. So why don't you leave things as they are? Don't think you can come up here and start to blackmail me out of a five-pound note, because you can't. Not with your own husband away in the Green Howards, and you sharing your bed with every man who has a couple of shillings in his pocket to pay for you.'

'You're a dirty old man, Mr James,' she said. 'You were a dirty old man even when you were only a young man!'

'Enough, Meg,' he said, his voice hardening for the first time. 'How much rent do you pay for that cottage I let you live in, that has a lavatory of its own and a separate kitchen? A shilling a week? You were a bonnie lass once, and your Elsie is a bonnie lass now. And if she doesn't like working in Tockett House, she can find herself another place, though I fancy there's not many who'd take her in with her reputation. As for me being a dirty old man, Meg, I'll let you say that to me and wouldn't let no other. But that's the end of it, you understand, the end of it. You can take it or leave it.'

She got up to go, thoroughly bested, but determined to try for the last word. 'Who do you like the best, then, me or my lass?' she said defiantly. 'Come on, I'm asking you?'

'Nobody could ever touch a candle to you, Meg,' he said, 'and that's God's honest truth!'

Sal Pearce came in last, and she was wearing black too, but her

47

collar wasn't fur-trimmed. She had that funeral look that comes from ill-fitting garments borrowed from friends and neighbours; the coat was baggy and had been tightly belted at the waist though the over-large shoulders dropped part way down her arms. Her dress bulged open at the neck and she'd stuck a scarf and a pin in it. This time he didn't open with 'What can I do for you?' He got up out of his chair behind his desk when he saw who it was, and conducted her with his hand beneath her elbow to a seat near the fire. He sat opposite her, his chin cupped in his hands. 'You have all my sympathy, Sal,' he said. 'He was a grand lad.'

Sal's son was one of those who had been killed in the potash mine. Now that the funeral was over, Sal had come, according to tradition, for the 'settling-up'. What is the value of a wage-earning son? How do you reckon it in pounds, shillings and pence? He was still living at home. He'd be paying his mother seven-and-six out of the ten shillings he'd been earning a week. It'd be a few more years before he'd be getting married and his 'housekeeping' payment would stop.

Say, three years, 150 weeks, at seven-and-six. Well, you had to take away half-a-crown a week because he wouldn't be eating at home, would he? That would be nigh on thirty-seven pounds, a lot of brass.

'What's it to be then, Sal? A lump sum, or a weekly payment from the office. We shall want to do what's right.'

'I was thinking of a lump sum, Mr James. I'll have to take in a lodger now, so I shall need to smarten up his room a bit, and buy a proper bed.'

'Yes, well, a lump sum would be best, in those circumstances.' His mind raced through the figures. She'd charge a lodger ten shillings a week, wouldn't she? The lads were earning high wages these days, on piecework and with a war on. And if she was going to give him a proper bed, and his three meals a day . . . Damn it, she would be making a profit, an extra two-and-six a week now that her lad was gone. And, if she played her cards right, her a widow woman, she'd find a lodger who'd move in with her, perhaps even put a ring on her finger. And then she'd be well away. 'I've a mind to be generous,' he said. 'Your lad was a good lad, and we don't want to besmirch his memory by being mean about his compensation, do we?'

48

Though Sal didn't understand the word 'besmirch', it sounded about right. 'No, we don't want to do that,' she said. 'What did you have in mind, Mr James?'

'Well, it may sound a fortune to you, and I want you to be careful with it, but since he was such a grand lad, I think I might stretch it to twenty pounds.' He could see the dismay on her face. 'Twenty pounds is a lot of money, Sal, in a lump sum. Think of all the beds, and curtains, and whitewash all that money would pay for. Of course, if you're not happy with it, if you're not satisfied that I'm being generous letting you live in one of my cottages with that big bedroom for a lodger, and a big sitting room with a sofa for yourself, and on top of all that, giving you twenty pounds in cash, we can always leave it to the solicitors to decide, can't we? They'll work out something satisfactory to both sides. I'll abide by what they say.'

Thrummell and Slade out of Whitby had acted for Tockett for as long as they'd been in practice. Good chapel men, they lived with the Whitby aristocracy on the hill overlooking the harbour. Rumour had it that Thrummell gave his wife two shillings a week for the housekeeping, and Nellie Clewson had stood behind him in a Whitby butcher's one time and had heard him ask for two ounces of liver. For a family of four!

'No, we don't want to bother the solicitors,' she said. 'I'll take the twenty – guineas, was it you said?'

'Pounds, Sal.'

'Pounds, aye.'

'And now, since you're the last in, you must have a cup of tea with me.'

Sal was boiling inside. The mean old bugger. The sanctimonious hypocrite. They said the tea he drank was as weak as a fly's piss, and you got half a spoonful of sugar if you were lucky! 'No, thank you, Mr James. I must be on my way. You've a lot to do.' She got up to go, her cheeks blazing, but that could have been the heat of the fire on which she saw he was burning what for her would have been a weekend's coal. So, he wasn't mean in all things, only when it came to handing out the brass.

She paused on her way to the door, determined on taking her revenge no matter what it might cost her. 'I see Meg Milner was in here before me, Mr James,' she said softly. 'That lass of hers, Elsie, is working up here, they tell me. Takes after her mother,

49

Elsie does. Big girl, very big. Still, for anybody who's not particular, know what I mean, anybody who doesn't mind biting a cherry that's been nibbled by a lot of other folk. . . . Some of us likes to keep ourselves a bit more decent, Mr James. Poor we may be, but we do have our pride to keep us out of the gutter.'

She had gone out of the door before he could fashion a suitable noncommittal reply. All right, so they all knew! It would be too much to expect that a slut like Meg, or her daughter for that matter, would keep her mouth closed. What was it his father used to say? – 'Sticks and stones may break my bones, but *calling* will not hurt me!' He'd guessed they were all 'calling' him behind his back. But the look of contempt Sal had given him hurt because it reflected, in a way, a contempt he had often felt for himself and his sexual appetites. That young and abundant flesh, so much more succulent than the flesh of the woman he'd married, so lewdly lascivious, so pleasurable.

He went to the door and called out. 'Agatha,' he shouted, 'has Elsie gone home yet? Tell her to fetch a bucket of coal in here, right away!'

The storm abated about six o'clock and the smoke from the coal fires rose straight into the starlit night. The wind had done an effective job of scrubbing the sky clean of clouds; the moon would be full later, the night air crisp and bitterly cold.

'If you're going out,' Hannah Godson said to Reuben, 'mind you wrap your scarf round your throat!'

He'd walked down the bank from the tops in a most curious state, after his afternoon spent mostly sitting by the Ducketts' front-room fire, with Emily by his side on the big stuffed sofa playing halfpenny knock on the green-baize-topped card table, for matches. Or so they pretended every time they'd heard her mother coming along the passageway. Once they'd been in such a hurry to disentangle themselves they'd sent the dominoes over with a crash, but bending down to pick them up off the carpet had allowed him to hide the confusion he felt must have been showing in his face.

When it came to half-past five, Amelia Duckett had come in, felt at his clothes spread on the wooden horse, and announced, 'Right, that lot's dry. You'll be wanting to get on home!' She'd beckoned to Emily to come with her, out of the room, while he dressed. Emily had seen him to the back door, looked quickly round, and dabbed a kiss on his lips. 'Are we courting, then?' she'd asked, with a forward, mischievous grin on her face.

'I suppose we are,' he'd said. 'Owt to keep you out of the hands of that Phil Naseby.'

'He never kissed us,' she said, without removing the grin. 'I just said that.'

'Yes, I guessed that!'

As well as the scones, his mother had fried a fishcake when he returned home – two slices of potato with chopped-up fish between them, fried in batter the way he liked them. Eleanor was home, with a face long as a fiddle. He'd tickled her in her back when she came past his chair to try to make her smile, but without success. She'd settled in the chair by the fire, Dad's chair, with her knitting in her hands, but both he and Hannah noticed the time she spent looking in the flames, her hands and fingers working the wool around the needles without apparent effort or attention, her eyes flicking from the fire to the mantelpiece clock incessantly. When the hands showed half-past six, she put her knitting in its cloth bag, and tucked it in the lower drawer of the sideboard. 'Half an hour!' Hannah warned her.

'She going out, then, at this time of night?' Reuben asked. After all, he *was* the male head of the house, with his father and brothers away.

'Nowt to do with you,' Eleanor said as she pulled on her green woollen coat.

'Where's she going?' Reuben persisted, looking at Hannah.

She put her hand on his shoulder. 'Mind your own business, lad,' his mother said. 'She's going to do a bit of an errand for me. Come on, you can help me clear the table.'

He glanced at the clock when Eleanor returned; it was five-past seven but Hannah didn't chide her. Her face was even longer than before. 'Quite cold out there,' she said, 'and that wind's enough to bring tears to your eyes.'

'Aye, wrap up well, Reuben,' Hannah said. 'We don't want you coming back home with tears in your eyes.' She was smiling at Eleanor, and put her arms round the girl's shoulders. 'Come on, lass,' she said. 'You can give us a hand with the rug.' She'd already spread the hessian-covered frame by the fire, and the basket with the strips of old clothing, each cut slanting about three inches long, that would be pricked through the hessian to make a gaily coloured rug for the floor.

Reuben put on his coat, wrapped a scarf round his throat as instructed, and went out. 'Keep out of the pub' was his mother's final injunction.

He walked down Godson Street, into the Lane and went on until he came to the side of the Cut. He walked along the Cut until he could look out over the sea. Now that the storm had abated, the waves creamed in slowly, boiling pale green at the tops but not with any enthusiasm. The storm had left a smell of iodine and kelp behind that hung in the air, tangible as woodsmoke. The moon was already up, and the stars hung low in the sky so that he could see High Batts clearly, and Tockett House. He went down the slip and out on to the scaurs, the moon bright enough for him to see the fissures in the slate clearly enough not to fall over them. The long slabs canted at an angle to the coastline, not quite horizontal, so that every ten yards or so he seemed to be going down a step. Below each 'step' the pools of water held fronds of seaweed that, he knew, hid baby crabs and the whole variety of sea life. He liked to stand out here at night, with a moon above, and think of himself not alone but in the centre of a teeming life. When he turned his back to the ocean and looked at Old Quaytown, or to the left to Newquay Town, he derived a sense of pleasure from knowing he was out there, solitary. Tonight, however, he wasn't alone. He saw the figure by the low-tide waterline, and walked slowly across the spit of sand towards him, watching as he threw the weighted line end into the water, paying the line back to the spike that had been driven into the slate of the scaurs.

Phil Naseby was lining, a lazy man's way of fishing, putting out a length of baited hooks at low tide that he hoped would make the catch for him when the tide came back in. He'd walk out again at low tide and pull in his line with the catch on it.

Reuben walked across to the dark-clad figure, realizing what force had drawn him out on to the scaurs at this time of night.

'Ah, it's you, Reuben,' Phil said. 'I'm just setting a line for tomorrow.'

'I can see you are,' Reuben said.

Something in his voice must have alerted Phil Naseby. 'What's up then, Reuben?' he asked, peering anxiously into his face.

'Nowt's up,' Reuben said. All right, Phil Naseby was three inches taller than he was, and a lot heavier. He was known as a fighter – all the Nasebys took after their dad in that respect and he'd even been arrested for it a time or two. But, Reuben told himself, I'm not afraid. 'I've come to give you a warning.'

'A warning?'

'Keep your hands off Emily Duckett!'

Phil Naseby grinned and dropped the line on to the scaurs. He wiped his hands down the seams of his tweed trousers and then held them loose at his sides. '*You're* giving *me* a warning!' he said. '*You're* trying to tell *me* to keep my hands off Emily Duckett!'

'Yes, I am. She's mine, and don't you forget it!'

'Why, you saucy bugger!' Phil said slowly.

Reuben had always known that Phil Naseby, like all the Nasebys, was a quick puncher and he'd been ready for it, but the speed of the blow still took him by surprise. It came up from Phil's waist, a bunch of fist so hard, so iron-like, that it took all the wind out of his belly, and doubled him over. He saw Phil's brawler's knee coming up towards his face and managed to slew to the side so that it hit his shoulder. Phil had whirled round and had thrown his arm round Reuben's neck, dragging his head beneath his armpit. Phil's right hand came in; Reuben ducked and felt it hit the bone of his skull, above his forehead. 'All right,' he thought, 'two can play the dirty game.' He jerked his elbow backwards, felt it ram into Phil's crotch. Phil howled, and his grip around Reuben's neck slackened. Reuben bashed his elbow in again, and this time Phil let go of him and danced with his hands clutching his balls, howling. Reuben didn't need to hit him again; he rushed forward and butted Phil backwards; Phil staggered a pace or two and then toppled slowly over the edge of the scaur to fall backwards into the low-tide sea beyond. 'Keep your hands off her, you mucky bugger!' Reuben shouted, though the sound of his voice was lost in Phil's snorting and gasping as the ice-cold water closed over his body. Phil lay flat on his back with the water lapping over him. 'You hear me?' Reuben said. 'Keep your hands off her, you mucky bugger.'

Phil didn't move; his body seemed to float in the water as the waves lapped over him, streaming his hair down his face. His eyes were closed, and his mouth open. Reuben watched horrified as a

53

frond of seaweed ran into that open mouth. He bent down. 'Come on, Phil,' he said, 'stop mucking about!' He reached down and dragged at Phil's jacket, holding part of his body out of the water. Then he jumped down off the edge of the scaur, put his arms under Phil's shoulders and heaved him back up the two feet of slate. Phil's body flopped on the edge; Reuben reached down to grasp the back of his legs and heave him up and over, twisting him so that he lay flat on his back out of the water. He jumped up and crouched over Phil, lifting his head and cradling it on his arm, wiping the seaweed away from his mouth. Then he felt the sticky seepage on his hand held beneath Phil's head.

He stood up, looked wildly back at Old Quaytown, panic-stricken. He couldn't leave Phil out here, bleeding. But, should you move somebody with an injury? Bloody hell; he wasn't going to leave him. He bent down and picked him up, the water streaming down his shoulder as he threw Phil over in a fireman's lift; he wiped the water from his eyes and face with his free hand, and set off in a shambling half-trot, half-walk, across the scaurs, the couple of hundred yards back to the slip. When he was about fifty yards away, he heard a shout, and a figure came rushing across the scaurs towards him. He recognized Bill Clewson. 'It's Phil Naseby,' he said. 'We had a fight and he fell and banged the back of his head. He's out cold!'

'Let me take him for a bit,' Bill said as he hefted Phil across his shoulders.

The shout had attracted other people from the bottom bar of the Raven and he saw the shaft of light from the open door, the men standing at the top of the slip, trying to see what was happening. Bill Clewson carried the body across to the pub and inside, and Reuben followed, the first time he'd actually been in the room. A wood fire was burning in the grate; they cleared the glasses from a couple of the tables and dragged them together, laying the inert body across them, on its side. Now they could see the back of Phil's head, and the blood that had soaked his hair from the gaping wound.

'That's a nasty one,' Bill Clewson said. 'Somebody'd better go up for the doctor, I should think.'

Reuben stood beside the fire, worry etched into his face. 'We were fighting,' he said. 'I only meant to give him a bit of a punch.'

Sam Gainer pushed a glass of beer into his hand. 'Sup this, lad,' he said, 'and hold your noise.' He looked across at Stanley behind the bar. 'Give us a clean cloth, Stanley,' he said, 'and dip it in the water.'

Stanley gave him the cloth. Sam had trained in first-aid with the St John Ambulance, and often went over to the hospital in Sleights to give a helping hand. He took the cloth and wiped the cut gingerly, sponging the blood away. The cut was deep and about three inches long, blood welling continuously from it.

'Is he dead, then?' Reuben asked, his voice small and frightened.

'Dead, lad? It'd take more than this to kill a Naseby. Made of old iron and leather, the Nasebys are.'

Somebody pushed another glass of beer in Reuben's hand. 'Sup this, lad, and stop fretting,' he said. Reuben couldn't have told you from whom the drink came but he downed it in one. The room was hot and he realized he still had his scarf wound tight round his neck. He took it off and dropped it on a chair. When he straightened up again, he saw a hand with another half-pint. Sam was working deftly at the back of Phil Naseby's scalp, making certain that nothing remained in the cut. He grunted, dug deep inside, and swabbed again. In his hand he held a sliver of bottle glass that shone green when he wiped it. 'See that,' he said to Reuben, who had some difficulty focusing on it. 'He fell on a broken bottle, that's what happened. I think I've got it all out.'

Phil Naseby shuddered and his body twitched. 'Give us a bit of dry rag,' Sam said. Stanley handed over a piece torn from an old flannelette sheet, and Sam wound it round Phil's skull, bringing it tight across his forehead to hold it firmly in position. 'Anybody got a safety pin?' he asked. Bill Clewson fumbled at his waist and produced a pin that had been doing duty as a button until such time as he could get one sewn on, and Sam used it to pin the bandage tight. They turned Phil on the table; he had recovered consciousness and they swung his legs down, helped him off the table to sit on a chair. Stanley came from behind the bar with a hot rum and lemon in a glass; he gave it to Phil, who was blinking his eyes, shivering now with cold and shock. 'Get that down you, lad,' Stanley said.

Phil sipped it slowly and the colour came back to his cheeks, which, Reuben had seen with fear, had been a mouldy white-green colour. Reuben walked across the pub. 'You all right then, Phil?' he asked.

Phil looked up at him, his eyebrows lowered. 'Gin me a right clout, you have,' he said. But then he smiled. It was supposed to be a smile, but because of the tension of the bandage it came out as a lopsided grin. 'I never touched her,' he said, 'nor never shall. She's a bit skinny for me!'

Reuben pushed out his hand tentatively. 'Like, I'm sorry you cut your head. I didn't mean you no harm!'

'I know you didn't, but you can dip your hand in and buy us a drink!'

Sam Gainer and Bill Clewson took Reuben home; Phil Naseby walked on his own across the bridge over the Cut to Newquay Town, where he lived with his father and mother, three brothers, his married sister, and her husband and baby.

Bill Clewson knocked on the door of the Godson house and it was opened by Eleanor. 'It's our Reuben, Mam,' she called, horrified by what she could see hanging between the shoulders of the two men.

Hannah came to the door rapidly. 'What's up then?' she asked. 'He been in an accident?'

They lifted Reuben over the threshold, and Eleanor and Hannah took hold of him and carried him across the room to the table. When they got him into the chair, his head slumped down on the tablecloth. 'It's all right, missis. He's already been sick,' Sam Gainer said.

Hannah sniffed, sniffed again, a look of wonderment on her face. 'He's been in the pub,' she said. 'You've brought the lad home drunk!'

She whirled to them, a look of accusation on her face. 'Drunk,' she said scornfully, 'you've got my lad drunk!'

'Nay, missis,' Sam Gainer said from the doorway. 'He's got himself drunk. But it was the best way. He's had a bit of a shock tonight.'

'Then you'd better come in and tell me about it,' she said, but he shook his head.

'The lad will tell you all about it in the morning,' he said. 'It's time I was getting on my way.'

Hannah and Eleanor carried Reuben up the stairs into the back bedroom, where he normally slept with his brothers. 'You can leave him to me now,' Hannah said, 'and get yourself ready for bed.' Since Silas had left, Eleanor had been sleeping in the big bed with her mother, keeping her company. Hannah stripped Reuben, putting his sodden trousers and shirt and jacket into a heap. She lifted his shoulders, wrapped his flannelette nightgown round him, and drew it down to his ankles before rolling him under the bedclothes. Reuben was out cold and didn't even stir. She turned him on to his side – Tom Baldwin had died the night he'd swallowed his own vomit when he'd laid down, blind drunk, with nobody to stick their fingers down his throat to make him sick.

'Daft lad!' she said as she drew the sheet up around the back of his shoulders. Then she went downstairs and sat for a minute in front of the fire, thinking. It had to happen, didn't it. Like all the rest, the young boy had to go, one by one, through all the patterns of approaching manhood. Already he'd taken to the coble on his own; he'd become the bread earner. Now it'd be the pub, and the painful task of learning to hold his beer without being sick. After that, God forbid it should happen soon, he'd be courting. She sighed deeply as she emptied the tealeaves over the blazing coals, damped them down with ash from the grate, and went upstairs to bed.

It was seven o'clock when Arthur Duckett pounded on the door of the Godson house. Hannah, already up, had made a pot of tea. 'Stop your knocking, lad,' she said as she opened the door. 'You'll wake the whole house.'

'Don't tell me he's still in bed?'

Reuben had heard the knocking; Arthur had barely put his hands round a pot of tea when Reuben appeared at the passage door at the bottom of the bedroom steps. He looked ghastly. He'd put on the dry trousers and shirt Hannah had laid out for him – his face was the colour of the off-white flannelette of his shirt. He came across and stood by the fire, warming his hands at it. 'What's up, then, Arthur?' he asked, his voice listless.

'No, what's up with you, Reuben?'

'Daft lad got himself into the pub last night, that's what's up with him!' Hannah said.

Arthur's face cracked open with a great smile. 'You never did, Reuben!' he said enviously. 'You never did!'

57

Hannah pushed a pot of tea into Reuben's hand. 'Get that down you, lad,' she said. She'd already been down to the slip and had had words with Stanley, intending to berate him for supplying beer to her lad in such quantity, but Stanley had told her about the encounter with Phil Naseby, and the way Reuben had been scared that he'd killed him. 'We didn't know at first as he hadn't, missis,' Stanley had said, 'so we thought it was better to put your lad out of his misery for a bit. Sam had a look at Phil's head – it was a broken bottle that did the damage.'

'And he's all right?'

Stanley had pointed out beyond the slip where the morning high tide was just receding. Hannah could see the figure on the scaurs, overcoat flapping in the early morning breeze. 'Right as rain,' Stanley said. 'That's him waiting till the tide goes out so's he can fetch in his line. It takes more than a broken bottle to stop the Nasebys – I thought you'd have known that!'

'What brings you down here?' Reuben said when he'd drunk half his tea. 'The way you went off yesterday, I thought you was mad at us.'

'Ah, get away. That was yesterday. I was talking with Willy last night. There's a shoot on today.'

'On the Sabbath,' Hannah said, disapproving.

'Yes, there's some big muckymuck up from London.'

'Where's the wind?' Reuben asked quickly.

'From the north.'

'Right, we're off then?'

'I thought we might. Just us though.'

'All right.'

The Tocketts regularly shot the land they owned, which was stocked with pheasant to profusion. Occasionally Tockett would bring people from the county, or from London, to shoot over his land. Mostly the beaters were drawn from the inhabitants of Newquay Town – it paid five shillings for the day's beating, with all the beer and sandwiches you could manage for dinner.

The lads from Old Quaytown didn't go beating. That would have meant touching the forelock to a Tockett, and they would never do that. But they did like to eat pheasant, whenever possible. Especially when they could get it fresh.

Hannah had given Reuben sandwiches to carry in his raincoat pocket, and a bottle of tea. 'I was going fishing today,' he said to

58

Arthur as they set out, 'but you know how Mam is about the Sabbath.'

Arthur had his own sandwiches, and his were corned beef. He also had his own bottle of tea. They struck north, climbing out of Ravenswyke to the high moor. The weather was unseasonal, and a pale sun was shining by the time they struck south across the moor, over the crest and out of sight of Ravenswyke and Tockett House. The heather, always springy, was wet from the previous day's rain; they tucked their trouser bottoms into their socks and wound the strips of canvas they'd brought, from an old boat sail, around their ankles, puttee-style. Reuben's head cleared rapidly in the crisp morning air, the exertion of quick walking across the moor drawing air deep into his lungs to drive out the smoke of the previous evening in the pub. 'How was it, then, in the Raven?' Arthur asked slyly, afraid that evening might have been an experience Reuben wouldn't want to share, even though they were pals.

'It were smashing!' Reuben said. 'I don't know how much I drunk.' And then he told him about the fight with Phil Naseby out on the scaurs, not mentioning, of course, the reason for the fight. Luckily, no one ever needed to explain a fight with the Naseby family. He told how he thought Phil had bested him until he smashed his elbow into Phil's bollocks.

'You never did!' Arthur gasped in admiration.

'Yes, I did. Right in the bollocks. Twice. With my elbow.'

He told about seeing him topple over into the water, falling backwards off the scaur, to crash flat into the shallow pool. Then lying still. Arthur listened to every word. When Reuben told about the seaweed floating into Phil's open mouth, Arthur swallowed as if he could taste it. 'By heck, Reuben,' he said, 'what a lad you are. What a lad!'

'I was afraid. Dead afraid. Bloody hell, I thought I'd killed him. I imagined myself having to go into the police station to tell them I'd killed him. It'd have been murder, you know, and they top you for murder.'

'Bloody hell, Reuben, you, a *murderer*!' Never had so much prestige attached itself to the young man. Arthur was awestruck at contact with such a person.

'Well, as it happened, he wasn't dead, though I thought he were right enough. Sam Gainer brought him round, and took a bit of glass from the back of his neck that showed a broken bottle had done it.'

They stopped by the sheepfold, stone-built, by a corner of the moor where a brook and the start of a steep escarpment made a natural boundary. They squatted with their backs to the stones, the early morning sun on their faces, the wind from the north lifting safely over their heads. Reuben could see the ocean to the left, and a few of the boats from Whitby moving slowly along the near horizon. The sea had calmed considerably during the night. The gulls had come inland, but that was no bad sign; he could see them busy over by Thwaites, where Amos was doing a bit of ploughing. More and more of the moor's acres were being reclaimed by the Tockett farmers. 'One day,' Reuben said, 'if Tockett has his way, there'll be no moor here. Just plough land.'

'They'll never do it,' Arthur said. 'The moor always takes back its own.'

'It'd be rotten without the heather.'

'Where would the pheasants live?' Arthur asked logically. 'They'll never get rid of the moor so long as there's pheasants.'

They sped to the right when they left the sheepfold, down into a long valley that formed the first of several slashes nature had made in the coast; down from the top the slopes were wooded, and heavy with brambles in the undergrowth. They turned east and made their way along the shoulder of the valley, down below sight from the high tops.

'If they shoot by Body's we shall be about right up on the edge,' Arthur said, instinctively adjusting his voice to a whisper.

Reuben wasn't listening to him. 'Get down,' he said. 'There's somebody up ahead of us.'

Tockett kept a staff of gamekeepers; all were hard men who shot first and questioned later.

They dropped into the base of a hazel clump, lying still, hardly daring to breathe. Whoever was ahead of them was moving quickly and quietly up towards the lip of the ridge, dodging from clump to clump, keeping his head down among the ferns. He was taking cover from the front, leaving his back exposed. Reuben got a clear sighting of him as he neared the ridge top. 'Come on,' he said to Arthur. 'That's no gamekeeper. It's Sam Gainer.'

They went quickly up the slope. Sam must have heard them

coming; he squatted in the base of a hazel clump and the first Arthur knew of him was when Sam's arm came out and grabbed his ankle to pull him down.

'You two young buggers are making enough noise to waken the dead,' Sam said.

He had no need to ask what they were doing there; they all shared a common goal – Tockett's pheasants.

'What do you reckon to the wind?' Reuben asked Sam when they were in position, hunkered down just below the crest.

'It'll be right a bit later on. Sky had feathers in it just after dawn.' Sam looked critically at Reuben. 'How are you this morning, lad?' he asked. 'Let's see your tongue?'

Sheepishly, Reuben stuck it out.

'I reckon you'll live,' Sam said. 'I thought you were trying to drink the taproom dry last night,' he said. 'I gin up counting when you'd had nine, and the two rums Phil bought for you.'

'I reckon I owe you summat,' Reuben said, shamefacedly.

Sam shook his head, smiling. 'There'll come a time,' he said. 'You'll have your arm round a young lad who's sniffing the apron for the first time, and you'll be obliged to stick *your* fingers down *his* throat. Just remember to make sure you wipe them first!'

They all heard the boom of the guns above and to the north of them.

No more talk.

The beaters would be working east to west, driving the birds across the guns. The guests would be on the edge of the copse by Body's, strung out in a line, seeking the moment to have their crack at the birds flying in the air in front of them. And the wind would be behind them.

'Watch it!' Sam cautioned.

The shooters had the sun in their eyes, but they blazed away nevertheless, each in sequence. The gamekeeper would be discreetly placed at the end of the line, taking the last shot, making sure none of the guests went home empty-handed.

Reuben listened to the shooting, neatly at intervals. He counted six guns, six double-barrelled bursts.

And then the first one came over. A dead pheasant will plummet to the ground if there's no wind. If there's a wind, the feathers of the wing will extend, and sometimes, not often, the bird will go into a dead glide. Down wind. Off the moor and into the gully where Sam, Reuben and Arthur were waiting. It happened only one in ten times. But it happened!

This morning the conditions must have been just right; four came over, one after the other. Reuben, Arthur and Sam scattered; each was carrying a pepper pot, and where the bird landed they quickly scattered pepper around – not much with the price pepper was, but enough to blunt the nostrils of any dog that ventured down here. The bird Reuben picked up was a plump cock that must have weighed anything up to four or five pounds; he made for the fourth bird but Sam was ahead of him. 'Come on,' Sam said quietly, and they sped west along the side of the gully. Within minutes, the first dog came over the top, a yellow labrador; then another, and another. They raced about in the undergrowth, quartering each section. The first one came to the pepper, sniffed, coughed and retreated. The second one found pepper and he too retreated, snuffling. The third one must have taken a nose full; he came out of the undergrowth making the nearest thing to a sneeze Reuben had ever heard from a dog. The three dogs went back over the top with their tails between their legs. Now the guns were blazing again as the beaters worked the other side of the square, but this time the pickings would be fewer, many of the birds already having taken fright at the sound of the guns. It's amazing, Reuben thought, how complacent a pheasant can be, when shotguns are blasting a hundred feet from its hide in the heather. Somehow the pheasant must have a built-in device that tells it when the guns are firing away, that warns it when the blast is coming in its direction. Then the pheasant panics, and takes to the air. If only they knew the code – that a bird is safe from human predators so long as it says on the ground!

This second shoot brought five pheasants over the edge, but now the wind was beginning to gust. They culled the shot birds quickly, peppering as they went, but lightly. Now they had three birds each, and Sam gathered them around him. 'I think it's time to call it a day,' he said.

Arthur dissented. 'Couldn't we try for just one more each?' he asked. 'They'll be beating Tor next.'

Sam shook his head. 'It's up to you, Arthur, but I'm away down on to the scaurs and home again. I'd rather take three home than have them send a policeman for me. Any keeper in his right mind will know what's happened to his dogs.'

They scattered down the gully, each choosing a different route. Reuben went straight to the bottom of the slope and worked his way along the banks of the swollen stream the quarter mile or so to Boggle Hole. There he could walk out on to the scaurs, with Ravenswyke a mere mile and a half away, and a straight walk below the cliffs. The pheasants were heavy in his raincoat pocket; the tide was going out; he'd lost his hangover; a winter sun was shining on his cheek; gulls screamed and cawed overhead, diving down when they saw the flutter of sprats disturb the surface of the ocean.

'Yahooo,' he shouted. 'Bloody yahooo!'

Most of the treetops of the orchard ahead had been splintered by gunfire, but a few had blossomed defiantly in the French spring, and now were fruiting. The farmhouse behind them had lost its roof long ago, and its walls were reduced to rubble around which brambles were already beginning to twine their persistent fronds. The sky overhead could not be touched by the petty affairs of men at war; it shone with a painter's palette of blues and no clouds, even absorbing the occasional puffs of explosions and dissipating them contemptuously before they could form shape and substance.

Flies buzzed constantly, large ugly devils flecked with bottle green and the purple black that denotes malevolence. They settled on open wounds, laying eggs that would maggot and consume the rotting flesh; they swarmed into the moist heat of dugouts and pestered living flesh, seeking entries in the dirty unwashed skins of the half-sleeping men. They landed on bandages on which the flush of inner bleeding was revealed, heads dipping, legs rubbing, defecating venom.

The men scratched and slapped, turned over, and tried to sleep again, bone-marrow-weary, bleary-eyed, consumed by fatigue.

A regiment of flies swarmed on the uncovered pot in which the meat stew they'd had for dinner, and would have again for supper and breakfast, slowly congealed. Byron Molesworthy, Private, waved his hand languidly across the top of the pot but the gluttonizing flies ignored him. He went back to sleep, his back jammed against the inner earth wall of the dugout.

For the past hour the world of Number 2 Company of that battalion of the Green Howards had known peace since the

Germans opposing them the short distance across the no-man's-land of orchard and tangled barbed wire appeared to be sleeping, offering an opportunity none of the Green Howards could resist.

Except those assigned to duty under the unforgiving eye of Sergeant-Major Silas Godson. He walked the length of the trench silently as if it were the deck of a boat, rolling with each undulation of the shattered earth, appearing round each of the blast corners like a sea wraith. Woe betide any man whose gun was not propped over the parapet ready to fire, any man not wearing his tin hat despite the sweltering heat, any man not maintaining his once-a-minute glimpse through the parapet's spy holes, despite the risk of a sniper having located that particular six-inch-square orifice.

Lieutenant Rupert Henry Tockett was sitting in the officers' dugout halfway along the trench, hollowed back into the earth down a short flight of wooden-capped steps, when Sergeant-Major Godson made his report. The officers' dugout was in two parts. The nearer, an orderly room, contained the terminal of the field telephone link back to company headquarters. There were even two tables improvised from ammunition boxes and doors removed from the farmhouse. Across the orderly room hung a brown military blanket to form a curtain behind which the lieutenant had erected his field bed, his canvas washing bowl, even a mirror for shaving.

Pinned beside the mirror was a photograph of a face Sergeant-Major Godson knew well. He'd known the lady when she was Gertrude Aspinall, of Aspinall House, Upper Stokeley, a prize among the county folk that James Henry, Rupert's father, had carried off by sheer force of personality and wealth. Certainly the Aspinalls had been in dire straits at the time, with the failure of their West India Trading venture, and the foundering of the *Lady Aspinall*, in which unwisely they had taken all sixty-four shares, and the *Lord Aspinall*, in which they had not only the sixty-four shares but also their own cargo of Hudson Bay furs. Rupert Henry had been fourteen when his mother died; he still remembered her as a quiet, wistful lady, fine-boned and fragile, delicate and often confined to her room by a wasting sickness. He could remember being invited to sit by her bed while she lay looking up at the ceiling, or propped on pillows, talking softly with him, telling him so much he could remember about thoughts,

64

ways of life, mores unknown in the hard Yorkshire household of the Tocketts. She didn't often speak about the death of his sister, Sarah Ellen, but when she did it was with an intense bitterness that often shocked him. Only later, when, as a good Yorkshireman, he read the books of the Brontë sisters, did he realize that his mother had cast herself in a role that could equally well have been played out in Haworth Parsonage as in the bleak Tockett home. If only she'd made the effort, he realized after her death, she could have developed the strength to make Tockett House into the home it apparently had been during the life of his grandfather and grandmother.

He watched Silas Godson come into the dugout; he still couldn't get used to thinking of this man as his inferior in rank or station. During his childhood, when he came home from school he always found his way down to the dock area over the Cut, the only Tockett apparently welcome there and easy with the fishermen. He'd watch the launchings and the returns, see the catches of fish, of lobster and crabs in season. Silas Godson had always been an imposing figure to him, a man among men, with individual strength and wisdom as opposed to his own father's corporate power. Over the years he'd come to understand the difference between strength and power, especially now that the cycle appeared to be repeating itself, when Silas Godson had the strength and the wisdom, and he, Rupert Henry, had only the power.

'The captain has been on the telephone, sergeant-major,' he said. 'We're to anticipate an assault tonight.'

Silas Godson smiled. 'I anticipate an assault *every* night, sir,' he said.

Rupert Henry smiled. 'I know you do, sergeant-major, but tonight they think it's more certain. You'd better get some sleep.'

'I was just going to suggest the same to you, sir.'

The two men were comfortable together, sharing the same geographic heritage, each recognizing the position of the other, knowing the common ground and the barriers without the need to impress the other.

'The captain had one other piece of news, sergeant-major,' Rupert Henry said softly. 'We're being pulled out of the line next week. The Lancashire Fusiliers are coming in. Colonel Britten says we're going back to England.'

Silas Godson smiled again. 'Home leave?' he asked. 'All that stuff?'

'That's what they say.'

'Don't build any hopes on it, will you, sir. If I could tell you how many times we were offered home leave while you were away in England.'

'It would be good to see Old Quaytown again, to stand on the slip by the Raven and look out over the scaurs. Your lad is making a grand job of the *Hope*, you know.'

'I guessed he might. I had a bit of a letter. The young devil's started courting already! I'll give him courting, when I get back.'

'You'll be buying another boat?'

'I reckon I will. I've a bit put by. Let's face it, the chances of spending are not very great out here.'

'Will you be giving sixty-fourths?'

Silas grinned at him. 'It'd be the first time, Mr Rupert Henry. You'd have to go to Whitby for that, alongside your father.'

'I wouldn't mind just one sixty-fourth of the new *Hope*. Give me a bit of an interest. Then, maybe, you might let me come out with you. . . .'

Both knew they were dreaming. The Godsons never gave sixty-fourths, always paid cash for their boats, and never ever took a stranger out with them.

'It'd be grand to be leaving the slip, just now,' Rupert Henry said.

Silas didn't need to think. He carried a clock in his head everywhere he went, every day of his life. 'Yes, it'll be high tide coming,' he said, 'and they'll be running off Boggle Hole.'

The nostalgia, the homesickness, hit both of them like a physical blow. They could see it, smell it, feel it. A June high tide, and the heaving water streaming into the centre of the bay, clashing back from Boggle Hole, rich with glistening fish. Without a word, Silas turned and left the dugout. Sometimes, thinking, he was that choked!

Sergeant Martin took over the duty, and Silas sprawled out on his palliasse in a corner of the trench he'd cut more deeply. Within a minute, despite the pain of his memories, he was asleep, snoring lightly.

He slept for three hours and was woken suddenly by the crash of guns and mortars as the evening offensive began, with both

66

sides pouring high explosives aimlessly at each other, two ineffectual giants snarling meaninglessly, posturing. The war seemed to have bogged down into the stupidity of routine, with each side so firmly entrenched that the other had no hope of shifting it. Silas knew it was only a pipe dream that they might go home the next week; somehow he was convinced they would stay here until the war could be ended one way or the other. He uncoiled rapidly from his sleeping position, stood up, went to the corner of the trench and squatted over the latrine bucket. He wandered down the trench, checking the duty men one by one. All were in position, all pretending to be super-alert as he passed. He knew they were as bone-exhausted as he himself, so completely bored and fed up with the war that it was all they could do to hold their rifles ready.

'Offensive tonight,' young Smart whispered.

'So they tell me, lad.'

'It'll be my first. . . .'

'Then make certain it isn't your last by keeping your head down.'

'Yes, sergeant-major.'

Miller had made a pannier of tea and Silas dipped his mug into it. It was hot, strong and sweet. He'd made sandwiches out of cakes he'd griddled from flour on a hot plate, with corned beef in them. Miller could be relied on to cook something tasty for the sergeants, unlike that nancy Byron Molesworthy, who cooked endless stews for the lads. 'I hear there's an offensive tonight, sergeant-major,' Miller said.

'So they tell me. I'll believe it when it comes. But you'd better make sure everybody eats in good time.' Silas examined the griddle cake, picked a piece of brown substance from it. 'And watch the flour, Miller. There are cockroaches in it again.'

Miller coloured. 'Bloody hell! I keep it hanging from the roof in a sack.'

'I know. Don't worry – a bit of a roach never hurt anybody.'

Silas was walking past the orderly room when he heard the field telephone ring, and the orderly, Watson, answer it. He pulled the blanket aside and went in. Lieutenant Tockett was emerging from behind his blanket wearing pyjamas and belting a dark blue silk dressing gown round his middle. He took the telephone, identified himself, and stood listening. Silas waited.

'Very well, major. If that's what they want. I must say, however, that to me it does seem rather pointless. . . .' He handed the telephone to Watson, still looking at the instrument as if the voice he'd listened to were the person himself. 'That was the adjutant,' he said. 'We're to put a fighting patrol into the far side of the orchard by twenty-one hundred hours!'

'In God's name, why?' Silas asked, aghast. By 2100 hours, it wouldn't even be properly dark. They'd be an easy target.

'Because battalion headquarters, in all its wisdom, has decided that if *we* don't push a patrol in there tonight the Germans will. They'll establish a forward spotting post in there which will permit them to direct their artillery fire with greater accuracy. We're to go in there, and keep them out!'

'It'll be volunteers, lieutenant?'

'Sergeant-major, greatly though I admire your sense of discipline, and the way you have kept this company together in the absence of the company commander, I don't believe for a moment that you, *even* you, could get twenty-five men to volunteer to commit suicide. Especially when rumour has it that we are withdrawing from the line in a week's time, and home leave! I'm afraid it's names in the hat, unless you have any better suggestion.'

Silas Godson had no better suggestion; he knew quite well he wouldn't have a hope in hell of getting twenty-five *genuine* volunteers – bribe, cajole, blackmail, threaten that number of people into accepting the job, but he wouldn't be able to live with himself afterwards if, as he suspected, the patrol were wiped out.

'Right, sir, names in the hat it is.'

Rumours scuttled along the trenches like rats and cockroaches. Wherever Silas walked he saw tight lips, bleak faces, eyes from which fear and hatred of authority stared naked. He took himself, alone, to the far end of the company position from which he could see through the parapet aperture the ground leading to the orchard, the orchard itself. How many times had he stared over that undulating ground. How many times had they advanced over it and been repulsed by the superior German fire power, their mortar accuracy, the sheer volume of shells from enfiladed guns. Granted they could get out of the trench, and could traverse the first twenty-five yards; he'd ordered a tunnel cut that let them sneak out *under* the parapet, out of sight of the snipers who operated right and left. Once outside the first wire strands they could use the shallow depression to get them twenty-five yards. But no further. The previous night they had sent out a probing patrol, a recce only, to ensure the Germans hadn't infiltrated the farmhouse. Six men out, one back, and the bodies of the other five lay plainly visible, bodies crawling with the damned big bluebottles that plagued them all even in the sprayed trench bottoms. One by one the men of the patrol had been picked off, and they'd gone out in the dark. Of course, the Germans had been using star shells, fired at random, and no matter how quickly a man may halt, some sniper's trained eye will spot substance where no substance existed before.

At 2100 hours, any figure would appear as a darkening of the surround; every movement would drag eyes, and rifle sights.

Damn battalion headquarters, those blasted theorists who spent so little time in the trenches, and cared so little for human life. Who moved markers on boards, plotted strategies, made maps, drew lines in coloured pencils. Did they use red for man, because of the blood? Did they draw black, without expectation of survival?

Silas Godson pushed these wayward thoughts from his mind knowing them to be as fruitless as the act of dropping a line into sterile waters. He studied the ground ahead, feeling the responsibility of command. Later he would send men over that ground, would give them objectives and targets, military commands laced with meaning, like tea fortified with brandy. And would have no hope they could understand.

They called the men for 8.30, though it was nominated as 2030 hours. The men lined in the trench beside the orderly room. Most were freshly shaven, wearing the desperate final air of impending doom like a badge of honour. 'Present and correct, sir!' Correct is a meaningless phrase in that context; it implies only that the man has the specified equipment with him. If the patrol orders specify small pack, then he certifies he is carrying packs, small, patrols, for the use of. Nothing more, nothing less.

That his rifle is clean, has been cleaned. That his ammo pouch contains the specified number of live rounds, all cleaned and waxed. That he has shit, and pissed, and otherwise prepared his body for the rigours of the voyage.

'Your job,' Silas Godson said, hating himself for dispatching these men on such a mission so calmly, so precisely, 'is to get to

69

that orchard, and hold it. It may be that when you get there you'll find a party of Krauts approaching, wanting to occupy it themselves. It's your job to stop them. Any questions?'

Sergeant Miller would be in charge of the patrol. 'If we have to use rifle fire to stop them, sergeant-major, won't that give away our position? Won't the Germans throw a lot of shit at us?'

'Good question, and you're right! They *will* throw a lot of shit at you, mark my words. It'll be up to you to keep your heads down, and make damned sure none of the shit hits you.'

'When do we come back?' This from Private Packer, from Goathland. Silas knew his father, a sheep farmer with a liking for beer.

'You come back before it gets light enough for them to see you.'

'You come back when I tell you,' Sergeant Miller growled.

'You're right, of course,' Silas said, cursing himself. Of course, they would only, could only, move on orders.

Silas anxiously watched the evening fade, willing the sky to darken, praying for distant vision to be impaired. Of course his fisherman's eyes could see longer distances than most, but somehow the day seemed to linger on, as if reluctant to leave the warm earth.

'You'd better go, Sergeant Miller,' he said finally. His watch showed 2145 hours; time to start the hopeful deception. He spoke to the orderly. 'Tell Number Three Platoon to open fire.'

The orderly used the field telephone, and immediately they all heard the crackle from the extreme left end of the company position. The men were using tracer rounds and the shots could be seen traversing the thin residual daylight, aimed a little high, like covering fire. The men of 3 Platoon lifted sandbags and plopped them over the parapet, one by one, hoping to convince any watching snipers that men's bodies were creeping cautiously into the no-man's-land. Several sandbags were hit by bullets when the Germans opened up, concentrating machine-gun and rifle fire at that end of the position.

'Right,' Silas said, 'out you go.'

The men of the patrol went quickly into the tunnel that would bring them up into the enfilade position; Silas tapped each one on the shoulder as he went, noting that young Smart's face was sickly green with fear and a stench of trench sweat hung over him.

Packer winked at him. 'See you on the moors, sergeant-major,' he said.

'Aye, you do that. But keep your arse down, meanwhile.'

Packer winked again. 'Home leave next week. I'll buy you a pint in the Raven.'

'We don't allow riffraff from Goathland in there!'

Sergeant Miller was good, and Silas Godson, standing beside Lieutenant Tockett, watched as he shepherded the patrol along the sides of the gully that would hide them only a few yards from the German positions. Silas had shown him the best route to take into the orchard, and watched intently as the men snaked along the ground. The men of the three platoons had their eyes to the watch-holes, seeking the German firing positions. A machine-gun opened up to the left, but concentrated on the Number 3 position, deceived by the sandbags into thinking the evening's action would come from there. Mortar fire sounded sporadically; the field telephone rang and Corporal Wainscott answered it. 'Four casualties in Two Section of Three Platoon, sir,' he reported to Lieutenant Tockett.

But he was looking at Sergeant-Major Godson when he spoke, and in his eyes Silas could see the thin shaft of accusation. 'Take two men from Two Section of Two Platoon,' he said, 'and make certain you get names and some details.'

The telephone rang again and the orderly called out. 'Battalion HQ, sir,' he said. Tockett went into the orderly room and Silas could hear him. 'Of course they've left, sir. They're about fifty yards from the edge of the orchard.' His voice sounded petulant and he muttered to himself as he came from the dugout. But he said nothing to the sergeant-major. It was not in his blood to complain of a senior officer to a junior. He tugged at his barathea jacket, straightened his Sam Browne, small self-indulgent signs of his irritation Silas recognized at once.

'The lads are in position, sir,' he said.

'Good. Let's pray they have a quiet night!'

'Sergeant Miller's not the man to seek medals.'

'Good. It's not our turn this month, anyway.' With the patrol safely launched, they could both relax. Lieutenant Tockett sat on an upturned ration box; Silas Godson wedged his backside into a step in the earth wall. Neither smoked. Rupert Henry appeared deep in thought, and Silas had a habit, based on a life at sea, of saying nothing that was not strictly necessary.

Both knew, however, that they were thinking of the same geography. Perhaps it was the earlier mention of Boggle Hole that wouldn't leave them in peace, or the fish leaping at high tide as they encountered the new, sweet taste of river water, drained from the moor tops, full of bracken minerals.

A star shell rose slowly in the sky with its minute red following trace; when it burst, it cast a blue-white light over the desolated scenery, the hard-packed ripples on the earth, the craters, the torn tree-trunks, the broken stones of the farmhouse. And the thick growth of the orchard.

A bored gun barked; its shell whined overhead, fell to the earth with an audible plop, and exploded there harmlessly.

The off-duty headquarters men started a game of solo whist around a table made from a flattened tin. The cards stuck together when Taffy Jones tried to shuffle them, and he was obliged to place each one separately on the table, peeling it from the pack like pound notes from a bundle. They remembered the habits of years, and smoked, with the cigarettes, Craven A, hidden in the palms of their hands. Frank Birch rolled a gob of shag in the palm of his hand, stuck it into his pipe, bent down and lit it, carefully closing the perforated brass lid. Desmond King, who'd been a boat constructor and thought he might get into the army as a carpenter – poor fool, since he wound up in the infantry – made the ritual joke. 'What you got in there, old socks?'

Frank grunted, puffed, and without taking the pipe out of his mouth said, 'You bidding, or not?'

'Prop,' Desmond said.

'Bloody adventurous tonight, aren't we?'

'I'll cop you,' Taffy said.

'Hang on, it's not your turn to call. I've got a bloody solo here,' John Metcalf said. 'Anybody going a bundle, or a mizaire?'

Frank shook his head, turned and adjusted the lamp whose unpainted two-inch square gave their only illumination. 'That's better,' he said. 'Now we can see what we're doing.'

Silas heard the men, isolated with their off-duty light behind the curtain. He turned on the step and his eye was level with the peephole. He looked out in the direction of the wood and could see nothing moving. The evening now had that grey-purple quality he'd come to know so well since that was usually the time of maximum activity. A flower grew miraculously twenty yards into no-man's-land, its white petals the only light in that evening landscape.

'When you go out on an evening tide, and you have no water sight to inform you, how do you pick your fishing ground?' Rupert Henry Tockett asked, as if it were the most natural question in the world in that surrounding.

Silas was not surprised – he, too, had been thinking of Old Quaytown. 'I dunno,' he said. 'Folks is always asking us how we know where the fish lie, but there's no real answer you can truthfully give. Any road, whatever answer you'd give, you'd be wrong half the time, since half the time you come back with empty baskets. Call it an instinct, a feeling.'

'You don't think there might be another force involved. You don't think that perhaps the force that made you a fisherman in the first place might not have a hand in how well you do it? You don't think there might be some other influence that touches your hand when it sets the tiller port or starboard, that guides you when the times comes to shoot your nets, or drop your lines?'

Silas turned. 'Some other *force*, Mr Rupert Henry? What might that be, then?'

Rupert Henry Tockett was fumbling for ideas. 'Oh, I don't know exactly,' he said, standing, but keeping his head below parapet height. 'You don't think it might be some sort of destiny at work? Some predestination?'

Silas thought about it for a while. 'Destiny? Well, Mr Rupert Henry, I've never been able to think of destiny as a sort of universal servant, keeping us all along straight lines like a railway train. And this predestination you talk about – well, I've heard people use that as an excuse for doing nowt too often to give much credence to it as a workaday idea. You've got what God gives you, good or bad, yes, I'll grant you there's that much of a force working inside each one of us, but what we do with what he's given us, how we utilize the good and throw out the bad, well, that's a man's own decision.'

'Even if the bad, Silas, is an incurable disease. . .?'

It was the first time Rupert Henry had ever used the name Silas on its own in the trenches. Of course, in Old Quaytown, everybody called him Silas. Even the gawky young lad wearing his short breeches fresh from school had been admonished when he called him Mr Godson.

Silas was silent. What could he say? Rupert Henry had told him the doctor's decisión when he'd returned from home sick leave, but Silas had brusquely said, 'Them doctors don't know everything, Mr Rupert Henry! They get their knowledge and education from books, like the rest of the folk. They don't have any special relationship with God that makes them speak the Universal Truth, any more than parsons have. It's an opinion, nothing more, nothing less.'

'But it was confirmed by a second and third opinion. . . .'

'Not *confirmed*, Mr Rupert Henry. If I say there's fish in a certain place, and two of my lads say there's bound to be fish there, that doesn't confirm it!' But Silas had known the doctors had spoken the truth. Dying men have an aura as positive as the aura that surrounds a bad fishing ground.

The attack on the orchard started shortly after the real dusk, with mortars giving heavy fire, artillery guns following, the spotters guided by star shells, and then the blackness that told Silas men would be advancing from the German trenches. He took the Very pistol, fitted a shell into it and waited, remembering the ground, the lie of the land. The Germans would move the second the star shell they'd fired went out, relying on the dazed vision of the British to help them over the first few yards. Sergeant Miller would have located each man in that orchard with a connecting field of fire, looking forward to the German position. Though unimaginative, the sergeant was a well-trained NCO. Fifty yards is a bit close, but the best range at which to fire on a dropping target. Silas waited, counting the seconds in his mind, traversing the ground with the Germans step by step. One hundred yards. Dead give-away that the mortar fire had lifted out of the orchard, that the artillery was punching away behind the lines. 'Thomas,' he whispered, 'set that Vickers at five hundred yards. Can you remember where the right-hand edge of that orchard is? Then aim the Vickers roughly there. When I fire this thing, make sure your eye is to the back sight. You get an extra hour's kip for every German you hit, right?'

'You're on, sergeant-major,' Thomas said with his soft, valley lilt. He hefted the Vickers handles, checked the feed, the catches, ready to fire.

Silas waited a few more seconds, allowing for caution. After all, the Germans were advancing over rough ground, corpse-strewn, pitted with mortar craters.

He squeezed the trigger and the star shell soared skywards. The pistol punched back against his wrist, but already he was shading his eyes with the flat of his left hand against his forehead.

The shell exploded and began its parachute descent.

The Germans were behind the orchard, not in front of it! 'Swing left, Thomas,' Silas shouted. From both sides of no-man's-land the fire power erupted – the Germans shooting at the British trenches to keep heads down, the British trying to down the fighting patrol that was approaching the orchard from the back.

Silas knew all too well that the unimaginative Sergeant Miller would have posted his men facing forward, in direct line with the Germans' positions. The advancing patrol would cut them to ribbons.

Thomas was already firing but his swing had been too far too fast, and the first rounds went behind the Germans, to the left. He compensated rapidly, and started to creep up on them from the left, from their rear.

A hundred yards from the British position, a solitary rifle barked from the earth, it seemed. The shot took Thomas in the centre of his brow, just above his nose. The back of his head burst into a soggy red mass that pushed his tin helmet up and over. He fell backwards.

'Damnation. A sniper. A hundred yards, ten degrees left of arc,' Lieutenant Tockett snapped loudly. Silas, concentrating on the patrol, hadn't seen the source of the shot that hit Thomas. But it was certainly a sniper's bullet, no mistake about that, and from close range. Thomas had been thrown backwards against the wall of the trench and then had slid down it. His number two, Phillips, was bending over him. 'Get back on the gun, Phillips,' Silas Godson shouted in his ear. 'Thomas is dead, and there's nothing anyone can do for him. But you can get that Vickers firing again.'

Phillips looked out over the terrain cautiously. A hundred yards, left of arc ten degrees. He sighted the gun instinctively at what he thought the point should be, and pressed the heavy trigger. The gun shuddered in his hands, but he held the sight.

The sniper's shot came from ten yards to the right of the Vickers burst. It took Phillips between the eyes, in the same place Thomas had been hit. He, too, was bowled over backwards, his blood spurting over Thomas's face as he fell in a heap on top of him.

Lieutenant Tockett leaped forward to grab the handles of the Vickers but Silas stopped him. 'Yon bugger's sighting on that hole,' he whispered. 'Keep away!' Silas pushed Wilkins to one side, looked out along Wilkins's Lee Enfield. At first he could see nothing, but then, gradually, he sensed rather than saw the thin line of shadow, the same indefinable line you get sometimes along a wave top just before it breaks. How the hell had a sniper got in so close without being seen? A hundred yards! Damnation! No one in the company position was safe. 'Pass the word,' he said to Wilkins. 'I'm going to put a tracer into that sniper's position and then I want everybody to follow it with ten rounds, rapid fire. Understand. Everybody!'

He opened the breech of the Lee Enfield, took a tracer from his pocket, and held the rounds down in the magazine as he slipped it on top. When he closed the bolt, the round was in the breech, ready to fire. The word Wilkins had passed came back as a 'ready' nod, and Wilkins whispered in his ear. 'Ready when you are, sergeant-major.'

'When I say "right", lieutenant,' Silas whispered, 'put a piece of paper behind the Vickers. But for God's sake keep your hand out of the way!'

Rupert Henry Tockett grabbed a page from the army message pad and stuck it in a split that had formed weeks ago in the end of his officer's cane.

'Ready,' he said.

'Right, now!'

The lieutenant thrust the paper behind the handles of the Vickers; the crack came immediately and Silas saw a puff of dust, a very faint glow. He aimed the Lee Enfield and fired rapidly. The tracer went short-arced and clean to where he had seen the telltale glow. Immediately all the rifles opened up along the company position, each pumping ten rounds at the place where the tracer had landed, devastating that small piece of ground, pounding it, pulverizing it with the impact of the steel-jacketed bullets. The noise rose to a crescendo, and then stopped suddenly, when the magazines had been emptied. Silas could imagine each man stripping the magazine from his rifle, loading it again with the clip of ten rounds.

The Germans opened up from their trenches, machine-guns and rifles sweeping the company position in savage retaliation. Star shells fired, and mortars began their creeping crunching explosions as they sought the thin slit of the trench. One exploded in the next segment from Silas and Lieutenant Tockett, and they heard the blast and the screams of the stricken men.

Silas had his eye to the peephole, and Wilkins's rifle aiming at the position where he'd last seen the German patrol. Sergeant Miller's men had not yet started firing, but perhaps he was holding them tight-hauled, waiting for the Germans to get nearer to him. If so, he was playing a dangerous game.

Silas never heard the sniper's shot that hit him.

Lieutenant Rupert Henry Tockett screamed in rage and frustration, realizing that all that fire power, all that effort, had been wasted.

He leaped behind the Vickers and squeezed its trigger wildly.

The sniper's shot took him in exactly the same position as it had hit Thomas and Phillips.

During the late autumn, it seemed to Reuben he'd never been busier in his life. He went fishing every day, since the weather stayed fine for that time of year. November was often a turbulent month with no possibility of leaving the slip, but this year the elements were at peace, and each day saw Reuben with at least three baskets of fish. For some reason, the haddock were moving closer inshore, and he caught more of them than ever before. Even Fearon was impressed. 'If this goes on, young Reuben,' he complained, 'you'll be buying out my business.'

'You sell 'em, I'll catch 'em,' Reuben said.

Twice a week he saw Emily and now it was established they were courting. Arthur had complained, but the mothers had met and talked quietly about it, and the new fact was accepted. A couple of times they passed Phil when they were walking at low tide along the scaurs – the first time he was wearing a bandage on his head covering the stitches Dr Gilchrist had sewn in him – but, beyond giving them a sardonic smile and wave of the hand, he'd said nothing to disturb their peace.

Reuben's major joy, however, was not the fish. Not even Emily. Every evening he went down into the taproom of the Raven, the local bar formerly closed to him. Stanley would serve him a half-pint of brown ale, and he'd take a seat in the corner, away from the privilege of the fireside reserved for the older men, and spend an hour sipping it. Nobody bothered him, nobody bought him a drink, nobody talked to him. He sat there, his head down but his ears and eyes open, listening to the chatter and the gossip, proud to be accepted, however probationally, as a man among men.

To his great surprise he discovered that often he could have contributed something of advantage to the conversation. The things his father had taught him about the ocean, about fishing, about the movement of the tides, and the way the sky will tell you the coming weather in advance, were all fresh in his mind and he could have offered some of that knowledge in conversation.

But wisely, he remembered the old Yorkshire maxim – hear all, see all, say nowt!

He never paid for his half-pint with money, but every day, when he came in from fishing, he'd bring a codling or some kind of fish wrapped in a bit of paper, and hand it silently to Stanley, who'd take it without a thank-you and put it beneath the bar top, winking at Reuben as he did so.

His drink finished, Reuben would wend his way slowly up the backs into Godson Lane; the sight of the name plaque under the gaslight never failed to give him a thrill, and he'd remember his grandfather, walking up that same narrow alleyway, with young Reuben perched on his shoulder. Once he arrived home, he'd go out to the back and spend an hour or so working on his lines, or preparing the pots he'd put down in the springtime for lobster and crab, before coming in to sit by the fire and drink his cup of cocoa. By nine o'clock, he'd be fast asleep in the unaccustomed luxury of an empty bedroom, all the blankets from his brothers' unused beds piled high on top of him.

Eleanor cried solidly for three days when Terrie Pitt went to York to join the army. Sam Pitt was in the taproom of the Raven every night, drinking beer and whisky. 'He's spending his boat money,' Sam Gainer said to Reuben one evening, and shook his head. By the time Reuben left the smoke-filled, hot, heady atmosphere to go home, Sam Pitt would be sitting slumped across the table-top by the fire, his head in his hands, looking deep into the flames. He'd re-rigged the *Jolly Lads*, but it still looked like a Christmas tree, and they said the seams had all sprung and needed recaulking. The *Jolly Lads* was a sorry sight, standing beside the slip, or out on the ocean, and Sam rarely came in with more than a basket of fish. Mostly he still went too far out, ignoring the nearer fishing grounds they were all using at that time of year. Sometimes there'd be six of them all within a radius of a mile, with Sam five or more miles off. But he no longer used a mizzen-mast or mizzen-sail. Reuben looked at him many times, sitting in the pub, comparing him to his father. Sam was a pitiful creature by the comparison, and Reuben determined he'd never let himself go like that.

One night Reuben was sitting in his corner seat, keeping himself inconspicuous, when Sam Gainer, Bill Clewson and Tom Featherby came in. 'Give us a bloody pint, quick,' Sam said to Stanley, and Reuben's ears pricked up. Sam was normally a quiet, polite man. Didn't he teach in the Sunday school at the chapel? The three men sat at the table by the fire and started talking low, but in heated voices from which, from time to time, Reuben could hear the name of Fearon. Sam Gainer's eyes lifted from the group after they'd been there a few minutes, and he saw Reuben as if for the first time. 'Here, Reuben,' he called across the room, 'this concerns you as much as us. Get yourself a drink and come over here!' Bloody hell, promotion to the high table, eh?

Reuben went hastily to the bar, got his second brown ale, and carried it to the table near the fire. Sam and Bill Clewson had moved aside to make a space for him and he settled his half on the table between their pints, not trusting himself to speak. 'That bloody Fearon,' Sam said. 'He's twisting us.'

'Twisting us?'

'Bugger told me the market price was tenpence; my wife's brother just come over from Whitby and says they're getting a bob.'

The selling of fish is a complex matter; Fearon would give them a price which reflected the state of the market. But that wasn't the firm final price. If, when he took the fish to market, the price had dropped, he'd pay less than the offer, but if he got in on a rising market he'd be obliged to pay more. That was the system the fishermen of Ravenswyke had always used with Fearon; it had been worked out by their grandfathers with Fearon's grandfather when he first came into the business. Fearon spent a lot of his time in Whitby, and was supposed to know what the markets were doing. Of course, the price paid for fish reflected accurately the amount of fish that was available at the market time, and it only needed one group of fishermen to bring in a large catch for the price to be depressed, sometimes by as much as a penny. But never twopence. It'd take a real glut to do that. Of course, they had largely to rely on Fearon's word, since they couldn't be there in the market at the actual time he made his sale, and the price of fish could change up or down radically within ten minutes.

But for Fearon to downgrade them twopence was nothing short of criminal.

'What'll we do?' Reuben asked.

'Whatever we do, we must do it together,' Bill Clewson said. 'We must all stand side by side in it.'

'I suggest we have a meeting,' Sam proposed. 'Here in the tap. Fearon never comes in here, nor ever will if I have my say.'

'When's the meeting to be?' Reuben asked, proud to be taken for one of them, side by side, with equal rank.

'Tonight's as good a time as any,' Sam said. 'You go round the houses, Reuben, and tell 'em to make their way down here; tell 'em to come singly, not all together, and keep it casual. We don't want Fearon getting wind of it.'

Reuben set off immediately. As he arrived at each of the fishermen's houses, he'd knock on the door quietly and usually the missis would open it. 'There's a meeting in the tap of the Raven. About Fearon!' That name was all he needed to say before he sped to the next place. He knew the fishermen would understand. They'd had a meeting once before, when Fearon had tried to charge them for the boxes. Fearon's father and grandfather had always kept the fishermen supplied with boxes, into which they tipped the fish from the baskets. Some of the bigger boats used to take a few boxes out with them and do a bit of sorting before they came back in, so's they could see how much was haddock, how much codling, or soles. Sam Gainer had taken four boxes with him one day, and a sudden storm had pitched him about. He'd lost three boxes of haddock over the side and arrived back angry. His anger was increased, however, almost beyond reason when Fearon had tried to charge him for the lost boxes. And then had said he was going to charge everybody! That had been in 1913, and Silas Godson had taken charge of the meeting, at which they'd voted to cut Fearon right out of it. They'd club together, buy a wagon, maybe one of the new ones with a motor on it, and cart the stuff to Whitby themselves. They'd take turns going there, and place the fish with Lington, an honest wholesaler. They'd have done it, too, but when they went to Fearon with a show of strength, though he called them all bolsheviks, he'd had to back down. Though they did say he'd brayed hell out of his missis that night, for spite.

When the meeting assembled there was an awkward silence, and Reuben was discomfited to find they were all looking to him. After all, he'd been the one to call them out, though the idea for the meeting had been Sam Gainer's. It was with a shock that Reuben realized that, in the absence of Silas Godson, his father and their natural leader, they were expecting some sort of overture from him. By now he'd drunk *three* brown ales, and though he was far from drunk he felt a certain light-headedness. It was only this that even permitted him to speak, since normally he would have retired quietly to a corner as the youngest one present. It wasn't his privilege to lead these men, not yet.

'Go on!' Harry Golding said. 'Say summat, young Reuben.'

There was a sinking feeling in the pit of his stomach, reminding him of the time he'd thrown out the line without securing the end of it. He stood on a chair and cleared his throat. 'Hold your noise,' somebody shouted, and the room fell instantly silent, all faces turned up to Reuben's.

He looked round at the sea-gnarled faces of the men below him, men who'd spent a lifetime going to sea for fish, men who'd lost children older than he was, who knew instinctively more about the tides, the wind, and the weather than he would ever be able to learn. 'Well,' he said. 'Like . . . I mean to say. . . .'

Sam Gainer leaned forward and touched his leg. 'Get on wi' it, Reuben,' he said, 'you're all right. You're doing fine. Just speak up a bit.'

'Yes. Well. . . .' Where did the surge come from? Where did the words form themselves and spring, ready-made like a Club suit, to his lips? He'd never know. 'Well, it looks as if Fearon's trying it on again. He's been docking us twopence on the price of fish and that's a lot of money, money we can ill afford. He tried his tricks once before, and we put him to rights, so maybe the time's come again to teach him a lesson.'

Now there were assenting growls from round the room – most

81

of them had suspected they were being twisted, but none had had the proof.

'It's not rightly for me to say, but I'd think we should work out a way together to do Fearon in the eye. To show him that if he can't play fair wi' us, then he ought not to be playing with anybody. We're all working men; we all know what it is to turn over in bed and wish we could have just another five minutes on a cold morning. We all know what it is to go out there in the sheeting rain, soaked before we're even off the slip. We know what it is to hold on to a rope with us knuckles cut, and the saltwater rubbing in. And we know what it is to haul up fifty fathoms of line and find the bait gone. If we're doing all that for the sole benefit of a twister who's ligging warm abed, I'd say none of us wants it. I know we'll be called bolsheviks, but, frankly, I don't even know what that word means. My dad never bothered to explain that to me!'

There was a laugh that rolled around the room like a wave bouncing off a cliff bottom.

'Maybe he had more important things to tell me. But I'm telling you all this – I'm not working, the Godsons have never worked – for the sole benefit of another. I'm working for me, for my family, for the *Hope of Ravenswyke*, and for the . . .' – the word came to him after only the slightest hesitation – 'unity of all of us here!'

They took the word and shouted it. 'Unity, that's it, Reuben, unity!'

Sam Gainer reached in and pulled Reuben down off the chair. 'That were grand, lad,' he whispered. 'You've done right well and got 'em started. Now take a bit of advice. Let 'em mull it over a bit. Let 'em make up their own minds about the best way to go ahead.'

Three half-pints were pushed simultaneously at Reuben. He laughed, thanked the buyers, and set them on a table, sipping cautiously at the first one. The atmosphere in the room was electric and he didn't want to miss a second of it. Fancy him, Reuben, getting on his hind legs and spouting all that! He couldn't remember a word he'd said except that one last inspired word – unity! And fancy them bothering to listen to him, a bit of a lad!

Clive Helliwell was standing next to Reuben in the buzz of conversation. He pointed to Sam Pitt, who was standing with his back to the bar, listening to the throb of sound with a vague, uncomprehending expression on his besotted face. 'I were watching when you brought the *Jolly Lads* in, Reuben,' Clive said. 'I mun say a right bit of seamanship, that were! Though looking at t'owd lad standing there wi' his sons gone to t'army, I'm not sure as it wouldn't have been kinder to let him go down. He'll never see them lads of his again, you know, and it might have been kinder to let the stones take him to the bottom.'

Reuben shivered as he heard Clive's words. The fishermen put stones in the pockets of their overcoats when they went on board in the winter; they'd rather sink quickly if they were washed overboard than try vainly to swim to safety. A cold death, but quick was the best a fisherman could hope for.

'He'd have done the same for me,' Reuben said. 'He'll get over it. And Terrie and Alf will come back, when the war's over.'

Clive shook his head. 'Mark my words, Reuben, you'll be going to foreign places to see that sister of yours wed. Likely Hull, Yarmouth, Lowestoft!'

'Wed? Who's said anything about getting wed?'

Clive laughed. 'Aye, you'd be last to know, I reckon. But I saw them holding hands – not doing nowt wrong, mind you – and I've seen that look on many a lad and lassie's face afore now! We shall be seeing 'em walk out of the chapel together. That's if we can afford the brass to travel to where they wed. But, mark my words, it won't be in Ravenswyke. Any road, enough of that. Your dad had the right idea years ago when he suggested we make a co-op to sell the fish. Why should we hand it to Fearon? We could handle it ourselves. One thing, though, I should warn you. Fearon has the Whitby crowd in his pocket. They'd gang up on us, with the bosses behind them, and we'd not get a price for owt. We'd have to take it further afield.'

'Where, do you reckon?'

'It'd have to be Pickering.'

'To the railhead?'

'Aye.'

'Are you going to suggest it, then?'

Clive laughed deprecatingly. 'They'd not take it from a Helliwell. But, coming from a Godson . . .'

The meeting appeared to be breaking into fragments, and sporadic arguments had broken out in several areas of the room. Sam Gainer was trying to talk to one group but was being shouted down by Harry Golding and several others.

'Go on, lad,' Clive Helliwell urged, 'afore it all goes to pot!'

Reuben felt the exhilaration of power. Yes, he truly believed he could carry them all along with him. He recognized he was substituting for his father, but if they'd listen to him . . . Anyway, he was a Godson. He'd try.

Clive banged his empty beer mug on the table; made of pewter, it was a family heirloom Stanley kept for him behind the bar. It made a shocking noise that stilled everyone in the room. 'Hold your noise,' he shouted. 'Our Reuben wants to have a few more words.'

And so it was proposed. The fishermen would form their own co-operative. Fearon would be starved out of Ravenswyke. The fishermen would use any means possible to take the catch to market in Pickering. When the Whitby merchants realized they were being done out of a profit, they'd come to heel, and Fearon's influence with them would be broken. Reuben's stroke of genius came at the end, when the vote had been taken with a show of hands that revealed unanimity.

'You, Sam Pitt,' he shouted across the room from the height of his chair top. 'Can you hear me still?' There was a kindly laugh, and someone pushed Sam a pace or two forward, away from the bar. 'That's the man to do it for us,' Reuben said persuasively. 'We need a man who knows fishing as well as any man in this room, a man who's spent his life at sea and can tell a haddock from a cod. Aye, and a man who's mean with a farthing. Because it'll be *our* farthings he'll be saving, from now on! We'll appoint Sam Pitt, Mr Samuel Pitt, as the agent for the co-operative of Old Quaytown.'

'He'll sup it all!' Harry Golding said disgustedly, but, despite Harry's age and bulk, his well-known muscular strength, Reuben, young, wiry, but charged with authority, turned on him. 'He'll do no such thing!' he said, his young voice ringing with conviction, eloquently sincere. 'He'll guard every penny of our brass until the pay-out. What he does after that is his own business. What about it, *Mr* Pitt? Am I right in what I say?'

Sam blinked his eyes and there were tears in the corners.

Reuben wouldn't let him back away. 'If we're going to be related by marriage, according to what they tell me, I'd better be right! Our Eleanor's not having a boozer for a father-in-law!'

The laugh that swept the room drove away all misgivings, even Sam Pitt's. And he was the logical choice. He had been a fisherman, he was as mean as a skinflint, he was a son of Old Quaytown.

'Right,' he shouted. 'Tha's bloody-well on!'

Nothing was said to Fearon, or to anyone else outside the taproom. They all clubbed together, and Sam Pitt went away with all of £100 in his pocket and bought a wagon. They went fishing, as usual, and brought their catches in, as usual, giving them to Fearon. Reuben was given permission to take Arthur Duckett into his confidence; Arthur was in Whitby and able to hang around when Fearon made the sales. Arthur recorded the prices meticulously without Fearon's being aware that the young lad who delivered telegrams was actually listening and watching. 'I shall get a job with the co-operative,' Arthur said. 'When you've got it all going, I'll speak to Sam Pitt to take me on!'

'I can't promise anything,' Reuben said. 'We've made a committee and it'll depend on them.'

Arthur had smiled his lopsided grin at him. 'I've been reading about the co-operative they've formed in Salford,' he said. 'I know how it works. I've been studying all about it, the shares, and all that sort of thing. Sam Pitt's not a book man. He'll need somebody like me, mark my words!'

They struck on the fourth day, a Thursday. Friday was always a good day for fish retailers; they bought desperately on a Thursday to satisfy the demands of their customers. The boats, by agreement, went off the slip early, around five o'clock, even though the weather was blowing up a bit and a cold wind lashing across the moor threatened to cap Tockett Top. It was agreed they'd work a line, each dropping three baskets of fifty fathoms. And then they'd come in, all at the same time. It was eleven o'clock when they started to come back in and the catch was good; that much was plain to see from the first boat to be dragged up the slip. Fearon was already in the saloon bar of the Raven, drinking a rum and black. He put on his coat, finished his drink, clapped his beaver hat on his head, and bid Stanley, who'd stayed in the saloon to serve him, good-day. Stanley grinned hugely. 'You haven't paid for your drink, Mr Fearon,' he said evenly.

Fearon's eyebrows shot up. 'I'll pay you tomorrow, if you're in a hurry or in need of a coin or two.'

'I think you'd better pay me today, Mr Fearon,' Stanley said calmly, his eyes twinkling. 'Which of us knows where he'll be tomorrow?'

'You're taking my credit away?' Fearon could hardly believe his ears.

'Happen I am,' Stanley said. 'You being a Newquay Town man, you shouldn't rightly be drinking in here at all. I only let you in because of the fishermen, you know!'

Fearon reached into his pocket, drew out a couple of coins, and flung them on the counter. 'That's the last drink I'll ever take in here,' he spluttered.

Stanley nodded, took the coins, found threepence change, and laid it on the mahogany. Fearon snatched it up, mustered what was left of his dignity, and left. When he reached the bottom of the stone steps that led out of the top of the Raven Hotel, he saw a wagon parked across the path. Sam Pitt was wearing a suit and an overcoat, and was loading the fish out of the baskets into boxes. On the side of the boxes someone had written with a red-hot poker, OQC. Fearon went across and looked at the new boxes, recognizing the maker as the same man who made his boxes, which had been stacked at the side of the steel railings overlooking the slip, out of the way.

Fearon's team of two horses, and his wagon, were backed up into the lane by the post office, next to the pub. It seemed as if the whole of Old Quaytown had turned out to watch; the women stood in their coats and shawls amid an atmosphere of expectancy. 'What's going on?' Fearon shouted to Sam Pitt.

Sam kept on tipping the baskets into the boxes and loading the boxes on to his cart. 'You'll have to excuse me, Fearon,' he said. 'I'm too busy now to talk with you. Come back in a couple of hours.'

'What are you doing with *my* fish?' Fearon shouted, his voice strident, his face mottled with anger.

'*Your* fish, Fearon?' Sam Pitt said, infuriatingly continuing with his work. 'Have you paid for it, then?'

'Of course I haven't, man.'

'Then how can it be yours? I think rightly, fish belongs to the man who's caught it, until such time as somebody pays him for it.'

'What's all this OQC nonsense?'

'OQC, Fearon,' Sam said, as if addressing a backward child,

'stands for Old Quaytown Co-operative. The sole agent for the fishermen of Old Quaytown. So you can put that in your pipe and smoke it!'

Fearon looked quickly round. The circle of women had pressed in close. Suddenly he realized what each one of them was carrying in her hand. A wooden rolling pin.

Sam Pitt stopped work and stood tall and proud in front of Fearon. For the first time since Fearon had known him, Sam Pitt had washed clean, had shaved close. His suit had been pressed. His overcoat was clean. His boots were polished. And on his head he wore, at a jaunty angle, a beaver hat!

'Fearon, you're finished in these parts,' he said. 'You're through, washed up. There's not a man in Old Quaytown as'll ever sell you a piece of fish, not even if it's wrapped in newspaper with chips and salt and vinegar. And you know for why? Because you're a twister, Fearson, you'd twist the tit out of a baby's mouth if you could.'

The fishermen had gathered behind Sam Pitt. They were an awesome crew. Each of them carried a twist of rope, with a knot on the end. Fearon swallowed hard. The fishermen ignored him after that first glance, and went to stand with their backs to the Raven, forming a line. The women went to the other side of the slip and they formed a line. When the line opened at the far end, there was an avenue. Fearon had two choices. He could go down the slip where the wind and the waves were lashing the sea up against the ramp. He could go into the sea. Or he could brave the tunnel of that avenue. He had no option. He tried to assemble the last tattered remnants of his dignity, gathered his coat tightly about him, clamped his beaver hat on firmly, and then set out in a sprawling shambling run, hoping to take them by surprise. Each fisherman, each fisherman's wife, each fisherman's dependant, gave himself the liberty of one blow, one strike, one gesture in which all the bitter hatred for this twister, this thief, this blood-sucker who had battened on them, was contained.

No man stayed his hand, nor woman, so venomous was the acid Fearon had instilled into them; all aimed for the back, the shoulders. Sam Pitt had the last blow and his was different from the others. He knocked Fearon's beaver hat, the hated symbol of his chicanery, flying from his head. 'Now get out of here,' he shouted, 'and don't ever cross that bridge again, or you're a dead man!'

Fearon walked slowly up the street, realizing for the first time that all had been done in a most terrifying silence, that no one had cried out in jubilation, that the hatred he had spawned was too deep, too intense, for the relief of words.

James Henry Tockett was in his study when Fearon arrived to tell him the story. He recognized the danger immediately and sent for Willy. 'We'll be going into Whitby, Willy,' he said, 'and don't let me have any nonsense with that magneto. I'm in a hurry!'

Fearon rode with him, though James Henry put him in the front seat next to Willy, as befitted his station, while he sat in solitary splendour in the back of the phaeton, his fur collar tight around his neck, a cigar in his hand, a silver flask on the seat beside him.

He had Willy park the car outside the fishmarket; Fearon hastened round the buyers who came quickly in response to Tockett's command. Tockett wasn't a man you ignored, or suddenly you found your credit at the bank not so good, your standing in the community eroded in subtle ways.

It took ten minutes, no more, to ensure that no Whitby wholesaler would handle Old Quaytown fish, any fish from the OQC, other than through Fearon.

Fearon took up his position in the market, waiting for the arrival of Sam Pitt with his wagon of fish, a smirk on his face. Tockett had left as soon as the embargo was clamped down. The wholesalers went about their business, buying the fish that arrived from Staithes, from the Whitby boats, from Robin Hood's Bay and Sandsend, on behalf of customers with hotels, restaurants, fish-and-chip shops. It was a cold midday, with the temperature dropping to freezing in the exposed fish-sheds. He went into the nearby pub, drank a rum to warm himself, flushing again at the humiliation he'd suffered at the Raven, and then in the street outside. Tockett had suggested he inform the police, but what was the point? If he accused an entire village, would the police arrest all of them, every man, woman and child? What would they do with them? The story would make good meat for the *Gazette* – it would be front-page news and then Fearon would truly be finished. He'd bring them all to heel in his own way. Once they realized they couldn't sell except through him he'd make them eat all their insults, make them suffer the pain of every blow they'd planted on him. He realized they hadn't struck him to injure him physically, or his back and shoulders would have been broken. The final insult had been that they'd all slapped at him, containing their anger, so that though his back and shoulders ached intolerably, nothing appeared to have been broken. Except, they hoped, his spirit. Well, he'd show them. After this day, his commission on every sale would be no less than forty, no, forty-five per cent. He'd been too damned lenient with them in the past. Well, now the time had come to show them.

That daft bugger Sam Pitt was taking a long time with the wagon. Ten to one he was stopping, drunken sot that he was, at every pub on the way.

Two o'clock came and went.

At three o'clock Fearon felt the first flurry of snow on his face, the first twinge of apprehension. Where the hell could Sam Pitt be?

At four o'clock the wholesalers came to Fearon. 'You and Tockett needn't have bothered,' they said. 'They've taken their fish elsewhere.'

'Elsewhere? Where else could they go?'

'Scarborough. Filey.'

'Nay, they'd never compete with the Scarborough or Filey fleets.'

But Fearon knew, in his heart, that somehow he had been bested.

Sam Pitt hadn't waited to give Arthur Duckett a job as his assistant and tally clerk. Truth to tell, he wasn't feeling the confidence he was trying to show; there'd been too many pints of beer, too many rums, passed down his gullet to let him face the world bravely. But he felt that even at his time of life, with the younger willing lad to help him, he could make something of himself. He chuckled as he remembered how young Reuben had called him a skinflint. Aye, he'd always been careful with money, up until the time the lads left him. They'd never given him credit for it – he'd wanted to save the money for them, in the first place. He'd wanted to keep a bit by so that his two lads could enjoy life. But then it had become a habit, a disease, and though he knew he was prejudicing the catch by not having his gear in trim, because he couldn't thoil to buy a new bit of rope, a new sail, there'd been nothing he could do. And saving money had resulted in their being poorer than ever, because they couldn't catch the fish. Well, now the lads had gone; at first he'd asked himself, what's the point of it all, and had started to drink the little bit of brass he'd put by, his 'boat money'. Reuben had brought him out of that by trusting him, and he wouldn't let them down.

Still, it was a comfort to have Arthur travel with him across the lonely moors, the sixteen miles to Pickering. Champion was pulling well with Bessie. Sam reckoned that in four good hours they'd be there. Just in nice time to catch the market before it closed. By gum, he'd create a sensation when he got there. He'd be able to sell at the Whitby price, saving the buyers a Whitby commission. Well, he'd put a penny on, for the transport. Arthur had explained to him in his bookish way that you have to have a return on your capital investment, that, by rights, the customer ought to pay bit by bit for the wagon, for the upkeep of the boats, as well as for the fish itself. It was all double dutch to Sam, but the young lad had his head screwed on right. No wonder they'd taken him into the post office.

It was cold, no two ways about it. He walked beside the wagon with his hands tucked into his overcoat pocket from which he'd removed the two heavy stones.

They headed due west, away from the coastline, down the tracks across the moor he'd known when he was a lad. It'd been a long time since he'd walked them – not in fact since he was courting Annie, who came from Goathland. His face twitched with sorrow when he thought of Annie, his wife. Aye, it was when Annie was taken away, and they'd buried her on top of the moor, that everything had started to go wrong, wasn't it? It was a poor mean life without her, without her laugh, and her pink cheeks, and the warmth of her fat flesh beside him day and night. Her roly-poly arms to come home to, and the smacking kisses, and her opening the fire oven and the smell of new-baked bread coming out, or a pot with meat and taties. Nobody could have told him the poor lass was living on borrowed time; she was that fat and jolly, with the high colour in her cheeks, you'd have thought she could have gone on for ever. And so she would have, if she hadn't been born, as they later said, with a faulty heart that had strained and strained to give Sam Pitt the best of everything, and then had burst. She'd even died with a bellowing laugh on her lips; in those days, even with the two lads and the lass, they were still young at heart and they used to lark about in the kitchen until sometimes they'd fall down with laughing, and him tickling her, and by God was she ticklish, and her howling and hooting with laughing and trying to twist herself away from him, but not very hard because she knew how it always ended with her sitting in the chair with her legs spread wide, laughing and saying, Sam, somebody might come knocking. And, suddenly, the laughing became a choke, and her rosy red cheeks turned purple with the strain, and she shuddered, and died. And most of what made Sam alive had died with her.

The first flurries of snow took him by surprise; at sea he'd have read the signs easy enough, but back here, crossing the moors, he was in a foreign element, alien and somehow frightening. 'Come on, Champion,' he said, 'let's get a move on! And you, Bessie, there'll be no hay for you, my girl, if you don't get a move on!' The wagon groaned under the pull of the horses and the weight of fish. By gum, he'd got a right load for the first day, nicely sorted. Weather like this, it'd arrive at the market in beautiful condition – they'd see how fresh it all was.

And so they did, clamouring around the cart to buy, some of it wholesale, but, as the word got around, even retail. And he'd put twopence on what he reckoned the Whitby price would have been, and certainly threepence and even fourpence more than Fearon would have given, and still the folks were happy. And quite right too, because they knew they were getting today's fish today, not tomorrow, and they were getting the best choice, not the remains after the big buyers had picked it over for York, Leeds and London.

When the cart was empty, and the boxes stacked again, they set off up the hill out of the market place. 'Nay, Sam, aren't we going to stop and have summat to eat?' Arthur complained.

'Aye, when we get outside the place.' Sam didn't want to stop anywhere within sight of a pub. Anyway, the night was coming down fast, and he wanted to get back to Old Quaytown. Today's run had been a proving trial; they'd shown, to judge from the jingle in his pocket, that it was the right thing to do. He wanted to get back, and show his money bag in the tap. He knew they'd be waiting for news, not certain yet whether they could trust him all the way or not. He wanted to show them, to re-establish himself. And then there was tomorrow and the day after, and every day until they had the buggers in Whitby licked, until the OQC was fully accepted.

Now they were travelling full east, the snow was driving hard at them, coating the fronts of their jackets and their faces. 'Get on the wagon, lad,' Sam said, 'and build yourself a bit of a shelter with the boxes.'

Arthur protested but Sam had found a new strength. 'Do as I tell you, lad. We've a long way to go home and I don't want to be worrying about you. Wrap yourself up as warm as you can, but get under the boxes out of this snow.'

The horses knew they were going home and clipped along at a fair lick. Sam saw he'd wear himself out keeping pace with them so he climbed on the wagon and rode the front bench. It became dark early, and turned even colder. Champion was sure-footed, even on the black ice that had formed, but Bessie, younger and less experienced, was not so deft. Once or twice she would have slid if Champion hadn't braced himself in the trace, giving her support, turning his head and nipping her neck to encourage, not chastise her. They followed the roadway for six or so miles, clopping along down and up hill in fine fettle despite the swirling snow and the freezing temperature. Sam was working out in his mind that they'd need to establish two teams once they'd got going. One team to go to Pickering and stay overnight there, resting. If they tried to do the journey twice a day, they'd kill somebody, if only the horses. Or perhaps they should buy a motor-car; that might be the answer. So concentrated was his thinking that he almost missed the moor turn-off. But Champion saw it in time and nudged Bessie over. Now they were on the high moor, with miles of open ground to cross, following a track. The wind howled up there, and the snow swirled, blocking his eyes, coating his face. He wound his scarf tight about his mouth and nostrils so that only his eyes showed; he'd forsaken his beaver hat in favour of a cloth cap, which he pulled well down about his ears. He held the traces between his knees, knowing Champion needed no urging, and slipped his hands into his overcoat pockets. By gow, it were cold, he reckoned. Well below freezing. The sea holds warmth, even in winter, and the temperature is never so low, never seems so low, as over the unyielding land. He hunched his shoulders forward, trying to see through the swirling snow mist. This track was unfenced and barely wide enough to take both sides of the cart but, if he could make it, if Champion could pull them through, it would save many miles. He hadn't dared try it with the full load and had climbed down into Littlebeck, and then up Blue Bank, the one-in-five climb that Champion had taken in full pride. Going back, however, he hoped to be able to forge his way across the moor top itself. The track dipped and rose, often hub deep in water in the becks. Ice had formed on the slopes leading out of the becks and once or twice only Champion's sure-footedness lifted them back on to the tops. Sam could feel that Bessie was tiring, not pulling her weight, and the cart had a tendency to slew to the right.

'How are you doing, lad?' Sam asked, and Arthur's voice came back at him, thin and tired. 'Very cold, that's how I'm doing!'

'Tomorrow, us'll bring a tarpaulin for you to get under!'

'Aye, we'll need that!'

Now the wind was really howling and the snowflakes were driven almost horizontal into Sam's face. Even Champion snorted and snuffled. Over the top they headed down a long steep incline, and Sam could just discern the gleam of water below where the beck had swollen. Half of him regretted having decided on this shortcut; the other half said the sooner they got home the better. Certainly they would never have made it down Blue Bank with all that black ice about; they'd have skated from top to bottom.

Perhaps it was fatigue, or her youth and nervousness, that caused her to skitter, but when what seemed like a rabbit flashed out of the heather under Bessie's fore, she rose up in the traces in a savage kicking, rearing movement that snapped the pole of the wagon in two. Champion whinnied and reared, too, and the broken end of the pole hit his flanks, running deep into his side. Bessie was enraged, now, out of her senses and kicking up and back. Sam bellowed at her and flashed the whip at her, but still she kicked and her hoofs landed smack on the front board. There was a terrible noise of splintering wood as the footboard smashed backwards, and Sam felt the force of the blow run up his legs to slam at his pelvis. The wagon tipped sideways as Bessie pulled it with the dead weight of Champion, who'd slumped down and sideways when that broken pole end had stuck into his side. Bessie was crazy with cold and fright, and kicked at anything she could find. Within seconds the front of the wagon was in ruins and Sam had been catapulted off it. He felt a tearing snap in his shoulder as he hit a rock at the side of the path, as if a bundle of straws had been rent apart by bending; Arthur was up and shouting as

Bessie kicked herself free and thundered off down the slope, sliding, running, snorting with anger and frustration. Arthur had a bump on his forehead the size of a duck's egg, where the corner of one of the fish boxes had hit him. He fell out of the ruins of the wagon into the snow-laden heather, in a daze, not knowing where the hell he was.

'Sam?' he shouted, half crying. 'Sam?'

Champion bellowed as the pole was driven in deeper, and tried to rear up on his back feet, Arthur saw a great rush of bile and blood pour steaming out of the horse's mouth, and the pool of red that drenched the horse's side before it collapsed on the ground in the midst of the splintered wood.

'Sam,' Arthur yelled. 'Bloody hell, Sam, where are you?'

He wiped the back of his hand across his face and began to stumble around.

Sam was lying up against the rock and half immersed in the heather. Arthur felt at his face, and Sam's eyes were closed. 'Sam?' he whispered.

There was no reply.

'Bloody hell, Sam? Talk to us, Sam!'

Only the howling wind spoke, telling Arthur he was alone on the high moor, in freezing temperatures, miles from the nearest human being, at night.

'Sam!' he yelled, trying to force Sam to come back from where he'd gone by the sheer volume of his cry.

That November night was the coldest that had been recorded for thirty-seven years, and five feet of snow fell on the high moor. They estimated that 300 sheep were lost that night.

It was two weeks before the snow thawed sufficiently for the outlines of the broken wagon to be discerned. When they dug down, they discovered the body of Sam Pitt, with his back to the rock, his shoulder and his thighs broken.

They never found the body of Arthur Duckett.

Walter Brackley hated the damned war more than any other man, but then he had good reason to do so. He'd been captured at Bloemfontein with a wound in his leg and broken bones. They'd healed the wound and botched the fixing of the bones. When Walter finally came home from South Africa, his right leg bulged outwards like half a question mark.

Oddly enough, almost as if he had a need to prove himself, he sought a job with the post office; they gave him one out of pity and admiration and from then on he spent his days hobbling about the streets of Ravenswkye with the letters. Despite the bow of his leg, daily he covered the ten or fifteen miles required, up the cobbled streets and down again, across the bridge into Newquay Town, then up to Tockett House. It was a matter of principle with Walter that the mail for Tockett House, even though it weighed by far the most, was always delivered the last.

The heaviest mail he ever carried, however, was not the Tockett bundle, nor the mail-order parcels, but the War Office telegrams.

He knocked on the door of the Godson cottage shortly after half-past seven. He'd waited until he'd seen Reuben go off on the early tide, so's he'd catch Hannah on her own, though with Eleanor somewhere about the place to comfort her.

Hannah always offered him a cup of tea. This morning he refused. She looked deep into his eyes with an instant understanding. 'One of *them*, is it, Walter?' she asked quietly. Walter couldn't bring himself to speak, and nodded.

'Well, you'd better let us have it,' she said.

'Not *it*, missis,' he said. 'Them! You'd better call Eleanor.'

'Nay, Walter. She has worries of her own. Give us 'em!'

He took the three telegrams out of his brown canvas satchel and handed them to her. He turned away, knowing she'd want to close the door.

She went inside, sat at the table, and placed the telegram envelopes side by side. All were labelled with her name in that curious printing the telegraph office used. She reached into the table drawer and took out the horn-handled carving knife, using it to slit the envelopes.

Martyn Godson.
John Godson.
Alan Godson.
Lost at Sea. Enemy Action. Letter of notification follows.

The names hit her heart with sledgehammer blows. Tears rushed to her eyes, but she was not crying. She bent her head over the table, cradled it in her arms. The tears ran down on to the telegram forms but still she didn't cry. Martyn gone, with his brother

95

John, both nineteen-year-old lads. And Alan, her lovely Alan, only eighteen. Gone. Lost at sea. Her mind couldn't understand it. They'd all joined the army, the infantry. Silas, God rest his soul, had said, 'We take our living from the sea; us'll fight the Germans by the land!' How can you be lost at sea if you're a soldier of the infantry?

Then she cried, and sobs from deep inside twisted her shoulders.

She'd cried for Silas, when the letter and the telegram had come. A woman must be prepared to lose her man; that's the inevitable way of life, living and dying. And, in a sense, when a girl marries a fisherman, she already accepts in advance that, one day, she'll stand on the slip waiting for a return that never comes, from a storm not even her own man can conquer.

But her three sons!

Eleanor must have heard Walter's knock; she'd thrown a dressing gown round her shoulders as she'd come eagerly down the steps from the bedroom where she'd been having a few minutes' lie-in, waiting for her mother to call that the tea was mashed. Every morning, she'd listened for Walter's footsteps up the cobbles, that uneven clack-click that came from his boots on twisted legs. Perhaps, this morning, she'd think.

She'd never believed the telegram that posted Terrie 'Missing in Action, presumed Dead'. Her mind refused to accept the word *presumed*.

She saw her mother's bent and heaving back, and the telegrams lying partially beneath her arms. 'Who is it, Mam?' she asked. 'Our Alan?' She'd always known her mother had a particularly soft spot for Alan among the other boys.

Her mother didn't answer and then Eleanor counted the telegrams. Three.

Four brothers away to war. Three telegrams.

'Our Lewis is all right,' her mother said between sobs, 'but all the rest, all, gone down.'

'I'll make a cup of tea,' Eleanor said. It was all she could think to say. She'd wept herself out for Terrie, and for her father. Two sides of love. Love of your man, love for your parents. She had nothing left for her brothers. Not yet. They'd been away too long while her life had changed from girlhood to womanhood, and now to impending motherhood. There'd been a fuss, of course, when she'd told Mam about the baby. They'd travelled to York, just the two of them, and Terrie, white-faced and fearful, had met them at the railway station. Alf had been a big help, large and cheerful.

'So, you've gone and done it, lad?' her mother had asked Terrie.

'Aye, Mrs Godson.'

'Well, you know that if my Silas was here you'd have him to answer to?'

'Aye, Mrs Godson!'

'Well, don't just stand there like a lump. Take us somewhere and buy us a cup of tea while we sort it all out.'

'We're going to get married, Mrs Godson.'

'Who says you are? You haven't got Silas's permission, have you?'

'No, but I thought . . .'

'That's the trouble. You didn't think. Else, our Eleanor wouldn't be missing, would she?'

Alf had been a big help. He'd settled her mother down at a table in the railway buffet, a very grand place with etched windows and marble-topped tables. He'd brought her a cup of tea and a plate with a paper serviette on it and three buns, one of them a cream one. He'd sat by Mrs Godson's side, touching her elbow, exerting his tremendous charm on her. She knew it, he knew it, but they played the game valiantly. After all, what's the difference when the baby's made, and where, so long as it's born right. 'Friend of mine's in the chapel,' he said. 'We've called the banns three times already.'

'Even though she's living away. . . .?'

'Well, I said that . . . you know how it is. . . .'

'No, I *don't* know your wicked ungodly ways. *Tell* me how it is.'

'I gave her the address of a young lady I've been courting, here in York, while I've been doing my training. Look, missis, the pair of them want to get wed. We're going over to France week after next. My friend in the chapel will marry them. . . .'

'I still don't understand why my Eleanor can't be married from her own house, like any decent girl.'

Terrie shook his head; on this point he had been adamant with Eleanor, with Reuben, with Alf. He wouldn't go back, he wouldn't ever go back, to Ravenswyke. He could never forget that last fishing trip with his father, then having to return on compassionate leave formally to identify, with Alf, his father's frozen and ravaged corpse. Though he said to himself that he would never return to a place that had done that to his father, he knew that, if he and Alf hadn't left when they did, his father would still be alive, still be fishing, however meanly, however inefficiently, in the *Jolly Lads*.

'Please, Mam,' Eleanor pleaded. 'We've been over all that.'

So they had been married in chapel in York, with her mother and Reuben her brother by her side, and Alf doing best man for *his* brother. And they'd managed a night of honeymoon together, in the grandeur, the unbelievable splendour, of the Station Hotel, before Terrie set off for France.

To be posted missing in action, *presumed* killed by everyone except Eleanor.

Her mother had stopped crying. 'You'll have to write to Lewis,' she said, 'and tell him what's happened. Then you'll have to sort all their stuff, and put it together for Reuben and Lewis to look through.' She looked wildly about the room as if seeing it for the first time. Eleanor poured the boiling water into the pot in which Reuben's tea had been made. She never needed to add fresh leaves to his brew, which came out of the pot like leather, strong and bitter.

She brought the tea to the table, picked up the telegrams, and placed them under the tea caddy on the mantelpiece, with the telegrams they'd received for Silas, and for Terrie. She sat beside her mother and put her arm round her shoulders, noting how worn and drawn were her mother's features, how deep ingrained the lines, how much of her mother's wispy hair had turned grey, even white in places. Her mother's shoulders were thin and it seemed as if the bones were sticking out with no protection of flesh. When she'd been a young girl she remembered her mother as fat, pink and jolly, with an indomitable strength and courage. Now it seemed as if the repeated blows of life had pounded away all the flesh, had drained her mother's cheeks of that high colour she could so well remember.

'We've still got Reuben and Lewis, Mam,' she said.

'Aye. Four down, and two to go, not counting Terrie and Alf.'

'I was talking with Alf last night,' Eleanor said, 'when I went down to the shop. He's not coming back fishing after the war. He's going to sell the *Jolly Lads* for what it'll fetch. It seems as if a man

98

in York has offered him a job after the war. It'd pay a lot of money, and regular. At least two pounds a week, perhaps even more.'

'He *will* be grand!' Hannah said.

'Yes. He told me, if Terrie doesn't come back, he'd like us to get wed!'

Hannah looked at her daughter incredulously. 'To get *wed*?' she said in surprise. 'What happened to that lady he was courting?'

'Oh, that was just passing fancy. . . .'

'And you, are you just passing fancy?'

'No, he said he loves me. He said, he always has, but Terrie spoke first for me, and he would never do anything to hurt him.'

Hannah heaved herself up from the table. 'And what, pray, did *you* tell *him*?' she said. She put the poker to the fire and stirred it, something she rarely if ever did. It rattled against the iron bars of the grate and the flames flared.

'I told him that I'd think about it!'

Hannah softened, came back to the table and made a show of setting the pots to rights. 'Aye, lass,' she said. 'You think about it. After this war is over life's going to be very different. Especially for young lassies. When I were young, we didn't stand much of a chance of anything. It was either go into service, or get wed and have your family. Now the world's going to be a more modern place, you mark my words. Think twice before you make up your mind to anything. One thing is certain. Don't, whatever you do, marry a man you don't love. And don't marry a fisherman!'

James Henry Tockett eyed the ruddy-faced young lad who sat on his chair as if he owned it, firm, strong and proud. If only he could have fathered sons like that, he thought. Rupert Henry had had a touch of that sort of strength, but Mark Adam, serving in the safe job his father had got for him in the War Office in London, was not a patch on either one of them.

'I don't usually see folk at this hour of the day,' he said mildly. 'You could have come later and taken your turn with the others. I'd have seen you.'

Reuben flushed. It had taken all his nerve and courage to come in the first place. And a hell of a lot of arguing in the taproom of the Raven the previous evening. 'I've not come to touch the fore-lock,' he said. 'I've not come to ask you a favour, either for myself or anybody else. I've come, like a businessman, to make you a business proposition.'

James Henry laughed, but carefully, so as not to give offence. 'Quite right, lad,' he said. 'I'll take you at your word, and you've no need to humble yourself.' His mind was whirling. What *business* could the lad possibly have with him? Since when did the Godsons do *business* with the Tocketts? Or wasn't he here as a Godson, but maybe as a spokesman? 'Are you speaking for your family, Reuben, or for somebody else?'

'I'm speaking for the co-operative.'

'Ah, I see! Then that'd be a different matter, wouldn't it? What does the *co-operative* want from me?'

After the tragedy of Sam Pitt's death, and the loss of Arthur Duckett and the two horses in the blizzard, they'd tried running the co-operative in different ways. The wholesalers in Whitby had relented and, disobeying Tockett perhaps for the first time in their business lives, had accepted the co-operative's fish at normal market prices. One by one the fishermen had taken turns to haul the catch there, and one by one had lost their enthusiasm for the journey. Gradually they'd come to learn how much actual organization Fearon had put into his business. How he'd rushed some things to market, knowing the demand and the price would be high. How he'd hold some things back during a glut, reckoning on being able to bring the price back up again with a few late orders, after the glut had been satisfied for next to nothing. The fishermen of the co-operative realized that now, on average, they were earning far less than they had been with Fearon.

Fearon himself had never got over the humiliation they'd imposed on him. His business appeared to be going rapidly downhill, and more and more he was taking to drink, almost as if the ghost of Sam Pitt wouldn't let him be. Everyone blamed him, blamed him directly for the deaths of Sam Pitt and the Duckett boy. Suddenly he found that old cronies turned their backs on him, that it took him a long time to get served in the Merchants' Club by the wharfside, that people pushed him rudely aside when he was standing by the bar waiting.

'Let me warn you, though,' James Henry Tockett said to Reuben sitting across the desk from him where many a suppliant had sat before, 'that I don't approve of your co-operative. I don't believe in this new socialism, this bolshevism. You're trying to interfere with the natural order of things. All right, you've bested Fearon, not that there was ever very much there to best, but I'll have no dealings with you, or any other of the co-operative people, on the basis of bolshevism.'

'I haven't come all this way,' Reuben said firmly, 'to talk about bolshevism. For one thing, I don't know what the word means. I've come to talk about a matter of business. Take it or leave it. We're fishermen. You're a businessman. We know how and when and where to catch fish. We can go out there for it, and we can bring it back, in good condition. Fish has to be sold. It takes a businessman to organize the selling of anything. You're a business-man. It's as simple as that. We want *you* to set up a business to sell our fish for us, in the best possible way, at the best possible prices. And we want fair shares.'

Right, he'd said it. It was an exact replica of of the speech he'd made in the taproom the previous evening. The fishermen were not businessmen. The co-operative was a nonsense. Fishermen had no sense involving themselves in a thing like that, he'd argued. All right, they'd done what had been necessary to get rid of Fearon. It had cost lives. But then, whenever did anything to do with fishing *not* cost lives?

'You're asking me to set up a business, selling the fish you catch?'

'That's it.'

'The Tocketts and the Godsons?'

Reuben shook his head vigorously. 'This has nothing to do with the Godsons,' he said firmly. 'This has to do with the collective fishermen of Old Quaytown. The OQC is only a name, no more. It isn't politics. It's an easy way to say, the lot of us.'

'One for all, all for one, is that it?'

Reuben wasn't to be trapped so easily. 'We leave slogans like that to other people, Mr Tockett. We don't talk in slogans, down in the Raven.'

'What do you talk about, down there?'

'We talk about fish and fishing, about catching fish and taking it to market so that we can get a price for it. We talk about the boats that have been lost, and the lives; we talk about the sea and the weather, the deep cold sea and the cruel relentless weather!'

James Henry shuddered as he listened to the young man's words. How he would love to have that freedom, that purpose, to

101

be able to go into the Raven, to talk with these simple, dedicated men, to be accepted as one of them. But that could never be. Damn it, he could buy the Raven if he'd a mind, make it modern with beer engines, coloured lights. Even bring in barmaids like they had in so many of the Whitby public houses. How bored he was with the false meaningless conversation of his own contemporaries in the district of Whitby. How much he longed for a bit of reality, a touch of veracity, honest simple truth and purpose not motivated entirely by brass!

'Aye, you've got yourself an education, I see,' he said, and could have bitten out his tongue. This young lad's simple eloquence had made him feel oddly inferior – he shouldn't add to it by making cheap jibes. He saw immediately the look of contempt on Reuben Godson's face, a look no money could ever eradicate. 'You're to be complimented on the way you express yourself,' he said lamely, trying to undo the mischief his rash words had caused.

'Some of us reads a book or two,' Reuben said. His eyes swept round the room, along the shelves packed with leather-bound volumes, as if knowing that not one of them was ever opened now that Rupert Henry and his mother were dead.

'I'm glad to hear it, lad,' James Henry said gruffly. 'If ever you want a book from the shelves, come up and take it. Make yourself at home. The books are gathering dust now that the lad is gone. He died beside your father; it reassures me to know they were together at the end. He always was a great admirer of your father, you know. I'd like to think that maybe a spark that was struck between them could live on, and pass between you and me. Let's face it, Reuben. This part of Ravenswyke is Tockett territory, always has been and, I suppose, always will be, but once you cross that bridge over the Cut, you're in Godson territory. Your father, and his father before him, they have ruled that territory as surely as if it belonged to them by bill of sale. Maybe you and me, together, could make a bit of sense out of what we've both got left.'

'I'd like that, Mr Tockett,' Reuben said respectfully. 'But first, we'll have to start in small ways. The co-operative would be a good beginning. And that copy of Walter Scott's *Ivanhoe* I can see on that shelf. I've always wanted to read it.'

'You shall have it,' James Henry said. Damnation, how did this slip of a lad manage to best him every step of the way. 'One thing

I should say, though. Selling fish is a technical matter. It takes knowledge and experience, like the commodity market. It means knowing when to go, when to stay, when to hold back and when to be liberal. Say what you like about him, the best man for that around these parts is Fearon. All right, I grant you he's a twisted sort of fellow, and not to be trusted unless you control him. But he's good at what he does. My idea of taking on your co-operative would be to put Fearon back in, but this time as an employee, under control.'

'They'd never agree to that!' Reuben said, worried. He could imagine the faces in the taproom if he even suggested such a thing.

James Henry smiled; now he was back on his own ground. Now he'd taken control again. 'It'd be your job, lad, to persuade them, wouldn't it? You want help from me; well, you have to give something in return. You've taken up a stand with this co-operative of yours, and it isn't working. You're asking me to invest my time and money to make it work for you. Not for myself. I can make more brass with one instruction to my office in London than I'll ever make out of selling your fish for you. All right, if you want it, we can work out an arrangement. But it'll have to include Fearon, and your co-operative will have to learn to live with him. When you can tell me they've agreed to that, you'll have my hand on it, and we shall go from there.'

Reuben got up to go, his eyes on the Walter Scott he coveted.

'Aye,' James Henry said, chuckling, 'and you can start borrowing the books when the contract is signed.'

There was nothing so far as the eye could see, in either direction, save the tangles of barbed wire rusting on the rotting earth from which all manner of vegetation had long since disappeared. The ground swept down and formed a shallow valley on the lips of which the trenches had been dug and fortified. The Germans were to the south, the British to the north. The sun rose to the left of the British position, hovered over the German trenches, set to the right. Day followed day as if by obligation unchanging. During the mornings nothing ever stirred. When the British served dinner at twelve o'clock, the Germans opened fire from behind the ridge. The British ate dinner stolidly, stoically. It was usually stew of one sort or another. Often they had bread but usually there were tiny mites baked into it and the soldiers had to take it apart almost

103

crumb by crumb to avoid eating them. The mites, it was reported, would cause tapeworms. It was rumoured that a man in 3 Platoon had discovered a tapeworm in his underwear over fifteen inches long, with hooks all along its back. When dinner had been eaten and the mess-tins cleaned with sand and soil, the men would man the parapets. At two o'clock, when the Germans took a *Mitta-gessen*, the British guns would open fire. The Germans ate wurst and sometimes had fresh cabbage with it, but they had to pick the cabbage clean since often it contained weevils and eating them could give you a painful anus.

When Lewis Godson finished his dinner, he cleaned his mess-tin and went to the latrine, which was very full, and stank badly. Lewis thought about the sea as he squatted, thought about the clean odour of fish and seaweed.

After the German trenches had been bombarded and the dead had been counted and removed, both sides settled to a long after-noon of slumber. Men easily learn to sleep standing up, propping their bodies into any niche in the sandbags. The major problem is the flexibility of the neck; one's head keeps dropping and jerking one awake again. Lewis always solved that problem by sleeping with his head supported by his hand, his elbow propped against a sandbag.

When the hot tea came at four o'clock the Germans, who didn't take afternoon tea, would fire sporadic rounds from rifles, and machine-guns switched to single fire. After tea, the British would count and remove their dead, report back to headquarters, and request replacements. Headquarters was efficient, and always sent more soldiers before the evening bombardment began. Which gave the unblooded young soldiers a whole half-hour to settle in before their first taste of the effects of the enemy guns.

On this particular night, Lewis Godson was standing more or less at the centre of the company's position. The lad to the left of him had just arrived, and Lewis had established that he came from Scarborough. They exchanged place names. The lad was called Peter. His uniform, Lewis noticed, was new and didn't fit him very well. 'When we go out of the line,' he said, 'you'll have to give that jacket to Nobby Clarke. Used to be a tailor. He'll make it fit you for five cigarettes.'

The lad on the right of Lewis was an old soldier. Lewis didn't care too much for him, since the old soldier was perpetually trying to be clever at the expense of the wartime soldiers. The old soldier was always telling tales about his service in India, implying that only men who had served in India had any strength, any guts, a commodity he seemed greatly to favour.

Dusk was approaching, and both sides, it seemed, had settled down for the nightly exchange of explosive compliments. The Germans started the firing first, and the British were puzzled to see the shells fall short.

A strong wind blew from the south.

Most of the shells seemed to be duds, since they landed and either just fizzled, or exploded harmlessly on the open ground in front of the company position. From them came a cloud of thin green and white smoke, which thickened as it made contact with the air.

Lewis's gas mask was faulty. It took them six weeks back in base hospital to wash the phosgene, chemical formula $COCl_2$, out of his lungs, one of which, they told him, he'd never use again.

'You're a very lucky man,' Dr Gilchrist told Lewis Godson, whom he saw on the slip by the Raven the evening he was called out to write a death certificate for old Mrs Patchley, who died aged ninety of complications caused by a broken hip. 'If they had been using mustard gas on your sector, we wouldn't have been seeing you in these parts again for a year or two. As it it, take life steady, don't exert yourself, and I don't see any reason you shouldn't live to be a hundred.'

Lewis merely grunted his thanks; he hadn't sought a consultation with the doctor and didn't cherish his opinion. He'd been embarrassed when the doctor confronted him and spoke with him, looking searchingly into his face. He'd been back in Ravenswyke only a day, discharged from the army with a pension pending, when they could work out the amount. They could easily assess a lost leg, an arm or a foot, but how do you rate the loss of the function of a lung? His thoughts were more concerned with the *Hope of Ravenswyke*, the Godson boat, standing on the slip. Reuben stood by it, an anxious look on his face. Of course, immediately on his arrival, Lewis had hastened down to the slip but Reuben had been out fishing. When he returned in the *Hope* with six baskets, Lewis had stared goggle-eyed at the boat. 'What in the name of bloody hell . . .?' he'd asked, but then had been

105

interrupted by the arrival of Dr Gilchrist, to whom he'd had to pay a certain amount of reluctant attention.

When the doctor had mounted his horse and had gone, Lewis turned back to Reuben. The evening had darkened rapidly, but he could still see every detail of the *Hope*, the frayed lines, the chipped mast, the battered hull. 'Now, young 'un,' he said, 'what the devil are you playing at?'

Reuben had always been in fear of his oldest brother, who lacked much of the kindly understanding of Silas. At twenty-one he was stocky and broad-shouldered, with a shock of black hair that crinkled unruly across his brow, giving him a perpetually lowering frown. His arms were short, and his big brawny fighter's hands were those of a fairground boxer. As if aware of the huge responsibility that faced him as the Godson heir, he was naturally suspicious of everything and everyone, resistant to change, harshly inflexible in many of his opinions. Of all the moments Reuben had faced alone during the war, burdened by assumed responsibilities, this had been the one he'd feared the most.

'What do you think, then?' he asked, lamely. It was quite obvious what Lewis thought – you could read it on his face like newspaper headlines.

'What do I think? I think you've taken leave of your senses, that's what. I go away, we all go away, and we leave you with a boat in good trim. All you have to do is take it out and fish it, keep it clean, give it a lick from time to time, and what happens. I come home with one lung busted and find this. . . .' Words obviously failed him as he eyed what looked to him to be a decrepit tub, the only clean part of which was the name newly painted on the stern.

'It was too good a chance to miss,' Reuben said, anxiously. 'And I had to make up my mind immediately. Lots of people were after it. Alf only let me have it at the price because of our lass being married with Terrie. That way, he said, it'd stay in the family!' He looked at Lewis in desperation, gave the boat that had been the *Jolly Lads* and now was the *Hope of Ravenswyke* a rap with his knuckles. 'Nay, Lewis, it's a good boat. You know that. Of course, Sam kept it rotten, but the hull's fair and square and sound as a bell.'

Lewis took hold of the mainstay and rattled it, loose in its fixing. 'And what's this, then? Sound as a bloody bell?'

'All right, I grant you the rigging's wrong. Old Sam never rigged it right. But we can rig it with the difference between what I paid for it, and what I got from Tallby in Whitby for the old *Hope*. Look, Lewis, this is four feet longer. And broader on the beam by two feet. It's easier to work. I've taken six baskets a day while I've been running it single-handed. Six. In the old *Hope*, I was lucky to manage four.'

Lewis was standing at the bows, looking down the vessel. 'I must say, she's got nice lines,' he said. 'She allus was a goer, before Sam got hold of her!'

'Still is, take my word! Once we've had the time to rig her right. And now that you're back . . . I've been that busy. . . .'

Lewis came round the boat and stood by his brother. 'Busy! I've been hearing about you and keeping busy. They say you've worn a hole in the Ducketts' back step, standing there nights dipping your wick.'

'I've never . . .,' Reuben started to say but then realized his brother was provoking him. 'It's all right then? About the boat?'

'Aye, Reuben, it's all right. I'd have liked to be asked, but I reckon with me in the hospital, and Alf wanting you to make up your mind quickly. . . . But us'll have to rig it sharp, else us'll be the laughing-stock of Old Quaytown!'

Reuben punched his brother's arm. 'Us'll rig it tomorrow,' he said. 'I've got all the stuff brand new!'

'And a bit of paint wouldn't be amiss.'

'I've got the paint, even.'

'By gow, you have been busy, Reuben. Looking after that young lady up the bank, fetching in six baskets a day, supping ale all night in the tap, organizing the co-operative. . . .'

'Nay, that's not me. . . .'

'It was you, they tell me, who went up the hill and took on Tockett . . .?'

'Yes, well that were easy. There's brass in it for him. And for us. . . .'

'I'm dying to see Fearon's face. Taking wages. . . .'

'He had to. It was that or the workhouse!'

Lewis put his arm round his young brother's shoulder as they stood by the *Hope*. The sea carried whitecaps; the evening air was keen and smelled just as he remembered it, of home. Tomorrow he'd get up early and take a walk on the scaurs at low tide,

107

listening to the gulls, watching them fish, hearing the sharp sound of their calls. Slowly he'd come back into the old ways again, after the horror of France, the nightmare of the trenches, the white-green gas rolling over him. Slowly he'd fill his sail with wind, the leader of the Godsons of Ravenswyke, the undisputed head of the family. He'd find himself a local girl to marry, move into the front bedroom, start a family.

'Aye, Reuben, it's smashing to be home again!' he said. 'Come on. They tell me you're a fully fledged member of the taproom society. You can buy us a double rum, to celebrate. . . .'

The co-operative had flourished, though James Henry Tockett rapidly grew bored and left the running of it more and more to Fearon, who'd even started wearing a beaver hat again. Fearon was never the same again, never arrogant, never cheated them out of a penny. Somehow, the experience had sharpened his business wits and, as if to prove himself to the fishermen, he got better prices than ever for them, playing the market in Whitby as if it was his private fief.

Mark Adam Tockett came home from the War Office, on indefinite leave from the army, though the word was that they'd sent him home in disgrace for some scandal with another young officer. But that was only gossip. He never came down into Old Quaytown.

They re-rigged the *Hope*, painted it, and Reuben and Lewis sailed it together. Reuben had been busy making lobster pots, and when the season came they went out first and dropped them before carrying on to do a bit of lining. The fish paid their living; the lobsters were pure profit.

Overcome by passion one evening, when he and Emily were sitting in the shelter at the top of the cliff where Jacoby kept his sheep in winter, smelling the warm earth about them and the comforting odour of animals, Reuben had his first experience of sex, when he slipped his hand up under the elastic of Emily's knicker leg. For the next half-hour she snuffled into his shoulder, hugging him close, kissing his mouth, her hands never still on his body. When he unbuttoned his trousers, she gasped with pleasure as she grabbed hold of him. Reuben was in paradise. Time and again, he felt her squirm and then give a little scream, time and again he felt her shudder beneath the touch of his hand and his exploring fingers. After half an hour, he could bear it no longer and directed her hand for her, and as she worked him backwards and forwards he arched, and finally ejaculated across the shelter in one long juddering spurt that seemed to drain him of all life.

'That should make you feel a bit better, love,' Emily said. 'Any time you feel like it, I'll always be happy to do it for you.'

'You'd better wash your hand in the trough,' he said gruffly. 'We don't want you having a baby.'

Hannah and Eleanor moved, one Sunday, out of the front bedroom, and Reuben and Lewis moved into the double bed. Reuben would rather have had a bed on his own; some nights when he was lying there before sleeping, disturbing thoughts of Emily wouldn't leave him, and he found himself growing hard beneath his nightshirt. He turned on his side, ashamed, the first time it happened, but Lewis must have sensed what was the matter. 'Wait till you go to the lavatory,' he said. 'We don't want you messing up the bed wi' that stuff!'

With their father and three brothers gone, Lewis and Reuben grew very close. It was assumed in the village that Lewis would take everything over from Reuben; he was the one the co-operative consulted, he was the one to decide when and where the *Hope* would fish. Reuben was happy to slip back into the old routines under the protection of his older brother; he went back to the corner of the taproom, watching Lewis sitting with the older men by the fire, conversing vigorously with them about the nonsense that was still going on in France.

'They say it's going to be all over this year,' the men would say, but Lewis would talk them down. 'You haven't been out there,' he say. 'I have and was gassed for it. I *know*!'

On 4 January 1917, Alf Pitt, coming out of a house in York, was knocked down by a charabanc carrying new recruits. The house was a brothel, and Alf was drunk at the time. He died two days later without ever recovering consciousness, though Eleanor sat by his bedside the second day, having travelled to York fat-bellied with her six months' pregnancy. 'Was he the daddy?' the hospital sister asked spitefully. 'All men are awful!' She was a thin, dried-out husk of a woman and Eleanor eyed her pityingly. 'No, he wasn't the daddy of this one,' she said, 'but he'd have been the daddy of the next.'

'Have you no shame?' the sister asked. 'You know where he'd been. It's the judgement of God, that's what it is!'

He died an hour later and Eleanor returned to Ravenswyke by train. On the way down the bank, in the snow and ice, she slipped and rolled about fifteen yards to the doorway of the Laurel Inn. Dr Gilchrist was brought, and saved her life as she lay on the long table in the saloon bar. But he couldn't save the life of Terrie's child.

Sir Walter Scott's *Ivanhoe* was among the secondhand books in the shop in Whitby. Lewis gave Reuben a shilling, but cursed him when he spent it buying a book, the first one Reuben had ever owned. 'It's better than spending the money the way you do, up in the Laurel,' Reuben sneered, aroused by Lewis's jibe. Lewis brought up his hand, and smashed the back of it across Reuben's face.

'What I do with my time is my business,' Lewis said. The hard blow brought on another spasm of his frequent coughing. Sometimes, recently, he kept Reuben awake half the night with it. It was about the time that his bad coughing had started that Lewis had abandoned the taproom at the Raven in favour of the Laurel, a halfway house between Old Quaytown and Newquay Town used equally by the inhabitants of both sides of the bridge.

Lewis was seeing Elsie Milner, who'd given up her job, apparently, at Tockett House. She'd even moved out of Meg's cottage after a row with her mother, and had rented what had been the Pitt cottage, empty now that Alf was gone. Of course, everybody had said she'd be going into the same business as her mother, and tongues really started to wag when she was seen going into the snug of the Laurel, the only room in which women were allowed to drink, hidden from the saloon or the tap where the men congregated.

Lewis had also been seen going into the snug, and word even had it he'd been seen going into Elsie's cottage after dark. Though that, too, was only gossip.

110

The two lads were fishing one day in May, about a mile off, with sunny weather all about them and the fish too lazy to feed, when Reuben decided to have it out with Lewis. They were eating their snap at the stern, the tiller tucked safe under Reuben's arm, the first three disappointing baskets lashed to the mast, when he tackled him.

'Something's wrong, our Lewis, isn't it?' he said boldly and bluntly.

'No, Reuben, it's the time of year. Never get much of a run in May. I reckon us is wasting our time.'

'I didn't mean with the fish. I meant with you. . . .'

Lewis bridled immediately. 'Wrong, with me? What're you getting at?'

Reuben was tonguetied for a moment and only his love of his brother and his resolution drove him on. 'I mean, since you came back from the army. At first, well, it was just like the old times before you went away. Now, somehow . . . They were asking after you again in the tap last night. I said you weren't coming out much, just now, and Bill Clewson said he'd seen you going into the Laurel again. . . .'

'Nowt better to talk about, I suppose,' Lewis said. 'I mind my own business. I wish other folk would do the same.'

Reuben put his hand on Lewis's thigh. 'I'm not *other folk*, Lewis,' he reminded his brother gently. 'I'm your brother. Our mam is very worried about you. I heard her and Eleanor talking last night, in bed.'

'I wish folks'd let me alone,' Lewis said. 'I'm all right.'

Now Reuben had the bit between his teeth and not even his natural fear of Lewis would stop him. 'No, you're *not* all right,' he said. 'When does a Godson start running about with the likes of Elsie Milner. You know what her mam is, and Elsie's no better. They say Old Dirty Tockett had his hand up there before she was fifteen. . . .'

'I'm telling you, Reuben . . .', Lewis said, his brow foreshortening in a deep scowl that brought his hairline and eyebrows almost together. He got up, moving easily in the rolling boat, and went forward before the mast, lugging one of the baskets out of the scuppers. As he bent over, the effort racked his lung, and he started coughing again. This was one of the worst attacks Reuben had ever heard. He left the tiller and went forward, seeing the

111

spume around his brother's mouth. 'Bugger off,' Lewis said. 'It's nowt to do with thee!'

Reuben felt helpless; he knew deep down that his brother's physical condition was responsible for the changes in him, but had no way of helping. Lewis had been up to see Gilchrist two weeks before, but when he'd come back he'd smiled and said, 'The doctor thinks I'll last another hundred years.'

'Lewis,' he said helplessly, 'come and sit down. Come on!'

Lewis allowed himself to be helped back to the stern, to sit with his legs spread out in front of him on the transom seat. When his chest had stopped heaving he wiped the spittle from his lips on the back of his cotton smock, looked at Reuben, and smiled. Reuben hadn't seen him do that for weeks.

'Ah, you've a lot to learn, lad,' Lewis said finally. 'But you'll be all right. Folks give Elsie Milner a bad name, and maybe they're right to do that, but she's not a bad lass. And she gives me a bit of comfort, right now when I need it.'

'How do you mean, right now when you need it?' Reuben asked, not wanting to hear the answer to his question, dreading what it might be.

'I don't mean nowt,' Lewis said. 'Let me be, Reuben, just let me be, will you?'

He started to cough again, and this time his lips and chin were flecked with red. He wiped his mouth without looking at it, as if knowing what he'd find. Reuben got the bottle of cold tea and held it out. Lewis took it and drank deeply but in sips, keeping his lips close together as if fearing what might escape.

The wind had freshened and the waves were piling one on the other in that uncomfortable summer way. Reuben looked at the baskets and the lines they'd brought back in. 'We're wasting our time,' he said, 'especially if it's going to blow up.' He looked over at Tockett Top but there were few clouds, though the air hung heavy with an unnatural translucence. 'Shouldn't wonder if we're due for a bit of thunder,' he said. The boat was wobbling from side to side, the waves getting under the beam. Reuben was holding the bows into the wind, relaxed. This new boat was a treat to work now they'd re-rigged it but, being broader on the beam than the previous *Hope*, it did tend to wobble a bit more.

'Aye, we might as well get on back, for all the good us is doing out here,' Lewis said. Reuben turned them on to the wind and let out the sail which filled instantly in the strong blow. The *Hope* went scudding along, riding the crests of the tall waves, the high stern taking the force of the weather comfortably.

One of the fish they'd caught was a fat juicy sole that would cook nicely. Lewis took it from the basket, brought the hook out of its mouth, and went forward to wrap it in a bit of newspaper.

'I'll take this, if it's okay with you?' Lewis said as he wrapped the sole. Then he grinned at Reuben. 'It's Elsie's birthday today. I promised her a bit of fish, to celebrate.'

Reuben could only grunt.

Lewis started to walk back along the caulked decking of the *Hope*, to the port side away from the bellying sail. Reuben was holding a straight line for the light at the end of the harbour of Old Quaytown, happy to be going back in for the first time he could remember, anxious to get Lewis on dry land where they could talk together. For he was determined to get to the bottom of Lewis's few cryptic remarks. What did he mean – 'right now when I need it'? What did he need, and why right now? Though Reuben felt he'd known a bit about Lewis – after all, they'd grown up together, hadn't they? – the man who'd come back from the war, from the hospital, had been almost a stranger to Reuben, someone it was impossible to understand. For a start, he was not kind to their mam, nor to Eleanor, and treated them like interlopers. And somehow it seemed as if he had no respect for the pride of the Godson name. In the pub, instead of giving a clear sharp lead on the issues they were all discussing, he'd adopted a cynical, sneering, outside manner, as if none of it was of the slightest interest to him, as if he was remote from the vital concerns of the fishermen. Ravenswyke, Old Quaytown, the fishing, the co-operative, were matters of life and death to Reuben and the men who'd not gone to war. Why did Lewis treat all these matters so casually, as if he couldn't be bothered any more?

Perhaps Reuben was preoccupied with his thoughts and not paying attention to helming the boat; perhaps because the boat was new he hadn't yet grown accustomed to the vagaries, the little traits of personality that all boats possess, but the backing wind caught him totally by surprise. The sail bellied up and backwards, snapped across the boat on its boom, viciously carried over, slicing at head height across the deck. Reuben heard the crack as it struck Lewis's neck and saw his brother seem to dive in a perfect

113

arc over the side into the tumultuous waters. With an instinctive reaction Reuben pushed the tiller away to bring the *Hope*'s bows into the wind. He ran forward past the boom, with the sail fluttering like a flag, streaming backwards, and tossed the anchor overboard. The rope and chain snaked over the gunwale while he dashed back to the stern, looking at the point of the ocean where Lewis had gone. Suddenly he thought he saw the fabric of Lewis's blue smock billow on the wave. He lashed a rope around his waist, made the end fast, and went over the side, swimming strongly though inexpertly towards that flash of blue. The waves carried him up and down, and dunked him beneath each trough. When he'd gone a dozen yards he saw the flash again, this time more positive, and made for it; it was Lewis's smock and it billowed upwards on the wave, then down again. Reuben dived beneath the waves' surfaces and plunged his body forward, grasping desperately at the blue cotton.

It must have slipped up and off Lewis's head, and now was floating free. There was no trace of Lewis.

Reuben swam around for a few minutes, but knew his quest was hopeless. He worked his way, hand over hand, along the safety line he'd tied to his waist, and then used it to scramble over the side of the *Hope*, which was riding in the wind serenely at anchor. Reuben stood in the bows as high as he could reach, searching the seas for any trace of his brother, his mind still in shock. A gull, seeing the stationary boat, flew cawking down and settled on the mast top, its beady eye staring quizzically at Reuben.

Six boats were out, but none was nearer than two miles away. Three of them had turned on to the wind and were running for the harbour. A black cloud, edged with grey-white wisps, had formed above the moor top but it was blowing inland. The bottom of the cliffs was laced now with a skirt of white whirling foam, spuming among the rocks, cascading back out again.

Reuben's face was drenched with tears of anger and remorse. How could he, how could he, have made the most fundamental error of any helmsman, to let his sail chinaman over on the run, whipping viciously from side to side like that, moving like a reaper's scythe to chop anything in its path. Where was Lewis? Where? Where?

He strained his eyes to search every wave top, every fragment of the ocean about him, wiping his eyes free of tears with his sleeve, having to wipe them again when the tears continued to pour out and down his cheeks.

After fifteen minutes he went back to the stern, the anchor warp in his hand. He sat on the transom seat and bawled in misery. As. so many generations of fishermen before him, Lewis must have carried the weights in his pockets to make sure that once overboard, he wouldn't bob back up again, but would die the fisherman's swift and merciful death.

Later that evening, when all the formalities with the police had been completed, when Hannah and Eleanor both sat dry-eyed again in the parlour of the cottage, when the taproom of the Raven had been closed as a gesture of respect, when arrangements had been made for the chapel service, Reuben, by now dry-eyed himself, climbed the hill and knocked on the door of Alf Pitt's former cottage, seeing the light in the front room burning behind the closed curtains.

When the door opened, Elsie Milner stood there, wearing a black dress.

'There's never shortage of tongues to bring bad news. You can come in, if you've a mind to.'

Reuben followed her into the parlour and sat across the table from her. This was the first time he'd actually been close to her. She had a strong face, with good features, a full mouth and well-brushed and shining hair. Now her eyes were dull with sadness. He eyed the green chenille of the tablecloth and felt awkard with the paper-wrapped parcel, not wishing to place it on the table top for fear of soiling it. 'Our Lewis picked this out for you,' he said, 'before he went. I thought you might like to have it. He said today was your birthday.'

She took the parcel; the sight of it and the simple words he pronounced brought tears to her eyes, but she blinked them back. 'Aye, he were thoughtful, your Lewis,' she said.

'He spoke well of you,' Reuben said timidly.

'He wasn't a man to speak bad of *anybody*! Not even me!'

He stretched out his hand and placed it on hers where it lay inert on the table. 'He told me, you helped him when he needed it.'

She nodded. 'Poor devil. He had a hard time understanding.'

'Understanding what? Will you tell me? He couldn't. . . .'

She thought for a moment. 'I'm not sure I understood it too well myself,' she said. 'It were all a bit deep for me!'

'Will you try? Please?' Reuben pleaded. 'I really want to know, if I can.'

'Well,' she said awkwardly. 'You know we met in the snug at the Laurel. That first time, he'd gone in for a packet of cigs, and didn't want to talk to anybody. When he'd got his cigs, he thought he might as well have a sup of something. While he was drinking, he was sitting down in the corner with such an expression on his face. I felt real sorry for him. Of course, I knew he was a Godson, and all that, and I were nobbut a bit of a Milner, but I thought I'd try to cheer him up a bit. And that's what I said. Come on, lad, cheer up a bit. Your face would turn a cow's milk sour. . . . Well, he give a bit of a laugh. I reckon it would, Elsie Milner, he said, and that's how it started. He came back here, natural and easy, and I had him laughing for an hour or two, telling him about some of the things that has happened to me in service up at Tockett House. Right dead comical, some of them are, and it made him laugh. Like the time I was carrying a damned great big piss-pot, and Mr James Henry came on me unawares and put his hand on my bum, and I turned quick, and he got the whole piss-pot full in his face. It makes me laugh now, thinking about it, and God knows, I can use a laugh!'

Her hand tightened round his, and the tears filled her eyes. 'I could do with a laugh, Reuben Godson,' she said. 'It's my birthday, my birthday, and the only man who's ever been halfways decent with me has been taken away, and if that isn't a great big bloody joke, and a face full of piss-pot, I don't know what is!'

Her head dropped down and the tears rained. He came quickly round the table and put his arm along her shoulders, trying to comfort her, but lacking the ideas and the words. 'He spoke well of you,' was all he could say. 'He spoke really well of you!'

She sat up straight. 'He was dying,' she said. 'Did you know that?'

Reuben shook his head.

'He was dying, and he couldn't understand why. He'd feared God all his life, he said, been to the chapel, honoured his mother and father, done everything he should have done and nowt he shouldn't, yet they sent him to some bloody awful hole in France and filled his lungs full of gas. One lung riddled with rot, the other one going slowly, lingering on. Can you wonder he couldn't understand *why*! He couldn't *understand* why! And, I'll tell you the truth, Reuben, neither could I. Because he was such a lovely lad. I've seen him for years, a lovely lad, and they sent him away and gassed him!'

Now she was bawling with anger, frustration, sorrow, her features screwed up in pain, her cheeks bright red with rage. Reuben was stirred that anyone could think so passionately, so openly, about his brother. His mother had cried, silently; Eleanor hadn't even shed a tear though he could see her deep feelings. But Elsie Milner, one of the village tarts, was crying openly with regret for the death of his brother and he was moved deep inside himself.

'He told me you comforted him at a time when he needed it!' he said.

'He was dying,' she wailed, '*dying*! That lovely young lad. You were talking to him about boats and co-operatives, about fishing and rigging, and he was *dying*! He was a Godson, a Godson of Old Quaytown of Ravenswyke, and he was dying, and the God-sons don't make a scandal about anything, don't make a fuss. So he came to me, and I comforted him the only ways I knew how, which was to make him laugh, and to put him in my bed and make him happy. And every time he went out on that damned boat, he tied a couple of lead pigs round his waist, under his shirt, and every time he went away from me, I said goodbye to him for ever!'

He drew his arm slowly from around her shoulder and went to stand with his back to the fire, looking across the room at her – without meaning to, comparing her to Emily Duckett, to his own sister Eleanor, even to what his mother must have been as a young lass. Had his mother felt this way about his father, Silas? Had Eleanor felt this way about Terrie, and Alf? And Emily, what did Emily feel for him? He'd never seen this sort of passion on the face of any woman, but did that mean it didn't exist? He was frightened and excited by it. He remembered Emily's squirming under his hand, remembered her hand on his, and the cold shock of – what had it been, disappointment, regret, sadness? – when she'd said she'd do what she'd just done any time he wanted it. That wasn't passion, the naked intense feeling he was now witnessing which so stirred his hitherto unknown emotions.

'Wipe your face, Elsie,' he said softly. 'Wipe your face and put your coat on. I'm taking you down home with me for a bit of supper!'

She smiled at him through her tears and her face cracked with what he saw as a wild loveliness, a look that must have tugged at Lewis's heart. 'Nay, Reuben, lad,' she said, 'that wouldn't be fitting. That wouldn't be right at all. Not tonight, when your mam and your sister are grieving. I shall cook that bit of fish, and bring it in here by the fire, and I shall think about him. We didn't have much time together, the two of us, but what we had is mine and I'll not share it. Though I'm grateful for your suggestion. You're a right lad, you are. You'll make Emily Duckett a good husband, in time. So long as you stop away from the likes of me!'

'That's bloody rubbish,' he said, 'if you'll pardon the expression.'

'You, a Godson, swearing. . . .'

'Rubbish is what I said, and rubbish is what I meant. All right, Elsie Milner, do your grieving on your own if you've a mind. But one day, very soon, I shall be coming up here, and you'll be putting on your coat, and you and me will be walking together down that hill in broad daylight, arm in arm. And I don't give a bugger who sees us!'

Women are inexplicable, he thought. He hoped his words would comfort her, but instead they caused her to burst into tears again, her head on her hands, the drops running down and staining the green chenille of her best tablecloth. Women! he thought, as he let himself out of the house.

But now he understood more about Lewis. And, in some curious undefinable way, he knew more about the Godsons, more about himself and his task as the head and sole male survivor of that long-lived family.

He walked slowly down the cobbled street, seeing the lights behind curtains, hearing the murmur of voices. The Laurel was busy and from inside he heard laughter and the clack of dominoes on the wooden table tops. The bright moon hovered over the ocean, sending ribbons of stirring silver light across the ocean towards him. As he walked down the steep hill, he saw the roofs of Old Quaytown spread out before him, lining the left of the steep bank and, to the right, the mean streets of the Tockett cottages in meaninglessly straight lines across the face of the rise.

118

Several strong lights burned outside Tockett House at the top of the hill above Newquay Town, as if the old man who lived there were driving out the darkness. Reuben remembered Elsie's story about the piss-pot and laughed mirthlessly. The Tocketts and the Godsons. What was it Tockett had said? You rule one side, we rule the other. Well, James Henry Tockett wasn't too long for this earth, and Reuben would see him out. What sort of a 'ruler' would Mark Adam Tockett prove to be, when he couldn't even hold his commission in the army, in a safe job in the War Office, when all the other lads were in France getting sniped and gassed. Or, like his brothers, being drowned when the boat bringing them back to England for a bit of leave ran into one of the mines the Germans had dropped in the Channel.

He looked down the hill at the buildings of the Tockett boatyard, that poor enterprise that had never proved itself. The factory had been going to bring prosperity to Ravenswkye, and full employment, but instead it had merely put half the population in mental, domestic and financial chains.

The future of Ravenswyke didn't depend, he knew for certain, on the boatyard. It depended on Old Quaytown, on the fishermen who gave a strong core, a definite lead. The independents who couldn't be bought or seduced by Tockett's money, the hard men who could meet Tockett, as he himself had met him, face to face as business equals, fearing nothing, touching the forelock to no one.

The odour of coal smoke assailed his nostrils as he walked down the hill, nearing the slip, seeing the Raven with no lights in the taproom. Now the coal smoke had gone, and most of the cottages on this side of the Cut were dark. Fishermen go early to bed, rise early to take the day fearlessly at its own value, treating fair weather and foul with equal caution but equal disdain. By God, today had been as fine a day as they'd known that year, but the day had taken Lewis. No, not the day. The sea. Reuben smelled it, an old antagonist, in the night air, giving off its familar sweat of salt and sea-wrack. He stood by the *Hope*, remembering the time he'd brought it back, named then the *Jolly Lads*, running his hands over the wood he and Lewis had varnished so carefully, rubbing it smooth with glass-paper, caring for it.

'I shall have that front bedroom all to myself,' he said. 'All to myself.'

119

When Reuben heard the knock at the door, he looked up at his mother.

'That'll be him,' she said nervously. 'Hang on a minute.'

She whisked the chenille cover off the table top, unfastened her apron from around her waist, smoothed her hair. 'Right,' she said, 'you can let him in.'

Tobias Liggett had the sort of lugubrious face often assumed by craftsmen in solemn contemplation of their unique abilities. Certain no one could duplicate the work Tobias did. His bag was made of a triangle of Wilton carpet folded catercorners and sewn with sail stitches. Its two handles were thick rope. Inside he carried a plane, a pair of chisels, two mallets, and a fine-bladed bow saw with leather thongs providing the stress across the wooden shoulders.

The pencil he used was oval in section, sharpened to a chisel point a quarter of an inch along the blade.

' 'Morning,' he said. 'Turned out cold.' Tobias wasn't a renowned talker. He eyed the beam on which he'd already carved two names, that of Silas and that of Lewis. He ran his hand over the name *Lewis* as if testing its permanence.

'You'll take a cup of tea?' Hannah asked.

'When we've done, missis, thank you.'

He ran his eye along the beam, expertly assessing its grain, then climbed on the wooden chair Reuben had provided, placing his bag carefully on the table, opened wide. The space beneath the name *Lewis* had already been planed smooth in inevitable anticipation; Tobias took up his chisel and the smaller of his two mallets. He pencilled in the figures 1917 with deft strokes of the flat-bladed pencil. When he tapped his chisel with the mallet the wood curled in the cut; a stroke in the other direction and the first chip fell out on to the square of canvas slub Hannah had spread on the floor. Tap chip, tap chip, tap chip. The one, the nine, the one and the seven were quickly formed on the smooth surface of the wood, cut a quarter of an inch deep, with a V-cut whose edges could have been drawn by a ruler. When he'd finished the date he stepped down from the chair, eyeing his workmanship. 'Aye, that'll do,' he said, without any apparent sign of enthusiasm.

Hannah had seated herself on the arm of her chair, looking deep into the fire's flames. Reuben put his arm around her shoulders without speaking, noting with shock how brittle she felt beneath his hand.

Tobias glanced at them, then climbed back on the chair. He used his plane to lick the beam flat at the level where he intended to carve. The wood curled neatly back beneath the sharpened blade, giving off an odour of old resin. As the plane bit in, the colour of the wood changed from a dark brown to a red-purple hue he knew would soon darken back again. Lewis's name had already toned down to match the rest of the beam in such a short time. He used his pencil, drew the name REUBEN deftly in plain characters, matching the rest of the names extending along the beam.

Then he started to chip away at the wood. The silence of the room was broken only by his concentrated breathing, the tap of his mallet on the head of his chisel, the crackle of the fire burning in the grate. The job took him half an hour, after which he climbed down from the chair, took up his plane, and used it to shave a couple of edges of chipped wood, standing proud of the rest of the carving. He shaved the space beneath. 'I seem to remember as you were born in 1900, Reuben,' he said.

'That's right.'

'Aye, it was a different world we lived in, in them days,' Tobias said as he climbed on the chair and began to chip again.

PART TWO

As long as Elsie Milner could remember, there had only been her mam. Granted, there'd been lots of men about when she was a young girl, and they'd all been old enough to be her father. For a day or two her mam would treat them with great affection, sit them down at the table and make them pots of tea and slices of bread and butter and jam. She'd cook meals for them, even clean their boots. They'd sleep with mam in the big bed in the front room, and that always seemed natural to Elsie because, if they didn't sleep in the big bed in the front room, where else could they take their rest and spend the night?

Until Elsie had been eight years old, this had seemed the normal pattern, this constant slow changing-over of men. On the very few days when there was no man about, her mother would be snappy and restless, bad-tempered and fiddly, and Elsie would long for another large, male-smelling, tobacco-smoking, loud-voiced, braces-trousered man to come and clump about the cottage where they lived.

She lost her innocence slowly. At first she noticed that the other girls in the school halfway up the bank in Old Quaytown had the same man as a father all the time. The same man, the same mam. Well, Susie Quill's mam died of tuberculosis and her father brought a girl from Whitby to live in as housekeeper, and when she started to grow fat a few months later married her and gave Susie a new sister. Janet Foster's father was lost at sea when the *Perspicacity* foundered with all hands; Janet's mam took another man and when *she* started to grow fat, at her age, she got married in the chapel, and Janet got a new sister. So many times, Elsie learned as a young girl, the change of father or mam was associated with a new sister or brother. But her own mam changed men all the time, and Elsie never had a new sister or brother.

When Elsie was nine, she went to a party in the school, the day before they broke up for Christmas. Everybody was given an apple and an orange, and a shiny new threepenny bit to go home with, but before that they had a tea of paste sandwiches, pies and jellies, red and green. They wore paper hats and sat on the floor round a big tree with candles on it, and sitting next to her was Harry Naseby. He was in the top school, at twelve, and a big lad. While they were sitting there, singing carols and looking up at the tree, he beckoned to her, nudging her in the ribs.

'Look at yon!' he said, and lifted the jacket he'd spread across his legs, since it was quite cold in the schoolroom. She looked under the jacket and for the first time saw a man's private parts. It stuck up in the air, seeming to grow like the branch of a tree out of his middle.

'Grab hold of it,' he whispered fiercely. She did as she was told. After all, he was older than she was, and already in the big school, and so she grabbed it and held on to it tight as if it were the handle of a pan. And he grabbed her wrist, under his coat, and waggled it up and down in a funny sort of way and when she looked up into his face he was all red and seemed to be gasping for air. She was so frightened she took her hand away and called out, 'Mr Jennings, I think Harry Naseby's been took bad!'

All the carol-singing stopped, and Mr Jennings came striding across the room, forging his way between the sitting bodies that littered the floor. Harry was scrabbling beneath his jacket and still gasping, and now Elsie could see his face was turning greeny white, as if he'd seen a ghost. And he got to his feet and ran out of the schoolroom, not waiting for Mr Jennings's help.

'What's wrong with the lad?' Mr Jennings asked her.

'I don't know. It looked to me as if he was going to be sick or summat.'

'Probably eaten too many sandwiches, the greedy little devil,' Mr Jennings said and turned round. 'Come on,' he said, 'you've got three more carols to sing before you can go home!'

There was a general groan, soon stifled when he started them off on 'Good King Wenceslas', which they all knew by heart.

When Elsie left the school with her apple, her orange and her threepenny-bit, it was already starting dusk as she climbed the bank. On the bend behind the Laurel, she turned up the steps to cross the bit of field before the start of the street of her mam's cottage, and they jumped on her from behind a bush – Harry, George and Phil Naseby. They tripped her up and pushed her down on the ground under, or at least half under, the bushes. 'You make a noise,' Harry said, the menace in his voice unmistakable, 'and we'll kill you and chuck you over the cliff top.' She didn't make a noise. One look at his face and she believed they'd do what they said. Everybody knew the Nasebys were a rough lot. George reached up under her dress, the nice one she'd saved for the Christmas party, and pulled down her drawers. He had a job to get them over the tops of her boots, and Harry, who was more experienced, cautioned him. 'Don't tear 'em,' he said. 'It's got to look voluntary.'

Elsie didn't know what he meant; she realized, however, that they were going to hurt her, and she could make it better for herself if she faced up to it, didn't resist them, or fight to make them angry. She looked at Phil. He was in her class. He couldn't look into her eyes but turned his head away.

Then Harry got it out again. 'I'll teach you to split on me to Mr Jennings,' he said. George held her legs apart, and Harry lay down on top of her, his weight hurting her. The pain between her legs was intense and it was all she could do not to cry out, but she bit her lip. It felt as if Harry was tearing the bottom of her stomach open as he pushed further inside her. He was grunting with satisfaction, the way she'd heard animals grunt up on Blakey's farm. And, come to think of it, the way she'd heard some of the men grunt when they'd been sleeping in the big bed with her mother. At least, up until this moment she thought they'd been sleeping, but now she realized with terrible clarity that they had been doing to her mother what Harry was doing to her now. George had let go of her ankles and was thumping Harry's back.

'Don't come inside,' he was saying, 'else she'll name the three of us.'

Elsie didn't realize exactly what he meant, but she lay still when Harry eased his weight off her and, a couple of seconds later, gave a muted shout.

Then George lay down on her, and this time, the pain was less, and she could turn her head and look into his eyes, and think about the times she'd seen him running about in the schoolyard with snot on his face and holes in his socks and his cap with its broken neb.

'Are you enjoying yourself, then?' she asked, but he merely grunted.

'Shut up,' he said. 'We'll teach you to split on our Harry!'

By the time it was Phil's turn, she'd begun to understand what it was all about. And had even begun to feel a bit of something herself, deep inside, between her legs. When Phil pushed himself into her, his eyes still avoiding her, she bent her knees slightly to make herself more comfortable, and then clasped her arms round his waist, and held him tight. That brought his face round, and his eyes looked into hers, and she could see what might have been the tortured misery in them. 'It's all right, Phil,' she said. 'It's all right!'

And then she felt the draught of cold air and knew he'd left her. She unclasped her arms as he broke away and turned his head, but not before she'd seen the tears in the corners of his eyes.

As she pulled her drawers back on, Harry squatted beside her. 'You tell anybody,' he hissed, 'and us'll come for you and kill you, understand?'

She nodded her head. She couldn't speak. Now she'd started to cry. Not because she'd been raped, or because these three lads had violated her in revenge, but because she'd suddenly realized, without being able to put a word to it, just what her mother was, what the men who'd been father to her had done to her, and had come to know with blinding clarity that, so far as the people of Ravenswkye were concerned, she'd always be an outsider, a brat without a father, a bastard stained by the sins of her mother.

She got up. The three lads were standing in an awkward group, not looking at her. 'If you've all finished,' she said, 'I'll be off.'

Only Harry tried to be brave. 'That'll teach you,' he said. 'Nobody splits on a Naseby and gets away wi' it!'

'Happen you're right,' she said, 'but I wouldn't count on it.'

Elsie went straight home and showed her mam the orange and the apple, and gave her the threepenny bit. 'No, you mun keep that,' Meg Milner said, 'that's for you. I reckon you've earned that!'

When the current man, George Willie, came home from the pub, Elsie was already in bed. She'd washed her drawers in the shed behind the lavatory, and had hung them at the back of a bush in the garden to dry overnight. She was lying in bed, still awake, as they came up the steps; when they'd been in bed ten minutes she crept out and listened at the door of the big bedroom.

George Willie was grunting, just as Harry Naseby had grunted. She turned the handle slowly and eased the door open a crack until she could see the bed reflected in the mirror of the tallboy, and they were doing exactly what Harry and his brothers had done to her that evening. She saw how hairy was George Willie's body and how gross his bum pushing up and down on her mam's fat flabby flesh; she saw her mam's face looking up at the ceiling with an expression of boredom. 'Hurry up and get it over with,' her mam said, 'I want to get to sleep when you've done!'

Sickened by what she'd seen and heard, Elsie went back to her own bedroom and lay on her back in her own bed, watching the motes in the moonlight across the room. She could hear the sea outside pounding at the rocks, and the rhythm of the creaking bed in the next room seemed somehow to fit in with it as a monstrous but necessary vulgarity, like farting and belching, having a pee and doing a number two, necessary things the body did and you didn't talk about. So that's what being married was, eh?

Well, she didn't think much to it, she said to herself, as she drifted into a deep, exhausted sleep.

Elsie never forgot that evening and night, and never forgave either her mam or Harry Naseby. During the next years she took her revenge on her mam in small ways, snubbing the men she brought home, making derogatory jokes at their expense, mostly deriding their manhood. She saved her revenge on Harry until she was sixteen and already a fully developed girl. Over the years she'd seen the Naseby brothers grow to manhood, but none of them had ever tried to touch her, or referred to that evening before Christmas. By then she'd known several men of her own and had wondered why her mam had found it boring that night; Elsie had developed a taste for sex, for the sheer enjoyment of it, that had surprised the men who'd been with her. They'd been amazed, and somewhat discomfited, to discover that she attacked them with the same vigour they applied to her, with none of the blushing naïve reluctance of most of the girls they'd successfully seduced. Elsie made one rule – she would never have anything to do with any man from Ravenswyke. She'd travel into Whitby on a Saturday afternoon, and wander round the market and the fish stalls looking demure and respectable. Inevitably some youth, some male, would offer to carry her shopping bag, buy her a cup of tea in one of the neighbouring teashops, even a little something stronger in one of the many alehouses open to the public, with snugs in which the ladies were increasingly permitted to sip a glass of port. Any who passed her rigorous scrutiny would be accepted, but in a demure way. She wouldn't go into a teashop or an ale-house, but 'had been thinking of taking a stroll up as far as the Abbey' and wouldn't object if the gentleman cared to accompany her. The Abbey was a fierce climb to the east of Whitby harbour; what more natural than, when in sight of the large edifice, they should walk a way across the fields to sit down and relax, gazing out to sea? And what man with blood in his veins and lust in his loins could resist the sight of such a well-formed, attractive young lady, sitting on the springy turf, remote from the prying eyes of the world beneath them in the gathering dusk. On the headland overlooking the silvering ocean, the fortunate pair could have been abandoned on another planet.

Elsie Milner was in the Old Folks' Party in the chapel when Harry Naseby, who'd heard there were three barrels of beer to give away free, and beef sandwiches, came swaggering in with Tom Malton and Wally Wicklow. 'This,' she thought as she saw them, 'is the night for my revenge.'

She saw Harry look across the room at her, as he usually did, and before he could turn his face away with that sickly grin he wore on it whenever he saw her, she winked at him and smiled. His eyes grew wide with surprise. She winked and smiled again, and beckoned with her head. He said a word to his two pals and came across the room like a hunting dog sniffing the air.

'Hello, then, Harry,' she said.

'Hello, Elsie. What's up?'

'Nowt's up, you gormless ha'porth. Are you going to spend the rest of your life avoiding me?'

'By gow, I'm not,' he said.

She was standing by the barrel giving out the pints of beer to the old folks. She filled a pot and handed it to him. 'Get that down you,' she said.

In the next hour she handed him, and he drank, twenty pints of the strong ale, and by the time the party was over, he was stagger-ing. 'Come on,' she said, taking his arm, 'let's have a bit of a walk in the fresh air!'

He winked owlishly at his two pals as they left together, arm in arm.

'It's all right for some,' Tom Malton said. 'Some of us is looking after the old 'uns!' Tom and Wally had both been press-ganged into helping Mrs Cartwright, who weighed at least thirty stones, down the steps of the chapel room, and up the bank to her cottage.

Once outside, Elsie and Harry turned up the bank, walking parallel with the fields that stretched towards the moor above Old Quaytown, a traditional courting spot. 'Wait here for me a minute,' Elsie said at the end of her lane. 'I'll have to tell my mam I've been invited. I shan't be a minute.'

He sat on the bottom step of the path that led to the field lane, the world spinning about him. When they got up on the top, he resolved, he'd stick his finger down his throat and get rid of some of it. He hadn't ought to have drunk as many pints as that. But it had all been free, hadn't it? When Elsie came back, she was wearing her topcoat.

'Give us something to sit on,' she said.

'By gow!' Words failed him, but he found expression in an enormous belch that seemed to start from somewhere deep inside him and gather force as it climbed. 'Better an empty house than a bad tenant!' he said and, as if to prove his point, followed the belch with an equally enormous fart. 'Over-much gas in that beer,' he said by way of explanation. It never occurred to him to apologize.

The way grew steeper as they headed up the path, across the field, down the side, until they were on the cliff edge overlooking the lighthouse. 'Tha's bringing me a long way, Elsie,' he complained, but she quickly silenced him.

'If you don't want to come, Harry Naseby, you needn't bother,' she said. 'I've a mind to get away from Ravenswyke, to look out over the water. But if you'd rather go back, on your own, don't let me keep you.' As if to emphasize her point, she skipped lightly a few steps ahead of him, a fairy dancing in the moonlight, infinitely provocative, infinitely desirable.

'Nay, I'll come,' he said, lumbering along the grass after her, his belly rumbling, his guts aching with the unaccustomed exercise on top of the drink.

Finally they reached the corner of the hedge, climbed over, and there before them was Statheby's Field, of which this hedge formed the boundary to the west, and the sheer drop to the ocean

129

the boundary to the east. Statheby's sheep were cropping the lush winter grass, ghostlike figures that wandered slowly through the moonscape. Elsie took off her topcoat and spread it on the ground, with her large canvas shopping bag beside it. She reached into the bag. 'I've brought a present for you,' she said. 'Something I've been saving!'

'What is it, then?' he asked.

She drew out a bottle. 'It's rum,' she said. 'Should settle your stomach!'

It *was* rum. Rum, and gin, and brandy, and whisky. It was the dregs of all the bottles her mam's men had brought back to the house, poured into one bottle and saved for this very occasion. Harry grabbed the bottle from her and drank deep. 'By gow, that's a bit o' good stuff!' he said. 'You have one.'

'You trying to get me drunk, Harry Naseby?' she said with the voice of a coquette. 'You don't need to do that, you know,' she said.

'Right! I've had thee once. I s'all have thee again!' Harry said.

She leaned towards him. 'Go on, let's have a look at it again,' she said.

He fumbled inside his trousers and she was shocked when she saw how much he'd grown in the intervening years.

'Go on, grab hold of it,' he said. 'Like you did that day in t' schoolroom.'

'Don't you want another drink?' she said.

'Drink's not what I want, Elsie,' he said, grabbing at her.

She sprang to her feet. 'Come on,' she said, 'sup up. I've been saving that for you. Don't tell me you're not man enough to drink it!'

He roared, grabbed the bottle, upended it over his mouth, and drank it down in gulps, emptying the bottle in one long pull. He put the bottle on the grass beside him, lifted his hands towards Elsie in a sort of pleading gesture, his face stricken. She could see the spittle running down his lower bristly lip as he sat on the grass, his trousers unbuttoned, his private parts hanging out, and the dribble running down his shirt front. And then he dropped backwards as if poleaxed.

Elsie bent over him, looking down at him. Harry was out, and would stay out for a long time.

'Right, you bastard,' she said, the long-concealed hatred gleaming in her eyes, in the tight set of her mouth, as she ran swiftly towards the nearest sheep.

Alf Neckridge had been the Constable of Ravenswyke for only a year. It was the first constable appointment he'd ever had, after his training in Whitby. They'd given him a cottage up-bank where he could look down on Old Quaytown and Newquay Town. Most of his business came from the latter; the residents of Old Quaytown were an early-to-bed, law-abiding lot who rarely if ever gave him any trouble, except the job of recording the accidental deaths of fishermen lost at sea. The Newquay Town lot were the source of most of his problems – a shifty transient lot; he seemed to spend most of his time wandering the mean streets in which they lived in their company-built, back-to-back houses in which, privately he thought, he wouldn't keep the rabbits that were his hobby and source of extra income. He answered the door at the first knock, and saw Elsie Milner standing there.

'Right, Elsie, what can I do for *you*?' he asked. She'd called him out once before, when one of her mam's 'men' had taken to beating her.

'Can I come in? It's a bit awkward,' she said, obviously embarrassed.

'You'd better,' he said.

The police station proper was a room off his parlour, but he took her into the kitchen and invited her to sit in the chair by the fire. 'My missis'll be back any minute,' he said. 'She's gone to look in on Mrs Partridge. We're not expecting her to last the night before she has the babby.' Molly was one of the local unpaid midwives, as well as being the policeman's wife. She also earned a bit laying out the dead.

'Can I talk to you, like, private?' Elsie asked.

'Yes, you can, lass,' he said. 'Would you like a cup of tea while you're doing it?'

'No, thanks. Well, what I've got to say mustn't get out. You see, I went for a walk up by Statheby's Field after the Old Folks' Social.'

'Nowt wrong wi' that, Elsie. I often take a walk up there myself. . . .'

'Aye, but I went with Harry Naseby. . . .'

'Ah, that's different,' he said. 'You coming to lay a complaint against Harry on account of something he's done to you?'

'No,' she said. 'It's nothing like that. You see, I was serving the ale at the social. Harry had a few too many, so I took him up there for a walk to sober him up a bit.'

'Yes, I can see your problem,' he said instantly. 'There's not many folks who'd give you a good name, if they knew you'd walked up there with him, whatever the reason. So, what do you want to tell me?'

'Just that I lost him. He fell down blind drunk, and when I turned round, he wasn't there. I'm just afraid he might have gone over the cliffs. . . . He were that drunk. . . '

'I'd better go up there, and take a look,' he said.

'And you won't say owt about me being up there?'

'I won't, lass. You've no cause to worry. Unless it should turn out,' he added with heavy humour, 'as you pushed him over. . .?'

She managed a smile. 'Now why would I do that, constable?' she said sweetly.

He agreed, looking at her, so sweet and demure, so different from that slut of a mother of hers. 'I'd better take a walk up there,' he said, 'and see what I can find.'

He found Harry Naseby lying on the ground with his private parts hanging out and a substance smearing them which the public analyst, in closed court, subsequently reported as coming from the interior of a sheep's organs. A sheep was also found, mewing piteously near Harry's unconscious body, both its back legs spreadeagled and staked to two bushes with Harry's belt and Harry's braces.

When Alf Neckridge was promoted sergeant, after the trial, he gave Elsie Milner a gift of half a sovereign. 'For your birthday,' he said.

Harry Naseby died in Wakefield Gaol, killed by a fellow prisoner in 1917.

Elsie had dressed herself very carefully in a plain, dark blue woollen frock with a white lace collar, and a bit of lace at the sleeves, when Reuben came to fetch her. 'I still think you're making a mistake, lad,' she said as he helped her on with her coat.

'Leave me be the judge of that,' he said.

When they left her cottage, the curtains in the nearby houses fluttered like warning flags, but he defiantly took her arm, linking it with his. She looked up at him and laughed. 'Lad, I never knew as you were a rebel,' she said. 'You've put more noses out of joint, and given more people summat to talk about by this deed, than I'd have believed possible. A Godson, walking out arm in arm with Elsie Milner! I never thought I'd live to see the day.'

He took her down the steep cobbled street between the cottages. The doors opened like the shutters of a cuckoo clock as the ladies came out, brooms in hand, to sweep already immaculate front steps. He said a careful and courteous good morning to each one of them, but few replied with anything other than an indecipherable mutter and a glance at his companion.

'You know summat, lass,' he said, 'I've a good mind to ask thee to wed me, just to see the look on their faces!'

She pulled her arm away from his, stopped dead, and squared off to face him. 'That's not a very good joke, Reuben Godson,' she said. 'I thought better of you than that.'

He was immediately contrite. 'Aye, Elsie, like I'm sorry. It just come to my tongue, you know, seeing all these old bats dying of curiosity.'

Mollified, she took his arm again. 'Any road, how do you know I'd have you?' she said. 'You're a bit on the skinny side for me!'

He let out a roar of pretended rage, happy now that their good humour had returned. Of late he'd been thinking a lot about Elsie Milner, more in fact than he cared to admit even to himself. His evenings with Emily Duckett had been plagued by thoughts of the other girl who'd begun to seem altogether more sophisticated, more desirable, more worldly than the plain, simple, even naïve Emily, who was always so ready to please, so anxious to say nothing wrong or do nothing selfish that it was impossible to probe beneath her bland and obliging surface to the real person beneath. For example, he said to himself, Emily would never have stopped him dead and faced up to him as Elsie had done back there, when he said something she didn't like. Emily would have pouted, gone quiet for a while, keeping her resentment to herself. And then, later, she would have found some excuse not to let him touch her.

Hannah had put on her good dress and had combed her hair tightly into a severe bun at the back of her head. 'It's nice to see you, Elsie,' she said when Reuben brought her into the room. 'Dinner's almost ready.'

Reuben saw, with some amusement, that a cloth had been laid on the table from Hannah's special drawer. It covered the chenille table-spread with snowy whiteness. Knives and forks had been laid in place, instead of being handed out from the drawer once they were sitting around. There were even glasses and a jug of water, a salt pot and pepper. And plates at the sides of the forks. A dish in the centre of the table carried a loaf of bread, but Hannah had already cut four slices from it.

No doubt about it, giving Elsie her dinner was going to be a posh do! He hadn't seen such a setting since they'd had the service for Lewis and had brought a few folks back 'after', as was the tradition.

They sat in the two chairs while Hannah bustled about them. She went to the door and called up the bedroom steps. 'Come on, Eleanor,' she said. 'Elsie and our Reuben's here already.'

She went back and opened the fire-oven door. A smell of roasting meat came out at them. 'By gow, that smells good,' Reuben said.

'It should do,' Hannah said. 'That's a leg of Fewster's best lamb!'

'You couldn't have got that while the war was on, Mrs Godson,' Elsie remarked brightly, making conversation.

Eleanor came into the room, wearing her 'best', as Reuben quickly noticed. Mind you, he shouldn't complain. He'd worn a collar and a tie and had scrubbed his hands. 'Hello, Elsie,' Eleanor said after her mother had looked severely at her. The greeting came out forced, with no warmth.

'Hello, Eleanor,' Elsie said brightly. 'What a lovely dress! That colour looks nice on you.'

Eleanor did look nice, Reuben thought. For once, she'd spruced herself up a bit. Since Alf Pitt had died, and she'd lost Terrie's baby, she hadn't looked after herself. She'd let herself go a bit to seed. And he could no longer trust her to bait the hooks properly – when she did the job these days, half the mussels dropped off when the line went over the side. Of course, he could understand that losing two fellows, and almost all her family, would have affected her, but it was time for her to snap out of it. One of the many reasons, half-formed in his mind, why he'd brought Elsie here this day was that Eleanor could be cheered up a bit by the other girl. Perhaps they might hit it off together. God knows,

Eleanor could do with having a girl pal instead of mooning about the house all the day long, with Hannah as her only companion. Elsie could show her a bit of life, that was certain.

But she sat there, as if frozen in a block of ice, with nothing to say.

Eleanor stayed the same all during the dinner. Elsie chattered away, and even Reuben talked. Hannah was busy dishing up the food but she replied fully when either of them talked to her. From time to time Hannah looked at Eleanor with exasperation on her face, but she said nothing. After dinner, Eleanor bent over the sink, refusing Elsie's offer to help her, rejecting her with little grace. Hannah busied herself clearing the table, then made another pot of tea and even provided a few cakes she'd bought from the local shop. To Reuben, used to his mother's home cooking, they tasted like sawdust but he knew that social etiquette demanded 'bought' cakes at a time like that. He was greatly disappointed. He'd hoped he'd be able to bring Elsie Milner down for dinner and see her accepted as one of the family, the way Emily was when she came to eat. His hopes had dropped when he'd seen the elaborately laid table, the way Hannah had dressed and furbished herself. Eleanor, of course, had put the kibosh on everything. She was always a wet blanket these days, even when Emily came to see them.

'It'll be high tide soon,' he said finally. 'I shall have to get changed if I'm going out to look at the lobster pots.'

'I'll have to get back home,' Elsie said. 'I haven't done a thing yet today.'

It was the end of the experiment. When he'd seen Elsie on her way he stood by the fire, reflecting that the visit had not been a success.

Eleanor had disappeared upstairs the minute she'd finished the washing up. Hannah was sitting in her chair, two knitting needles in her hands. She was never still, never sat down doing nothing. She looked up at him and saw the disappointment on his face. She put her knitting needles in her lap. 'You've got to give us time, Reuben lad,' she said. 'We've got to get used to the idea.'

'What idea? I don't know what you're talking about!'

'You will, Reuben lad,' she said. 'You've got a hard road ahead of you.'

135

'I don't know what you mean!'

'Aye, well, some of us has eyes that can see further than our noses. You'll be chucking Emily Duckett, mark my words. And you'll be hanging round Elsie's doorstep. You'll be breaking one lass's heart, and another lass will happen be breaking yours. Elsie's four years older than you, Reuben. She'll never take you, mark my words. Already folks is talking, and Emily Duckett isn't daft. The gossiping tongues don't spare anybody, and she'll be hearing all about this day's doing, how you brought another lass home for dinner. Why did you have to do it, Reuben? Why couldn't you have her for tea, on a day when Emily herself was here? You've humbled Emily, but you wouldn't know that. No man ever would.'

She picked up her knitting again, but didn't start it.

Reuben couldn't understand fully what his mother was saying. He had no intention of 'humbling' anybody. He'd wanted to bring Elsie for her dinner to thank her in the most practical way for being so nice to Lewis all that time ago. In the year since Lewis had died and the war had ended, he'd thought a lot about Elsie and the conversation he'd had with Lewis that last day, that fatal day, on the *Hope*. Now he felt he could understand what Lewis had meant when he'd said that Elsie comforted him at a time he needed it. He'd known he was dying – the doctor had told him that – and Elsie had accepted him as he was. A human being. Not a fellow who already had one foot in the grave. Reuben told himself he wanted to give Elsie Milner the best thanks he could by leading the way, by showing the evil gossips and the spiteful crones that the Godson family was prepared to accept Elsie for what she was, to forget the bygones and treat her as a human being, irrespective of the soiled reputation folks may have put on her.

'I just wanted us to be nice to her,' he said lamely.

'Aye, that's what you tell yourself,' Hannah said. 'You're a man. A man's man at that, though you'll never have problems with the lasses. You've got to give yourself some kind of reason for what you do. A woman, well she does what she knows she must, without seeking reasons for it. But a man always has to tell himself he has a reason. Mark my words, you're storing up trouble for yourself and for Emily Duckett, if you go with Elsie Milner. Don't misunderstand me, Reuben. I'm not standing judgement on

136

her. She is what she is, what her mother's made her. I must say, I found her pleasant-spoken, and decent enough. And she's certainly bright! She brought a smile or two to my lips and it's a long time since anybody's done that. Only one thing I ask, Reuben. For all of us. For the family. Think carefully before you let Emily down and when you do, as I'm afraid you will, do it nice. Let her down gently, because she's done nowt to deserve what's going to happen to her. She's been good with you, and good for you. She'd make you a good wife, and a good mother for your bairns, but I can see you're too besotted with the other to see that, just now.'

'Besotted? Who said I was besotted?'

'I did, lad, and keep your shirt on. Like I said, some of us can see further than the end of our noses!'

Eleanor must have come downstairs and have been listening behind the door. She pushed it open violently and stood with her hands on her hips, no longer the calm, placid, distracted person she had been at dinner.

'You can't be going to throw over Emily Duckett, our Reuben, for that ... that slut!'

Reuben's anger flared. 'You watch your mouth when you're calling somebody a slut,' he said. 'It was a good job you had Terrie on hand to marry you when he did, or that's what they'd have been calling *you*, with some justification!'

It was as if he had slapped her on both cheeks, where patches of red now glowed. No one in the Godson family had ever referred to the fact that she'd not been a virgin when she and Terrie were wed. Hannah stood up.

'Now that's enough from the pair of you,' she said. 'Reuben's a grown man, Eleanor, and he's a perfect right to go his own way. And you, Reuben, you've no call to be unnecessarily cruel. That was a *cruel* thing you just said. You've no call to be bringing up old tales like that. No call at all!'

Reuben turned on his heel and would have marched out of the cottage had they not heard a loud knock on the door. 'I wonder who the heck that can be at this time of day,' he said.

Hannah beckoned for Eleanor, who was standing with tears streaming down her face, to go back upstairs. She followed her, and Reuben opened the door. He recognized the man standing there as Terence Batsford, whom everyone called Batty. Batty lived in Newquay Town and worked for Tockett in the boatyard as a carpenter. A couple of years before, he'd asked Reuben to take out a recently completed boat to test its seaworthiness, and a nodding acquaintance had developed between them.

''Afternoon, Reuben,' Batty said. 'Do you have a couple of minutes to spare?'

'Aye, you'd best come in,' Reuben said. 'We were just supping some tea, if you've a mind.'

Batty sat awkward at the table, looking up at the beam, scanning the names. 'Bit of good carving, that!' he said. 'I'd heard about it.'

Reuben handed him a pot of tea from the big teapot, took one for himself, and sat in his dad's chair which now, of course, was his by right. 'What can I do for you, then?' he asked.

Batty looked a mite uncomfortable, but he'd obviously screwed up his courage to talk. 'I've been watching you with the new *Hope*,' he said. 'It's a lot of work for one pair of hands. I was wondering, like, if you'd take me on.'

Reuben was surprised. 'Take you on?' he asked. 'You've a good job in t'Yard, surely. Carpenter? He must be paying you at least a pound a week by now.'

'That's the trouble,' Batty said, the words spilling out of him. 'T'bugger's not paying me owt. He's given me my cards. Aye, and lots more like me.'

'James Henry's given you your cards. . .?'

'Not bloody James Henry, though he were bad enough. No, he's turned the Yard over to Mark Adam. Him as is fresh from t'army and knows nowt about it. Aye, and the old man's told him he's got to make a paying proposition out of it by the year's end, else it'll be closed down, and they'll all be out of work. Mark Adam's started by cutting the jobs. One carpenter where there was three, one engineer where there was four. I'm only one of the first. There'll be a lot of unemployment in Ravenswyke now, mark my words. There'll be a lot of folk asking if they can come fishing with you. I had in mind you might teach me. And then I could build a boat of my own and go independent, know what I mean? I'd not be a stone round your neck while I was learning, Reuben, I'll give you my word on that. You'll only have to speak and I'll do as you tell me, even though I'm old enough to be your dad.'

138

Reuben thought about it for a moment. Batty was a clean-living sort of fellow, and didn't drink heavily as so many men in the Yard did. 'You'd want wages?' he asked. 'Regular wages, every week?'

'No, I know how it is with fishing. I know sometimes you can go a week and catch nowt, especially in the changing seasons. I've got a bit put by, enough to keep the club going. I'd be willing to take wages when we caught summat, go home empty-handed when we came in without owt. Maybe, if we got on together and pulled in a bit extra because there was the two of us, you might manage a bit of a bonus? But I'd leave that entirely up to you,' he added hastily, not wanting to queer his chances by seeming to be greedy. 'It's work I want,' he said. 'Work now, with maybe a chance of being independent of buggers like the Tocketts.'

'What are the rest of them going to do?' Reuben asked. 'You must have talked it over.'

'Well, a few of 'em are going down Tockett's potash mine, though you'd never get me slaving underground for the sort of money he's paying down there. And some of 'em is talking about moving away, to Whitby, Scarborough, anywhere there's work. Mark my words, Reuben, Newquay Town will be a ghost town, a shambles, before long. I don't know how long it's been since you were last up there?'

'Nigh on a couple of years. . . .'

'Aye, well, you know, a lot of 'em never came back from the war. You've cause to know how many men were killed in that little lot. But what you maybe don't realize, because you don't live among 'em as I do, is that a lot of 'em scarpered when they got out of the army. A lot of 'em took their demobilization in York, and with the bit of gratuity they had in their pockets, and the new suit, they went back down south. Travis, they say, has gone back to France and is living in a bar with the lady he met while he was over there. She owns the bar – her old man was killed in the fighting – so he's on a good wicket there. Lots of 'em has sent for their wives and families, of course, but I'd say that one house in three, on t'other side of t'Cut, is empty, derelict. And it's going to get worse, mark my words. You know summat, Reuben. You ought to come over there and have a look. You ought to come into t'Yard and see the way the Tocketts have let it run down. I'm not criticizing, you understand, but sometimes I think you folks over here in Old Quaytown don't know how the other half, we folks on t'other side of t'Cut, are living. Folks look up to you, Reuben, and the Godsons. They admire what you did with the co-operative when Fearon was twisting you. They admire the way you went up to Tockett and got the best deal for your fishermen. By gow, if we had somebody like you over there, to stand up for our rights! If we'd had somebody all these years, talking sense to that old skinflint who doesn't realize, who's never learned, that to make a bob you have to invest a bob. I wish you'd come over and take a look, though me, I'm outside it all now, wi' my cards. . . .'

Reuben knew that what Batty was saying was right. He didn't know how they lived over there. He'd never bothered to find out, had he? He'd taken the Nasebys and a couple of other families as his example, and had never ventured to find out how life was for people like the Batsfords.

'What are you doing right now?' he asked.

'Right now. . . ? Well, after I'd seen you, I was going to see if I could scrounge a bit of wood here and there, make a rabbit hutch. I thought I'd get hold of a breeding pair, try to make a bit of money that way – though, when everybody's in it, there'll be a glut on the market. They're all talking about starting with pigs and rabbits, owt to make a bob or two. And then, if you'd turned me down flat, I was going to see if any of the other fishermen would take me on.'

'Let's go and have a look at that Yard,' Reuben said. 'But first you can take me on a tour round Newquay Town.'

Reuben was shocked by what he discovered once he'd crossed the Cut into the other half of Ravenswyke, Newquay Town. It was as Batty had said, but worse. The unoccupied houses stood out like bad teeth along the mean streets, with old scraps of curtain left at the windows, sometimes old newspapers yellowed already with age. There were many slates missing from roofs, many windows broken, even a couple of doors broken down. At the far end of one of the streets, an attempt had been made to provide better housing, perhaps for foremen and chargehands, and the houses there, though still pinched together, had bits of gardens in the fronts and backs. The gardens were derelict. 'First thing Mark Adam did when he came was get rid of the foremen and promote

140

lads without giving them the same wages. The foremen moved out – they were the lucky ones with a bit saved,' Batty told him, seeing the way Reuben was looking.

'I've seen enough,' Reuben said grimly. 'Let's go and take a look at yon Yard.'

The Yard was a repeat of the same story. Many of the worksheds were semi-derelict, and it was obvious that nothing had been spent on maintenance for some time. The stacks of wood on which a boatyard depends were sadly depleted, with only small stocks of oak being weathered for the future building programme. Much of the power machinery was belt-driven from the central steam boiler; some of the belts were rotten and all were unprotected. No wonder they had so many accidents in the Yard when they were on full shift. Only two boats were being built. One, a forty-footer, was for a firm in Whitby; the other, even bigger, was for Filey. 'It's already three months late,' Batty explained, 'and the company as ordered it is in dispute with the Tocketts over it. They were promised oak boarding and most of it is elm. They were promised copper nailing, and it's being done in galvanized throughout, and you know what that'll mean in a few years, once the seawater gets through the zinc. Nay, Reuben, it's a botched job. Those of us working on it knew it, but there was no way we could protest about it – one word out of turn and it'd have been t'cards.'

Reuben eyed the general air of dereliction and wondered, as he had in the streets of Newquay Town, how man's spirit could be so crushed that he would consent to continue in such circumstances. Surely one of the workmen could have grabbed hold of a bit of a broom and swept the floor. And that bench of tools could have been sharpened, with the rust taken off, and oiled. He compared the way the workmen kept their working spaces with the way he kept the *Hope of Ravenswyke*, spick and span at all times, just like the rest of the fishing boats, with all the lines coiled, all the bright-work polished till you could see your face in any bit of brass or bronze on the vessel. Aye, and could eat off the deck.

'Men's got no pride,' he said involuntarily, not meaning to create offence.

'How can a man have pride in these circumstances?' Batty demanded heatedly. 'They're underpaid, they're forced to do

141

shoddy work because somebody's breathing down their necks all the time, and they're given inferior materials to work with. Where can you find any pride if that's what you live with day by day? And then go home at nights to a house with slates off the roof, and a bailiff who refuses to do anything about it but tells you to catch the water drips in a bucket?'

Lots of the men had looked up and smiled when Reuben walked his way round the Yard; one or two greeted him diffidently without stopping work. They were standing by the laid keel of a third boat, on which little progress had been made, when Mark Adam came bustling down the steps from the Yard office.

'What are you doing here, Batsford?' he demanded imperiously. 'I thought you'd collected your cards?'

Reuben looked at Mark Adam Tockett. It was the first time he'd seen him standing on his own two feet for many a year. Mark Adam would be twenty-four, twenty-five, something like that. He was wearing a thick tweed suit in green, with a stiff white collar and a thin green tie. A watch-chain hung across his already big belly. And he was already using glasses, which hung from a cord round his neck. Reuben eyed his podgy pink hands with distaste – each finger looked like the pink sea slugs he sometimes found clinging to the bottom-feeding fish he caught, the slugs that quickly went grey when they were exposed to sunlight and air. Mark Adam had something of the slug about him, so unlike Rupert Henry, his brother who had been killed in the war, whose features had reflected the delicate lines of his mother. Mark Adam took after his father, gross and coarse.

'I left some of my tools here, Mr Tockett,' Batty said, improvising. 'At least, I think I might have left them. I can't find them at home anywhere.'

'Tools of your own? More likely company tools you've helped yourself to. I know you men. I've seen the money my father's been spending to replace the hand tools you've all made off with so freely,' he said, his voice loud and nasty.

Several of the nearby workmen heard his words. One of them, Frank Dobbs, another carpenter, was a man six foot three tall who weighed fifteen stones. Strong as a horse, it was said he'd once lifted a full stagecoach out of a ditch with his two bare hands. Another of his reported tricks had been to hoist one of Fewster's live bulls into the air and throw the squealing, snorting beast

142

over fifteen feet. The clatter he made as he slammed down a mallet he'd been using could be heard all over the Yard.

'Pinching t'bloody tools as no self-respecting tradesman would have in his hands, is that what you're accusing us of, Mark Adam Tockett?' he bellowed, loud as the bull they said he'd thrown. He threw the chisel from his left hand; its blade penetrated an oak plank three-quarters of an inch thick. 'That's it; I've bloody well done the last bit of work I'll do for thee, or any other Tockett, until tha apologizes and takes it back!'

The men downed tools, rebellion and mutiny spreading among them like moor fire. They gathered round Frank Dobbs, as if grateful, at last, to have found a spokesman. Frank pointed his mutton-chop thumb at Reuben. 'There's a lad as told your owd dad where to get off, these years ago. And what he can do, we can do! We're all going out, and we're stopping out, aren't we, lads, until tha pins a note up on t'gate, withdrawing your remarks.'

The men, their spirits aroused, were with him. He grabbed his coat from the peg at the side of the shed; they grabbed theirs. He picked up his snap tin and his cold tea bottle, and they picked up theirs; he led them, marching together out of the Yard, to gather on the side of the Cut, by the slip down which the boats would be launched. 'It's a strike,' they were saying, muttering it at first as if afraid to speak the word aloud, but then growing in confidence and strength until finally they were chanting and shouting. 'It's a strike, it's a strike, it's a *strike*!'

Reuben had watched them go and looked back at Mark Adam in time to see the gleam on his face. 'That bugger's up to something,' Reuben quickly thought.

'Come on, Batty,' he said, 'let's get out of here.'

The office staff, two cripples and the tea lady, came hobbling down the steps.

'What's going on, Mr Mark Adam?' old Wainsford asked, his voice quavering.

Mark Adam looked grim. 'The rest of them have walked out on strike. You'd better be away and join them. You, Maud, go and tell the boiler man to shut down and then he can join them.'

Wainsford looked anxiously at Mark Adam. 'General strike then, is it, Mr Mark Adam?'

'It's not a strike, Wainsford. Tocketts has never had a strike in its history. You can tell them out there, when you join them, that it's a lock-out. And, so far as I'm concerned, they can all go to the dogs and starve!'

The men shouted with rage when the boilerman left the Yard after he'd damped down the fires and opened the steam-cock valve. They gathered aimlessly beside the Cut in two main groups. One of them contained Frank Dobbs, Reuben and Batty. The others were led by Wainsford, the old crippled clerk. The two groups had quickly polarized into opposite factions; Frank Dobbs let out a mighty roar when Mark Adam himself slid the heavy gate across the Yard entrance and they heard the rattle of the chain being locked. 'Go to hell, Tockett,' Frank Dobbs shouted, and fists were raised in the air from the group about him.

Wainsford and his group groaned. 'We ought to go in there and ask him to give us our jobs back,' Wainsford said in his thin whining voice. 'Maybe if we go back right away he'll forgive and forget and we shall still be in work.' The group surrounding him agreed with him, but not one of them dared cross the intervening space in the face of the anger of Frank Dobbs and his group.

'We'll have no scabs in this,' Frank Dobbs shouted, waving his fist threateningly. 'We're all in this together, lads. Look at Reuben Godson, here. He and the fishermen over there in Old Quaytown know what you can do if you hang together. Look at the way they faced Fearon down, and now they've got him working for them, instead of t'opposite way round. We've got to face Mark Adam Tockett, God blast his soul, we've got to face him down over this.'

'Aye,' Wainsford screeched, 'and what happens to us wages in the meantime? Most of these lads have bairns, Frank Dobbs. What'll they feed the bairns on, while we're making the grand gesture of snapping our fingers in Mr Tockett's face? I say, let's go back, nice and peaceful. Let's ask him, nice and polite, to give us back our jobs. There'll be no victimization, I can promise you that. He's a fair man is Mr Tockett. You don't know him as we do, in t'office.'

Batty and Reuben had withdrawn a little to the side. 'What do you think, Reuben?' Batty asked quietly. 'Do you think they'll do it? Do you think Mark Adam will give in?'

Reuben's heart sank as he looked round the faces of the men in both groups, as he read the anxiety that lurked behind the bravado even of those who had allied themselves with Frank Dobbs. It would seem that he alone had seen the gleam on Mark Adam's face, had realized what it meant.

'I'm afraid they're on a loser, Batty,' he said slowly. 'Did you say the Yard was in dispute over one of the boats?'

'Aye. They're already late. The buyers are invoking the penalty clause for late completion. It doesn't seem as if the Yard has a leg to stand on – at least, that's what Wainsford told me the chap from Thrummell and Slade had said.'

'Well, you realize what Frank Dobbs has just done? He's given the Tocketts a perfect excuse. All these contracts have a clause in them which makes them invalid in the event of war or industrial disputes. Well, Frank Dobbs has given the Tocketts a get-out. How can they finish the contract if the Yard is in an industrial dispute. Mark Adam won't take 'em back. He doesn't *want* 'em back. He'll keep 'em out until such time as Thrummell and Slade have fixed the contract in the Yard's favour, you mark my words. I'm afraid they've all played straight into his hands.'

Batty went across to Frank Dobbs and whispered in his ear. Frank came over and stood in front of Reuben. 'What's that you've been saying to Batty?' he asked, his voice bellicose. Reuben repeated his words. 'The only reason I know about it,' he explained, 'is because it cropped up when I bought the new *Hope* and sold the old one while the war was on. The lawyer explained about the two clauses and we both agreed to wipe 'em out of the contract.'

'And you think we've played into his hands?'

'I wouldn't be surprised if he didn't say what he did just to provoke somebody. I wouldn't put it past him!'

Frank looked about him, bewildered. This double-thinking was far too much for his simple mind in which a man did his work for the Master, got his wages, kept himself decent. The other men had gathered around, listening to Reuben's explanation. 'He's *right*,' they said, 'Reuben Godson's *right*! It was all a trap to get us to walk out!'

The two groups coalesced, surrounding Frank Dobbs and Reuben. Wainsford shook his puny fist in Frank Dobbs's face but Frank ignored him, deep in thought. 'We've got to go up and see the old man,' he said finally. 'We've got to put the matter to the old man. He may be hard, but he's fair. Not like that slimy bastard of a son of his.'

The side door of the Yard opened, and Mark Tockett's car emerged. He looked across at the group of strikers when he got out of the car and shut the Yard door behind him. The strikers stood immobile, none of them geared for physical violence. Mark Adam climbed back into his car and drove it slowly up the road at the side of the Cut, turning left on to the road that climbed through the top of Newquay Town on its way to Tockett Top and Tockett House. The strikers were silent as they watched him go, knowing he took their livelihood with him.

James Henry Tockett was seated behind his desk. He didn't ask them to sit down. They were the last ones in at the end of the afternoon session. He was looking at Reuben, an amused expression on his face.

'You've got yourself some new friends, Reuben?' he said.

'Understand, Mr Tockett, that this has nothing to do with me personally. I've been asked by these lads to come up here with them and speak for them. I'm speaking for *them*, not for myself.'

'Right, Reuben. The point's clearly understood. You're the spokesman, and you've got the floor, so get on with it. I don't normally see *delegations*, but when they told me you were here with them I felt I owed it to you. To my way of thinking, any group of men that needs to band together to gather strength from each other is a group of weak men who can't individually stand on their own two feet. Normally, I wouldn't give such a group the time of day, but seeing as you're with them. . . .'

'They want the Yard opened again. They recognize that perhaps they were a bit hasty in misinterpreting a remark Mr Mark Adam made to mean they were stealing. . . .'

'If it's to do with the Yard, Reuben, I'll have nowt to do with it. I've handed the Yard over to Mark Adam. It's his affair, not mine. I'm not one to hand over responsibility and then go behind a man's back listening to a group of complainers, of self-seeking bolsheviks. As I understand it, these men walked off the job and made certain demands. Personally, I think those demands are unreasonable and designed just to stir up trouble. But it's nowt to do with me. It's a matter for Mark Adam. You'll have to make your appointment with him, not with me.' He shuffled the papers on his desk to tell them that was the end of the interview. Frank Dobbs had been standing beside Reuben, shifting from one foot to the other as Tockett had talked. Now, no longer able to contain himself, he let out a frustrated yell, bounded forward, reached across the desk, and grabbed James Henry Tockett by his shirt-front. One heave and he picked him straight out of his chair and dragged him across the desk. Then he forced him back on his desk. 'I'll kill you, you rotten bloated bugger,' he shouted. He brought back the ham of his left hand, preparing to smash it forward into James Henry's face, but Reuben and the others grabbed his arm and held him back, though it took all their strength. In the struggle, he let go of James Henry's shirt-front, but brought his fist up under his chin. James Henry's head snapped back, his eyes glazed over, and he fell back across the desk. 'By gow, you've buggered it now, Frank,' Batty said. Wainsford scrabbled forward, fanning James Henry's face ineffectually. 'Oh, Mr Tockett,' he wailed, 'what has he done to you, what has he done?'

Reuben went across to the side of the fireplace and pulled the bell-rope. They'd managed to quieten Frank Dobbs, and had sat him in one of the chairs. He was sitting with his head in his hands, looking down at his feet, realizing that his temper once again had got the better of him. 'What have I done,' he said, 'what have I done? I've buggered it, that's what I've done!'

'You'd better all get out,' Reuben counselled. 'I'll have a word with whoever comes in and try to smooth it all over!'

As if he'd been expecting trouble, Mark Adam came into his father's study with the chauffeur and the housekeeper. He was carrying a double-barrelled up-and-over shotgun. By then Reuben had lifted James Henry into an armchair and he was recovering consciousness. He rubbed the underside of his chin and his throat, silencing Mark Adam's screeching with a gesture. He coughed and spat into his handkerchief; Reuben saw the fleck of blood.

'Put that damn shotgun down, Mark Adam,' he said, his voice weak and strained. He looked up at Reuben, folded his hand-kerchief, and put it away in his pocket. 'My grandfather always told me, Reuben, that if you lie down with dogs, you'll get up with fleas. You've just had a demonstration of what he meant. I shall see that yon ruffian Dobbs goes to prison for this day's work. And, I warn you, I'll be calling you as witness. If you'll take a bit of advice from me, Reuben, you'll be a bit more careful in the future who you give your hand to. They say you know a man by the company he keeps. Just now, it seems to me, you're running with a strange pack of hounds. And I don't only mean Frank Dobbs and his bunch of bolsheviks. If you can't understand what I'm getting at, have a word with your mam. And, if you've a mind, with Emily Duckett!'

The three magistrates were sitting behind the long mahogany table, with the clerk in front of them. Dobbs had been brought from the police station and charged. He'd pleaded 'Not guilty', on the advice of Philip Lazenby, who'd been hired after the village had held a whip-round to pay his fee. Lazenby had already addressed the magistrates. 'Common assault,' he'd said, 'requires the intention of the accused to inflict bodily harm on his victim. My client had no such intention. He merely wanted to emphasize a point and, in the manner of his class, seized the plaintiff's clothing to claim his attention. Gentlemen, have we never taken a man's arm in an attempt to emphasize a point in our dissertations and our arguments? My client does not deny that the back of his hand came into contact with the plaintiff's throat in a somewhat violent manner, but makes the claim, which will be verified by eye-witnesses, I can assure you, that such contact was purely accidental.'

Batty was the first witness called. He drew a laugh from the spectators, if not from the bench. 'Frank Dobbs can't have meant to hit him,' he said. 'Frank's as strong as an ox. If he'd meant to hit him, he'd have knocked his block off!'

John P. Mulroyd, JP, looked round the court at the chortling crowds, tapping his mallet on the table at which he and the other two magistrates sat. A bit of humour helped the proceedings along, though it didn't do to let it get out of hand. He looked round the tall polished room, with the long high windows down one side, the spectators' gallery running like a horseshoe round the other three sides. All his life he'd wanted to be a magistrate and, though it had been inevitable, thanks to his station in life and the position of his family in local social circles, that one day he'd be invited to 'sit on the Bench', he'd waited out his time with great impatience. Now that he was here, now that he'd arrived, the excitement of it all and the drama fulfilled his greatest expectations. He turned to look at his two fellow magistrates – Lord Humby on the left, now eighty-four and, some said, quite gaga; and Percival Minton-Hughes on the right, a man, it seemed, without a brain in his head, the scion of the Minton-Hughes ship-building family whose father had been wise enough to leave the management of the firm in other hands.

They smiled back at him, though neither had understood the source of this evident good humour that ran through the court-room.

Mulroyd's eye caught that of James Henry Tockett; he was grim-faced and not smiling at all, his glare seeming to demand that Mulroyd pull himself together and get the proceedings back to order. Well, as the aggrieved party, he'd feel like that, Mulroyd thought. He turned to the court, admiring yet again its heavy mahogany panelling, the leaded windows, the sense of order, with the accused standing in the dock surrounded by the railings with their spikes, the public on benches behind, the tables and seats for defence and prosecution, everything neat and orderly, arranged with precision for the highest function of mankind, the dispen-sation of justice.

Now the accused, in his spiked enclave, was laughing, chortling at the joke the last witness had made. That would never do! He hammered the mallet on the block that had been placed on his table top for that purpose.

'I will have silence,' he said, 'or I will clear the court.' It took two repeats and two more sessions of gavelling before the noise died down.

'I would remind you, Mr Dobbs,' he said firmly, 'that we are gathered here today to discuss the question of your future liberty. In that circumstance, I cannot see any opportunity for levity. My colleagues on the Bench and I would be much obliged if you would compose yourself.'

'He means *stop laughing*,' one of the gaolers whispered.

'I cannot see that this witness has anything further to offer, Mr Lazenby,' Mulroyd said. 'Perhaps you'd be kind enough to take him down and offer us someone with something more pertinent and, I might add, less impertinent to say?' It was the nearest he could come to a rebuke.

Grinley was next. 'No, your honours,' he said. 'He didn't mean to hit him. It was, like, an accident.'

'Don't tell us what you *think*, Mr Grinley,' the exasperated Mr Mulroyd said reprovingly. 'Just confine yourself to telling us what you actually *saw*.'

'I didn't see him hit him, that's for sure.'

'Did you see the accused's fist come into contact with Mr Tockett's throat?'

'No, I didn't!'

'Then you can't be very much help to us either, Mr Grinley.' He turned to Mr Lazenby. 'I would suggest, Mr Lazenby, that this witness might also step down!'

Wainsford was next, in a lather of frightened sweat. 'I'll put it to you simply, Mr Wainsford,' Lazenby said. 'Did you see Mr Dobbs strike Mr Tockett?'

Wainsford gulped and swallowed. 'I saw him. . . .'

'Saw him *what*, Mr Wainsford?' Lazenby prompted.

'Saw him . . . grab Mr Tockett's shirt-front.'

'That's not the question I am asking, Mr Wainsford. My client doesn't deny that he grabbed Mr Tockett's shirt-front in an attempt, possibly a little too enthusiastic, I'm sure, to emphasize a point. Did you see Mr Dobbs actually *strike* Mr Tockett? A simple yes or no will suffice.'

Wainsford remembered the meeting in the pub the previous evening. 'You split on Frank,' they'd said, 'and it's you finished in Ravenswyke!'

He closed his eyes as if hoping that way to translate himself to another place where all eyes were not upon him, all ears not waiting for his words. 'No!' he whispered. 'No, I didn't actually *see* him hit him!'

'That will be all, Mr Wainsford, thank you,' Mr Lazenby said in triumph.

A buzz ran through the court when they called Reuben Godson. James Henry Tockett, who'd been sitting in a chair placed specially beside the bench, looked up as Reuben walked into the court, following him with his eyes. Reuben's mind had been in a turmoil during the days preceding the trial. He'd seen Frank Dobbs grab Tockett's shirt-front and lift him across the desk. He'd heard him threaten to kill Tockett. He'd seen the hand come away from Tockett's shirt-front and, as if in slow motion, he could still see that hand suddenly bunch into a hard-knuckled fist and jab upwards into Tockett's Adam's apple. He took the oath, stated his name, and his profession as self-employed fisherman, and then faced Lazenby, conscious all the while of Tockett's eyes on him, the faint suggestion of a smile on Tockett's features.

'You were present during the entire incident resulting in this trial, is that correct, Mr Godson?' Lazenby asked, his voice slow and pitched low.

'I was.'

'In fact, I believe that, though you were not directly involved in the dispute, you had been requested to act as spokesman?'

'That's right.'

'Now, Mr Godson, I think it's safe to say this is not the first time you've been asked to act as spokesman for a group of villagers during representations with Mr Tockett, is that not correct?'

'Yes, they've asked me before.'

'Would you say people respected you?'

'I suppose you could say that.'

Mulroyd looked at the defence counsel. 'The character of this witness is not in question, Mr Lazenby,' he said mildly.

Lazenby nodded without speaking to the Bench. 'Now, Mr Godson, it's safe to say that you are not a man who would voluntarily consent to take part in a violent demonstration?'

'Nowt to be gained by violence, is there?'

'Precisely, Mr Godson. Did you see Mr Dobbs strike Mr Tockett?' Lazenby had skilfully come to the question without anyone, particularly Reuben, being aware of the direction he was taking. The quick question demanded a quick answer. One word would do it. One word, and the case against Dobbs would collapse. He'd be reprimanded, no doubt put on probation, for adopting a menacing attitude by grabbing Mr Tockett's shirt-front.

'Tell the truth in that court,' Hannah Godson had said. 'Tell the truth and fear no man! That's the Godson way!'

'You can't let them get Frank Dobbs,' Eleanor had pleaded. 'Tockett deserves everything he gets, the damn old skinflint.'

Elsie had looked at him when he'd talked with her about the case, a half-smile on her face. 'This is where it shows,' she said. 'This is where we find out if being a Godson means owt at all. Batty'll lie, you know. So will Grinley. For them it's *us* and *them* – *us* is always right, *them* is always wrong. Wainsford'll pee his pants but, in the end, he'll lie too. He's too much afraid of what'll happen to him one dark night if he says what he saw. But what about Reuben Godson, of the Godsons of Ravenswyke? Is he afraid of what might happen some dark night, like the rest of them?'

Reuben looked across the court and his eyes held Tockett's. Tockett looked steadily back at him with that faint smile of contempt. Us and them? He looked at Frank Dobbs, standing between the two constables, leering at him, confident that Reuben would get him off with one word, just one word.

'Yes,' Reuben said, looking straight at Frank Dobbs. 'Yes, I saw him clench his fist and hit Mr Tockett under the chin.'

The court erupted into uproar and again Mulroyd hammered the table with his mallet. Reuben watched the look of anger crease Frank Dobbs's face. 'I'll get you, you bugger,' Frank Dobbs shouted across the courtroom, his voice clearly heard above the hubbub and the hammering of the mallet. 'I'll bloody well get you, Reuben Godson!' Mulroyd beckoned imperiously and the two policemen reached in to grab the accused. Frank Dobbs shrugged them aside, his elbows jabbing into their stomachs; he started forward as if he would jump over the rail but the two policemen, despite what must have been the pain in their guts, held on to him, grabbing his wrists, twisting his arms up his back. He reared up, trying to tear his arms free, his head stretched up into the air. They pulled him back down and he jerked forward, a crazy man.

This time, when they pulled him down, one of the spikes on the railings in front of the dock stuck straight up his throat. His mouth opened in what started as a yell but became a gushing gout of blood. His eyes were open but then, as the spike rammed into his brain, the pupils of his eyes rode up into the top of his skull, leaving only the grey-green whites of his eyeballs exposed. 'Clear the court,' the magistrates were yelling. 'Clear the court.' Women in the gallery were screaming, and the Clerk to the Court, whose table was only six feet from the dock and that spiked head, was suddenly and violently sick all over his papers. One of the policemen put his hand under Frank Dobbs's chin, and together they lifted him back up and off the spike. The blood spurted out of the hole in his throat but only from the built-up pressure. His heart had already stopped. Frank Dobbs was dead.

Reuben sat on the bench in the witness box, his head in his hands, tears running down his face. He could still see the look of fury on Frank Dobbs's face when Reuben had denounced him, the anger as he tried to get away from the two gaolers, the shock when his head had come down violently on to the spike which, mercifully, had driven straight up into his brain, killing him instantly. Reuben felt a hand on his shoulder. He looked up and saw Elsie standing there, next to James Henry Tockett. 'Come away home, Reuben,' she said. 'It's finished for today.' He reached up his hands and put them around her waist, burying his face in the firmness of her belly, the tears still rolling down his cheeks staining her skirt.

'Look after him, lass,' James Henry Tockett said as he turned to walk away.

Stanley Baxter drove his new car slowly down the road through Newquay Town, over the bridge across the Cut, along the side of the houses to the Raven Hotel by the fishermen's slip. 'Now isn't that very pretty, Emma?' he said to the woman sitting beside him. She had barely got over her fear at sliding or so it seemed to her, down the steep bank from the moors above, with Stanley holding on to the long handle of the hand-brake to stop the car's downhill rush. 'We shall never get back up that hill,' she said plaintively.

'Of course we shall. Now stop worrying. If we can't get up under our own steam, I'm sure some local will break out a team of horses to pull us up. Meanwhile, what do you think to trying this hotel? Perhaps they can accommodate us for a day or two.'

'Without a booking, Stanley? Whatever will they think?'

'I'll tell you what they'll think, my girl. They'll hold as how we're not married, that we're travelling together for immoral purposes, that you're a high-priced courtesan.'

'Stop it, Stanley,' she said, slapping his wrist where it showed between his pigskin driving gloves and the grey cuff of his elegant suit. It had all seemed a wonderful lark, to go off in the motor-car, letting the roads take them where they would. They'd been on the road a long time, and now she would so like a bath. But what *would* the people in the hotel think if they arrived that way without a booking, and stained by a day of travel in this Morris motor-car.

The landlord was most accommodating, as if people turned up every day in motor-cars seeking lodging without booking. 'I can let you have the front room,' he said, 'which overlooks the water. There's a sitting room next door where you can take your meals.'

'Is there a bathroom?' Emma asked timidly. 'I would so like to clean away the dust of the roads.'

'There's a bathroom, er, Mrs . . .'

'Baxter,' she said, waving her hand gently to display the solid band of the wedding ring on her finger.

'. . . with plenty of hot water.'

'Good. If someone could bring in our trunk?'

'Right away, ma'am,' he said, 'right away.' He went to the door behind the reception counter. 'Jack?' he called. 'Jack Dobbs?'

A ginger-haired lad of fourteen came through from the back. 'Get this gentleman's trunk off the back of his motor-car and take it up to Number Three, sharp as you can!'

'Yes, Mr Wilcox,' Jack said. He was a slender lad who didn't take after his big burly father at all. After his fathers tragic death, his mother accepted the job of cook in the Raven, which was starting to build up its trade as a resort hotel. Shortly after, Mr Wilcox had taken Jack in, as general factotum and boots. The lad was willing, though the manner of the death of his father had made him shy and withdrawn. Still, he did his work well, and was quick and willing. He took the heavy trunk from the back of the car, hoisted it on his back, marvelling that people could possess so many clothes, and carted it up to Room number 3, the best room in the hotel. Well, with the sitting room next door, and the bathroom, it was a suite really. Just think, folk paying a guinea a night, just to sleep. . . !

Mr Baxter gave him a sixpence, would you believe it, a whole sixpence just for carrying up a trunk. . . He rushed down to the kitchen to tell his mum.

'Aye, they'll be a couple of Johnnie-come-latelies from Leeds or Bradford,' she said disparagingly, 'trying to buy their way in. If he was the proper quality, he'd have given you nowt until he was leaving!'

Jean Dobbs was more correct than she knew. Stanley Baxter came from Leeds, where he'd built a substantial business during the war, weaving and dyeing the cloth for soldiers' uniforms. Now he'd invested his fortune and owned a spinning mill in Huddersfield, and a small tailoring chain in Leeds specializing in the new ready-made clothing. And he continued to prosper. This was the first holiday he and Emma had taken since before the war, when he was a cloth salesman for Levisson's of Leeds, Makers of Fine

Worsteds. Stanley always had an eye for the main chance – all his life he'd known that one day, inevitably, he'd make a fortune. But now he was going to take a holiday.

'Look at that view, Emma,' he said, when they'd both bathed and changed and were waiting for supper. He was standing in the window, a thin cheroot between his lips, looking out over the ocean and Ravenswyke Bay to the sandy beach that had formed to the south side, with the grassland above it, the cliffs on either side rising sheer to Tockett House on the top. 'What would you think to a house like that, Emma?' he said, slipping his arm round her waist. 'That'd be living in style.'

'You'd have to marry me first,' she said, 'and not just by slipping a ring on my finger as we're driving out of Leeds!'

'I shall marry you, Emma. All in good time!'

'You'd better,' she said, 'and pretty quick, I'd say.'

He looked down at her, standing head and shoulders beneath him. Such a small delicate creature, such fine bones. And, truth to tell, such well-shaped limbs and abundant breasts. She'd been working in the factory he'd bought, lock, stock and barrel, a very superior young lady who'd had a fine education before her father went bankrupt. 'What do you mean, Emma? Pretty quick.'

'I think it's time you knew, Stanley. We're going to have a family!'

'A family?' His eyes gleamed at the thought, then he quickly set the cheroot down in the ashtray and grasped her waist, lifting her up until her face was level with his. 'A family? Are you sure?'

She nodded, tears in her eyes. 'You're not angry with me?' she asked.

'Angry, my love? I'm delighted! Well get wed, right away. I'll buy you a big house, big enough to bring up a family. We'll have a piano, a coach and horses. . . .'

She stopped him speaking by the simple expedient of kissing him. And she went on kissing him until the knock came on the door of the sitting room, and the maid wheeled in the trolley containing the light supper they'd ordered.

Emma and Stanley Baxter slept that night in the Raven Hotel, locked in each other's arms, while outside the sea advanced and retreated, the waves lapped across the scaurs, the moon scudded across an almost cloudless sky, and Ravenswyke slumbered, waiting for the morrow in blissful ignorance.

Reuben Godson had risen with the tide at four o'clock and had launched the *Hope* with the help of Bailey, another early riser, and his two sons. It was cold on the water, though Reuben knew he'd warm up once the sun rose. He checked round the *Hope*, seeing that everything was pulling well. Bailey had installed one of the new engines in the *Victorious*; the throb of it and the stink of fuel were an offence to Reuben's ears and nostrils, but he supposed that was the future. He was in no hurry; Bailey had given himself difficulties when the seawater got into his magneto the previous week, when he was lining under the cliff. Only a quickly dropped kedge anchor had kept them off the rocks while they stripped the motor down and cleaned and dried it. Reuben had studied the specification of the new motors but didn't like them because of the danger of seawater stopping them at the wrong moment, and the risk of the fuel exploding on board if anyone threw a careless cigarette. Still, it would have to come, no doubt about that. They were trawling the bottom with steam winches on the bigger boats out of Whitby, firing the boilers with coal just like a railway engine. And some of the petrol engines were a mammoth size. There was also talk of the new diesel they'd used in submarines during the war. Apparently diesel didn't flash and explode the way petrol did and, since it didn't use a spark-making magneto, it was unaffected by seawater, they said, unless you got the water mixed up with your fuel. Reuben tightened his mainsheet – there'd be time to make up his mind later on, when the engineers had worked a bit more on the problem and had come up with something a bit less vulnerable.

The sun was just rising over the lighthouse when he came to his first bobbin, and began to haul the first bank of lobster pots. The surface of the ocean was flat as a table top, the water flecked with patches of sheen that looked like oil, glistening iridescent. The morning was clear, with only a few light clouds; the mist had lifted off Tockett Top within minutes of the sun showing itself. Now the day had broken clear and it'd be warm for May. Slowly he hauled on the line and the first pot broke the surface empty. The bait had been eaten and that was a good sign. He examined the twine net, all of which seemed in good nick spread over the withy frame. He checked that the lump of iron that would sink the pot was securely tied – sometimes rust seemed to eat through

156

the twine and the chunk of metal would free itself during the pot's shifting tidal movement on the seabed. He opened the bait bucket he'd brought ready, cut a lump of codling and rolled it into a ball with a couple of mussels before inserting it into the inside of the net, pinning it through with the sharpened withy stick that held it secure. Then he dropped the pot over the side again and used its sinking weight to help him lift the next. Some fishermen lifted all the pots and stacked them before baiting them again. If Reuben wasn't going to move them to another location, he preferred to re-bait them one at a time. He did the work automatically, looking out over the familiar water as he hauled, checked and re-baited. Already he could tell this was not going to be a good catch. He could be philosophical about it – all that week he'd done well with sixty per cent, or thereabouts, of his pots containing either crabs or, surprisingly in view of their position, lobsters. Perhaps, he reflected, it was a sign of his growing maturity that he could be more patient with the bad days. Next week, he'd be twenty-one, and sometimes he asked himself where all that young eagerness had gone, all that bubbling, tearing force to solve all his problems at one go, to remake everything the way he himself thought it should be.

The problem that taxed his mind, however, this beautiful May morning, had nothing to do with crabs or lobsters, with the ocean or the boat. It had to do with the totally inexplicable, totally unpredictable, totally irrational reactions of women!

Reuben was caught between two fires; one was sombre and smouldering but, he suspected, could have an intense effect on his life. 'Of course I love you,' Emily Duckett had said the previous evening. 'Why do you keep on asking? Haven't I showed you that I love you? It's deeds, not words, that counts.' Emily did love him: one part of him was quite certain of that. She was always available when he wanted to go for a walk on the moor top, would always come into his arms when they sat in some sheltered corner on the springy turf, away from prying eyes. And, though they'd never committed the final act of sex, she was always ready and willing to give him ease and comfort, to bring him to the release he frequently sought, now that he was feeling his sap rising. But, always, he had to *ask* her! The desire for sex never seemed to spring from within herself. 'If you want to . . .' she'd say. 'If that's what you want.'

157

'How about *you*?' he'd ask despairingly. 'Don't *you* want to? Don't you feel an ache, a pain?'

She'd look up at him with a pitying look on her face. 'Well, you know, Reuben,' she'd say lovingly, 'it's *different* for women. If you want to do owt, it's all right with me. I've seen you sometimes, couldn't wait to sit down on the grass, so big you've already grown. But it's not like that for us. We don't grow big like that. If you want to, it's all right.'

'But when I play with you, you know what I mean, when I stroke you down there between your legs, doesn't it, like, get you all excited? It makes you all wet.'

'Hush, Reuben, you shouldn't talk about things like that!' she'd say reprovingly, as if he'd accused her of some monstrous indecency. 'Just do what you want to, that's all I ask. If you want to go further, you know, like, do everything, well it's all right with me! Just be careful, that's all I ask. You know what I mean. Just be careful!'

And he'd groan with despair. How could he tell her he wanted to be wanted, he wanted to be *desired*. He wanted flame, and passion, because part of him suspected that flame and passion could be, even should be, part of human relationships. Not simply silent acquiescence, compliance.

Sometimes, on a Saturday afternoon, they'd go into Whitby and walk through the streets window shopping, and he'd see some household item he liked, a chair perhaps, or a table, or an attractive fabric, and he'd say, 'My, that's grand, what do you think about that!' And she'd look at it and say, 'If you like it, Reuben, that's all that matters!'

And he'd want to bang his head against a wall, because getting Emily to express an opinion, getting her to speak out and say what was in her mind, *was* like banging his head against a wall.

Sometimes, in utter frustration, he'd go to see Elsie Milner, would sit there entranced, listening to her conversation, hearing her loud and uninhibited laughter, seeing the glisten of her eyes and the way she'd toss back her hair and tell him what she thought. And, sometimes, she'd look at him with a softening of her eyes, especially after they'd had a couple of bottles of beer together, and she'd say, 'Count your blessings you're younger than I am, and keeping company with Emily Duckett, else I'd

158

have you in that bedroom, lad, and I'd show you a few tricks that'd make a man out of you!'

And he'd long, desperately, for her to make a man out of him.

The last time, when he arrived, she'd just finished washing in the tub in front of the fire and the smell of steam was in the room. She'd put on her rough cotton dressing gown and tied the belt roughly round her waist. In that circumstance, Emily would never have permitted him to see her; she'd have bolted upstairs and stayed there for twenty minutes, dressing herself and towelling her hair dry so that she could 'make herself presentable', as she'd call it.

Elsie wound the towel round her head like a turban, lifted the tub of water, refusing his offer of help, and emptied it out of the back door. Then she came back and sat with him, just as she was, and poured him a glass of beer from her seemingly inexhaustible supply of bottles. And as they sat and talked, his eyes grew wider and wider, and his trousers tighter and tighter, as the loosely tied knot came slowly apart, until her dressing gown fell apart during one of her more extravagant gestures and he saw the full length of her body, her heavy full breasts, even the hair at the bottom of her belly. And she laughed even louder.

'Eyes like chapel hat-pegs, you've got,' she'd said. 'Aye, and I'll bet you've a cock to match!'

Now that he thought about it, he realized it'd been a challenge. He, damned fool, had done nothing about it! Compounding the evil, he'd even struck out self-defensively. 'Well, you're the one to know about that!' he'd said, the words blurting out of him. He'd watched her face harden, the disappointment clearly registered. Not disappointment that he'd failed her sexually, but that he'd broken the rule that had enabled them to establish and maintain their friendship, the rule that said he wouldn't refer to her reputation as a loose-living woman.

'You'd better go,' she'd said. 'We don't want to damage your reputation, sitting here supping beer with a woman who looks like a tart, do we, Mr Godson!'

'Nay, Elsie,' he'd said lamely, 'you know I didn't mean that!'

She'd pulled her dressing gown firmly across her body and had tied the knot viciously. 'You should have taken a better look,' she'd said, taunting him. 'Happen next time you see all that, you'll have to pay for the pleasure!'

159

'Oh Christ,' he thought, sitting in the *Hope* with his pots up and down again, his sail pulling tautly back to the bay, 'where is a man to put himself with women?' He didn't know which woman he wanted, which way of life. He wanted one of them, badly, but which was it to be? Emily Duckett, who'd follow him about like a lapdog all his life, agreeing with everything he said, giving him a family and keeping his home spick and span for him, accepted by his mam and by Eleanor and by everyone else in Old Quaytown as the perfect wife for him. Or should he take a chance with Elsie, who'd challenge him every inch of the way of every day of his life. Who'd fight him when she didn't agree with anything he'd say or do, but who'd give him a fierce sexual kind of love, yes, and sex was an important part of it, that would stimulate him in ways Emily would never understand.

A stranger was standing by the top of the slip when the horses came down, were hitched to the trailer they'd made to slip under the boats at the low-water mark, and started to heave the coble over the scaurs to the slip. The stranger was a city man; Reuben could tell that instantly from his dress, from the soft flabbiness of his skin and his muscles. A right dandy, too. A woman was standing beside him, with her hair elaborately combed on to the top of her head, wearing a blue silk dress in the new calf-length fashion, trimmed with broderie anglaise down the front, and the neckline tipped with a white and obviously genuine and expensive fur. Reuben knew nothing of these fashion points, only that the woman looked extremely dainty and attractive in a delicate way.

'You'd better stand back, missis, else you'll get splashed,' Reuben said, feeling coarse and rough in his fisherman's togs. She walked away from the side of the boat and Reuben carefully sluiced the decks with rainwater from the barrel outside the Raven Hotel. He wondered idly where Eleanor had got to; idly, because these days you could never rely on her. When she wasn't in the house sewing or knitting or helping Mam, she walked the bank and often spent hours alone on the moor top, sitting on a fence, or crouched on the grass. One or two of the lads had come to the house, on the pretence of chatting with Reuben, and had tried to draw her respectfully into the conversation. Reuben had encouraged them, but Eleanor, the moment she had been addressed directly, would gather her sewing or her knitting and make for the bedroom she now occupied on her own. The lads would linger for a minute or two but then they'd leave, disappointed by the snub.

Reuben had placed the few crabs he'd caught in a basket with the two lobsters, and covered the basket with a bit of sacking. Fearon came down the steps from the bar of the Raven, where he'd been accepted again as a customer, wiping the froth of a pint of stout off his big heavy moustache. Reuben fingered his own upper lip. The last few days he hadn't shaved it, thinking that he, too, might start one, but so far the results were disappointing.

'Not a lot, Fearon,' Reuben said. 'It's hardly worth a journey.'

'Aye, there's not much about.'

When he lifted the sack from the top of the basket the stranger and the lady, who'd pressed in closer, both exclaimed. 'My, that's a good catch,' the stranger said.

Reuben was feeling in a provocative mood after his thoughts of Elsie and Emily. 'Does your lady like crab then?' he asked.

'Yes, I do,' she said eagerly.

Reuben reached into the basket and, without being pinched, expertly picked the best-looking one out of the squirming mass. He took a piece of twine from his pocket and tied its claws together with a single knot. 'There you are, missis, you can have that for your tea,' he said, holding it out towards her.

She eyed it with mock horror. 'Laws, I wouldn't know what to do with it,' she said. 'I've never seen one alive before.'

'I'm sure Mr Wilcox can handle it for us,' the stranger said. He stepped in closer, obviously a man used to handling situations. 'My name's Baxter,' he said. 'Stanley Baxter, from Leeds. We're taking a few days' holiday here in the Raven Hotel. I'd be much obliged if you would sell those two – lobsters, aren't they? – to me and I'll ask Mr Wilcox to have them prepared for our supper!'

Mention of the word 'sell' brought a gleam to Fearon's eyes. He nodded to Reuben and stepped forward. 'Happens I'm the agent for the fishermen in these parts,' he said. 'I'd be very happy to let you have the lobsters, if you've a mind. One thing is sure, you've never had any as fresh as these two, in Leeds!'

'And freshness is something you pay for, is it?' Stanley Baxter said. He knew a businessman when he saw one.

Reuben had turned away from the negotiation. What had his father said all those years ago? Only a fool keeps a dog and barks hisself! He was coiling the warp at the stern of the coble, laying it neatly on the deck, when he smelled the perfume of the woman beside him. 'What's your name?' she asked boldly.

'Reuben Godson, ma'am.'

'Mine's Emma,' she said, and then for some reason she couldn't understand, added, 'Thoroughgood. Emma Thoroughgood.'

He turned to look at her and saw her eyeing him boldly. 'I've never met a fisherman before,' she explained. 'Is this your boat?'

'Yes, it's the family boat. The Godsons have always had a boat.'

'Why is it called the *Hope*?'

'I dunno. The Godsons' boat has always been called the *Hope of Ravenswyke*. Kind of in the family – know what I mean.' He felt tonguetied in front of this city-bred, smart young lady with her neat figure, her expensive clothes, her open manner. In a way he could sense she was like Elsie. A woman who laid everything out on the surface, so you could tell who and what she was, instead of hiding everything deep down. Though, given the right occasion, she'd have her depths, too. 'I've never seen anybody like you!' he said guilelessly. She had a gentle tinkling laugh that pleased him and caused him to smile.

'That's better,' she said. 'You looked so fierce when you came in, like the old man of the sea. Have you ever read *Moby Dick*?'

He shook his head.

'I don't suppose you get much time for reading?'

'Not a lot.'

The lobster business had been concluded and not, it would seem, entirely in Stanley Baxter's favour. No doubt he'd been hoping to pick up a cheap bargain from these locals, but Fearon had shown him otherwise. 'Come along, Emma,' he said, his voice sharp. 'If you want to take that walk we'll have to be quick before the tide comes in.'

Reuben and Fearon stood side by side and watched them step out on to the scaurs. Emma squealed delicately as she slipped with her high-buttoned boots into a shallow puddle, but Stanley Baxter seized her hand and dragged her forward, heading across the edge of the bay towards the base of the cliff. 'I heard him asking Wilcox if there were a path over there,' Fearon said. 'They'll have to move if they're not to get that pretty dress wet!'

Reuben couldn't take his eyes off her.

'Smitten, are you, lad?' Fearon said, his face crinkling with a smile. 'Aye, and you're not the only one. They've been here nobbut three days now, and the business in the saloon, Wilcox was telling me, has trebled. After dinner, they come down of an evening. She sits there like a queen, sipping a glass of port, while he lights a cigar and drinks brandy. He's a fellah used to his creature comforts, I'll be bound. Wilcox says as he doesn't think they're wed, but Baxter's spending money, and that's what matters these days, the way the price of everything's going up.'

'She told me her name,' Reuben said, still marvelling. 'Emma Thoroughgood. That's a nice name.'

'Used to be a family called Thoroughgood lived in Staithes,' Fearon said. 'I wonder if she's related. . . ?'

Reuben wasn't thinking of her relations. He was thinking of those bountiful breasts beneath that delicate embroidery, the round swell of her backside as she stepped down the slip to go out on to the scaurs, that tinkling laugh when he'd said – naïvely, perhaps, but truthfully – that he'd never seen anyone like her.

Fearon was speaking to him again, disturbing his reverie. 'I'm glad I've got you on your own, Reuben,' he was saying. 'I wanted to have a word with you.' They walked together to the edge of the slip and looked out over the scaurs, standing side by side at the fence. Reuben couldn't take his eyes off the receding form of Emma Thoroughgood, but was prepared to listen to Fearon as he watched.

'You know Sam Gainer's selling his boat?' Fearon asked.

'I've heard him say so a dozen times.'

'This time, he means it. Seems a relative has died and left him a bit of property in Middlesbrough.'

'I remember him going over there for the funeral.'

'Aye, well apparently he was the favourite nephew or summat. The old lady as died had three cottages side by side. She lived in one. She's left them to Sam. One of them has a bit of a shop in the ground floor, newspapers, tobacco. Sam's going to sell his boat and go to Middlesbrough to live.'

'Bloody hell!' Reuben said. 'I can't see Sam behind a counter selling packets of flake and boxes of matches.'

'Well, that's what he'll be doing.'

'Have you heard owt about who's buying the boat then?'

Sam's boat was a fifteen-footer, and hard to manage, with very little room aboard. It was hard to make a living out of anything

163

that small. Sam had made up for the boat's deficiencies by his personal energy. Whoever bought it would have to be strong and willing.

'Aye, that's what's bad,' Fearon said. 'It's been bought by a lad called Smitherson. Lives in Whitby. We shan't see the *Red Rose* around here no more.'

Now Reuben could realize what Fearon was getting at. Three boats in the last year had been sold and their owners had left Ravenswyke. The *Red Rose* would make four, a lot to lose from the Ravenswyke fleet. The income for the co-operative would go down yet again. And Fearon's money, which depended on the total catch, would be reduced yet again. 'None of us is getting any younger,' Fearon said. 'I've had an offer from a big wholesale fish merchant in London. He wants me to be his buyer in Whitby. It'd be a steady wage.'

Reuben turned to look at Fearon, realizing immediately how much the man had aged in the last three years. Gone were all traces of his former cockiness. Reuben had put that down to the way the co-operative had bested him, but now he could see that, inside, Fearon was a worried man, and the worry was ageing him rapidly. 'I'm coming up to forty-five, Reuben,' Fearon said. 'The fishing here in Ravenswyke is going down and down, instead of up. More and more men are selling their cobles, and nobody's coming along to replace them. Do you realize, you're the only young lad who's fishing on his own. . . ?'

'Nay, Fearon. There's lots of us. . . .'

'On your *own*, I said, Reuben.'

'I can't see the difference.'

'Well, I can. Tom goes out with his brothers and his dad. But Tom's heart's not in it. Do you know, he's studying in his spare time? He wants to get with somebody like Wakeham's of Whitby, or Turnbull's, and eventually get a Master's Certificate. I was talking about it with him. Well, truth to tell, he was talking with me. He was asking me to use my influence in Whitby to get him in to see somebody about it. He's prepared to start as a cabin lad, to get the experience. He wants to visit far places, that lad does, not be stuck here in Ravenswyke for the rest of his life. And the same could be said for Walter's lad, Billy, and Bill's lad, Mark. With the younger generation casting its eyes further afield, what's going to happen to Ravenswyke and the fishing business, Reuben? Have

you thought to yourself about that? Have you thought what's
going to happen to your fishing grounds now they're trawling the
bottom. You've seen them otter boards. . . ?'

'Have I ever,' Reuben growled. The trawlers carried two heavy
metal-tipped boards, which they dragged along the bed of the
ocean. Behind the boards was a long net, shaped a bit like a
funnel. Everything in the way of the otter boards was scraped up.
That meant, among other things, that the feeding spawn, working
the bottom, were being systematically destroyed. Already
Ravenswyke Bay had felt the effects and the liners had to go
further out. No wonder he couldn't bring in a full quota of crabs
and lobsters if the boards had destroyed everything on which
they fed.

'Us'll just have to take a strong hand against the trawlers,'
Reuben said. 'We were talking last evening in the tap. Some of
the lads were talking rough, like cutting the lines, ramming them,
that sort of stuff.'

'It might even come to that,' Fearon said.

'So, you want to get out of it,' Reuben said bitterly. 'Nay,
Arthur, Ravenswyke's given you a living all your life. I know it's
a bit hard now, and we're all going through a bit of a difficult
time – you can blame the war for that. But there's no call to be
tucking your tail between your legs and running.'

'A man's got to look after hisself,' Fearon said darkly.

Reuben turned, and cursed. The delicious arse of Emma
Thoroughgood was no longer in view. 'Come on,' he said, 'I'll buy
you a drink, Arthur, to cheer you up.'

'Won't your mam have your dinner ready?'

'Aye,' Reuben said, 'but it won't spoil, will it, while we sup a
glass of beer.'

Arthur Fearon was in the glummest mood he could remember,
and it took several glasses of beer, and several rum chasers, to
cheer him out of it. Reuben kept company with him, drink for
drink. 'They your lobsters?' Wilcox asked from behind the bar.

'Aye, they were.'

'Haven't got any more? I've got one or two in for supper tonight. I could put it on the menu.'

'And charge a bob or two, I'll be bound!' Fearon said owlishly,
the beer and the rum already getting to him.

'They were the only pair,' Reuben said, obviously having diffi-

165

culty focusing his eyes and pronouncing his words. 'And a right pair they were!'

'You talking about the lobsters?' Fearon asked.

'No! I wasn't!' Reuben said.

Hannah Godson took one look at him as he came in and slumped in his chair by the fire grate, empty in the warm May weather. 'Quick, get his boots off, Eleanor,' she said.

She ladled stew from the blackened pot that had been bubbling on the gas stove, a recent acquisition now that Ravenswyke had its own gasworks. She fetched a piece of board from the back and placed it across the arms of the chair. She took a square of bleached cotton and placed it round his neck, as if he were in a barber's shop, and handed him a spoon and a fork. There was room on the board for a chunk of bread and a pot of tea. 'Get that down you, lad,' she said. 'Then happen you'll feel better!'

She looked at him, slumped in his chair after he'd wolfed down his meal. Fishing and drinking always seemed to go together. A man on the salty ocean became dehydrated, especially in the summer. What more natural, with the Raven taproom only a step away when they came in, than that the fishermen should slake their thirst with a pint of ale? Fishermen were mostly alone on the ocean, with no opportunities to talk. When they came back and sat in the tap, it was often as if the floodgates had been opened. Talk about fishwives gossiping! The fishermen themselves, safe back in harbour, were even worse!

Two minutes after he'd finished eating, he was sound asleep in the chair.

Hannah wrapped a blanket round his knees then, on impulse, bent down and kissed his forehead. 'Just like your dad, you are,' she said, 'just like your dad!'

Reuben woke at four o'clock, considerably refreshed. 'I've *never* been asleep an hour!' he exclaimed when he saw the clock.

'Yes, you have. And us tiptoeing around you like elves. Now stir yourself so's I can get a bit of work done!' Hannah said in mock reproof. A fisherman depends on the tides. She'd heard Reuben get up just after five, had called out 'Do you want any tea mashed?' In the days of Silas, she'd have got up without question to help her man out to sea with a good hearty breakfast, but Reuben seemed happy enough cutting himself a bit of bread

166

and making his own tea. He'd be down and out of the house in ten minutes.

Reuben came out of the chair and stretched, then went out to the back, doubtless to relieve himself and have a wash. He'd had one of the new copper hot-water gas boilers installed in the back; a big unwieldy contraption they'd bolted to the wall, it started with a whoosh of flame that never failed to scare the living daylights out of Hannah. But it did deliver hot water, gurgling from its pipes, and that was a help when it came to bathtime and washing days. Though she still liked to light a fire under the clothes boiler and give the garments a good possing with the wooden three-legged stool on the end of a stick she'd used since first she was married, adding a cupful of washing liquor bought from old Harry, who brought it round with stones for colouring the edges of the front doorstep and exchanged it for bits of old rags. Old Harry with his horse and cart had been a familiar sight in Ravenswyke and the surrounding villages for as long as she could remember. By now he must be getting on for seventy, but he still came around once a week, looking for old rags he supplied to the shoddy and felting mills of the West Riding. They said Harry had hundreds of pounds stuffed in his mattress but then, Hannah mused, they said that about anybody who was in business for himself, even Alicia Pentyford who sold the mints she made herself in her back kitchen. According to the gossips, the Godsons were sitting on thousands!

When Reuben came back into the sitting room, after his wash, Hannah asked him about money for the first time since he'd taken the account over on the death of Lewis, being the sole inheritor as was the Godson way.

'How are we doing, Reuben, at the bank?' she asked. 'That gas boiler and the stove must have cost a penny or two.'

'How are we doing?' he asked, as if to say, What's that got to do with you?

'I was just curious.'

Reuben didn't need to get out the bank book. He'd inherited the Godson caution about money. 'We're doing nicely,' he said. 'There's one thousand four hundred and seventeen pounds on deposit. I was talking to Blakey at the bank. He thinks we ought to invest a bit of it somewhere. Get more interest that way, he said. But I don't know as I've a mind to start mucking about wi' money. So long as it's earning its keep, I'm quite content. And it's there, for a rainy day. I *have* been thinking about buying a motor. I've heard these new diesel engines are good and reliable.'

He could see the dismay on her face. Only a month ago Silas Bredford had been caught at the base of the cliff when his petrol motor had taken a dousing and had stopped. Bredford's anchor warp had been all twisted – he was never a neat sailor – and, before he could get it down, the waves had thrown him up on the rocks. The boat had been a ruin and Bredford himself, two legs broken and his pelvis fractured, was likely to be in the hospital at Whitby for a couple more months.

'You'll keep the sails, lad?' Hannah asked anxiously.

He put his arm round her waist. 'Aye, Mam, I'll keep the sails. The motor would only be for days when there was no wind, and to get me back quick.'

'I'll bet it's expensive. I was hoping you might stretch as far as a new frying pan. This old one – it belonged to your father's grandfather – has practically got a hole in the bottom under the fire-soot. I daren't scrub it too hard lest I push my hand through it.'

Reuben laughed. 'You can have a new frying pan, Mam, any time you want. I'll get one for you. I'm going into Whitby.'

'When, lad?'

'Right now.'

'Whatever are you going all that way for? At this time of day.'

'Never you mind,' he said, 'never you mind.'

The idea must have come to him in his sleep because it was already fully formed when he woke. He'd have to get a bit of a move on, though, if he was to get there before the shops shut. Whitby was five miles away. With luck, he'd be there before half-past five.

It was half-past seven by the time he got back, having walked and trotted both ways, on the return journey with a parcel in his arms. Hannah eyed the parcel curiously when she gave him his belated supper. When he'd finished eating he reached inside the outer wrapping paper and produced a large cast-iron frying pan. 'How will that suit you?' he asked, smiling.

Hannah took it from him, weighed it in her hand, twisted it to test its balance, examined its surface carefully as if for flaws in the metal. 'That'll do champion, Reuben,' she said. 'Champion. You *are* good to me!'

She cast a glance at the parcel which still bulked large, but would rather cut out her tongue than ask what was in it. Whistling innocently, he picked it up and went upstairs to his bedroom. She heard him moving about, heard the well-remembered clomp of his heavy boots on the floor. How many times had she heard Silas take off his boots and throw them down like that?

When he came down, he stood diffidently just inside the door to the stairs. 'Well, what do you think?' he asked.

She looked across the room at him. 'Come forward a bit into the light where I can see you.'

As he moved out of the doorway Eleanor, as if sensing something unusual was happening, came down from her bedroom where she had been knitting, sitting alone as, more and more, she did these days.

'You've got a *suit*?' she said accusingly.

'Hold your tongue, Eleanor,' Hannah said. 'Turn round, lad, let's have a look at the back.'

He turned round awkwardly. She came up behind him, pulled his collar up, pulled the back down, held a bunch of spare cloth at the waist. 'The trousers are a nice fit,' she said, 'but the jacket's a bit on the loose side. Never mind, we can soon deal with that.'

'You're not touching this suit,' he said anxiously. 'Tailor-made, this suit is!' He turned back round and she stepped back, overwhelmed with emotion as she looked at him. By the Lord, he was handsome. The suit was dark grey, made of a very nice tweed — she'd been able to feel the quality when she'd been trying to fit it to him. His shirt was new and crisp white cotton broadcloth, by the look of it. His tie was string, a four-in-hand. 'Where ever did you learn to tie a tie?' she asked.

'The tailor showed me.'

'Did he make the suit special for you, then? If so, you've kept very quiet about it.'

'No, I was passing his shop about a week ago and he happened to be standing in the door. You know the place, Michaels on Baxtergate, Michaels and Tuppitt.'

'My Lord, Reuben, they make clothes for the quality.'

'Don't I know it. Well, I was passing and saw him eyeing me up and down. And he said, "Young man, I've just made a suit for a

169

member of the gentry whose name I shall not disclose, who alas has just passed away. That suit would fit you perfectly, I think. I've a mind to let you buy it from me at the cost of the cloth, rather than have it hanging about in my shop. You look like a prosperous fisherman to me. How would you like to own a suit that was made for one of the gentry?" '

'He never . . .' Eleanor said.

'I thought about it all week,' Reuben said, stretching the point a bit. In fact, without being rude, he'd laughed at the tailor. 'Suits for the gentry are not for the likes of me, thank you, mister,' he'd said, and put the thought out of his mind. But he'd woken today with a lust for the suit; his heart had beat faster and faster the nearer he had drawn to Whitby, praying the tailor wouldn't have disposed of the suit elsewhere, and that the suit would, in fact, fit him. He needed have no fear. Mr Tuppitt, as the man had turned out to be, had not disposed of the suit, and had offered, once Reuben had worn it a few times to 'let it hang on him', to reshape it to fit Reuben perfectly. But already, Tuppitt said, it was 'a remarkable good fit, a remarkable good fit, young man'.

Reuben stood six foot tall and appeared to have stopped growing. His chest had barrelled out during his late teens, with all the hard work in the coble. His black hair always shone naturally, thick and silky and brushed well back from his forehead. Working the boat, ever up and down, had given his body a natural grace when he moved and a perfect sense of balance. His eyes were dark blue, almost black, but they, too, shone with an alert perception that revealed Reuben's vital interest in everything about him. Hannah swallowed hard. Wearing that suit and tie, and the new elastic-sided boots he'd bought to go with it, he looked every inch a gentleman. And that was something no Godson had ever achieved before. They'd always looked like good, reliable, sturdy fishermen – proud, perhaps a little arrogant, but certainly sure of themselves, their abilities, their strengths. It was as if you'd taken a piece of perfect wood, and laid a polish on it to reveal the hidden grain. Hannah clasped her arms about him.

'It'll do, Reuben,' she said, 'it'll do. My, don't you look handsome!'

'One thing I must say,' Eleanor added spitefully, 'he looks a right masher!'

'You're never going *out* in your suit?' Hannah said anxiously. 'On a week night?'

Reuben winked at her. 'I shan't be late, Mam,' he said.

'Going to show off somewhere, I'll be bound,' Eleanor said.

'None of your business, young lady,' Hannah said. 'If you'd comb your hair and dress yourself up a bit, you could show off somewhere, instead of always looking like summat a cat's brought in.'

Fearon had been right. The upstairs saloon of the Raven *was* crowded when Reuben arrived. And Emma Thoroughgood and Stanley Baxter were holding court in the centre of the room near the fireplace, Emma blushing prettily, but that could have been the heat or the wine she'd probably drunk with her supper. Stanley was clasping a large fat cigar in his hand, waving it as he expounded to a group of merchants and fishermen. On the table beside him was a large balloon glass containing a liquid Reuben took to be cognac, a drink he'd never tried.

Reuben stood by the bar, which was placed strategically across one corner of the room. The saloon was a pretty room, much decorated with red damask seats and a thick burgundy-red carpet. The pub had already been fitted with gas, and the lights fluttered on the walls behind red glass shades, shining white above and below and twinkling in the pendant prisms and drops that hung beneath.

Reuben recognized only half the people in the room; the rest, he judged, had come down the bank from the Tops. He saw Cudworthy, a retired master mariner who'd sailed with Turnbull's out of Whitby for thirty years before retiring and building a cottage on the edge of the moor above Old Quaytown. He looked at Cudworthy's suit. 'No better than mine,' he thought proudly.

'What'll you be having, sir,' Wilcox said, his glance taking in the new, smart, urbane Reuben.

Reuben was at a loss. Could hardly order a pint of ale in that room, he thought, though many of the men were drinking beer. 'I'll take a brandy,' he said, 'yes, that's right, a large brandy, in one of them glasses.'

Wilcox tipped him a wink. 'They're called balloons, Reuben,' he said conspiratorially, 'and we always serve brandy in 'em. That's so you can sniff it before you sup it. Some folks call 'em snifters. "Have a snifter, Jebediah," they say. Don't let me catch you starting to talk like that, though!'

Reuben took the 'snifter' in his hand, then saw Stanley Baxter lift his glass and quickly changed his own hold to match. He put his nostrils into the top of the balloon and was nearly asphyxiated by the strong odour. Without drinking, he walked across to the group by the fire. 'Good evening, captain,' he said to Cudworthy, who looked up at him from behind bushy white eyebrows, not recognizing him for the moment.

'Ah, young Godson, isn't it? Which one are you?'

'Reuben, captain.'

'Reuben, that's right. Knew your father, young Reuben, and his father before him. Grand sailors, both of them.'

That had been Cudworthy's standard remark for the past ten years or more.

Emma was looking at Stanley Baxter and smiling. Baxter looked at the newcomer, then frowned. 'Don't I know you, young fellow?' he said, unconsciously imitating Cudworthy's style of speech.

Emma tapped Stanley Baxter's arm and whispered to him. 'Of course,' Baxter said effusively. 'I didn't recognize you for the moment in this light. That was a good pair of lobsters you brought in today, young man,' he said condescendingly. 'Keep fetching 'em in like that and you'll make a success. Quality of merchandise, as I was just saying to these gentlemen, is what I've built my businesses on. That, and a good reputation for delivering on time.'

Emma patted the banquette beside her. 'Won't you be seated, Mr Godson,' she said, smiling up at him. It thrilled him that she could remember his name. He sat beside her. 'I can't blame Mr Baxter for not recognizing you,' she said. 'After this afternoon, you look so grand, if you'll pardon me for saying so.'

'Aye, well, er, different occasions needs different styles!' Reuben said, trying to appear smart and sophisticated. 'What goes for the deck of a boat wouldn't do for here, now, would it?'

'And vice versa?'

'You could say that.'

Baxter had paused in his oration of the qualities that had made him successful. He removed his cigar from his hand, placing it on the cut-glass ashtray Wilcox had given him, no doubt in deference to Baxter's bill. 'Now, Emma, don't go being forward with that

172

young man. We can't have you turning his head!' he said.

Emma ignored him. 'I shan't turn your head, shall I, Mr Godson? It seems to me to be too well fixed for that!'

Reuben blushed, suddenly realizing he had no small talk, no banter he could offer this girl. As if aware of the effect it would create, she had chosen this evening to wear a white dress, completely embroidered, with a deep scooped neckline that showed the start of the cleft of her bosom. Round her delicate throat she wore a black ribbon, on the centre of which was a painted miniature, no larger than his thumbnail. It looked more beautiful than any jewel would have done.

'Any man would be happy to have his head turned by a beautiful woman,' he said.

She rewarded him with that pretty tinkling laugh. 'Why, Mr Godson, I do believe you're a ladies' man,' she said, 'paying them compliments and turning *their* heads.'

Reuben was – in the local expression – dead chuffed. It was the first time he'd played this social game, giving tit for tat. He wouldn't have been able to do it, of course, but for the confidence his new suit inspired in him, the feeling of correctness he'd acquired along with the boots, the shirt, the tie. He sat by Emma's side for an hour and they chattered together. He found her remarkably easy to talk to since she was a practised listener. She'd have to be, spending time with Baxter, who never stopped talking about his many successes. The others were willing to listen. Several times Baxter called for all their glasses to be replenished but each time Reuben refused. He'd had his share of drink that day, and, in some strange way, he didn't want to be beholden to this man, wanted to maintain his independence. Not solely on account of Emma, around whom his imagination was weaving a most delicious but impossible fantasy, but because he suspected Baxter's monologue was not entirely without purpose. Whatever that purpose might turn out to be, Reuben wanted to preserve his own integrity. He'd learned his lesson from Tockett and the Walter Scott novels – men of that type give nothing for nothing. And just as Reuben had never availed himself of the opportunity to borrow Tockett's books, so he was determined to avoid drinking Baxter's drinks. But, his mind told him, he wouldn't mind having a crack at Baxter's woman! Not that he'd ever have a chance of that! It was a brave, daring thought to keep in his mind, to fuel his tongue in their heady private conversation, to set his imagination on fire.

Baxter finally stood up, and took Emma's hand. 'Time *we* went off to *bed*, my dear,' he said, stressing both words deliberately while looking at Reuben. 'Nice meeting you again, lad, though I'm sorry you wouldn't have anything to drink. Just keep bringing in the fish, lad, just keep on bringing it in!' The warning was plain to read – 'and don't go getting ideas above your station!'

The men of the group were silent after Baxter and Emma had gone, then Cudworthy spoke. 'Talks a lot of sense that fellah does,' he growled. 'We're backwards in these parts, that's for sure.'

'Come on, captain, what would an old salt like you know about business?' asked a man Reuben recognized as a successful farmer from near Knowlton.

Cudworthy's features darkened. 'I'll tell you what I know,' he said. 'For years I wandered about the world on the bridge of my vessel, as faithful a skipper as ever you'll find, loading cargo, unloading it, bringing tons of stuff from one place to another. And who made the brass, answer me that? Not me. Not the man who loaded and carried it across the face of the earth. But the businessmen behind it; the families who chartered out their vessels, the agents who secured the cargoes, the people who obtained the goods for their own purposes. Not me. When I retired, I had enough to build a little house you wouldn't want to keep rabbits in, and a pension that'll last me out if I'm careful. Take my word, if you want to make money in this modern world, you've got to find other men to work and do it for you. Take you, Reuben,' he said, his eye lighting on the youngest man present. 'If you want to make a bit, you'll invest in other boats, get other folks to fish 'em for you *for wages*, and keep the profits for yourself. Believe me, lad, it's the only way if you want to go on wearing them fancy clothes you've got on. Aye, and supping your own brandy, instead of taking any handout that comes along like some of us does that hasn't got your pride!'

Baxter was a man who moved quickly once he'd made up his mind. In the seven days he spent at Ravenswyke he plodded over every street in Newquay Town, and even had himself shown round the boat-building yard by Mark Adam Tockett. At the end of the seven days he didn't bother to pack his trunk, but departed, for

Leeds presumably, in his Morris motor-car, leaving Emma behind with a promise to be back as soon as possible.

Reuben spent every evening in the saloon of the Raven, wearing his suit, looking elegant. On the Thursday, he even missed a tide, something he'd never done for as long as he could remember. Gradually he and Emma withdrew from the other folks in the room to an inglenook bench at one side of the fireplace in which no one could hear them, and they could hear no one but each other. Promptly at 9.30 each evening Emma would rise, offer her hand, which Reuben would shake formally, and retire to her suite. And the rest of the patrons would wink at him as he sauntered to the bar after a decent interval, paid his bill, and left the saloon.

The gents' lavatory was situated to the right of the saloon on the ground floor, with the door to the steps leading down to the slip on the left. Directly ahead were the kitchens and the small dining room. On the second evening after Stanley Baxter had departed for Leeds, Reuben came out of the saloon and made for the lavatory only to meet Jack Dobbs coming out with a rubber-tipped plunger in his hand. 'It's all bunged up in there, Reuben,' Jack said. 'You'll have to use the one on the front of the first floor. Just go up them stairs, and turn right, and it's the second door.'

Nobody would ever have believed Reuben if he'd told them he made a mistake in the doors, and the one he opened and stepped in through was the door to the bedroom of the suite. Emma was sitting on the bed. 'I thought you'd come up last night,' she said simply, as she held out her arms. Reuben walked across the room, not daring to believe his eyes, thinking this was a continuation of the dream he'd had every night since he'd first seen her on the slip and had offered her a crab.

Reuben lost his virginity that night and, under Emma's expert tutelage, he learned that people can do things to each other that he and Emily Duckett would never have believed possible. As dawn rose over the sea, flooding the room with light, he lay back exhausted beside the naked body of Emma, his arm around her shoulder, and realized what Elsie had meant when she'd said she'd make a man of him. He felt like a man now, spent and dry, but still a man. 'What are we going to do, Emma?' he said. 'What *are* we going to do?'

175

She turned in bed so that she could look into his eyes. She was as pretty to him as ever, even though the make-up she'd applied around her eyes had smudged during their marathon passion. 'Don't you go getting ideas, Reuben,' she said. 'We're going to make the best of the time we've got, that's what we're going to do. And after that, when Stanley comes back, it's a quick kiss and bye-bye!'

'Nay,' he said, 'you can't mean that!'

She twisted up so that she was half sitting, looking down at him. 'I *do* mean it,' she said. 'Stanley Baxter means something to me, and I'm not going to throw it all away in bed!'

He sat up, too. 'Funny, I thought maybe you loved me?' he said, and this time, when she gave that tinkling laugh, the sound of it ran through his skull.

'Reuben,' she said, when she'd stopped laughing at the sight of the hurt in his eyes. 'Let me spell it out for you. For a start, you're three years younger than I am. For the second, we come from different walks of life. And third. . . .'

'Go on, then . . .,' he said when she hesitated, 'what's the third?'

'Why do you think I said it was all right for you to stay inside me when we were making love?' she asked. 'You don't know much about women, do you? The reason I let you stay inside me, come inside me, was because I'm already pregnant. Me and Stanley, we've been living together, Reuben, for over a year. We're going to go on living together. We're going away somewhere and we'll get married.'

'But you don't love him?' Reuben asked, perplexed. 'Else why would you let me come to bed with you?'

She clicked her teeth, exasperated. 'I *do* love him, Reuben,' she said gently. 'I love him because he loves me, because he's wealthy, because he'll give me and my baby everything we want in life. Can't you understand? You don't get married because you have a good time in bed with somebody. You get married for security, for position. . . .'

The next evening, he delayed going to the Raven for a whole half-hour before, cursing himself for his weakness, he finally arrived and sat beside her. She said nothing about his being later than usual. His replies were all monosyllabic at first but, true to her art, she charmed him out of his mood and, after she'd gone upstairs, he followed her, feeling like a thief. It was five o'clock when he let himself out of the side door and walked up the cobbled streets to his home.

Hannah was waiting for him, with a cup of tea ready in the pot. 'They'll be talking,' she said. 'Let me give you a bit of advice. Wherever it is you go at nights, take your fisherman's clothes with you, and change into them before you come home. That way, folk'll think you've nobbut got up early, and been down to t'slip to look at t'weather!'

'We were playing cards,' he said, and would have gone on but his mother stopped him.

'The one person in the world you need never tell the tale to, Reuben, is your mother! I'm not asking where you've been. I'm just giving you a piece of good advice. Just don't get nobody into trouble, that's all I ask. And don't ruin anybody's good name! Especially your own!' She glanced up at the beam as she spoke, as if reminding herself of the Godson line. Well, there was nothing in what Reuben was doing that hadn't been done before. She could hardly suppress a giggle when she thought of Silas in her bedroom one night on the farm just outside Raunds where she lived until she was wed, the sound of her father's heavy footfall on the steps that led to her attic room, and her last sight of Silas's big white bottom disappearing out of the window, to crash down the slates and fall into the tree. Her door had burst open and her father had stood there, a loaded shotgun in his hands. 'What was that noise?' he'd demanded and, pretending sleepiness, she'd said, 'Ginger was in here. When he heard you coming, he jumped out of the window!'

'If I've told you once, I've told you a hundred times not to let that cat in your bedroom!' And merciful providence had arranged that at that very moment the cat had jumped on the windowsill. 'Here the devil is, back again,' her father had said and let out a roar that probably took two years off the cat's nine lives. And probably sent the fleeing Silas helter-skelter into the nearest hedge, fearful of a shotgun blast.

'You'd better go up and have an hour,' she said. 'Shall you be taking out the *Hope* on the tide?'

'No,' he'd said, smiling at her with complicity, 'today I think I'll give it a miss!'

That was the Thursday. Stanley Baxter came back the following Monday and, though he would have admitted it to no one, in a way Reuben was glad to see the car standing above the slip when he came back from fishing. It had taken Emma's voracious sexual appetite to teach him the truth of the old adage, you can't burn a candle at both ends.

He went into the saloon that evening, but wore his clean fishing clothes and stood at the bar with a glass of beer in his hand, listening to Stanley Baxter hinting in his broad West Riding voice that 'mark my words, there's going to be some changes made, but all for the better!'

Emma looked across the saloon once at Reuben and winked hugely. He surprised himself by being able to wink back, his infatuation now well in perspective. By God, she'd given him a wringing, that was for sure, but he was sailor enough to know that the bigger the blow, the sooner the storm ends. No gale can last for ever, and what they'd shared had shaken him more than any lashing winds or waves.

The following evening, he went back to the tap. Nobody passed any comment about his absence. He hung his suit in the wardrobe – for weddings and funerals.

Stanley Baxter's plan was a simple one. He'd take over the boat-building yard and the land on which the cottages in Newquay Town that Tockett had built for the workers were located. He'd buy the strip of meadow beneath Cliff Top, in the gap of the cliffs themselves. He wouldn't pay anything for the boat-building yard, but assume responsibilities for its debts and liabilities, on an agreed basis. He'd pay for the land on which the back-to-back houses had been built – in yearly instalments, as the tenants could be induced to leave.

Tockett leaned back in his chair, eyeing the man from Leeds cautiously. He hadn't sought this interview, but Hebblethwaite, the solicitor who had many West Riding connections, had asked him to see Baxter. 'You won't like him, James Henry,' he'd said one evening in the club of which they were both members, 'but he's earning himself quite a reputation in the West Riding as an up-and-coming businessman who's made his first fortune and is well on his way to a second.'

'The higher they jump, the harder they fall. . . ?'

'No, James Henry, I don't think he's one of those. He's a good Yorkshireman, born and bred!'

Looking closely at the smiling man sitting opposite him, Tockett realized one thing Hebblethwaite hadn't bothered to tell him. Baxter may have been born a Yorkshireman but not all his antecedents were. Baxter was a third-generation Englishman, of that Tockett could be sure.

'I don't like propositions that don't have money attached to them,' he said mildly. 'This paying a bit at a time. Assuming-debts-and-liabilities stuff. In my way of doing business, you state your terms and you put up cash. Hard cash. Not bits of promises. Any debts and liabilities the Yard may have are Tockett business. If we sell you the business, it'll be as a going concern, with good-will. No debts or liabilities. If we sell you the land, and, mark you, I'm not saying we will – I've got my lad to think about and his future – we'll sell it to you for cash. What you do after that about getting the tenants out will be your affair, not mine. I must say, your offer comes at an interesting time. I've been thinking – only thinking, mind – of pulling my money out of Yorkshire, at least some of it, and putting it to work for me on the Exchange. My lad seems to favour spending more of his time in London. You know what the young folk are? They like the fleshpots and you can't exactly call this end of the world very conducive to sowing your wild oats.'

There it was, a statement of intent that was not a statement, an offer that was not an offer. Stanley Baxter cursed the woolly-minded provincial, as he thought of Tockett. In the West Riding you went to a man with a proposition and he heard you out and said yes or no, not a lot of guff about his son sowing his wild oats.

'I'm told you'd have to raise a lot of cash to settle your debts and liabilities in the Yard,' Stanley said insidiously. 'But that may only be gossip. What isn't gossip, of course, is this case you've got against you. I understand Thrummell and Slade have not been very successful about pleading "civil disturbance" as your reason for non-delivery!'

'You know how it is with solicitors,' Tockett said expansively. 'They huff and puff and wait for the clients to tell them what they ought to be doing, ought to know in the first place. I wouldn't concern yourself too much about the court case, if I were you. If you come up with the cash for the purchase of the Yard, I can guarantee we'll have that case settled out of court before you can draw up a contract.'

'I see none of the men have gone back to work, and it's been a hell of a long time . . .'

'Lazy devils don't want to work. They've got their rabbits, their pigeons and their chickens. A lot of them have found alternative employment. I could empty those cottages overnight – they're all tied, you know.'

'Yes, I did know.'

'One thing I must say for you, Mr Baxter, you've done your homework.' Tockett came from behind his desk, went to the cabinet and poured a couple of glasses of sherry. He beckoned for Stanley to come over and sit by the fire, which he gave a poke with the iron, despite the warmth of the sun flooding in through the windows. 'I think my blood's getting thin,' he said. 'Happen I'm not long for this world. That's why I'm anxious to see the lad settled. Now, drink your sherry, and then tell me what you think would be a good offer – in cash, mind you – for the lot.' He pulled the bell-cord by the fireplace before he sat down.

When James McCloy, the Irishman Tockett had recently taken on as butler, came in, he heard Baxter say, 'If I'm to buy all those houses and get rid of the people in them, and if I'm to buy the Yard – to pull it down, you understand . . .' He fell silent when he saw the butler, not yet having acquired a gentleman's habit of completely ignoring any servants who might be about.

'We seem to be running low on sherry, James,' Tockett said.

James put the decanter on the silver tray he'd brought into the room and left, his face impassive. Sure and the damned decanter was half full and there was the Master, using him as a prop again to impress that upstart tyke from Leeds!

James McCloy did his social drinking in the Laurel, and before he'd been there half an hour and had drunk his second stout, the news was everywhere. 'That fellah from Leeds is going to buy Newquay Town, and throw everybody out.' The speculation ran rife. What, in God's name, could he want with all that land? What could he intend doing with the Yard? Would Tockett sell to him now that the Yard was empty, the workmen spread far afield. Many of them were walking five miles every morning to Whitby, working long hours, then walking back again. Many of

180

them had already moved away and now two-thirds of the cottages were empty and had started falling apart, as unoccupied cottages will. The biggest complaint came from the people who lived just behind and around the Yard itself, people who'd already been there when Tockett built the back-to-back terrace cottages. Their houses were all detached from each other with a bit of garden around. Johnson, the grocer, had one. Fewster, the butcher, had another. Linham, who ran the post office. And Captain Walham, who'd sailed out of Filey for Debenham's, had bought himself a strip of land along the coastline itself, starting at the Yard's slip, and going for a quarter of a mile. On it he'd built a three-storey stone house called Broadholme and some said his bedroom was shaped and decorated like the cabin of the last vessel he'd mastered. It was a small enclave of lower-middle-class success between the Yard and the tawdry streets of workers' houses. Would they be isolated if Baxter bought the land all around them?

Captain Walham received the first intention of what might happen when Baxter came to see him the following day. 'Nice house you have here,' Baxter said, 'but being so low down and close to the sea, I bet it's damp and cold in winter.'

'Happen it might be, but I don't see as that's any concern of yours!' Captain Walham said.

Baxter smiled; in business you get used to initial opposition. 'See the Cliff Top up there,' he said, pointing to the heights of Newquay Town and the strip of land that lined the skyline. 'You'd be better living up there, wouldn't you? A retired sea-captain like yourself with a distinguished record shouldn't be living down here among the works. You ought to be up there, on the bridge, captain, with a view of the ocean as far as the eye can see, not near a smelly yard where you get the noise of work all day long. Aye, when I think of what it must be like on the bridge of a vessel, looking down on everything, seeing the horizon as far as the eye will reach, I can imagine you well up there.'

'I see,' the captain said, a gleam in his eye. 'And what about my house down here? What would I do; put it on a magic carpet and float it up there?'

'You've hit the nail on the head, captain. Oh, I can see you're a perceptive man, all right! No, what you do is, you take your house apart, stone by stone, and you have it carted to the top, and there you have everything erected again, stone by stone. And, incidentally, while they're putting it together, they repair that gable end that I can see needs a bit of work, and they straighten the line of that roof, which I can see is sagging a bit in the middle. They redecorate it, when they've done, dig and plant the garden for you, and before you know what's happened, you're living in the same house, with the same flowers growing in the garden, but you've got a view from the cabin that's unsurpassed. You'd be the envy of every retired skipper in the district! And, what's more, if you'll forgive me touching on a personal note, when your rheumatism gets worse – and there is no real cure for rheumatism, is there? – you won't have to climb up and down the bank to get to your home when you attend the Mariners' Club in Whitby.'

The captain's eyes gleamed. 'You've had your thinking cap on, I can see that!' he said, laughing. 'And this dream of yours, carting the stones up the hill and all that, who's going to pay for it, answer me that? It'd cost a pretty penny!'

'That's the nice thing about it,' Baxter said. '*I'm* going to pay for it. I'm going to pay to have this house transported, exactly as it is now with a few necessary repairs, up the bank. And, when you get up there, you'll have cash in the bank, *and* a lifetime tenancy!'

'You've got it all thought out, then?' Captain Walham said.

'Look, captain. You don't try to bring a vessel into port without first of all studying the charts, knowing about the anchorage. Sometimes you realize, in advance, that you can't get in on your own and you engage a pilot. Think of me, if you like, as a pilot who would bring you to safe anchorage for the rest of your life up on the top of that bank on the bridge of Newquay Town where an old salt like you belongs. . . .'

The captain chuckled. 'You've got silver fish in your mouth,' he said. 'A right gift of the gab! I shall think on what you've said, and if you come back tomorrow I'll give you an answer. Now good-day to you. I've a few things to attend to, and you're holding me back.'

Fewster and Linham were easier propositions. Both were offered the construction of two-storey houses *above* their existing shops. Fewster, in addition, would get a larger and more modern ice-cold storage room, with a bank of the new ammonia freezing pipes worked off an electric motor, and Linham would get a burglar-proof vault. Both immediately indicated their future acceptance, when Baxter could come up with the contract.

One by one, Stanley Baxter personally called on each of the six house owners. By the end of that first day, he had five future acceptances, five handshakes that he knew were as good, in Yorkshire, as a written contract.

That evening, by invitation, he took Emma to Tockett House to dine with James Henry and Mark Adam Tockett, Mr and Mrs Thrummell, and Mr and Mrs Hebblethwaite.

It was a grand social occasion; all the men wore evening dress, of course, and the women sparkled in their heavy brocade and velvet gowns, trotting out their best jewellery as if for a ball at the home of the Lord Lieutenant of the county.

At first sight, Emma looked woefully underdressed. She was wearing a simply cut full-length gown in black shantung silk. Around her throat was a collar of diamonds set in thin gold. She wore black slippers, but no one noticed them. It would be a safe bet that, beneath the shantung silk, she was wearing no other garment! She smiled sweetly, spoke only when she was spoken to, and then in a soft, well-modulated voice that compared favourably with the harsh, moneyed tones of the other matrons, both of whom were twice her age. The men, with the sole exception of Mark Adam Tockett, were enchanted by her. Mark was sulking; he hated these business dinners, hated the stuffy formality of life in Yorkshire, would infinitely have preferred to be in his flat in St James's with his few cronies. Mark Adam was an unmitigated snob. He'd disliked Baxter on sight, as his father had done, but lacked the unscrupulousness to realize that the man, however coarse he might seem, could be used to their own financial advantage. He was not yet old enough, or ruthless enough, to realize, as his father had many years ago, that men of Baxter's type were there to be *used*. And, if they brought a delicious morsel like Emma into one's drab life, then so much the better.

James McCloy had brought two of the village girls in to help serve at table, though he masterminded the entire operation. James Henry's eyes lit up when he saw that one of them was Elsie Milner, who'd left his employ the day after her mother had been up to see him. She winked at him when no one could see, and he winked back.

'Ah, Elsie, we haven't had you for some time now, have we?' he asked.

'No, sir, you haven't,' she replied pertly. It was a private joke that sustained him through the tedium of Mrs Hebblethwaite's discourse on the declining morality of the serving classes.

Elsie took the opportunity when they were all eating and she was waiting to 'clear', standing demurely by the sideboard, to study Emma. Her woman's instinct told her immediately that Emma and Baxter – loud-mouthed masher, he was, she thought privately – weren't married. So, how did she do it? How had she achieved Elsie's own private ambition, of hitching herself to a wealthy, successful and tolerably good-looking and acceptable young man? One thing was certain: Emma had learned dress sense. She was a stunner. Every time she bent forward to sip her soup, old Tockett's eyes practically dropped out of his sockets. He'd seated Emma next to him on his right and the overdressed and yet dowdy Mrs Hebblethwaite on the other side of Baxter on his left. That had been a mistake; Mrs Hebblethwaite held the centre of the table and no one could get a word in against her loud and overbearing voice.

There had been talk about Emma and Reuben Godson and, of course, it had come straight to Elsie. 'I see your fancy man's got himself another dove to coo over,' old Mrs Farnham, forty years a rasping widow, had said. Well, Elsie thought, if Reuben is cutting himself a slice off that little cake, good luck to him! The thought only intensified the care with which she studied Emma's every gesture, listened to every word, absorbed every detail of her commanding yet demure presence.

James McCloy brought the meat in on a trolley. He wheeled it to the head of the table. 'Shall you carve, sir?' he asked.

Tockett was far too busy enjoying the sight of Emma's shoulders. 'No, James, you do it,' he said.

James McCloy carved the meat with a sure touch, wheeling the trolley round the table, the girls following him with the tureens of vegetables. When he came to Mrs Hebblethwaite she turned to examine the carcass, pausing briefly in her denunciations. 'Make certain the meat you give me is well done,' she said. 'I want none of this raw stuff.'

He tapped the baron of beef with the edge of the carving knife.

'Yes, there,' she said. 'Let's see what that's like.'

He cut her several generous slices and placed them on her plate on the warming table of the trolley. Elsie heaped on veget-

184

ables and the plate was put before Mrs Hebblethwaite, who was again in full chorus.

James McCloy reached under the trolley top and brought out a gravy boat containing a thick brown liquid. 'A little gravy, madam?' he inquired politely.

'Yes,' she said, 'lots of gravy.'

He poured it liberally over the meat, restored the boat to the underside of the trolley, and carried on his way. No one else was offered the 'special' gravy.

Elsie appeared to be having a coughing spell, which she quickly overcame under the glare Mrs Hebblethwaite gave her. When all the guests had been served, the two girls and James McCloy left the dining room.

'Your place is inside, my girl,' McCloy said to Elsie, 'in case they need anything.'

'Oh, I couldn't, Mr McCloy,' she said. 'I couldn't stand there and watch her eating that meat, with all your special sauce tipped over it!'

He winked at her. 'You're a bright girl,' he said. 'You'll go a long way!'

'I don't know what you're talking about,' Amy, the other girl, complained.

'Never you mind,' McCloy said, restoring his dignity. 'Now we'd better get the puddings ready! Immorality of the serving classes, indeed! Just too bad I couldn't get hold of a bit of horse's and was obliged to use my own.'

'His own *what*?' Amy asked Elsie, perplexed.

'Piss, you dummy, piss. It's in the special sauce he poured over gabby Hebblethwaite's meat.'

After dinner the ladies retired and the men went into Tockett's office and library. The chairs were drawn in a circle around the fire. McCloy came in, and offered brandy and cigars. He stood to attention in the corner, and would have stayed there but Tockett saw him and dismissed him with a wave.

'We've considered your proposition, Mr Baxter,' Tockett said without preamble. 'I must say as Mr Hebblethwaite has drawn it up very well for you. Shall you continue to use him in this matter?'

'Most probably,' Baxter said. 'He has the local knowledge I shall be needing.'

'Aye, and the local contacts to open a few doors. . . . Only one thing. The clause that makes the entire arrangement conditional on you acquiring ownership of the strip of land and the houses thereon between my property in Newquay Town and my Yard. I can't see rightly how the one affects the other.'

Baxter looked around the room at the two Tocketts and their solicitor, Thrummell, and his own retained solicitor, Hebblethwaite. Of course, he wasn't tipping his hand but Hebblethwaite would go, the minute he'd opened the doors Tockett had been talking about. He'd be fobbed off with a minor part of the job. The rest would go to the lads Baxter always used, Burton and Green in Leeds, who clearly understood Baxter's method of doing business. 'Gentlemen,' he said, 'I'm sure you'll agree that, whatever I may decide in the future to do with the land I am acquiring, I shall have to have freedom of movement. And, to do that, I shall need *all* the land, not two pieces of land cut through the middle by a strip of independent houses and gardens. I anticipate no difficulty acquiring that land – I've already got a handshake on most of it. But in these matters we're all well advised to be prudent. I want a firm guarantee from you that, in view of the money I am prepared to pay, in cash, I can have the land I want the minute I advise you that I have acquired all the other land. As between gentlemen, of course, I need hardly remind you that this information is quite confidential. I wouldn't like to have to bid against anyone in this room. . . .'

Tockett laughed. 'That's a Leeds trick, Mr Baxter. We don't go in for those games here. No, do what you can to acquire the land you want, and then we've an agreement for cash along the lines stated in the draft contract and letter of intention our joint solicitors have prepared for us.' He downed his brandy in one gulp. 'And now, if you gentlemen don't mind, I think we should rejoin the ladies.' Thrummell, Hebblethwaite and Mark Adam looked at him with undisguised surprise. Once they got into the library after a good meal, they rarely left to rejoin the ladies until at least two decanters had been disposed of.

'Here we are, ladies,' Tockett said gaily as they returned to the drawing room. 'Now you, Mrs Baxter – may I call you Emma? – come and sit on this settle next to me.'

A vastly different assembly was taking place at that very moment in the tap of the Raven, where a number of people never normally seen there were drinking beer. Reuben was sitting in the centre of a group at the table in the middle of the room. 'So, Baxter's buying the Tockett houses and the Yard, is he? Well, there's nowt we can do to stop that. Happen he'll repair some of the roofs, make the houses fit to live in. And happen he'll get the Yard back into full production again and you'll get back your jobs – them as wants 'em. But I can't see why you're bothering to tell me all this!'

Jean Dobbs had come down the inner steps from the kitchen of the Raven, where she'd finished cooking dinner for the three guests staying in the hotel, and for Mr and Mrs Wilcox, herself and her son Jack. The barmen provided their own meals. 'You forget what McCloy heard, Reuben,' she said firmly. 'McCloy's no reason to lie. He said, in the Laurel, that Baxter had told Tockett he intended to kick everybody out and pull the houses and the Yard down!'

'Were you there, Mrs Dobbs?' Reuben asked mildly. 'I mean, were you there and actually heard him yourself? I don't want to cause offence, but something like this always attracts rumours, you know.'

'Nay, Bill Clewson heard it, didn't you, Bill?' she asked.

Bill was standing by the door but came forward through the room. 'Right enough, Reuben. I heard what McCloy said, there in the Laurel. Well, I know he's a bit of an old woman, but there's no love lost between him and Tockett.'

That created a pandemonium of approval, and Reuben had to hold up both arms to get them to be quiet. 'He definitely said that Baxter was going to pull down the houses, kick the people out, pull down the Yard buildings. . . ?'

'I can't swear to it that he said he was going to pull down the houses. Just that he was going to get the people out. And close down the Yard.'

'And what do you want *me* to do?' Reuben asked. 'A man has a perfect right to buy anything he's a mind to, provided he has the brass.'

Jean Dobbs came forward. She had to; the contingent from the Laurel pushed her forward and all their eyes were on her. 'Go on, missis,' they were saying.

She stood in front of Reuben, twisting her apron. 'Well, like, Reuben. They've asked me to speak. Now, understand, the past is the past, and once before you was asked to be a spokesman, which ended in tragic consequences so far as I'm concerned.'

'You know how I feel about that,' Reuben said awkwardly, the memory of his visit to Jean Dobbs still with him, the visit when he'd gone to offer her his help, the Godson help, and she'd chased him out of the house with a carving knife, even slashed his arm in her grief and rage. Reuben had not been deterred from his purpose; he, it was, who'd gone to Wilcox and asked him to take her on. She was known throughout Ravenswyke as a good cook – before she'd married she'd cooked up at the Manor House for a time – and Wilcox was glad of the suggestion now that more and more people were travelling about in motor-cars and coming to stay overnight.

'Aye, well, one thing I can say, Reuben. The past *is* the past. Bygones *is* bygones. And I'm asking you, on behalf of us all as lives in Newquay Town, to do what you can for us any road you see fit!'

Reuben would have refused out of hand. He felt he'd burnt his fingers over the matter of the closing of the Yard, and had taken Tockett's advice. For a few months, the villagers had shunned him for speaking out against Frank Dobbs, but then gradually the animosity had faded as they saw the other side of the coin – that Reuben hadn't compromised, hadn't lied, and was therefore a man to be trusted. Even though his proven honesty might, sometimes, be difficult and painful for them. Reuben wanted no more of delegations, and being spokesman, but they'd chosen wisely when they'd asked Jean Dobbs to speak to him. Reuben still felt he owed her something for the death of her husband. 'What is it you expect me to do?' he asked helplessly. 'I can hardly go marching up to Tockett and tell him he can't sell his own property!'

'Just give it a bit of thought, Reuben. We've every confidence you'll come up with something.'

As he left the tap he felt awful. What a responsibility! What on earth could he *do*? He'd given his word and that meant he'd have to do something, but *what*? In his perplexed state of mind he didn't feel like going home just yet so he walked up the road at the side of the Cut, then turned the steep dog-leg of the bank, striding ever upwards with the roofs of Newquay Town stretching to his left below him. He paused at the top where the road divided, one way going to the moors, the other to Tockett House along the cliff top. The road was fenced on his left; he climbed the rails and sat on the top one, with the whole of Ravenswyke spread out before him, the ocean beyond. There were no clouds and the heat of the day rose gently from the land. The sea itself looked heavy as lead, glistening sickly as if slicked with oil, barely a ripple marking the surface as far as his eye could see. Tockett House gleamed with light to the right; he saw the lights of a motor-car leaving, and then the sidelamps of a carriage and pair. From above he could see some of the gaping holes in the roofs of some of the abandoned cottages and his heart was heavy without his knowing why. Reuben had been brought up in a state of order, where a man's pride wouldn't let him live in deteriorating surroundings without doing something about them himself. He had been repelled by the obvious apathy of these people, who appeared to want everything to be done for them, who thought that, because the houses actually *belonged* to someone else, they should play no part in maintaining them. The sheer squalor of Newquay Town depressed him – it was as if the people living there had given up all hope. What's a man to do, however, the reasonable half of Reuben said, when nothing stretches before him but an endless succession of wages and rent payments? At least Reuben had his destiny in his own hands. He could fish more skilfully, catch more, earn more money, invest in a larger boat, which would enable him to go further and catch even more. Maybe one day he could earn enough to get himself a small inshore trawler, though that would mean the difficult decision of leaving Ravenswyke to work out of Whitby. The important point, he argued to himself, was that his future, and the future of the Godson family and name, was firmly in his hands. One other thought, however, as yet ill-formed, kept intruding. The Godsons of *Ravenswyke*. The *Hope of Ravenswyke*. The combined Old Quaytown and Newquay Town that comprised Ravenswyke had been home to the Godsons, had been good to the Godsons. Did he owe it nothing to think so easily of going away, presumably to become a Godson of *Whitby*?

So deep were his thoughts that he didn't hear the light footfall beside him.

'Hello, stranger,' Elsie said. 'Not thinking of throwing yourself over the bank, are you?'

He turned quickly and saw Elsie Milner. She was wearing a black wool coat over a long black dress with a white pinafore at its front. The tips of white cuffs showed at her wrists. 'I've been skivvying for old Tockett,' she said, 'waiting at table and washing up.'

'You look nice with your hair done like that,' he said. It was all he could think of, since he hadn't seen her after that night she'd thrown him out for his unfortunate remark. She leaned on the rail by his side. 'What are you doing up here?' she asked. 'Moongazing?'

'No, I was looking at Newquay Town and thinking what a mess it's become.'

She shrugged her shoulders. 'Always will be a mess,' she said. 'Folks never learn to look after nowt until it's their own!'

'You keep your place nice!'

'Aye, well, I'm different, aren't I? I mean, I've got all them fellows coming in to see me, haven't I? Trade would fall off if I kept the place dirty.'

He could see she was determined to have it out with him, one way or the other. 'Look, Elsie,' he said firmly. 'I'm sorry for what I said. I was caught off balance, seeing what I could see. That's the first time I'd ever seen a woman's body.'

'But you've been gawping at one since, so they tell me. And a nice body it is, I'll be bound, from what little I saw of it at supper tonight. Old Tockett's eyes were hanging out further than yours were.'

He held her wrist to stop the flow of words. 'Elsie, I've said I'm sorry for the words I spoke,' he said. 'What's happened, or not happened, since then is my own affair.'

She made no attempt to pull her wrist away. 'Aye, you're right, Reuben. I was just a bit jealous, I suppose, a bit envious! My, she's got some lovely clothes, that one has, and a diamond choker that must have cost him a king's ransom. And she knows how to talk and behave herself in company, and that's something nobody's ever bothered to teach me.'

He saw the sorrow on her face, the regret at youthful opportunities lost, perhaps for ever. He leaned forward and kissed her forehead, taking his hand from her wrist and putting it round her shoulder. 'If you say, there, there, Reuben Godson, I'll kill you,' she said. There were tears in the sound of her voice and he hugged her tighter, feeling the warmth and strength of her body. It was a feeling he'd learned recently when he'd held Emma close in his

190

arms in the bed in the Raven Hotel. He brushed her hair back from her forehead and kissed it again, gently. 'My,' she said, 'you have learned a thing or two!'

'Come on,' he said, 'I'll take you home. You must have had a busy time of it, knowing the way the Tocketts wallow in their food!' He slipped his arm through hers and they turned to go down the road. At that moment, a motor-car came along from Tockett House, and went to turn right. As it drew level the driver honked his horn, then leaned across his companion to shout, in his wine- and cognac-soaked voice, 'You'll not catch any fish up here, my lad! Or maybe you've caught one already!' The car accelerated round the turn and quickly, too quickly it seemed to Reuben, started the descent of the hill. The screech of metal as it rubbed alongside the stone wall of the dog-leg could be heard right up the hill.

'One way or another,' Reuben said, 'I'm going to do that devil down, you mark my words.'

When all the guests had gone, James Henry and Mark Adam sat in the library sipping a last brandy together. These moments, Mark Adam knew, meant much to his father who liked to be alone with his son, liked to talk with him in general terms about their family enterprises. Mark Adam had little stomach for these tête-à-têtes, in which he never seemed to shine very well. He was more confident when he was in London, away from his father's prying eyes, when he could take his time about things and think them out slowly. Living in London stimulated him, made him more alive and, he believed, more alert. There were more business opportunities there, with people coming forward with sound propositions. Mark Adam hadn't realized how much he depended on his name and his father's reputation on the Exchange. His father had been known as a raider from the north, shrewd and astute, a bad man to tangle with but an easy man with whom to discuss a sound investment. And, in the aftermath of the war, most of the investments were sound, golden opportunities for the men with cash to play with, as Britain and the countries of Europe went crazily in search of the goods of which the war had deprived them. Men like Tockett, who could buy and sell cargoes, could take shares in vessels to carry those cargoes, were on an easy wicket. In approaching Mark Adam Tockett, most people with opportunities thought they were approaching the father. Mark Adam was astute enough, when he presented these ideas in Yorkshire, to propose them as his own ideas, his own findings. When James Henry recalled Mark Adam to Yorkshire, beginning to feel his increasing age and, at seventy, wanting what was left of his family near to him, the younger man was on less certain ground with the eyes of his father constantly upon him. The decision to stage a lock-out at the Yard had been Mark Adam's. His father admired the ruthlessness, the unemotional way in which his son, in one action, had solved their legal problem, even though it had meant putting so many men out of work. But part of him recognized that his son had gone further than he himself would have done. Ruthless he could be, yes, but not as ruthless as that.

'What do you think this lad Baxter has in his mind?' Tockett asked.

'In what way, Father?'

'Come on, Mark Adam, you know what I mean. Why does he want the Yard and the cottages? Surely he's not going into production again?'

'I don't know, Father. Perhaps he thinks he can build boats to rival those they build in Whitby.'

Tockett groaned with exasperation. 'Really, lad,' he said. 'I don't know what's happened to you since you came home. All those bright ideas that used to flow from you like tap water when you were in London seem to have dried up here. I'll tell you what he's up to. He's going to pull the lot down, clear all the land, and build seaside homes for the folks of the West Riding. And where the Yard is, I'll bet he's going to put some kind of resort place, like they have in Blackpool, I'm told, to appeal to any Tom, Dick and Harry that cares to come here for his holidays. Wake up, Mark Adam. Now that the motor-car's been invented, and the railway is coming, people are going to have a lot more mobility. Baxter's thinking on the lines you should have been. He's got his eye to the future. Work it out for yourself. On a plot of land it'll cost him a mere fifty pounds to acquire off me, he'll put up a nice little seaside house he'll sell for two hundred and fifty pounds. He'll make himself a clear four hundred per cent profit before building costs!'

'Then why are we selling him the land, Father?' Mark Adam asked, bewildered.

'I'll tell you, lad, just why! It's easy to talk about a deal like that, but to put it through takes a lot of energy, a lot of effort, a lot of business acumen, a steady hand and nerve, and the confidence of those people who back you.'

'Then why don't we do it, Father?'

James Henry rose in his seat, his mottled face marbled even deeper by anger and disappointment. 'Because, you blasted nincompoop, I'm too old, and you haven't got a single one of the qualities I've just listed. Not a single one! You don't think I let you loose in London without safeguarding the family investments, did, you? I knew the source of all those "business opportunities" you handed on to me as your own bright ideas. And I'll tell you one more thing. Just to test you, to see if, in fact, you had *any* brains in your head, I had Stone slip you a proposition that was so spurious, so worthless, that if we'd acted on it we'd have been bankrupt within a fortnight. Remember the Cretan sugar deal? We were going to buy Cretan sugar, sight unseen, and ship it on the Charavaris Line to Jamaica and make a fortune? And you approved it? Well, lad, they don't grow sugar on the island of Crete, take my word for it, and they *do* grow more sugar on the island of Jamaica than they know what to do with. And, what's more, there's no such thing as the Charavaris Line sailing out of Piraeus! You said yes to the whole deal, would have bought futures on sugar that didn't exist, to ship on a nonexistent line, to a country that didn't want to buy it. You authorized a deal with Stone that would have left us penniless. Stone could have cleaned us out! Thank God he works for our interests in London!'

He slumped back in his chair while Mark Adam sat there, stunned. Of course he remembered the Cretan sugar affair and couldn't, at the time, understand why his father had vetoed what seemed like such a brilliant investment. Why, the deal had been offered to him by Lord Bradley, a member at Boodle's. Who, come to think of it, was a senior partner in Stones. . . . Damn it, they'd set him up. Lord Bradley, Stone and his father had set him up!

He rose to his feet, offended dignity his only weapon. 'Very well, Father,' he said frostily, 'I'm certain you'll agree there can be no point in continuing this conversation.'

Something terrible in his father's eyes stopped him moving. 'Take that jacket off, lad,' his father said.

Without comprehending what was happening, Mark Adam did as he was told.

'Now take off your weskit and your shirt.'

'Father. . . ?'

'Do as I tell you, lad.' His father's voice was weary and resigned, as if in anticipation of some hard task to come.

When Mark Adam was standing there in his trousers and vest, his father rose from behind the desk. He walked to the cupboard set in the wall while Mark Adam watched with apprehension. From the cupboard, his father produced a horsewhip, and Mark Adam's fears were confirmed.

'You're not . . .,' he gasped.

Without even testing the heft of the whip, his father swung it backhand in a savage arc. The whip end cracked against Mark Adam's chest and he cried out in pain. His father didn't speak, but drew the whip back again; the lash streaked forward but now Mark Adam, shrieking with fear, had turned his back to his father, and the knotted end cracked across his shoulder blades. 'Father,' he sobbed, 'what are you doing?'

His father spoke for the first time. 'You know well what I'm doing, lad,' he said. 'I'm giving you the horsewhipping you deserve.'

Back and forward the whip went, all James Henry's considerable force behind it. Mark Adam fell forward across the desk but his father did not spare him until the blood began to seep through the cotton of his vest, until his back was a mass of weals and gashes and the tops of his arms and his shoulders, unprotected by the cotton, were running with the blood of opened wounds. Slowly Mark Adam stopped shrieking, but shuddered with convulsions each time the lash fell, cutting deeper, drawing more blood. Deep sobs were forced from him with each blow, and grunts of inexpressible pain. Finally, Mark Adam slumped down and down until he slipped off the edge of the desk and fell in a heap. His father drew back the whip, snapped it forward, and the lash bit savagely into Mark Adam's neck, slashing a cut that would mark him for life. Then James Henry coiled the whip slowly and, heaving with the exertion, placed it back in the cupboard. Beyond that one sentence, he hadn't spoken during the horsewhipping.

'Get yourself back up and sit in the chair,' he said. 'Come on, do as I say and sharp about it.'

194

Mark Adam levered himself off the floor and sat on the edge of the chair, facing his father's desk. James Henry went behind the desk and seated himself. 'I never thought I'd witness the day when I had to take the horsewhip to a son of mine,' he said. 'Why the gods had to take Rupert Henry and leave something like you to pollute the land, I'll never know.'

'Father!' Mark Adam said, his spirit broken.

'Hold your peace and listen to me, though I can barely bring myself to talk to such as you! I know all about you and your friends in St James's. Every time you've gone there during the past year, I've had a detective watching you. You are a *sodomite*. My son, a *pederast*!'

Mark Adam was silent. Now he knew the reason for the horse-whipping. He bit his lip. My God, why hadn't they all been more careful? His mind shuddered to realize that, if his father had been able to find out about him, then surely it would have been as easy for the police. The regiment had hushed up his only discovered transgression by letting him resign his commission; the civilian authorities wouldn't have been so protective.

'This is what you'll do,' James Henry said. 'You'll give me your word you'll never again have that sort of relationship with any male person – for I can't call them *men*. If you break your word I swear to God, as sure as the name you've defiled is Tockett, that I'll have you shot down like the dog you are. Secondly, you'll call as soon as your wounds have healed on Mr Gramond of Goathland. You'll make yourself civil to him and his wife, and his eldest daughter Hester. You have more luck than you deserve. She's a pretty little thing and, I'm told, quite intelligent. She doesn't know you're coming, but you'll talk nicely with her. You'll make it your purpose to win her over. Do you understand, *sodomite*?'

'No, Father,' Mark Adam gulped, hardly able to speak for the pain of his back and his shoulders.

'Then you're a bloody fool as well as a *sodomite*. You'll pay court to her, as if you've fallen head over heels in love with her. You'll do all the things a *man* – a normal man, that is, and not one of your sort – would do when he's wooing a pretty virgin. By a year from this date, you'll be wed with her. Within a year after that, you'll bring a grandson into this house, do you understand? And the grandson, make no mistake, will be *your* son, and the son of Hester Gramond. Just so you understand me, if you fail me in this, then though it might kill me I'll marry again, a young lass, and I'll sire another heir to cut you out of the estate. On the day the new bairn is born – and I've still got enough juice left in me for that – I shall give the detective's dossier to the London police. It's got everything in it. All the names and addresses of your fine friends, all the dates when you were bestializing each other. You need new curtains in that flat of yours in St James's. It's your choice, *sodomite*! It's either Hester Gramond, and may God have mercy on her poor innocent soul for what her father and I are doing to her, pairing her off with a thing like you, or it's cut off without a farthing, prison and disgrace for you and your sodomite friends. Aye, and one more thing. If you ever tell her it was a put-up job, if you ever repeat a word that's been said in this room tonight to her, if you ever give her a moment's anxiety or treat her badly, then I'll take the gun to you myself.'

There was no doubting his father's ferocious sincerity.

Only one hope remained. One thing his father didn't know. Mark Adam liked both boys *and* girls. He stood before his father's desk, holding the last shreds of his pride about him. Though he was almost fainting from pain, he held himself erect as an army officer. 'Very well, Father,' he said. 'I'll do as you ask on two conditions. . . .'

'Conditions. Who the hell are you to be talking to . . . ?'

'Shut up,' Mark Adam said, as if he were addressing one of his sergeant-majors, 'and pay me the courtesy of listening to *me* for a change. I'll do as you ask: I'll give you my word not to go with men; I'll marry Hester Gramond provided she'll have me; I'll try my best, God willing, to produce an heir to the family name, if you . . .'

'If I what . . .?'

'If you *stop calling me sodomite*! And stop messing about inside the servant girls' underwear!'

James Henry glared at him, then threw back his head and laughed fit to split the ceiling. 'So,' he said, still choking from his laughter, 'so you *have* got a spark of summat in you, after all!'

As Elsie Milner and Reuben walked together down the bank, it seemed natural for her to link her arm in his. As they went, he told her about the deal Baxter was rumoured to be making to buy the cottages and the Yard and pull them down. He told her about the 'committee' that had come to him and had asked him to intercede on their behalf. She laughed, but in a companionable way. 'My, Reuben, you are growing older, aren't you, and taking on responsibilities. They'll be having you on the Parish Council next. . . !'

'Aye,' he said, 'that's all very well, Elsie, but what the devil am I to *do*? I can hardly march up to Tockett Top and tell 'em they can't do business together, can I? It appears that Tockett has something he wants to sell, and Baxter has something he wants to buy, and what's to stop the pair of them getting their heads together? Certainly no words of mine. They'll tell me, and quite rightly so, it's no business of mine. It's nowt to do with me!'

They had reached her cottage. 'You coming in?' she asked.

'Nay, lass, tha mun be tired,' he said, unconsciously lapsing into thick speech.

She looked provocatively at him. 'Not so tired I can't make thee a cup o' tea,' she said, imitating the sound of his voice.

He flushed; why could Elsie always touch him, as if with the flick of a whip, on a raw nerve-end. He tried hard not to talk too broadly; during his conversations with Emma in the saloon of the Raven he'd listened to her and, in a sense, tried to emulate the neat way she spoke, with no 'thee and tha', no 'mun', no 'aye and nay'.

'Come on in,' she said, 'and stop mullacking about here on t'step.'

She'd left a fire well banked down with tealeaves and coal slack, covered with ashes from the ashpan. It was the work of a minute to stir it with the poker and bring back a crackle of flame among the heavy green-white fire smoke. He sat in the chair by the fire, his mind still occupied with his problem. She scalded a pot of tea, then went upstairs to her bedroom while it mashed on the hob. When she came down, she was wearing the same dressing gown that had caused his trouble before. 'Don't worry, I've got it pinned this time, *and* I've got summat underneath. There'll be no fireworks tonight. That's the only dress I've got for work, and I don't like to sit about in it.' She poured the tea, his in a pot and hers in a cup with a saucer, put milk and sugar in both, and stirred them before she handed his pot to him. 'It occurred to me while I was upstairs changing,' she said when she'd sipped her tea, 'that

197

yon Baxter's going to have a problem with the folk of Grinkle-gate.'

'You mean Fewster and Linham? Captain Walham? All that lot?'

'Aye. All the snot-noses. After all, they own their own places. Always have. They've always held themselves above the rest of the folk on the other side of the Cut. Aye, and a bit above you lot in Old Quaytown!'

'You live in Old Quaytown, remember! You're one of *us*.'

There was an edge of bitterness in her laugh. 'Nay, Reuben, that I'm not! If the old biddies around here could have their way, they'd ride me out tomorrow on a broomstick! Any road, that's a sidetrack. It seems to me that happen the key to the selling of this land might be in Grinklegate. If I was you, I'd go down there and have a word with them. See what their thoughts are on Baxter taking over beside and behind them. Happen they might not like it and you'll get yourself a few supporters to help you!'

'By gow, you're right, Elsie. Grinklegate must be the key to all this. I can hardly see somebody like Baxter buying *part* of any-thing. He'll want the lot, or none at all.'

She smiled smugly. 'There, you see, two heads are better than one, aren't they?'

He reached out impulsively and put his hand on her arm. 'You've taken a great load off my mind,' he said. 'When you hap-pened by this evening, I was at my wit's end, not knowing how to get started on this affair.'

'Aye, Reuben,' she said mischievously, 'starting an affair is almost as difficult as finishing one!'

He flushed beneath his sailor's tan. 'I wouldn't know what you mean, Elsie Milner,' he said.

'Tha knows, right enough!'

He downed his tea in one long draught, looking deep into her eyes over the rim of the pot. She held his regard steadily. 'You've changed,' she said when he put the pot down. 'I reckon some-body's done you some good. Afore, you were like a young stallion champing at the bit but not daring to make off on your own. Now, you've learned a bit of patience, it seems to me. You've got con-fidence in yourself from somewhere. Or someone.'

'Happen I have, Elsie, happen I have!'

'That Emma,' she said, 'she must be quite a woman!'

198

'She couldn't hold a candle to thee.'

'How do *you* know. You've never tried owt!'

He stood up. 'There'll come a time, Elsie Milner! A time we'll both be ready. Right now, you've an evening's work behind you, and I have things on my mind. It won't always be like that!'

'Don't count your chickens. . . .'

'I'm not, I can tell you that.'

'Get on home, you young bantam-cock! You're quite right; I *do* have an evening's work behind me. And you *do* have things on your mind.'

She saw him to the door and stood in the bright moonlight watching him go down the cobbled path along the narrow alleys in the maze of Old Quaytown. A bedroom curtain twitched on the other side of the street, and a voice floated down. 'When I were a young lass us didn't stand at the doorway in us nightie watching us fancy men go away!'

'Go on, you old witch,' she said, but without rancour. 'When you were a lass, you didn't own a nightie. You slept in your drawers and your coms!'

She closed the door and went to bed chuckling at old Mrs Farnham's screech of outrage.

Reuben sat in Fewster's kitchen the next morning with mounting apprehension.

'I haven't a lot of time,' Fewster said when Reuben, seeing the early light in his window, had tapped on the door. 'We're slaughtering today. But you can come in for a few minutes while I finish off my breakfast.'

'No wonder the fat bugger goes twenty stones,' Reuben thought to himself, watching while the butcher consumed six eggs, a couple of chops, two slices of liver, a couple of lamb's kidneys, and two thick slices of bread fried in the pan fat, all washed down with a bottle of beer and a pot of tea so black and thick you could have stood a spoon in it. When Fewster wiped his mouth on the back of his sleeve, he confirmed Reuben's worst fears. 'Yes, Baxter has made us an offer, though I can't see as it concerns you or anybody else but him and me. It's a grand offer and I've not a mind to refuse it.'

'You mean, you've accepted.'

'We've shaken hands on it, lad, shaken hands. It's only got to be worked out in detail.' His wife bustled into the kitchen wearing her outside coat. 'We'll have to be going, Jack,' she said. On slaughtering day she helped in the back of the shop, preparing the sausage skins from the intestines, grinding the sausage meat, working the stuffer. She made potted meat, cleaned the chitterlings and the tripes, boiled the cow-heel, while Jack Fewster, and his brother Ronald, who worked the shop with him, walked down each morning from his house at the top of the bank. The eldest of the three brothers, Peter, looked after the Fewster farm, rearing stock and pigs, chickens for meat and eggs in season. Since half the farm was arable, they grew a lot of their own feedstuffs and were almost self-contained. Rumour had it that the tight-fisted Fewsters were among the richest men in the district.

She collected Jack's plates and dumped them into the sink for washing later, when she'd lighted the fire to warm the water. Folks said she was so damned mean she couldn't thoil to leave the fire banked down overnight, as most folks did, but cleared the grate out before they went to bed and dropped the hot coals into a bucket of water to use again the next day, pouring the heated water into a stone jar to warm their bed, which, folk said, stank of sulphur.

'Before you go,' Reuben said, 'do you know if Baxter has made an approach to anybody else in Grinklegate?'

'Aye, lad,' Jeck Fewster said, 'he's been to see everybody. Of course, you understand, we keep to ourselves and mind our own business along here. He's made 'em all an offer and, so far as I know, they've all accepted.'

When Reuben called on him, Linham agreed that he, too, had accepted. 'I reckon if t'others were offered an arrangement as advantageous as mine, then they'd be fools *not* to accept.'

'You wouldn't tell me what your deal is?' Reuben said desperately. If he knew the details, perhaps that would give him a clue as to how to react.

'Nay, lad, you won't be expecting me to disclose the nature of a private business transaction in advance, now would you? That'd never be sound commercial sense, I think you'll agree?'

Reuben did agree.

Captain Walham invited him in to a parlour more spick and span than any room Reuben had ever seen, with the mahogany furniture polished to a bright gloss, the crystal of the handsome lamps on the mantelpiece glistening even in the early morning light. 'Not disturbing you at breakfast, am I?' Reuben asked diffidently, but the captain laughed.

'What time did you break your fast today, Reuben?' he asked. 'Six o'clock.'

'Then you were half an hour after me, young lad. I've already cleaned the cabins, dug the rose patch, cleaned the windows of the chapel and polished the door knobs. I don't hold with ligging abed! Now, what is it you wanted to see me about? Tell me that first, and then I'll be asking you why it is we never see you in chapel these days. . . !'

'I hear tell that Stanley Baxter is making offers along Grinkle-gate to buy the properties. Has he approached you, and have you agreed to sell?'

This was Reuben's last chance – he feared the reply. If the captain said yes, he knew that would be the end of the matter.

The captain eyed him shrewdly. 'What is that to do with you, Reuben?' he asked. 'What's your interest in the matter?'

Reuben knew he was on sticky ground. The captain was a stickler for preserving his privacy. You could count on one hand the people who'd be welcomed inside his house, and nobody had ever been invited to venture beyond the parlour.

'It has nothing to do with me!' Reuben said, knowing he'd have to put all his cards on the table. 'I've been asked by a few of the people in Newquay Town to find out what's happening – it appears this fellow Baxter is buying property fast as he can lay his hands on it. The folk are afraid they'll lose their houses and, if he pulls down the Yard, their livelihood!'

The captain snorted. 'They haven't had a livelihood there since they let Mark Adam outsmart 'em and lock 'em out on strike. Strike indeed. At sea we used to call it mutiny. And it was punish-able, at the captain's discretion, by keelhauling! They're a lazy lot of devils – who gives a penny damn what happens to 'em?'

'You do,' Reuben said boldly. 'How many of them come to the chapel?'

'Ah, you've got a clever head on your shoulders, and a quick tongue in you, lad! All right, there's no point in tacking about. Yes, Baxter has made an offer. Yes, he has approached me. No, I've not agreed to sell. Not yet.'

Reuben's heart leaped, only to be dashed down by the last two

201

words, which the captain had said after a pause, and with a twinkle in his eyes. 'Not *yet*? Does that mean you're going to accept his offer?'

'Now, that would be *telling*, wouldn't it, lad? You still haven't told me the full story of your interest.'

'Quite simply, captain, I was asked to try to find some way to stop Baxter buying the houses and the Yard.'

'That's simple, lad. Take him out in your boat, and drop him over the side. Wait for him outside the door of the Raven and, when he comes out, fire two barrels of a shotgun into his belly.'

'Nay, captain. Not that way. I'll not be a party to anything illegal!'

'I wondered. It seems to me last time you tried to help the ne'er-do-wells of Newquay Town, a man wound up dead.'

'That wasn't my fault,' Reuben said truculently.

'Reuben lad, all I'm trying to do is make you see you must accept the ultimate responsibility for your own actions. If you take a hand in this matter between Tockett and Baxter, between Baxter and me, between Baxter and the rest of the lily-livered grasping commercial cowards who live here in Grinklegate – you'll see I don't have too high an opinion of my neighbours, Reuben – then you must be prepared for what happens. Are you prepared?'

'Of course I'm prepared,' Reuben said. 'I spoke the truth about Frank Dobbs in the court, didn't I?'

'Aye, you did, lad, and you're to be commended! I went down on my knees when I heard about that. But you might have to be prepared for some rough stuff if you take a hand in this one. . . .'

'What kind of rough stuff, captain?'

'Commercial interests, that's what! Once a man sees a profit on the horizon, he's like a shipwrecked sailor sighting a boat. He gets a lust. Shall I tell you something? We were out in the Pacific Ocean one time, bound for Australia with a cargo of nitrate from Chile. The Pacific is dotted with islands, aye, and shipwrecks. We were blown about all one night and went twenty miles or more off course, running before a hurricane-force wind. When dawn came up and I took a sighting, I saw a tiny island off our beam. We'd had some damage – the mizzen was rent like paper before we could strike it – and I thought to drop the anchor near this island to give us time for a bit of refitting and maintenance. I was looking through the spyglass and saw two men on the shoreline, a-dancing up and down. Well, straight away, I said to my mate, them's two shipwrecked mariners. They'll be pleased to see us, no doubt. You see, we were well off the trade route there on account of the hurricane. . . .'

Reuben was fascinated, as always, by Captain Walham's tales of the sea, but impatient to hear about the sale of Broadholme.

'Now, this is the point I want to make,' Captain Walham said. 'If the two mariners had stayed where they were, we'd have launched the tender for them, and brought them safe aboard. As it was, they couldn't wait. They leaped in the water and started to swim when we were at least two sea miles off. . . .'

'And what happened to them? Did they drown?' Sailors are seldom good swimmers.

'No. Sharks got 'em. Both of 'em. That was shark water. I hope you're not planning to swim through shark water, Reuben!'

Reuben shuddered at Captain Walham's picture of the two men so desperate to be saved that they'd abandoned all caution. 'Nay, Stan Baxter, whatever his faults, is certainly no shark. . . !'

Captain Walham's hand crashed down on the table. 'That's the first lesson you have to learn, my lad!' he thundered. 'In the commercial world, there's sharks and fishes. The fishes gather together for protection, but the sharks eat 'em just the same. Baxter, Tockett, these men are the sharks. And the folks of Newquay Town, even with you to pilot them, are still the fishes.'

'You, Captain Walham, are you a fish or a shark?' Reuben asked innocently.

'I'm neither, lad. I'm outside of it all. Though I'll allow that, if I decide to sell Broadholme to them, folks will brand me as a shark along with the rest. But that won't bother me one little bit. I shall continue as I've always done. I'll keep my trust in the Lord and fear no man. Now, when are we going to see you in the chapel?'

The interview was over. Reuben knew that Captain Walham would not tell his decision to sell or not until he'd informed Baxter. He left Broadholme with a heavy heart and walked slowly up the dock. Naseby was waiting to go out, though the low tide had not yet arrived. Reuben, preoccupied, walked past the three men struggling with the boat.

'Is tha blind or summat?' Naseby bellowed after him.

Reuben didn't hear, but kept on walking.

'Happen he is, and deaf too!' Naseby's eldest lad Percival said.

Reuben walked up the side street leading out of the dock to the patch of grass at the top which overlooked the scaurs. Somebody, ages ago, had dubbed it the Cockpit. From there you could get a good view of the condition of the landing and the ocean beyond. Wives often stood there when their men were coming back in through a storm. He sat on the wooden-slatted iron bench, pondering. What could he do, what could he do? If Captain Walham decided to sell, that would be it. Stanley Baxter would have the whole parcel of land. The folk of Newquay Town would be rendered jobless and homeless. The whole country was in turmoil. While some people were making fortunes abroad, so Reuben had heard, there was growing unemployment throughout the land which the government of Stanley Baldwin was doing little to assuage. Reuben had little interest in politics, and, in general, the folk of Ravenswyke were more interested in local problems than those of the nation. But, if jobs were so scarce throughout the land, where would the men of Newquay Town find work and homes? This rabbit-breeding and odd-jobbing wouldn't keep them going for long – they knew that as well as Reuben. They were all hanging on, waiting for the Yard to open again, making ends meet as best they could. Tockett, for once, was being most understanding, give him credit for that. One or two of them, Reuben knew, had knocked on the rent a week or two and he'd let them work it off in the gardens of Tockett House. Of course, being Tockett, he'd extracted three shillings' work for a one-shilling rent, but you couldn't blame the man for that! But he wouldn't give any man work for cash wages.

Reuben made up his mind swiftly and walked back down past the dock, skirting the Yard, down the shallow hill to the office of the Gas, Light and Coke Company. Tockett, he knew, owned forty per cent of the shares of that company. Nellie Helliwell, Olive's daughter, had got herself a job sitting in the outer office. She was wearing a satin blouse and a long black skirt and her long blonde hair was done up nicely on the top of her head. 'Nellie,' Reuben asked her, 'who's the man really in charge, here?'

'In charge of what? Joe Baker's in charge of the ovens and what you might call the works, but Mr Smithells is the Office Manager. He's the one who talks to the Board when they meet every month.'

'That'll be him. Do you think you could get me in to see him?'

Nellie looked doubtful. 'I don't know,' she said. 'He's a very busy man. Usually, folks that wants to see him writes in first and gets a letter.'

'I don't have the time, Nellie!'

'I'll try,' she said. 'Why don't you take the weight off your feet?'

He sat on the bentwood chair in the outer office while she rose from her seat and went through the half-glazed door behind her. The door was ominously marked in gold lettering, PRIVATE, KEEP OUT.

She was back in three minutes. 'He's asking me, what's it about?' she said.

'Tell him it's very important.'

She went back again and this time came back with her worried frown replaced by a smile. 'He'll see you,' she said, 'but he told me to tell you it's only for five minutes.'

'You told him it was important, then?'

'No! I told him you were a customer who had a gas cooker *and* a gas boiler, like your Eleanor said!'

Smithells was wearing a plain grey cravat, a dark alpaca jacket with shiny elbows, and striped trousers. He'd covered his collar and his cuffs with celluloid and, when Reuben arrived, was busy taking the cuffs out, to place them in the drawer of his sit-down desk. Behind him the three accounts clerks worked standing up at sloping desks, each writing in ledgers that were at least fifteen inches square. Reuben recognized two of them who turned round when he came in. Miles Fordington and Trevor Lennam came from the top of the bank, and had both been educated in Whitby. Both were the sons of sea captains and their ancestors had plied the whaling fleet out of Whitby. Above the front gate of Fordington's house a whale's-jaw arch had been erected.

'What can I do for you?' Smithells asked in the brisk no-non-sense voice of self-important minor functionaries. 'Having trouble with your supply, are you?'

Reuben looked at him. Smithells had not invited him to sit down, though there was a chair placed in front of his desk. How did you tackle a man like Smithells? What arguments, what per-suasion, would reach through his vain pomposity?

'It occurs to me,' he said, 'that the Gas, Light and Coke Company is in for a lot of expense if matters take their present course. I didn't know if you'd been kept informed, as you should have been, about what's happening.'

'Expense? Kept informed? Well, of course, I like to keep abreast of things. Nothing much happens round here that I don't know about!' Smithells said. 'What, particularly, did you have in mind? Is it to do with our loading docks. . . ?'

It was a natural assumption, since no one could mistake Reuben for anything other than a fisherman.

'No!' Reuben said. 'It has to do with your gas main. It strikes me you're going to have to dig it up and bury it somewhere else.'

'Our gas main? What do you mean? Our main is perfectly safe, buried underground.'

Sitting up at the Cockpit, Reuben had suddenly remembered being told when he was a lad that Captain Walham had agreed to let the newly founded Gas, Light and Coke Company dig a channel through his ground to carry the gas main up into Newquay Town. It seemed to him that, if the company knew what was afoot, they might raise some kind of objection.

'Oh, you mean this excellent scheme of Mr Baxter's,' Smithells said. 'Mr Baxter and I have been in consultation,' he said. 'Very forward-looking man, in my opinion. It seems to me that, whatever happens when he starts his scheme, he's going to want a lot of gas. I've told him he can have our full support!'

He looked at Reuben expectantly. Where was this difficulty Reuben Godson had been speaking about? There was no difficulty so far as Smithells could see. If Baxter could shift those paupers, none of whom could afford the new gas appliances or buy any gas from the company, out of Newquay Town, the demand was bound to increase. Why, they might even have to put in another main to cope. Smithells had rosy visions of the future. With doubled, perhaps even trebled, consumption the Board was bound to rate his position more highly. Perhaps, instead of Office Manager, they might even consent to him being called, simply, Manager. Perhaps – but this was a dream – even General Manager! With an appropriate increase of wages, of course! He looked at Reuben interrogatingly. 'Excuse me, Mr Godson, I really don't see that you have any cause, any cause at all, to be worried about your own source of supply. Believe me, the company will not deprive any of its long-standing customers to service this new scheme. We'll maintain the pressure to your house, come what may. You have my word on that,' he added dramatically. 'And now, if you'll excuse me. . . . ? So much work in connection with the new plans. I'm sure you understand. . . ?'

Reuben left the office of the Gas, Light and Coke Company feeling truly beaten, and more depressed than ever before. Oh why had he agreed to try to help them? It truly was no concern of his. He looked out over the water and saw Naseby's coble already fishing. He had enough to worry about, trying to decide about putting an engine in his own coble, and what sort of engine it should be. He had enough to worry about with the steam trawlers out of Whitby and Scarborough scraping the bottom of Ravenswyke Bay so that this year even the crabs were scarce. He had enough to worry about with Eleanor, who wouldn't stir herself in life, but day by day went more into herself and became more potty, more old-maidish. And, finally, he had enough to worry about trying to make up his mind about Emily Duckett. Aye, and Elsie Milner. These days, Emily was hardly polite to him when he went up there and sat with her, or took her out for a bit of a walk across the moor top. Gone was all the former tenderness, and gone was all the sex, too! Now she'd hold his hand if he took hers, and she'd answer his questions, but you could hardly call it a stimulating conversation. And, when they'd sit in the front room, she'd take up her knitting or her sewing, and sit there silent. Sometimes half an hour would go by without either of them speaking a word to each other, him looking into the fire, her knitting, and sometimes he'd catch a fleeting look on her face like that of an animal that has been hurt and carries a pain inside. Sometimes she'd go with him when they had a bit of a social in the church or the chapel hall, and she'd dance with him, but he'd take his chance to drink with his cronies on the ale-bar that was usually set up across a corner of the room, and she'd sit with the girls, chattering away a hundred to a dozen so that, even if the lads had been so inclined, they couldn't have penetrated that aviary of chirping.

And now he had this lot to worry about, on top of everything else!

He'd already missed the tide and there was no one about in the dock to help him launch the *Hope*. He could go knock on a few doors, but that was beneath his dignity. Or so he told himself. In truth, he didn't want to have to make the excuse that he, a Godson of Ravenswyke, for the second time in recent months, had missed the tide. Lig-abed was not a reputation he cared to court.

He knew he'd earn it anyway; on his way up the bank he passed all the gossips; old Mrs Farnham cackled as she walked past him on her way to Johnson's, the grocer.

'Keeps you up late, doesn't she?' she wheezed.

Normally he would have ignored her, but he growled, 'Shut your gob, Mother,' and then was sorry for it. No Godson talks that way, he knew. Mrs Farnham was astounded and brandished her stick at him. 'Did you ever. . . ?' she repeated as she carried on her way.

He met Walter Brackley, the postman, near the turn to Fewster's shop. 'What's all this, then?' Brackley said good-naturedly. 'Taking a holiday, are we?'

'Shut it!'

'By gow, got out of the wrong side this morn and no doubt!'

By Linham's, who should happen along but Harry with his horse and cart, on his weekly journey. 'Now then, lad,' he said, a typical moors greeting.

'Now then, Harry,' Reuben replied, determined to put a good face on things.

Harry stopped the horse, took a plug of tobacco from his pocket, and cut a slice with his knife before rolling it and sticking it in his pipe. 'How's the crabs?' he asked. 'Wouldn't mind a nice bit of fresh crab for me tea?'

'Not a lot about, Harry! But happen I'll save you one next week.'

'You're not out today, then?'

'No, Harry. I've a bit of business to attend to'.

Harry had managed to get his pipe going. 'Aye, there's a lot of business in the air these days. But not much of the cash is getting very far down. Folks is just as hard up as ever. I've been thinking of going to Ameriky.'

Harry had been threatening to go to Ameriky for many a year and, once, had even sold his horse and cart, and his business, and had set off. He'd got as far as York when he changed his mind, came rushing back, and bought his horse and cart back from the

208

purchaser, who stuck a pound on the price 'for the inconvenience'.

'Aye, well, maybe this time when you leave, you'll take me with you?' Reuben suggested.

Harry looked at his troubled face, saw his dejected manner so different from the Godson he knew. 'By gow, Reuben, not got a lass in trouble, has tha?' he asked solicitously.

Reuben laughed. 'Nay, not yet,' he said.

Harry moved closer. 'Tell you summat, Reuben, as I've never told a living soul. The first time I was going to Ameriky, it was for that very reason!'

Reuben laughed. 'Well, what happened? You never got married?'

'Married, me? Nay, that whole business scared me off. It seemed she'd made a mistake and weren't in t'pudding club after all. Women, Reuben, puts the mortal fear into me. I hear as how there aren't too many women in Ameriky. It's mostly cowboys and Indians!'

His encounter with Harry had put Reuben back into good humour and he walked steadily up the bank, whistling part of the way. But soon the one-in-four climb put an end to that! It took a good half-hour to walk the top road to Tockett House along the road that skirted the top of the cliffs by the stretch of land known as Cliff. Soon he saw workmen holding a tripod, and the surveyor using his telescope, which was mounted on a stand. They seemed to be putting poles into the ground, marking out the ground of Cliff into square chunks. Mark Adam was standing there, supervising the work. His car was parked beside the road and the door was open. As Reuben approached, Mark Adam and the surveyor walked to the car and took a drink in silver cups from a silver flask that had been stored in a wickerwork basket on the back seat. As Reuben drew near, the two looked up at him without curiosity, but when it became apparent he was approaching them directly, Mark Adam finished the sandwich he'd been eating, and put down his silver beaker.

He murmured something to the surveyor, something Reuben didn't catch, but he lip-read the words 'a bit of a troublemaker'.

' 'Morning, Mr Tockett,' Reuben said as he stood before them, his feet spread apart, his thumbs tucked into his waistline, his manner respectful but in no way subservient. He saw the white bandage Mark Adam was wearing round his throat.

209

'Good morning, Godson,' Mark Adam said, his voice mumbled no doubt by whatever the bandage covered. 'What can I do for you?'

Reuben paused a moment before dropping his bombshell. 'You can build me a new boat, Mr Tockett, if you've a mind. With a diesel engine in it.'

Reuben had calculated, coming up the hill, that if he sold the *Hope* – and he would, he knew, be able to get a good price for it in Whitby – and added the money they had in the bank, he could just afford to have a new boat built.

Mark Adam tried to laugh, but was unsuccessful. 'Is this some kind of a joke, Godson?' he asked. 'I'm too busy at the moment for humour!'

'No, Mr Tockett. It's not a joke. You've got enough oak in the Yard, and enough beech for the decking!'

'In case you've forgotten, Godson, you were there the day they all walked out of their jobs. I've always thought you had a hand in that! Or,' he added with heavy sarcasm, 'were you planning for me to take off my jacket and build the boat for you single-handed?'

'No, Mr Tockett. If you agree to build me a boat, I'm certain I can talk the men into coming back to work for you. You could have that Yard open and working by the start of next week. Aye, and a new order to get you going again. I'll tell you summat else. I was alongside Liversedge a day or two ago, as sails out of Whitby, and he was saying he's thinking of having a forty-footer built. Happen, if I talk with him, I could swing the order your way! But there'd be no galvanized, mind you. It'd all be copper, in the proper way!'

'You've worked it all out, Godson, have you? You're going to order a boat from me; you're going to act as salesman selling the Yard's services. By the way, how were you planning to pay for the boat? With baskets of fish. . . ?'

Reuben would not be provoked, he told himself, by the sneer with which Mark Adam accompanied this witticism, the glance at the surveyor to make certain he appreciated the humour.

'In the usual way, Mr Tockett. I'll be giving you five hundred when you take the order, five hundred when the hull is finished, and the rest on delivery.'

'It's going to be an expensive craft, then?'

'Mr Tockett, it's going to be the best boat that's ever been built on this stretch of coast. It's going to be a showpiece, one that'll make your name as a boat-builder one to be reckoned with. I reckon, if we get it right, that boat could bring prosperity back to the Ravenswyke Yard, and to the people who'd go there to work. I've made a drawing of the boat I'd like. When you see it, you'll know what I mean. There's never been a boat like it, never!' And there never had. Reuben had laboured for hours with his pencil on a sheet of brown paper, drawing lines, rubbing them out, drawing them in again, using all his practical seagoing experience to design a fishing boat that would be perfect to work, easy to sail, easy to berth, and could take engine or sail. There wasn't a boat on that part of the ocean he hadn't studied in detail, milking out the best bits, working out methods, rejecting improvements he wasn't convinced would work.

But the sneer hadn't gone from Tockett's face. 'It's a charming idea, Godson, the thought that one boat, one boat by your design, could bring back the prosperity of an entire community. But it ignores the fact that you would understand if you knew a bit more about the ways of the world, especially the modern world, as I do, that a place like Ravenswyke is finished if it tries to rely on local craft. Boat-building, fishing, coaling, all those seaborne crafts, are things of the past, Godson. Lads like you, dropping a bit of line over the side of a boat, are an anachronism, out of date, dead, finished. Why, the boats out of Hull can go to the North Sea fishing grounds and they can match, in one scoop, more than you'll ever see in a lifetime. Take my advice, Godson. Go away and learn a respectable trade, before it's too late. It's too late for the Yard, and that's certain. We're in the process of selling it; we've shaken hands on a contract and even you must realize what that means. And now, if you'll excuse us, we were taking a bite when you interrupted us!'

He turned his back on Reuben, bent inside the hamper, and handed a sandwich to the surveyor. 'This French white wine is rather jolly, isn't it?' he said. 'Would you believe, the peasants round here used to smuggle it?'

As one of the 'peasants', Reuben wanted to reach in, spin Mark Adam round, and smash a fist into his sneering face. But he knew that would do no good. He turned on his heel and walked quickly away, back towards the road junction. He'd been certain, so damned cocksure certain, that Mark Adam would accept his offer, be grateful for it. They could have worked together on the boat. It would have redressed the balance, restored the good name the Ravenswyke Yard once had when James Henry took an interest in it. It would have been the best bloody coble....

As he turned the dog-leg going down the hill, where the stone still showed the scrape of Stanley Baxter's motor-car, he met Jean Dobbs. 'Oh, missis,' he said, 'I wish you hadn't asked me to take a hand in this business. I've racked my brains, trying to work summat out, but I've failed, I'm afraid, I've failed....' His voice tailed away when he saw the joy on her face.

'You'd better get yourself down and see Captain Walham,' she said. 'Tha hasn't failed, Reuben, tha hasn't. And us'll be eternally grateful to you, eternally in your debt.'

She hurried on into the shop, buying produce for the hotel. Mystified, he hastened down the hill. Before he could knock on the door of Broadholme it was flung open. 'Come in, Reuben,' Captain Walham said. 'Mr Baxter's just leaving....'

Baxter was standing in the parlour door. 'You're sure you...'

'Good-day to you, Mr Baxter!' Captain Walham said firmly. 'Give my respects to your lady. We are more than pleased to see anybody, *anybody*, in the chapel, you know. Remember St Luke, chapter fifteen, verse seven; aye, come to think of it, St Luke, chapter fourteen, verse eleven, might interest you.'

'I'm afraid I have so little time for such frivolities, captain,' Stanley Baxter said, trying to clutch his tattered dignity more tightly about himself as he stormed out of the house.

'What's all that St Luke business, captain?' Reuben asked as they entered the parlour.

'You, too, should read your Bible, lad. St Luke, chapter fifteen, verse seven, says, "joy shall be in heaven over one sinner that repenteth, more than over ninety and nine just persons, which need no repentance"! If Baxter and that young lady are married, I'll eat my sextant!'

'And that other bit?'

'Don't you know *anything* about the Bible, Reuben?' Captain Walham asked in mock exasperation. 'You'll have cause to remember St Luke, chapter fourteen, verse eleven, all your life, because it was only when *I* remembered it that I decided what to do about Broadholme. "For whosoever exalteth himself shall be

212

abased; and he that humbleth himself shall be exalted." That's what St Luke said. I was toying with the idea of exalting myself to look down on Ravenswyke and the ocean from the cliffs above. The sea has been a friend and provider all my days, Reuben. That's why I bought Broadholme and settled here, to be by her side, to hear her voice, be it raging in the storm or silently murmuring in the night. Happen you'll think I'm being a bit fanciful but, sitting here, I still feel joined with the sea. Why should I want to move up to the top of the bank among all those purse-proud and falsely exalted, long-nosed folk? It was you, Reuben, gave me the key to this.'

'Me?' Reuben asked. 'How?'

'Because you *humbled* yourself, Reuben, to come here at break of day, to anchor the irascible old sea-dog – I know my reputation – in his cabin and plead the cause of your fellow men. I'm not selling, lad, not now, not ever. I shall be here for the rest of my days, you can be assured of that. Now, when are you coming to chapel?'

'On Sunday,' Reuben said, with a sparkle to his eye. 'I want to read this St Luke, see if you got it right!'

When Reuben arrived at the dock the following morning, Batty was standing by the slip looking out to sea. 'That's a good thing you've done for us, Reuben,' he said. 'Happen they'll open the Yard again, now!' Reuben could sense how dispirited Batty was and, acting on good-humoured impulse, he said, 'Come on, I'll take thee out!'

Bill Brawnham and his son Mark were preparing to launch their coble; as Reuben walked forward, Walter Clegg and his son Billy shuffled down the lane in their sea-boots. 'Grand day,' Walter said. 'Us'll do well today.'

Bill Brawnham looked daggers at him; no fisherman likes tempting fate by predicting what the day will bring. 'Happen it'll blow up over t'Top,' he said darkly. 'There was enough cloud about, earlier.'

Reuben looked at Batty. 'Well,' he said, 'make up your mind. Are you coming? If you are, give us a hand. But, I warn you, if you're going to spew, make sure it goes over the side, downwind!'

Reuben was in bounding spirit, filled with cheerful good

213

humour. Now, with one problem solved, he could at least forget that and get on with his major interest, fishing, confident that the other minor problems he faced would eventually sort themselves out.

It *was* a grand day for fishing. They carted each coble in turn down to the water across the firm sand strip to the horseshoe landing that always formed at low tide. Brawnham was first off, his new diesel engine chugging nicely, though he'd gone red-faced turning the handle that whirled the weighty flywheel. Clegg looked contemptuously at him as he started his petrol motor with a quick flick of the starting handle.

Reuben held his nose as he went off, his sail set wide with the offshore wind behind him. 'What with these engines, and the gasworks behind us, the place is getting to be a midden.'

'Hold on,' Batty said. 'Who's that shouting at us?'

Reuben looked to the right where the arm of the scaur stretched out to sea. Standing on the scaur, waving his arms, he could distinguish a figure wearing a thick sweater knitted in the traditional Ravenswyke pattern, the sort Mrs Humble, one of the residents of Grinklegate, sold in her shops in Newquay Town and Whitby. The man was wearing thick black tweed trousers, heavy boots, and had a large cap pulled so low down on his forehead that Reuben couldn't see his features. He couldn't recognize the man, but knew there was something familiar about him. The only reason to stop a fisherman sailing out of harbour would be to tell him of an emergency, or to alert him of some local condition that may have escaped him. Reuben pushed his tiller to the left, then as he came just past the flat scaur on which the man was standing, he gybed the *Hope* around so that its gunwale touched neatly alongside. The man lifted his cap.

'Oh, it's you,' Reuben said, recognizing Baxter who'd obviously been to Mrs Humble and had said, 'Kit me out as a fisherman.'

'Yes, Reuben. I thought I might come out with you today, and learn how it's done. I'll bet you can teach me a thing or two, eh? Of course, I'll make it worth your while financially. I expect a few shillings extra won't come amiss, eh?'

Reuben was dumbstruck, unable to believe his ears. '*You* want me to take you out with *me*?' he asked incredulously.

'Yes. I see you have Mr Batsford with you. You can probably

214

use an extra pair of hands.' Baxter stepped out with one foot, and placed it on the gunwale.

'Tell you what you do,' Reuben said slowly and clearly. 'You take those few extra shillings, hold 'em tight in that extra pair of hands, and slowly shove them as far as you can get them up your arse-hole! This is a fishing boat, not a midden!' He brought the bow over; the wind caught the bow and swung it round, widening the gap between the boat and the scaur. It was a toss-up whether Baxter would try to hold on with his right foot and jump aboard, or step back on to the safety of dry land on his left foot. Or, of course, split his body from stem to stern. The boom solved the problem for him by swinging round in the wind, catching his midriff and hurling him arse first into the water. By the time he climbed back on to the scaur, the *Hope of Ravenswyke* was already a hundred yards out to sea. Looking back, Reuben caught the flash of a telescope lens from the porthole-like window of Captain Walham's top room and couldn't resist shaking his hand above his head in a victory salute.

Baxter emerged from the water and climbed on to the scaurs in time to see the gesture and mark it as a sign of defiant derision. He held his fist above his head, too, and shook it angrily before he turned and stomped away across the scaurs towards the Raven Hotel.

Batty was shaking his head. He, too, thought Reuben was shaking his fist at Baxter. 'Nay, lad,' he said, 'but I think tha's made a mistake there. He nobbut wanted to be friendly and come out for a day's fishing. Tha could have explained that it's not the Old Quaytown way to take passengers. But tha's made an enemy there, mark my words!'

'And tha's supposed to be looking over yon baskets, to make sure as the lines have been laid properly, and the hooks baited secure,' Reuben said, imitating his broad vowels but without malice. 'If tha's going to be a mate o' mine, tha's got to learn to do t'right thing at t'right time! And this is the time we check the lines.'

'I thought we were going out for the pots!'

'Well, you thought wrong, didn't you, *mate*!'

'Aye aye, *skipper*!'

'That's better!' Both were playing a pantomime they couldn't support. Batty looked at Reuben's face, Reuben looked at Batty's, and suddenly they both dissolved in helpless laughter. 'Did you see his face?' Batty said, laughter tears streaming down his cheeks. 'First as his feet went wider apart – I swear I thought he was going to split from top to bottom. . . !'

'Aye, but did you see the way he looked when the boom came round and smashed him in the belly, and him waving his arms around like Punch and Judy?'

The sound of their laughter echoed across the stillness of the ocean until they were over the fishing grounds and Batty had to control himself to lean over and grasp the buoy. As it was, a last-minute uncontrollable chortle nearly pitched him clear over the side.

The lamps that had been hung in the trees and shrubs around the house spread a twinkling carpet of fairy lights, inviting one out into the balmy September night. As the couples walked across the lawns, leaving the sound of the band behind them, their voices added a graceful note to the night air. Occasionally there'd be the bright tinkle of a girl's laughter, the swish of a girl's taffeta ball-gown, the rustle of petticoats. The walks were dotted with the flash of light-coloured dresses against the dark of men's tailcoats, the white of their collars and cuffs. Occasionally a waft of cigar smoke would hang on the air, and an agreeable whiff of an exotic perfume. Hester Gramond and Mark Adam Tockett stood on the first-floor balcony, looking out across the grounds of the Manor, their shadows cast on the stone balustrade by the bright lights behind them. He held a glass of champagne in his hand; she had put her glass of port on the silver tray the waiter had placed on the flat balustrade top for their convenience.

'It's a dream world, Mark Adam,' she said.

'And you, the perfect fairy to flit through it!' he said gallantly, raising his glass to her. She was, in truth, a delicious morsel. In her peach-coloured taffeta dress, wearing her rope of green emeralds around her tender neck, her black hair gleaming elegantly and set in demure curls around her face like an aureole, she looked exquisitely young, virginal and pure. He was reminded of a painting he'd seen of a young girl reading a book, standing by a tree, with a dog sitting waiting behind her. For the life of him, though he'd puzzled his mind about it all evening, he couldn't remember the name of the artist or where he'd seen it.

She uttered the social, deprecatory, 'Oh, la-la, Mark Adam,' but he could see she was pleased by his compliment. And yet, in ways he couldn't understand, she'd been somewhat withdrawn since they'd left the ballroom of the Manor, to walk up here for a breath of air. With all the bustle of the hunt ball, the boisterous Scottish dances, the waltzes and polkas, both had felt a need to get out to somewhere cool and quiet, to think and to talk.

They walked along the terrace to the corner, where a large stone urn containing varieties of upright and trailing fuchsias made something of a screen with a seat beyond. He went to brush the seat with his handkerchief, but a thoughtful servant had already placed a travelling rug on which they could sit.

'Do you object to my smoking a cigar, Hester?' he asked courteously.

'Lord, no!' she said. 'Sometimes, I warn you, I even take a puff at one myself!'

'Hester!' he said, pretending to be shocked, but vastly amused by the thought of this slender young morsel with a Havana clamped between her delicate lips.

Mark Adam was a sybarite. He enjoyed pleasure inordinately, especially when it was allied with beauty. To dismiss Mark Adam as a homosexual was a grave error – he would have enjoyed being with a race-horse if it were a beautiful one. He could see no reason to restrict his sexual pleasures to members of the *opposite* sex; to love a beautiful boy, to make love with a beautiful boy, was, to him just as desirable, just as pleasurable, as to make love to a pretty girl. And, let's face it, he'd often said to himself and his hedonistic friends in London, how many young boys' faces, lips, bodies, are indistinguishable from those of a young girl. Only later, when the girl began to grow breasts and the boy's parts to extend, did the differences become more apparent. Hester Gramond had passed the adolescent stage; her breasts had grown and her features had set in a delicious feminine mould. Untouched by apparent artifice, which may have been the greatest artifice of all, her face was open, her eyes bold, her lips a delicious cherry red that exerted a magnetic effect on his mouth.

'You are commanding much of my time these days,' Hester said to him with a quick glance. She cast her eyes down again to her hands, folded on her lap.

'It is no accident, Hester, I can assure you of that!'

217

'Do you intend to continue to command my time?' she asked quietly. 'I know you'll think me forward in saying such a bold thing, but I have to know.'

'Are you asking my intentions, Hester?' he said, a smile on his lips.

'Dear me, no. That wouldn't be proper, that wouldn't be proper at all,' she said. Her face lifted slightly; her eyes looked impishly in his direction and belied her protestations of propriety.

'We've known each other since the early summer, Hester,' he said gravely. 'Now it is the early autumn. I would like to marry you in the early spring!'

'Oh dear!' she said colouring slightly but not actually blushing. 'Are you so sure, Mark Adam, that you want to *marry* me? I had thought that perhaps you were seeking a companion, a dancing partner, perhaps, even a friend?'

'I want you to marry me. I want to be married, with you, Hester,' he said firmly.

'Are you saying, Mark Adam, that you *love* me?' she whispered. He leaned forward so that his lips were brushing her ear framed in curls. He paused for a long moment, ordering his words to express his thoughts. 'Hester,' he began diffidently, 'we must never be false with each other. We must never lie, never exaggerate, never change our words to suit the occasion. Please try to understand what I say exactly. I want to marry you. I want to spend my life with you. I find that you and I are exactly compatible, and can totally complement each other. I derive more pleasure from being with you than I would ever have thought possible. You are beautiful beyond words and I want beauty about me, for ever!'

'But you don't *love* me?' she whispered.

'I don't yet know what is *love*,' he said. 'Truthfully, I don't yet know how one crosses the boundary between total admiration, total desire, and *love*. I know I will learn that, if only you will agree to marry me! Will you, Hester? Oh, please say you will let me speak to your father tomorrow!'

Now it was her turn to be silent, to think about what he'd said. He pulled his head back until he could see her profile. He didn't hurry her, didn't importune her. Finally she turned and looked into his eyes. 'You've been very honest with me,' she said, 'and I thank you for that. Thank God that, since the war, people have begun to speak more freely and frankly with each other about their thoughts.'

'You're very emancipated,' he said, using the word that seemed to be on everyone's lips since women secured the right to vote in 1918.

'Don't worry. I'm not thinking of going into politics!' she said, smiling for the first time since he'd begun to speak to her. 'May I give you your answer tomorrow?' she pleaded. 'I'll tell you what. Come to Maisie's to tea tomorrow, and I'll tell you then. How's that?'

'That will be capital!' he said warmly. 'Simply splendid! Now, shall we dance again?'

'No,' she said, 'if you don't mind, I'd like you to take me home. I have much to think about before I see you tomorrow!'

Maisie de Peybeau-Scargill could not have lived in the manner she did had her mother not been a French countess and her father a Yorkshire ship-owner of such known wealth that he was above local susceptibilities. As a young man, John Foster Scargill had taken the Grand Tour in style, encountering on the way the widow of the Comte de Peybeau, whom he promptly married and brought back to Yorkshire at the end of his two years' world trip.

The local people, especially those with eligible daughters, had been scandalized at first, but the countess soon won them over. When she gave birth a couple of years later to a daughter, she had won their esteem completely, and Maisie was born into the top echelons of a wealthy society. When Maisie, to whose surname the name de Peybeau had been added with a hyphen, was twenty her father and mother, cruising in the family steam yacht, were both drowned when the yacht hit one of the mines left over from the war and sank with all hands within sight of Scarborough.

Maisie, of course, inherited everything and became possibly the wealthiest lady in the district. And the most sought after. Though she had more suitors than she knew what to do with, she was serious with all of them and none of them. She maintained a house in Berkeley Square in London and the family seat on the moors overlooking Danby, in North Yorkshire, and applied herself, with enormous energy, to the pursuit of pleasure. She was the first to wear a short skirt, to dance the Charleston, to show her knickers in her wild and exaggerated steps. She was the first to smoke a cigarette in public through a long holder, to wear a cloche hat, to drink cocktails, to swear! Her absolute gesture of contempt and dismissal was to refer to someone as 'a drag'.

Scargill Hall, Danby, became the local rendezvous for all that was modern in that most modern of eras, the years after the Great War. The drinks bill would have supplied gas for a modest town, the food consumed would have served the army in the Crimea. Scargill Hall was the first local building to have complete electricity; day and night, it throbbed with expended energy, noise, gramophone music, and the new sounds of jazz that were emanating from the wireless.

And at the centre of it all Maisie de Peybeau-Scargill twirled the most, drank the most, ate the most, talked the most, and laughed until she had to flop, each early morning, into exhausted sleep.

Her one true friend was Hester Gramond. What the two ever saw in each other no one could tell. Hester was a quiet English North-Country beauty, with a keen sense of humour but a firm sense of propriety. On any other person, the clothes she wore would have been dismissed by Maisie as 'a drag'. For anyone else to refuse a drink as often as she did would have been 'a drag', or to push a laden plate away. Perhaps it was that old and well-tried formula, the attraction of opposites. Or perhaps it was Maisie's certain knowledge that, whatever she did, in whatever scandal she involved herself, however often she fell down completely drunk, sated, exhausted, sometimes sick from her overindulgences, Hester would be there to pick up the pieces, never judging, never condemning, never reforming.

Maisie agreed to Hester's request at once. Lights glinted in her eyes. 'Don't tell me you're coming to life at last, *ma chérie*?' she said.

'That's none of your affair, Maisie!' Hester said firmly, and Maisie recognized that iron barrier she knew she mustn't cross if she were to keep Hester's friendship.

Mark Adam could hear the sounds of the gramophones as he approached the door of Scargill Hall, set in its hundred acres of parkland, the following afternoon. He'd hung about all day in a fit of anticipation, had wanted to delay his arrival until the more respectable hour of 4.15, but had been unable to stay away after four o'clock. He parked his Morris among the several other similar cars in the drive, the de Dion Boutons, the Bentleys. Music blared at him from the long windows of the library to the right of the heavily porticoed door; other music came from the drawing room to the left. The door was flung open by a man he didn't recognize.

'Maisie's somewhere around,' he said vaguely. 'Library, I think.' His collar was crumpled; his eyes stared owlishly as he sipped a drink from a conical glass in the bottom of which lurked a red cherry, an olive *and* an onion.

Mark Adam walked past him. Maisie's guests were something to accept, if you accepted Maisie herself. He found her in the library, winding the gramophone, which was playing the inevitable dance tune. He presented himself to her; she lurched into him smelling of tobacco, alcohol and strong perfume. He was shocked by her appearance; he hadn't seen her for months and was staggered by the lines that ran from the corners of her eyes, the coarseness of her skin. Maisie de Peybeau-Scargill had never been a ravishing beauty, but she'd always made up in vivacity what she lacked in looks. Certainly her money made her attractive to a large number of people. In a word, to Mark she looked *sodden*, sodden with food and drink, with the endless roundel of enforced gaiety. He was sorry, and somewhat displeased, to locate Hester in such surroundings. He greeted Maisie as civilly as he could in the circumstances, but her eyes hardened as she realized he was being no more than perfunctorily polite with her. After her attempts to entice him to food, to a cocktail, had failed, she said sharply to him, 'Mark Adam, you are on the verge of becoming a drag, I suspect. The Lord knows how you've changed since those days in St James's when, at least, you did have a little *something* about you, though no *girl* of my acquaintance knew what it was! Hester is taking her tea in the cottage. She asked me to direct you there, though for the life of me I can't think why if you're going to bore her as much as you're beginning to bore me! Now, light my cigarette, and be off with you!'

He looked coolly at her. 'Why, Maisie,' he said, 'you're beginning to sound like you look. Alas, I don't carry *matches* about with me, but I'm certain any *servant* could satisfy you!'

He turned on his heel and walked swiftly out of the room, knowing, but not caring, that he had perhaps made an implacable foe but determined to seek out Hester and take her out of that hornets' nest as soon as possible.

The cottage was a folly Maisie's mother had had built. Set at the edge of a copse far away from the main house in the grounds, a place where she could be alone with her books, her harpsichord, her thoughts, it was a one-storey building, more what the French would have called a *pavillon*, with a long vista across a sweeping pasture to the moors beyond. Now the pasture was dotted with sheep as Mark Adam drove across it, but he saw the welcoming plume of smoke which rose from its chimney. He parked the car to the side and walked round the gravel to the pavilion's main entrance, climbed the three steps, and crossed the paving in front of the French windows. His brow wrinkled in puzzlement as he heard the sounds of music coming from within, a popular waltz of the day whose name he didn't know, played on a scratchy record on a gramophone. He stood in front of the window, unable to see inside since the curtains were drawn across that side of the cottage, and knocked. He heard the voice from within. 'Come in,' Hester said. 'It's open.'

He went through the door, shutting it behind him. The room beyond was in darkness except for the crackling flames of a large log fire, some six feet across, in a fireplace that had been installed in the centre of the back wall. Beside the fire were two inglenooks and in front of it, with its back towards him, was a large sofa.

'Come in,' Hester said impatiently, and he saw her head appear above the sofa's back. He strode across the room and found her sitting on the sofa, her legs tucked up beside her. The record came to an end and the gramophone started to click rhythmically. 'Turn the record over,' she said, 'and let's hear the other side.'

'Must we?' he asked petulantly. 'They had nothing but music up at the house.'

'Oh, a bit of music helps pass the time,' she said. 'Turn it over, there's a dear.' There was no mistaking the sharp command in her voice, the underlying steel.

'Well, if that's what you want,' he said. He walked to the grand cabinet by the fireplace, opened its top, stopped the green-baize-covered wheel with his finger, and flipped the record over. He reached to the side of the machine, found the handle, and wound the spring until it was tight. 'At least let me close the doors,' he urged, then pushed both of them together to diminish the sound coming down the interior horn and escaping into the room. This side, too, was a waltz – he recognized the rhythm but not the tune as he walked back to the sofa.

Hester, too, was wearing what had become the standard uniform of the 'flapper', the enlightened young lady of the 1920s, a dress so short it revealed her knickers, thin white stockings and high-heeled shoes, a band round her forehead and a multistranded string of small beads hanging round her neck. She was wearing very dark lipstick, and her eyes had been made up. Her hair had been frizzed. He thought she looked awful, though he said nothing as he took his seat beside her.

'I thought it would be a gas to have our tea alone here,' she said, 'unless you'd like a White Lightning!'

He turned on the sofa to look at her. 'All right, Hester,' he said. 'I like a joke, but what is this all about?' He reached his hand forward to take hers.

She evaded him by jumping off the sofa. She went quickly to the gramophone and flipped off the record, replacing it with another whose rhythm he also recognized. He also knew the tune. 'Everybody's doing it,' it was called. 'Come on, Mark Adam,' she said. 'You can Charleston, can't you?'

Very well, he thought, if that was the way she wanted to play. 'Of course I can,' he said. 'I have all the social graces.' He stood in front of her, waited for the break in the rhythm, and then started to flap his lower legs about in time to the music. He was, it turned out, a rather deft dancer. The dance grew wilder and wilder but still he maintained it, throwing himself into all the dance's subtleties with considerable verve. When the record ended, he stepped quickly to the gramophone and turned it over to play the other side. Again they danced, clapping their hands, 'vo-di-oh-doh'-ing as if they were the centre of attraction of a ballroom of people.

When that record was over, he quickly chose another, which turned out to be a Viennese waltz. He spun her round the floor, eight times clockwise, eight times anticlockwise, whirling her in ever tighter circles until she was gasping for breath. But he would give her no stay; he turned that record over, too, to another Viennese waltz, and whirled her round in that one, too, now using the whole room as a dance floor, swirling around the sofa before the fire, round the numerous enormous deep chairs with which the room was dotted. It was a salon of comfort and repose but on that afternoon they turned it into a battleground, on which each strove to triumph over the other in the energy of dancing, the tightness of turns, the fleetness of foot, and the depravity of the abandonment of each's wild expressiveness. For Hester, who gritted her teeth resolutely, it was a marathon she seemed desperate to run, almost a competition, an examination she was determined to pass with flying colours. Her upper lip was wet but her eyes lost none of their lustre. Her cheeks were flushed but roselike in their heightened colour rather than red with effort.

Both heard the dip in the music's key as the clockwork spring began to run down, and now the music began to sound so comic that both began to chuckle. He manoeuvred her round the room in a decaying tempo, still keeping time to the failing music, but when the gramophone finally expired and the needle stuck into the groove in blissful silence, they found themselves, as if by accident, alongside the seat of the sofa. She clasped both his hands tight and fell backwards on to the cushions, pulling him down on top of her. She released his hands but fastened hers behind his head, drawing his lips to hers and kissing him hungrily. He responded instantly and crushed his lips against hers in ardent passion. As he lay there, he felt her body beneath his hands and clasped her breast, feeling it flattened beneath the constraint of the garment fashionable at the time, which reduced girls to apparent flat-chestedness. She writhed beneath him, not content with his putting his hand on her breast but seeking to rub herself beneath him. He felt an enormous shock as suddenly the tip of her tongue went into his mouth and began to caress the tip of his tongue wildly; now her mouth was wide open and he could feel the warm moist sweetness of her breath. She pulled her mouth away from his. 'Quick,' she said, 'take off all your clothes!'

She wriggled from beneath him and began to tear at the buttons of her dress, impatient to remove it. He eyed her for a brief moment in amazement, astounded by her seeming experience and wantonness, but then he quickly did as he was commanded. When he was naked, she lay along the sofa beside him, and he drew her to him and kissed her again. Now there seemed to be less urgency, less immediacy, as if, now that each was assured of the outcome of their voyage, they could take more time over the journey. He kissed her eyes, her delightful nose, her mouth, the sweet hollow of her neck, the nipples of her breasts. Neither spoke, as if consumed by what they were doing. She reached down and grasped his body, running her fingers through his pubic hair until she found him. Already he was hard and as her hand closed over him she gave a deep sigh. He had found her, moist and delicate, tender as an unopened rosebud. He lifted his body and she opened her legs wide so that he could lie between them. She could feel him hard against the outside of her, hard and thrusting. He lifted his hands, placed each beside her face, and gently held her cheeks, raising his shoulders so that he could look into her eyes. 'You're sure you want to do this, Hester?' he asked tenderly. 'You're sure?'

'Yes, please,' she whispered. 'I want you to make love to me.'

He tried to enter her, and was unsuccessful. He used his hand to open her wider, and again was unsuccessful. Patiently, he stroked her, kissing her lips, nibbling them, rubbing his well-haired chest across the nipples which stood out so proud from her breasts. He used his fingers gently to open her, partly inserting himself, and then pushed slowly and delicately, sliding himself into her with all the care he could command, even though, now fully aroused, he felt like ramming himself like a piston, deep inside her. Now she was moaning and then, as he felt himself go inside, he looked at her face and saw the tears in the corners of her eyes. 'I'm hurting you,' he said. 'I didn't want to hurt you.'

'It doesn't matter,' she said.

He started to withdraw himself but she clutched her arms around him. 'No, don't stop. Don't go away,' she said.

His voice was broken as he said, 'Darling Hester, I can't bear to hurt you.'

'You must,' she said, 'you must!'

So, resolutely, since she seemed to want him to continue so desperately, he began to move inside her, thrusting himself slowly into her, withdrawing slowly. She bent her knees and that seemed to ease the pain for her. Now he could see that she, too, was becoming as excited as he was, and she was breathing slowly and more deeply, as he was, and then he knew that neither of them could stop. Now he was kissing her and rubbing one hand across her breasts, supporting his weight on his elbow, and she started to moan again, but this time the sound was different. Now he knew that he, at least, was approaching a climax and he remembered suddenly that he had used no protection. 'Hester,' he said, 'I have to come.'

'Come,' she said, 'please come. Inside me. Deep inside me.'

When she said that, he knew he couldn't withdraw from her, and the pace of his thrusting increased until all the activity became a blur, until her mouth on his, her tongue on his, his hand on her breast and the indescribable feeling of himself deep inside her became one ecstatic sensation from which the blinding spurt of his orgasm, the repeated muscular spasm as he continued to come, feeling as if all his nature were being pumped out of him, became a relief of a height he had never known before.

He lay on her, his diminished manhood flabby but still contained within her. She was wet with perspiration, as he himself was, but her eyes were shining up at him, her hands were pressing against his sides, her mouth was part open as if to permit her to breathe. 'Mark Adam,' she said. It was a paean of love.

'Now answer my question,' he said. 'Are you going to marry me?'

'You bet I am!' she said.

They lay side by side, he looking into the fire's flames, she looking at him, seeing the fire's reflection in his eyes. They didn't speak for a long while, each conscious of the other's breathing returning more and more to normal.

'You arranged this, you minx,' he said finally, turning to her.

She was smiling smugly. 'Yes, I did,' she said. 'Is that so bad?'

His face was troubled. 'Why?' he asked.

'Oh, you asked me a question and I wanted to give you the answer here,' she said offhandedly. He reached out and seized her wrist, turned, and placed his other hand beneath her shoulders. Now his eyes blazed with something other than sexual passion and, for a moment, she felt frightened. He pushed her hand down his body until her fingers felt his pubic hairs again, until she was touching him again. Now he was wet and sticky, soft and flabby. She mistook his purpose and opened her hand, holding him. Then she began to rub him, slowly, and felt him harden almost instantly beneath her touch. When he was hard, he took her hand away, stood up from the sofa and towered above her, his manhood sticking out in front of him. She turned quickly until she was sitting on the sofa. Something in his eyes frightened her, some new expression she'd never seen before. 'Look at it,' he said, his voice harsh and unkind, 'look at it!'

She did as he told her. Seen like this it was a fearsome-looking object. She remembered, as a young child, seeing her brother in his bath. Sometimes her brother's would harden and stick out and they'd all joke about it, but it was nothing like this. She had nothing with which to compare it, of course. Mark Adam was the first man she'd ever seen naked, though she had seen paintings and statues and knew what men looked like. But she'd never seen a painting or statue that looked like this. She was drawn towards it, fascinated. As she moved forward, so Mark Adam moved forward slowly until she was near enough to kiss it. She thought she probably would have done so, too, if he hadn't suddenly turned and flung himself on the sofa beside her. 'Why, Hester?' he asked. 'And this time remember what I said to you last night. We must never lie to each other. We must never be false with each other. Why *did* you *arrange* this? And tell me the truth!'

She hugged her arms about herself, left the sofa, and sat in the inglenook, still hugging herself as if she were cold. Her hair was disarranged and the frizziness seemed to have gone out of it. He thought how petite, tender and vulnerable she looked. When she started to speak her voice was so low he could hardly hear her. 'When you started to come to see me,' she said, 'it was all right. I thought you wanted a friend. I liked you, you were courteous and, unlike some of the young men from around here, you were cultured and amusing. But then, when you started to command my time, when you asked me out so frequently I had no time to spare for other friends, people started to hint things to me. I didn't understand, at first, what they were saying, but then Maisie eventually spelled it out for me. She said you were not normal. That you were not – how can I say it? –normal. . . .'

'She said I was a sodomite!' he said cruelly, supplying the word she couldn't bring herself to use.

Now she was crying but he could not be merciful. 'She said I was a sodomite who would never be able to be a complete husband to you, who would have his disgusting affairs with men, who would eventually end his days in prison, or in a lonely hotel room, spurned by society. She probably referred to Oscar Wilde. . . .'

Hester couldn't speak for the tears, but nodded her head.

He went across the room and sat beside her, but didn't touch

227

her, didn't obey his instinct to put his arm around her and comfort her. 'Listen to me, Hester,' he said. 'I promised last night not to lie to you, not to be false with you. What Maisie de Peybeau-Scargill told you was true!'

She lifted her head instantly, stared at the couch on which they'd made love. 'True,' she said. 'How can it be *true*!' The last word was wrung from her.

'I *was* a sodomite,' he said, punishing himself with the use of the word but determined to leave no uncertainty in her mind. He looked down and smiled at where his erection had been. 'But I am one no longer!'

'I *was* a virgin until this afternoon!' she said. 'But I am one no longer!'

He gathered her into his arms and hugged her. 'Then it's all right, Hester?' he asked. 'It's all right?'

'I love you, Mark Adam,' she said. 'I want to be your wife! I want to be married with you. And I never want us to speak about the past again!'

He could find no words to express his feelings. He scooped her from the inglenook, carried her over and placed her full length on the sofa. He went behind the sofa and pushed it nearer the fire, then flung a couple of logs in the basket. There was a shower of sparks, one of which landed on his chest and he brushed it off, howling in mock pain. Then he flung himself down on the sofa beside her.

Half an hour later, both heard the footsteps on the stone of the paving outside the door and heard Maisie's voice calling, 'Hester, Hester? Are you all right?'

Hester looked up at him, then grabbed him round the waist. 'Don't stop,' she said. He was outraged by the thought initially, but then smiled. They heard the door open, the swish of Maisie's feet across the carpet. When Maisie appeared behind the sofa and looked down, she saw Mark Adam's buttocks rising up and down. 'Oh, Maisie!' Hester said. 'Don't be a drag – do leave us in peace! Can't you see that Mark Adam is *fucking* me!'

Emily Duckett sat in the scullery behind the kitchen of their house with tears running down her face, contemplating, or so she thought, the ruins of her life. For four whole days and evenings, she'd seen neither hide nor hair of Reuben. She assumed he was busy! He seemed to get himself so involved these days in other folks' affairs. But she'd just learned, when she went to the shops, that Reuben had been seen going into, and coming out of hours later, Elsie Milner's. 'And we all know what goes on in there!' old Mrs Farnham had said to her with a leer. 'I've seen her, time and again, standing on t'doorstep in her nightie saying good-bye to the men she's been keeping company with!'

The thought of her Reuben *keeping company* with Elsie Milner brought a fresh flood of tears from her eyes and she sat with her head bowed and let the drops run off her face uncaring into her pinnie.

Her mother had gone to Whitby; there was no one to whom she could confide her tragedy. Once she'd been able to talk to Eleanor Godson but these days Eleanor was that strange, as if she'd been tapped by spirits – nobody could get any sense out of her. Deep sobs racked Emily Duckett. She'd given everything, everything, to Reuben Godson. Well, not quite everything, thank God. She was still a virgin. She could understand a man couldn't be with his woman all the time. He had to go out fishing, according to the time of the tides. A man had to go to see his pals in the pub – he couldn't be tied to a woman's apron strings, not if he was a real man. And he had to do what he could for other folks, and that took time and interest. She'd been proud when people turned to Reuben to help them in their troubles. Look how he'd helped the people of Newquay Town with that business of the sale of their houses – why, they all owed a debt to her man, Reuben Godson, for what he'd done! But why, why didn't he come to see her? And why, why *did* he go to spend time with that Elsie Milner! The thought brought on a new outburst of tears, a new paroxysm of sobbing and weeping in which she saw clearly that her life was over, that there was nothing for her to live for any more.

She stood up and blindly reached out for the bottle of washing liquor that stood on the shelf, seeing it blurred by her streaming tears. Nothing to live for. She took the cork out of the bottle, tipped the liquor into her mouth and, despite the instant burning sensation on her lips and her tongue, on the inside of her mouth and the back of her throat, she forced herself to gulp it down. Her mouth and her throat, her entire windpipe, felt as if there was a fire in it. She dropped the bottle to the floor, empty, and the glass smashed. She felt a sharp prick on her legs where one of the glass shards had bounced off the hard stone floor. She was swaying, near to unconsciousness, but the fire in her mouth and her throat was growing, and now it was nearly unbearable. She started trying to scream but only a froth came out of her throat and slimed down the front of her dress, stinking of bleach. She reached up her hands and clutched her throat, all her thoughts commanded by the intense pain inside it. She clutched at her throat, trying to tear it out. She felt her nails dig in and the warm trickle of blood, turned, and ran out of the kitchen.

Mrs Duckett had just come in from Whitby, and was taking off her hat, removing the pins one by one, thinking of that cup of tea she'd make for herself since Emily didn't seem to be about, when the door from the scullery flew open and her daughter stood there, a weird bubbling coming from her mouth, a heart-rending screech coming out of her throat. Mrs Duckett abandoned her hat as she raced across the room and held her daughter's face, pulling her hands away from her throat which was lacerated, and streaming blood. 'What have you done, Emily, what *have* you done?'

But then she smelled the washing liquor and the harsh bleach, and suddenly she knew. 'Oh, my God,' she screamed. 'Oh my God!'

The sister came along the polished linoleum of the corridor of the cottage hospital on the hill overlooking the docks at Whitby. She was wearing her dark blue uniform, with its white cap. Pens and pencils, Reuben saw, were clipped into her top pocket and she carried a clipboard as if it were a membership card to some ultra-exclusive club. 'Reuben Godson?' she asked. For a woman so bulky, so big, so overbearing in the manner of her approach, her voice was surprisingly gentle.

'Aye, that's me,' he said, nervously.

'You can come in. She's expecting you.'

She led the way into a ward containing six beds, three on each side. As she entered, the sister beckoned to the nurse who drew the screens around the centre bed on the right-hand side. He stood at the foot of the bed, isolated from the rest of the ward, just him and Emily. 'Hello, Emily,' he said.

'Hello, Reuben.' Her voice was a croak, a harsh sound that rasped in his ear.

'Like, I came to see you before, but you were asleep.'

He'd rushed to the hospital as soon as he'd heard, but had been denied admittance. They were still battling for Emily's life and couldn't permit any visitors, though Emily's mother had virtually set up camp in the waiting room. Mrs Duckett had shot him a look of pure hatred when he'd come in. She'd worked out the reason her daughter had drunk the washing liquor intending to take her own life. It could only be Reuben. She'd questioned the doctor in a roundabout way and he'd surprised her by telling her that Emily was still a virgin. So it couldn't have been the shame of a premarital pregnancy that had caused it. It had to be Reuben's neglect, his seeming indifference over the past few weeks. Mrs Duckett assumed that Reuben had jilted her poor girl, and hated him for the thought.

He'd been to the hospital every second day while she'd been in there. Now, two months had passed and, at last, she was able to sit up and recognize him. At first the doctors had thought she would have lost the power of speech, that the fierce washing liquor would have destroyed her vocal cords. They had been impaired – 'I'm afraid, my girl, you'll never sing contralto in the choir,' the young doctor had told her, smiling – but, at least, she could speak well enough to make herself understood. 'Don't worry,' the doctor had said. 'The body renews itself. If you don't talk too much, if you give your vocal cords a rest, eventually they'll renew themselves and that croak will go out of your voice.'

But she'd lost her sense of taste and that, the doctor gravely said, would never come again. Nor would her sense of smell. 'You'll have to be careful all your life about gas,' he explained. 'If you leave the gas stove on, you'll never smell the gas so you'll never know the danger!'

The poor kid, he knew, would never again smell a rose, or perfume. She'd never taste a glass of wine, or a fresh crab. Tea and coffee would be the same to her. During her life, without realizing the extent of it, he hoped, she'd pay the price in small ways for what she'd done.

One day he'd come back into the hospital after normal rounds and had sat beside her bed. 'Do you want to tell me why you did it?' he'd asked gently. 'If it's any consolation to you, a young man has called at the hospital every second day during the time you've been here. Was it because of him?'

She'd turned her face away but not before he'd seen the tears

231

form in the corners of her eyes. 'When we're young,' he'd said, seeking to console her, 'we think that everything that happens to us is a tragedy. We think our life is ruined. But, Emily, as you can now see, life goes on! Part of growing up is the painful process of learning to live with the difficult things that happen to us. Trying to build up the strength within ourselves to fight these bad things and carry on. When I was a student, I was deeply in love with a girl. She was my whole life. She wouldn't wait until I'd qualified as a doctor and married a solicitor. At the time I thought my life was over. I very nearly gave up my studies because I said to myself, why go on? I don't want to be a doctor if I can't have that girl. Well, I went on as you can see, and after I'd qualified I met a wonderful girl, and we were married. We've just had our first baby. A girl. Looks a bit like you!'

Emily had turned her head back towards him. 'None of that is true, is it, doctor?'

He shook his head. 'I'm afraid it isn't,' he said, 'but, at least, it stopped you crying, and turned your head back again. You'll meet somebody else, Emily. You're a very attractive young woman. Soon, you'll see, all this will be behind you. I give you my word on that! Now, when are you going to see this young man?'

'Next time he comes,' Emily said. 'I'll see him. I might as well get it over and done with!'

'Hello, Reuben,' she said. 'I'm sorry I've given you all this bother. Coming all this way to see me.'

'Nay, lass,' he said awkwardly, 'it's been no bother.'

'Well, now that you're here, you may as well sit down,' she said, indicating the chair beside her bed. He walked round awkwardly, producing the flowers from behind his back and the bag with grapes in it. 'Grapes!' she said. 'They must have cost you a fortune, Reuben! You shouldn't have. . . .'

He sat there with nothing to say but a million thoughts teeming inside his head. 'I can't stop long,' he said finally. 'I've got to get back to catch the tide.'

'It's nice, just to see you,' she said. 'How have you been?'

'Aye, I've been right enough. I got a fish-hook stuck in my hand and it festered, but that were nowt. Mam fetched it down again wi' a bread poultice. There were so much stuff in it! You'd never have believed it!' It was hardly a cheering topic of conversation, he realized, but he had to say something.

'Oh aye, I've just thought of something. We've got the Yard open again, and I'm having a new boat built with a diesel engine in it. It's going to be a grand boat. All copper nails, mind you. No galvanized!'

'That should be good!' She hesitated before she spoke but she'd been giving much thought to what the doctor had said. A body had to face her problems squarely, he'd insisted, not tuck them away in a drawer of the mind. Bad thoughts put away were like all living things that were shut up. They rotted, went bad.

'Have you been seeing much of Elsie Milner?' she asked. There, it was out.

'Elsie Milner? Nay, I haven't. Has nobody told you? Elsie's gone away. The cottage is empty!'

Her heart leaped with joy. 'Gone away?' she said, controlling herself. 'Where to?'

'Leeds. She seemed to get the idea the chances were better for a young lass in Leeds. She got to know that Emma, you know, the one that was supposed to be married with Stan Baxter but wasn't. They became thick as two thieves. Some say as Emma has taken her in, in Leeds. I haven't heard owt, myself!'

All right, she told herself, you've faced up to one thing. Now face up to the rest. 'You and me, Reuben,' she said. 'Are we still courting?'

His reply sent a chill through her. 'No,' he said baldly, 'we're not!' But then he added, 'We're engaged. The minute you stir yourself and get out of here, we're going to call the banns and get married!'

PART THREE

The twenties brought a measure of prosperity to Ravenswyke. During the recession that followed the war, fish took a leading place as a cheap food and the catches seemed to become more plentiful to meet the demand. The offshore trawlers that had plagued local fishermen fitted their boats with diesel and were now able to undertake the longer voyages out to Dogger Bank and up to the Faroes, where they could hope to net more haddock and halibut as part of the catch. The humble cod, the herring when they were shoaling, the mackerel, were plentiful inshore, and often, with his new boat and Batty to help him, Reuben would return to the slip with as many as fifteen to twenty laden baskets.

Fearon died in 1928 from a chill he'd doubtless caught hanging about the dock waiting for the fishermen to come in, running in and out of the warmed saloon of the Raven Hotel, which also was doing boom business in visitors. The fishermen let bygones be bygones, and gave Fearon a fisherman's send-off, six of them hoisting his coffin on their shoulders and carrying it from his house, down to the dock, where the minister said a few words, then all the way up the one-in-four to the cemetery at the top. Reuben Godson, father of five, was one of the pall-bearers. Mark Adam Tockett, himself the father of three girls, attended the funeral, doffed his hat, and showed respect.

The Yard had stagnated since they had built the new *Hope of Ravenswyke* and had received orders for several similar boats. Somehow, Mark Adam's heart wasn't in it and he'd installed a series of managers, none of whom had the force and the drive to make a great success of it.

Newquay Town itself had improved. For a long time, the Fewsters, the Johnsons, the Linhams and the other residents of Grinklegate had shunned Reuben, accusing him of denying them a good investment opportunity. They all behaved as if selling their properties to Stan Baxter would have been the gateway to instant prosperity. As it was, several of the houses had been leased by companies anxious to get a foothold in Ravenswyke; they'd changed the properties, knocking down walls and opening windows, and now all the established shopkeepers had competition on their doorsteps. Of course, they blamed Reuben for that, too. Others of the unoccupied houses had been rented, and – this was the surprising thing – by West Riding families who used them as holiday cottages, travelling there four times a year on public holidays, tending the gardens as best they could. One or two families made the journey most weekends in the summer when they finished work on a Saturday, thinking it worthwhile to weekend there rather than back in the mill towns. There were new faces to be seen in the pub, new faces along the sandy strip by the scaurs. Sometimes, when the low tide was early on a summer's day, you'd find a dozen or more families with rugs spread out on the sands enjoying a picnic.

Ravenswyke, like it or not, was becoming a holiday resort!

When Bill Clewson developed a severe bronchitis that nearly killed him, the doctors told him he could no longer stand the rigours of fishing in all weathers. He started a little business, tending the gardens of the town folks while they were absent, doing a few property repairs for them, keeping the places aired, lighting fires when he knew they were coming, or when they sent him a postcard. In the summer, when most of them were in Ravenswyke anyway, he took his coble, across which he'd nailed a number of wooden seats, and rowed folks out into the bay, where he'd show them how to bait a line and where to drop a hook. Nothing delighted the townies more than to catch their own mackerel for tea, though they never reckoned that, for what they paid Bill to row them out there and back, plus what they paid in bait and tackle, they could have bought a stone of fish caught from that very selfsame bay by professional hands. Bill, in the local phrase, was coining it!

About the same time that Fearon died, the railway was extended to Ravenswyke, and now the fishermen could send their catch, suitably boxed, into Whitby by train. The wholesalers ran a regular service of picking all the fish boxes off the various trains, and that made selling the fish considerably easier. Since the boats all left at the same time, more or less, but came in at different times, and since there were several trains a day, it didn't make sense to wait until the last boat was in. Slowly the co-operative dissolved and each fisherman began handling his own affairs. Obviously the sooner a man could get in, the earlier the train he could catch and usually the more he could earn for his fish. Since Eleanor had grown too dotty to seek employment, she was given the job of wheeling the boxes of fish on a flat cart up the hill. If the catch Reuben brought in was heavy, many a lad standing by would be glad to earn a coin giving her a helping hand. Eleanor was supposed to keep her eyes open, looking for the *Hope* coming back in, but often Emily had to find her, in her bedroom, which she shared with two of the Godson babies, or sitting alone out in the backyard, and shoo her down to the dock, threatening her with Reuben's anger if he landed and found no Eleanor waiting. Sometimes she would fail to find Eleanor, and then she and Hannah would be waiting at the dock when he landed. Emily, however, was usually pregnant, and Reuben would rage and he and Batty push the handcart up the hill cursing. When Eleanor was eventually found, he'd curse at her and often fetch her a back-hander, despite Hannah's protestations. 'You're a Godson!' he'd shout. 'You're supposed to be one of us. That means you take an interest; it means you're standing on the dock with the handcart ready to get up that damned hill!' Sometimes he'd soften, and add, 'The only road tha can get out of it, Eleanor, is to get your-self a husband as'll put a babby inside you. Then tha wouldn't have to push t'cart up t'hill!'

Now that Reuben had married and had taken charge of the family – or it could have been the companionship of Emily and the five babies, and Amelia Duckett, who often walked down the hill to take a cup of tea – Hannah seemed to grow younger and more lively with each day. She was an enormous help to Emily with the work that five babies entailed. Wilfred had been born in 1922; Arthur followed in 1923. Next they had two girls, Eliza in 1924 and Anne in 1925. Amos was born in 1926, and by then the hand-me-down baby clothing and the layette were beginning to look a bit threadbare. Emily was pregnant again, and due in a couple of months, but by now she took pregnancy and childbirth in her stride. The years of motherhood had been good for Emily, and she was a mature woman, with a strong hand on her children and the Godson household. Hannah had learned to defer to her since, by Godson tradition, Emily and not Hannah was the head of domestic affairs. Since Emily's 'accident', as they had called her stay in hospital whenever it had been mentioned in the early days, she'd found an inner strength based, no doubt, on the good advice the doctor had given her. The quality of her voice seemed to improve with each pregnancy and already she'd lost the harshness of her former croak. Her voice was deep, almost like a man's, but it had good tones and she no longer felt embarrassed to speak to people. Occasionally, going about the house on some chore, she would break out into a song she'd learned from the gramophone Reuben had bought for her.

Hannah was a happy woman. She and Amelia Duckett had much in common. Both prided themselves on being clean and respectable, on having maintained good homes for their menfolk and families. Sometimes they went out together to Whitby for shopping, once to Scarborough on the train, but they hadn't liked the larger city. They preferred York, where Hannah had gone at the time of Eleanor's wedding to Terrie Pitt. She and Amelia went for the day on the train and walked in awe round the Minster. It was the grandest building either had ever seen, frightening in its size, terrifying in its conception. 'I wouldn't like to kneel down in a place like this,' Hannah whispered to Amelia, 'for fear I might have a hole in my stocking!' Long ago, Hannah had ceased to worry about Eleanor. The girl was touched, that's all there could be about it, she'd decided. She'd discussed Eleanor with Amelia, who'd said, 'Leave her be. Eventually she'll snap out of it! There's no cure for the sickness of love!' Which was a little unkind, though neither of them realized it. Eleanor, without their knowing it, was suffering from acute depression caused by the successive deaths of the two men in her life and her miscarriage. And it wasn't helping her to see Emily producing babies as if off a factory assembly line. Each new pregnancy, each new baby, left Eleanor more and more depressed, shut her more and more inside herself, where fantasies grew, could be followed, and never turned out bad. Eleanor was pining, could they but know it, her spirit wasting away.

Ravenswyke had just recovered from a scandal that had shaken the normally peaceful village; on Christmas Eve 1929 the police in Whitby had apprehended a man so drunk he'd almost fallen into the river Esk. They'd taken him to the police cells and had locked him in overnight. On Christmas morning, when the beadle had taken his breakfast, he'd noticed stains on the front of the man's clothes, many of which seemed to be neither vomit nor urine. The sergeant had pronounced his opinion that the stains had been caused by a copious flow of blood. Yet the man appeared to be unhurt. The sergeant missed his Christmas goose that year, not that he would have had any stomach for it when the man finally led them to a house in Ravenswyke and the sergeant saw the butchered remains, lying in the bed, of what once had been a human being.

They tried to locate Elsie Milner to tell her what had happened and for her to make arrangements about the funeral, but Elsie had gone away from Leeds and her present whereabouts were unknown. Emma Baxter, as she now was, knew where her friend Elsie was going, but she knew Elsie would have no interest in returning to Ravenswyke. She and her mother had had nothing in common for many a year, and, now that Elsie had achieved her ambition of finding a man for herself, Emma wasn't going to spoil it for her. Stan Baxter had brought the man to the house to try to influence him in a business deal. Rich as Croesus, Harry Bennett of Huddersfield seemed as cautious in business matters as he was incautious in his private life. He took one look at Elsie and swept her off her feet. Now, Emma knew, they were on their way to Venice. They'd been to Paris, Rome and Florence on an extended tour. She was eagerly anticipating their return, since Stan had promised to take her on the same tour as soon as their second child was born and she had recovered. The first birth had been a difficult one and Emma knew she wasn't destined for motherhood. Stan had been very good; they'd engaged a nurse as well as a housekeeper, cook and maid when they set up residence in Roundhay, and Emma rarely had anything to do with Winston George Henry Baxter. It was a bore being pregnant again, she thought, dreaming of Elsie and Harry on their Grand Tour, floating along one of the canals of Venice in a gondola, with the – what did they call them, gondolier – singing an Italian love song!

Emma thought of her friend Elsie with a certain pride. She'd taken the unformed country girl and had made her over into a smart, even sophisticated, woman of the world. She'd taught her dress sense, the art of conversing. She'd toned down her more obvious vulgarities, like the horse laugh she used to use, and had brought out her good points. Along the way, she'd earned herself a loyal friend, something Emma had never had before.

After the land purchase fiasco, the Baxters had never returned to Ravenswyke. They preferred Robin Hood's Bay, Runswick Bay or Staithes'whenever they felt the need to get out of the industrial atmosphere of Leeds for a few days' bracing sea air. She'd talked Stan into buying a cottage for her overlooking the sea at Robin Hood's Bay. It dated back to the fifteenth century. Quite delighted with it, she had filled it with beautiful furniture. Often Stan permitted her to take Elsie to the cottage on their own for a day or two but, in the presence of her friend and protégée, Emma behaved herself and indulged in none of the kind of affairs she'd so enjoyed with Reuben Godson. By unspoken agreement, neither of them talked with the other about Reuben, though Emma knew Elsie had felt a soft spot for him.

For his part, Reuben had put all thoughts of Elsie Milner out of his mind. When he learned that Emily had tried to commit suicide on his behalf, he realized he had not even begun to plumb the depths of her feelings for him. He'd understood that beneath her placid compliant surface a storm of hidden feelings raged. Perhaps his manhood was flattered; from the moment in the hospital when he asked her to marry him, he gave no thought to any other woman, and had no longing for the passion he imagined could come from Elsie or Emma. Emily amply justified his faith; she was a good wife and helpmate to him, a good mother to their children. Yes, and like a daughter to Hannah. She'd taken to being a Godson with the ease a coble takes to water! During the lean years of the twenties she'd managed the household with efficiency. It seemed to Reuben that the soups and stews she made were every bit as filling and as tasty as any he'd ever enjoyed; he had no conception of the lengths she went to, to get him the cheaper cuts of meat, the way she used bones and tripe, pigs' and calves' feet to nourish them all. Since he was catching plenty of fish, which found a good ready market, and Emily managed the household money carefully, the Godsons prospered. The new boat turned out to be a good investment; never once did the engine fail Reuben and now he was quick on and quick off the mooring. Many summer nights he left the coble in the water instead of dragging it up the slip to the dock. In his design, he'd made the stern flatter and higher, and the beam wider for the length, so that the *Hope* rode more comfortably at anchor during high tide. He'd set the mooring in concrete with a length of galvanized chain – it would have served an ocean-going liner! With the motor, he could often run out quickly and check his lobster pots, bringing in any crabs he might have caught for the early train, and then run out again to try his luck with a couple of hundred fathoms of line. Batty was a great help to him and had taken to fishing as if born to it. Reuben paid him wages. He knew Batty would have liked a share of the profits, a partnership of some sort, but Reuben was even more careful with authority than he was with money. Though he had to pay Batty's wages even when they caught nothing, to him it was still preferable to keep the ownership of the vessel and the fishing enterprise in his own hands. He knew that, if he'd made Batty a partner, Batty would have started arguing with him, disputing his choice of fishing grounds. As a family man, with five kids already, Reuben wanted the sole, absolute mastership of the *Hope*, as it had always been, until the day he would hand it on to his son Wilfred.

Wilfred was growing well and, in Reuben's proud estimation, a grand chap. He was sturdy and stocky in the fisherman's way and had Reuben's black hair. Already Emily was finding him a handful but that could have been because Reuben invariably spoiled him and his younger brother Arthur, naturally favouring them over the two girls Eliza and Anne. Now Reuben would race home as soon as the catch had been dispatched to the station, and the two older lads would be waiting for a pretend boxing match or a ride on their father's back. Sometimes he'd stop at the post-office by the Raven Hotel and buy them each a string of ever-lasting toffee, or a lollipop, or a stick of licorice. Emily, ever wise, always kept a few boiled sweets in a cupboard so that, when the two lads were tucked in, she could give something to the little wide-eyed, envious girls.

The two girls shared Eleanor's bedroom; the boys slept with Hannah, but Emily insisted on having each new baby with her and Reuben, in the cot in the front room.

Reuben still liked to go into Whitby on a Saturday afternoon, remembering the times he'd walked there with Arthur Duckett, but now he took Wilfred and Arthur with him on either the bus or the train. They preferred the train, and would stand on the seats and look out of the windows on the landward side, exclaiming with delight when the smoke and steam curled back past the windows as they were running through a cutting. Their cries of joy would be even louder when they passed the flocks of sheep and the many cows that now grazed the upland pastures. Cattle had joined horses and sheep as a profitable local endeavour and now, each day, the milkman came around Ravenswyke, calling at each house in Old Quaytown with his metal cans mounted on the sides of an old moorland pony, whose shaggy hair almost covered its eyes. Though they were familiar with the world of fish, crabs, lobsters and the marine life they found on the scaurs at low tide, the animals roaming loose in the fields were a revelation to them. They loved going to Whitby on a Saturday afternoon with their dad, each clasping one of his hands until Arthur became tired and asked to be given a 'horsey'. Then Reuben would swing the little one up on to his shoulder; they'd thread their way through the town or along the side of the harbour past the fish stalls and fishmarkets, seeing the large fishing vessels, the coalers, the timber boats from Scandinavia, the general cargo boats that had begun to throng the port. Whitby was booming, no doubt about that, Reuben thought, even though the number of actual fishing boats seemed to be on the decline. It was on the decline, he knew, all along the Yorkshire coast, and Ravenswyke had only half the fishermen actively engaged that he could remember from when he was a lad. Mind you, the catches had increased since the new engines made the boats faster and more efficient. Now they could risk going out in weather that would have been impossible in the days of sail alone and could head straight instead of tacking about. That didn't matter so much when they were going out, but it meant an awful lot to a fisherman, when he was exhausted from hauling his lines in adverse weather, to be able to make a beeline straight for the slip, the dock, and a pot of hot tea.

He was larking about with the boys on the bank one Saturday after he'd been to Whitby when Eleanor passed him, heading up-bank under a full head of steam. 'You'd better get on home quick,' she said. 'Emily's started and we think summat's gone wrong! I'm fetching t'doctor!'

He grabbed the two boys under his arms and raced down the steep bank, cutting through the backs to the Godson cottage. Emily was upstairs in the big bedroom and Amelia was with her. Hannah was sitting in the kitchen, nervously watching a big kettle of water on the fire. She had another, he noticed, on the gas stove.

'What's up then, Mam?' he asked, as he deposited the two boys in the big chair. 'Now you two just settle there and hold your noise!' he told them.

'She doesn't seem to be managing so well this time,' Hannah said. 'I warned her that the more you have the more difficult it can be. I remember well I had such a time with you! Seems as if your muscles get tired or something. Any road, I've sent Eleanor up for t'doctor. Can't do no harm to have him take a look at her!'

'She was all right when I left with the lads for Whitby.'

'Aye, it came on sudden. I guessed it'd be tomorrow or Monday, but it's come a bit sooner.'

'I wouldn't have gone if I'd known!'

'Nay, don't reproach yourself, lad,' Hannah said, seeing the troubled expression on his face. 'It took us all by surprise, me included, and I should have known better, having had six of my own.'

'Do you think we ought to fetch Alicia?' he asked. Alicia Pentyfold, besides making mints and mint toffees, was also the local herbalist. Many's the young girl she'd helped out of trouble with her special 'tea'. Alicia had a remedy for everything. Yarrow as a love charm and for curing colds, tansy for the stomach, horehound for coughs, betony for worms. 'I've already been to see her,' Hannah said. 'She's given me some feverfew – she gave me the same thing thirty years ago when I was having difficulty getting you out. It worked then; I'm hoping it'll help Emily now.'

He could see, however, that she had no conviction. 'What's really wrong, Mam?' he said. He knew her too well for her to conceal the depth of her worry.

'Well, I don't think it's anything we can help with feverfew,' she admitted. 'I think it's a matter for the doctor. Happen he'll have to use the knife!'

'Bloody hell!' he said and sat down in the chair by the fireside.

'Can we get down now, Dad?' Wilfred piped. 'Arthur wants to go to the lavvy.'

'You take him then,' Reuben said absently, 'and mind he gets it out before he starts. We don't want him wetting his trousers again!'

He stared into the fire. Poor Emily. He'd thought – he knew

243

she thought so too – that this sixth birth would be just as easy as the other five. If not easier! There'd been no indication of trouble other than the slight swelling of the varicose veins in her legs, but that, she'd said, was nothing more than the strain of lugging all that extra weight up and down the bank.

'I'll go up to her,' he said.

'I wouldn't, lad,' Hannah said. 'There's nowt you can do until the doctor's been and she'd not like you to see her as she is now!'

'If you think it's best!' Reuben had a distaste of any form of sickness, any suggestion of ill-health. The two boys came back from the lavvy. 'I've done him up,' Wilfred said proudly. 'I fastened his buttons myself!'

'There's a good lad,' Reuben said absently. 'Now I want you to go in t'yard and play quiet. Your mam's not feeling too well, so don't make a noise!' The boys went out, already planning a game. Reuben sat in his chair with a deep sense of foreboding. Emily, not well! It'd be the first time for a long while. He realized how much strength had come from her over the years, how she'd always been there, managing everything with a deft efficiency. He'd never once heard her complain, or make any demands on him. Since her 'accident', she'd learned to speak her mind and, whenever he did or said something she didn't agree with, she made no bones about telling him, straight to his face, never leaving him in any doubt about what she was thinking. Restless, he went out to the back and looked in the shed. He had three lobster pots that needed the mesh repairing and he took down a coil of tarred yarn and a long net-mending bodkin. When the lads saw him, they came across to where he sat on a three-legged stool but were hurt when he rebuffed them. He sat on the stool, staring across the yard at the cottages opposite, working at the lobster pots almost without looking at them. He saw the foundations he'd already laid for the new bedroom; they'd need more space with another one on the way and he'd planned to put a whole new house up, with a room down and a kitchen, and two small bedrooms up. It'd be grand, Hannah said, for her and Eleanor and would get them out from under his and Emily's feet. Then, when Hannah had gone, the kids could occupy it. Reuben had already ordered the stone from the quarry; it'd be a long heavy job hauling it down the bank, and then carrying each piece up the backs where they couldn't get a cart through. All the houses of Old Quaytown

244

had grown in this manner, except the houses up in the square, where the schoolroom was situated. They'd been built all of a piece. Over the centuries the fishermen had gradually spread across the face of this steep hill, often with the new room up the bank higher than, and overlooking the roofs of, the main house lower down. The two bedrooms Reuben was planning would be at least three feet higher than his present roof. He looked round the property, more to give his mind something to think about than anything else. The house behind him had been little changed since the first Godson had built it, though, four years before, Reuben had had the roof stripped off and new timbers let in under the pantiles to replace the old ones, reputed to have come from a fourteenth-century ship. They'd finally succumbed to old age and the worm had got into them, with the boring beetle. The L-shaped piece to his right had been added in the seventeenth century. Its roof stood a clear six feet above the original roof and, when the timbers of that had been checked, they'd been pronounced as sound as a bell. On one of them, the seventeenth-century carpenter had set a monogram, presumably of his own initials, and had carved 'Fear the Lord'. Reuben had negotiated with Mapham, the boat-builder in Whitby, who was also a boat-wrecker and had a stack of timbers in his yard he'd taken from vessels he'd purchased to use the wood. The timber in the new extension would be over a couple of hundred years old, most of it sound hearts of oak from a couple of old Whitby-built 'pinks'. Reuben had already ordered the doors and window frames from the carpenter, who'd use the old wood.

To Reuben's right was the long building his grandfather had built; a storeroom for lines and pots, for the charivari of boats and fishing, it contained a long bench carrying the carefully preserved tools the Godson family had accumulated over the years. Its two doors had been built like those of a stable, so that in summer you could work inside with the top part open to admit more light. It even had a blacksmith's fire, with foot-operated bellows for forging the iron they used, though the links and shackles they made had to go to Whitby to be hot-dip galvanized if they were to be exposed to seawater for any length of time. In his grandfather's day, the iron was forged and used in its raw state. It'd be a very foolish fisherman who didn't replace his anchor and chain every second year!

The yard itself, where a line constantly hung carrying the babies' washing, was paved with flagstones set in cobbles. Since Emily had come, she'd brought wild flowers from the top of the bank, and had trained wild roses, clematis, even a fuchsia, across the back wall. Each winter she nurseried daffodils and crocus, picked wild from the woods, and she even grew herbs in a long stone trough that once, they said, had sat on the dock for the horses; its centre was hollowed out from one block. There were few of the common ailments that Emily couldn't tackle!

Once again, Reuben thought wryly, his thoughts had come back to Emma with the inescapable knowledge of the good choice he'd made those years ago, when he was a foolish headstrong young lad with most of his brains between his legs, or so it seemed to him in retrospect.

He got up and went back into the house. 'Doctor not here yet?' he asked Hannah irritably.

'Yes. He came five minutes ago. I took him straight upstairs.'

'I wish he'd hurry up!'

'Nay, Reuben, you can't hurry a *doctor*!'

Still restless, Reuben prowled about the house, poking the fire, picking up the *Gazette* and putting it down again, lighting and forgetting the pipe he'd taken to recently. Finally Hannah said, 'If you want something to do, you can fetch in them lads and get 'em ready for bed.'

He went to the back door and called out into the yard. When the lads came in, Wilfred looked sheepishly at him. His hands were covered in tar, and Arthur's too. 'You've been in my shed!' Reuben said. 'I told you never to go in there if I'm not about!' Almost absentmindedly, he fetched the lad a clout on the side of his face. Wilfred gritted his teeth but didn't cry, though Arthur began to wail in anticipation of the punishment he was certain would follow their escapade.

'Now listen to what you've done,' Hannah said. She took the two boys across to the table and smeared their hands with butter. This was a grand game, and Arthur forgot his tears as he worked the butter into his hands, the only sure way to remove the black sticky tar. Hannah took the two boys out to the back scullery, and Reuben could hear her talking to them as she washed their hands and faces, preparing them for bed. She took them upstairs. 'I'll come in to say good night,' Reuben called out softly as he heard their murmuring voices. A pall hung over the whole house, of whispers, murmurs and the certain knowledge of Emily's difficulties.

Reuben had been sitting there for half an hour, looking into the fire, when suddenly he heard a shriek from above that sent him racing up the stairs.

Hannah was already standing in the door of the bedroom. 'Tha mun't go in,' she said. 'It's going to be all right!'

'What was she shrieking about!'

'He had to cut her in a hurry. But it's all right.'

As if to confirm her words he heard the muffled smack and the thin wail of a new-born baby, followed by coughing. 'There, I told you it was all right,' Hannah said. He could see the relief on her face and realized that she, despite sounding confident, had not been so sure that everything was going to work out.

Amelia came out and went downstairs, returning with the kettle of water from the gas stove. She still looked grave. 'You've got another son,' she said.

'Aye, right, but what about my Emily?'

'We don't know yet.'

She went inside, and he went downstairs to sit in front of the fire again, feeling a chill in his bones that had nothing to do with his body temperature. He had no interest at all in the new son – his only thought was for his wife. Five minutes later he heard Hannah's frantic shout from upstairs. 'Reuben,' she yelled, 'come up. Come up quick.' He raced upstairs as fast as he could go, past Eleanor standing in the door of her room with a book in her hand, and into the front bedroom. The scene that greeted his eyes from the bed was unbelievable. Emily seemed to be covered from her waist down in blood, to be lying in a pool of it. Her legs were spread wide apart and blood seemed to be gushing out from between them. The doctor was standing beside the bed with surgical instruments in his hand. 'Give him that towel, there,' he commanded, and Hannah handed Reuben what seemed like the only clean piece of cloth in the room. 'Come on, lad!' the doctor snapped. 'This is no time to be nervous. Your wife's having a massive haemorrhage. I need you to press down on the artery while I stitch it!' He took the towel from Reuben, and folded it quickly, staining it with the blood from his hands and arms. Reuben hadn't even looked at Emily's face. When he did so, he

was shocked to see it a greenish shade of white, completely without flesh colour. The doctor had taken a pebble they kept on the
dresser. Multicoloured normally, it had a natural blow-hole in it;
Yorkshire superstition said such a pebble would ward off the
Devil, but the doctor was thinking of it only as a hard lump. He
placed it exactly on Emily's side, covered it with the folded towel
and beckoned to Reuben. 'Press down there,' he said, 'as hard as
you can. And, whatever you do, don't let the pressure go until I
tell you!'

'I tried,' Amelia Duckett whimpered, standing beside Reuben
and wiping her daughter's brow with a damp cloth, 'but I got the
cramp.'

Reuben understood what was needed of him. Press down and
block the artery. Stop the flow of blood. This would give the
doctor time to do what he had to do, whatever that might be. He
pressed, gently at first and then more firmly. He was looking at
Emily's face; her eyes were closed and he could smell the strong
odour of ether, or was it chloroform? He shuffled his body round
so that it was half turned away from the doctor. He heard the
sound of instruments lightly tapping against each other and scraping together, setting his teeth on edge. But still he maintained the
pressure. Fifteen minutes later, he was still pressing down, though
now he realized why Amelia's arm had gone into a cramp. He'd
never tried pressing down on a small object for so long; he could
haul a rope endlessly, pulling up great weights of cod. He could
haul the mainsheet of the boat, hanging on for grim death in a
storm while the *Hope* battled to get back to port through the
heavy seas. Often he'd looked down at his fingers and had seen
them white as ivory from loss of the blood cut off by the ever
tighter mainsheet. Then he'd had to take the sheet one-handed,
and flex the other painfully stiff fingers to get back some kind of
life in them. Pressing down steadily on this pebble, on which he
could only use a thumb and two fingers, was harder by far than
all the mainsheet hauling!

The doctor was humming now as he worked, a tuneless dirge
that could mean either hope or despair. His blood-covered
instruments were thrown in a heap on a towel on the chair that
had been placed beside the bed. Twenty minutes passed. Twenty-
five. Then the doctor grunted out loud – it was almost like a belch
– and stood up straight. 'There, that should do it,' he said. 'You

248

can let the pressure off the stone. But don't move it; I may have to tell you to press down again quickly!' He turned to Hannah. 'If you can get me some more water, Hannah?' he asked.

Reuben slowly stopped pressing downwards, though, in view of what the doctor had said, he didn't move the towel. The doctor put his stethoscope into his ears and moved up the bed on the opposite side to Reuben, placing the horn cup on various parts of Emily's inert body and then listening for a minute before moving to the next location. The final place was over her heart. Reuben felt a quick surge of resentment when he saw another's hands lift Emily's full breast, but mentally kicked himself for the idea.

'I think we're going to be all right,' the doctor said. He went back down the bed out of Reuben's view and Reuben heard the scrape of the instruments again and the doctor's expressive grunt, which this time, he knew, signified satisfaction.

'Right, Reuben,' he said, 'you can relax.'

Reuben took his hands away, lifted the towel, and took out the stone. He knew it was something he'd never part with for the rest of his life, a true 'lucky' stone. He'd take it to the jeweller's in Whitby when Emily was better, and have it mounted, somehow. It'd become a family heirloom.

The doctor was speaking again. 'If you could do your best to clean her up,' he said, 'I'll take another look at the baby.'

Reuben left the room; he knocked on Eleanor's door perfunctorily before he went in. 'Stir yourself,' he said. 'Get down to t'Raven and fetch us back a bottle of whisky. And be sharp about it!'

'Is Emily all right?' she asked timidly. Reuben knew she was a coward when it came to blood – she couldn't even see a nosebleed without going all over faint.

'Aye, she is,' he said, adding cruelly, 'no thanks to thee! Now fetch that whisky else I'll take my belt to thee!'

When the doctor came down, after two more kettles of hot water had been taken up, the whisky bottle was standing on the table, with four glasses. The doctor sat on the chair at the table, spread his arms, and let his head sink into them, completely exhausted. 'They're both going to be all right, Reuben,' he said, 'but it was a hard fight. Your Emily must have a constitution of iron! To survive all that loss of blood! You'll have to look after

249

her, see she gets plenty of rest. Hannah will feed her up, that much I know. And you'll not stop Amelia Duckett from galloping down here with beef tea, if I know her!'

Dr Gilchrist did know her. He knew every childbearing woman in the whole of Ravenswyke, though normally he wasn't required to assist at the birth of their children. Esther Blakey, the local midwife, did all that. As well as laying out all the dead. Reuben poured two generous measures into two of the glasses. Dr Gilchrist heard the clink of the bottle on the glass and raised his head, then slowly sat upright. He took one of the glasses and held it before his mouth for a moment, no doubt savouring the anticipation of the fiery spirit, before downing the entire contents with one movement of his wrist. Reuben knew the doctor would take one more, and that would be it. He poured the drink, then raised his own glass. 'It's always the hardest thing to say, doctor,' he said. 'It always seems to be giving back so little for so much. So, I'll just say it again. Thank you.'

The doctor lifted his glass in salute and sipped at the whisky. 'Yes, well that's all right, Reuben. I know what you mean,' he said.

'Can you tell me what it was?' Reuben asked diffidently.

'The baby was in a right mess inside your wife. Somehow he'd got himself all tangled up in the umbilical cord. And he'd started being born when I arrived, so it was a rush job. Somebody ought to have notified me sooner, instead of giving her the herb medicine! One of the cords was round the baby's throat, so I had to cut it in a hurry, to save the baby's life. Your wife immediately started to lose blood – not from that cut cord, but from an artery that ruptured. I couldn't get to it to sew it because we couldn't stem the flow of blood. Amelia would hold the stone but then she'd let it slip. No fault of hers, you know. It needed a strong man. In the hospital, we could have put a strong clamp on it . . .'

'Should she have been taken to hospital?'

'There wasn't time, Reuben. By the time I got here, the baby was trying to be born. We could hardly slap its bottom and say, get back inside until we're ready for you. . . .' After his attempt at humour, the doctor looked gravely at Reuben. 'There's something I have to tell you, Reuben!' he said. 'You've had a good innings now. Six children altogether. All fine. I'm afraid that

Emily won't be able to have any more. You'll have to make do with the family you have.'

Reuben felt a current of relief run through him. The thought of Emily having to go through that lot again would be a nightmare to him. 'As you say, we've had a good innings, though I was hoping for a round dozen. . . !'

The doctor smiled, wearily. 'The days of the big family are over, Reuben,' he said. 'Believe me, there'll come a time when every family will have four children and that will be that! Count your blessings you have six.' Professional ethics wouldn't let him disclose to Reuben how many people were going to their doctor these days and saying, how can you prevent us having any more family? It was rapidly becoming a moral issue and doctors were talking about it among themselves. The more religiously minded of them regarded it as a sin to remove either a man's or a woman's ability to reproduce – in either case it could be a simple piece of surgery. Of course, an equal number were strongly against the use of these modern contraceptives, the pessaries for women, the rubber goods for men. Soon, however, it would all be academic to Dr Gilchrist.

'I shan't be seeing you much longer, Reuben,' he said. 'I've a young doctor starting with me next week as a locum.'

'What's a locum?' Reuben asked.

'He'll come in and study the practice with me. I shall take him round on all my calls. Then he'll start doing calls on his own. Eventually he'll take over the practice and I shall retire!'

'But that won't be for a year or two?' Reuben asked anxiously. The idea of Ravenswyke without Dr Gilchrist was as unthinkable as the dock without a *Hope*.

'I have only six months left,' he said. That was the life-span that the specialist in York had given him. Ironic, he'd thought on his way back, that fate would give a doctor one of the diseases for which there was no known cure!

'We shall all be sorry to see the day,' Reuben said sincerely. 'Happen you'll have another whisky?'

'Yes, tonight I think I will, Reuben,' Dr Gilchrist said. 'And we'll toast your new lad. Has a name been picked yet?'

'Yes. We decided if he was a boy we'd call him John. We don't hold with these fancy names.'

'Neither do I!' Dr Gilchrist said. He had a reason for his conviction. He'd spent his youth fighting his own two names, Cecil and Claude!

'You've got to stir yourself,' Reuben said to Eleanor. 'You've got to pull your weight and take a bit of the load off Mam and Emily!' The disturbed birth and the extreme loss of blood had left Emily weak and she had to spend a lot of time in bed resting. At first, she'd got up and had tried to carry on as normal – when the other children had been born she'd been cooking for all the family within twenty-four hours. She tried to do the same thing this time, and promptly collapsed in the kitchen, burning her hand on the hot fire oven. Hannah, though still an active woman, was starting to feel her age. After all, she had brought six children of her own into the world and knew how childbearing ages a woman and makes her less strong, less resistant to illness. She herself had suffered for years from very bad backache, though she'd concealed it for a long time from the family. Living in a place like Ravenswyke, built into the slope of a steep hill, didn't help with that one-in-four bank to be climbed every time a body wanted to go somewhere. Three benches had been installed next to the road up the bank; during the mornings the benches would be filled by pregnant women on their way up the bank, taking a rest and drawing a breath. Amelia Duckett didn't come down the bank so regularly now; since Emily had had a bad time she appeared to have taken against Reuben for some reason, as if the difficult birth had been Reuben's fault. Of course, she too was getting on in years, growing more fussy, more picky, as she grew older.

Eleanor sat at the kitchen table, playing with a pencil and a piece of paper. 'It's no good you hiding yourself away in your bedroom,' Reuben growled. 'Bedrooms is for sleeping in. During the day, your place is down here, helping. What I'm going to do is to make you responsible for the kids, since Emily's not well. So, you can set your mind to it. You'll get 'em up in the morning, make sure they wash and dress themselves. You'll send – no, you'll take – Wilfred, Arthur and Eliza up to school, and fetch 'em back for their dinner. And put that damned pencil down when I'm talking to you. If you're so keen on drawing, you can do a few for the bairns to keep 'em amused. Are you listening to me?'

It was always hard to tell if Eleanor heard what was being said.

Her face wore a perpetually lost look, as if she were a stranger in an alien land hearing a language she'd never been taught. 'Do you understand me?' Reuben asked, exasperated with her.

'Yes, Reuben,' she said in a small thin voice, 'I understand you!'

'Then do something about it. Mind you do as I tell you! There's places for people like you, you know!'

He looked at Hannah, standing by the fire stirring a pot of bones she was boiling to make Emily a broth. He knew he'd gone too far when he saw the misery in Hannah's eyes at the thought her daughter might be put away. 'Let her be, Reuben,' she pleaded. 'I can manage.'

'No, you can't manage, Mam. Not all on your own. And, after all, it won't be long before Emily's back on her feet again. In the meantime, Eleanor can give a hand. Dammit, we feed her, give her a lodging, her clothes, and she gives nothing back except half an hour's work shoving the cart up the bank. And, half the time, she's nowhere to be found when that job needs doing! I tell you, if my dad was still alive, he'd have taken his belt to her years ago!'

He got up, pulled on his jacket, and left the house. Women! he thought. There was just no accounting for them! Reuben lived his life according to a set of simple rules he'd derived from his father, from being a Godson. You did what you had to do, the best way you knew how. You pulled your weight, shared in the labours as well as the luxuries. And you kept yourself a bit cleaner than Eleanor did – why, he'd been able to smell her sitting across the table from him. He walked downhill towards the Raven. Men passing, women washing doorsteps, even the kids, all greeted him with a word, a nod, a smile. The recognition only made him madder at Eleanor. Didn't she realize she was a *Godson*, not some Newquay Town trollop, to sit smelling across the table! It was high tide; he could smell the salt in the air that came from the breakers crashing against the rocks of the landing. He walked down the road and stood beside the Raven Hotel for a few moments, savouring the sound of the water, the sight of the spume rising and hissing across the landing. October winds were un-reliable. Some days the sea was flat and still warm, like a bake-oven after the bread had been taken out. Other times, the wind came down from the north, curling viciously round the lighthouse at the end of the mole that marked the north-easterly limit of the bay, and the running waves were molested by it into an angry tormented fluke of grey-green water with power in it beyond the belief of land-living men. Power to smash a wooden boat into matchsticks in minutes, to tear out the plates of even the strongest steel-hulled vessel. Every year, or so it seemed, at least one vessel would be caught either in the lee of that lighthouse, or off the treacherous cliffs below Tockett House. Some mariner would lose his engine power at the wrong time and be blown inshore at the mercy of the ripping wind and the hammering lashing waves. It looked as if it would be such a night tonight, he thought. The wind would delay the coming of low tide by stacking the water artificially on itself, creating deep clefts and chasms of waves twenty, thirty feet deep into which a coble could vanish for ever. He doubted he'd be out the following morning – his experience told him the wind was in for a blow that would last through the tide. He looked right to the Yard, then turned his head away in disappointment. The Yard could have done great things, if only Mark Adam would have put his energies behind it. Reuben felt a curious ambivalence towards Mark Adam Tockett. In so many ways he had recovered from the bad reputation he'd brought back from the war and the unfortunate way he'd provoked, so Reuben still believed, that first strike and subsequent lock-out. Being married seemed to have humanized him, and often he took the trouble to walk down the road, down the bank, into the heart of Ravenswyke. Once or twice he'd put his face inside the Raven for half an hour, drinking a couple of brandies, buying a round, then leaving. He was often to be seen on the landing when they came back in, chatting away with them. He was the one man Eleanor would talk with. She'd be standing there with the flat-topped barrow and he'd tease her. And, surprisingly, she'd respond, and tease him back. When a bit of muscle was needed to get a coble off the cradle in the dock, he'd roll back his elegant cuffs and set to with the rest of them. Once a boat slipped and rubbed down the front of his grey coat, smearing the fine cloth with the green algae, but he laughed it off and hadn't seemed to mind. No one ever saw old Mr James Henry, as they now called him, who was in his seventies and kept very much to himself, except for the occasional trip he would take, riding in the back of the car, to Whitby.

Mark Adam, though he had become a more sociable person,

had not changed in one respect. In anything to do with money or business, he was still even more ruthless than his father had been. Any suggestion of the men of the Yard banding together to form a union and he'd sack the first one out of hand. If any one of the Newquay Town cottagers was late with the rent, he'd give them a week, no more, and then his bailiff, a much-hated man called Grimthorpe, would arrive. Some said that Grimthorpe had been a sergeant-major in the army police – he was not a man anyone tangled with voluntarily. The rents were usually paid the second week, or the cottager was evicted peremptorily, the bits of sticks of furniture thrown in a heap on the roadway irrespective of the weather. Gradually the Newquay Town people were being weeded out and replaced by people who came from all over the West Riding, or from North Yorkshire. As a holiday chalet, the cottages were perfect. At £300–400 each, they were also a good capital investment, and a few in favoured positions had already changed hands a couple of times, for cash. Ruthless efficiency seemed to be the hallmark of Mark Adam's administration of the wealth that one day would come to him. He was hoarding it, protecting it, like a miser.

One of the new men was standing at the top of the landing when Reuben came down to smell the water. 'You'll not be fishing tomorrow?' the man asked sociably.

'If you can tell me that,' Reuben said, smiling, 'you're wasting your vocation. You ought to be a fisherman yourself!'

The man coloured, but Reuben's smile removed any sting from his words. 'Happen you're right,' Reuben said, realizing that thoughts of Eleanor had caused him to speak a little too sharply.

The man took his courage in his hands. 'One thing I've always wanted to ask you,' he said. 'When we buy a piece of fish, or a crab, off the boat, it tastes marvellous! But when we're back in Leeds and we fancy a bit of fish, it never tastes the same. Can nowt be done to get us some of that fresh fish back inland, like? It's got so's we only buy fish when we come here. You might say as this place has spoiled us!'

'Well, by the time it gets to the market in Whitby, and they sell it to the wholesalers, then they carry it inland and sell it to the retailers, who sell it to you, you'll see that the fish has got to be a bit old, hasn't it? That's why the muck they catch on them trawlers is like a bit of old rubber! When you think how long it's

255

been lying in the hold of the trawler. Of course, some of 'em has ice now, but it still takes a while.'

The man thought for a moment. 'You know, when I go back to Leeds, I allus take a fish with me, a bit of cod, haddock, whatever you've landed. And I sell it to people. I'll tell you this, I sell it for more than I pay for it here. That's how I reckon to make a bit of baccy money! You could do the same, I would have thought. Instead of sending your fish into Whitby, couldn't you sell it straight to somebody in Leeds? And get a bit more for it?'

Reuben immediately thought of the sum of money they'd found on Sam Pitt all those years ago, when his body had been uncovered, frozen solid in that storm. It had been a *lot* of money, more than twice the amount they'd expected him to earn in Pickering.

If he could make *twice* as much for his fish. . . ! If all the Ravenswyke fishermen could. . . ! Reuben never thought of himself alone; what was good for the fishing community of Old Quaytown was good for him. He had neither ambition nor desire to prosper either in isolation or at the expense of the others. One key to Reuben's character was that he had no competitive urge other than the one that had been bred into him by being a Godson. He wanted to be first off, first home, with most, but only as a continuing proof of *himself* and the integrity of his family, and not to defeat anyone else, to do them down, to take advantage of them. It was like being in a competition in which he wanted them all to be winners, with no losers. All together.

A few of them were sitting around in the taproom when he went in and ordered his pint of ale. Now he sat near the fire, not away in a corner, and folks made room for him. He was a full-grown man with a handsome face. His dark hair was thick and glistened without any need for the pomades and creams some of the men had taken to using. He'd had a year-long flirtation with a moustache, but had never grown used to having hair sticking out on his upper lip. The wind and weather had beaten his complexion to a ruddy tan; his hands with the large spade-end nails were cracked and cut from handling fishing gear, but he kept them scrupulously clean and his nails, of necessity, cut short, level with the ends of his fingers. He was at the peak of his fitness and strength – it'd take a foolhardy man to tackle him or challenge him to a fight. One of his most attractive features was his ready slow smile, and his even temper. It took a lot to make Reuben lose his wick but, once he did, look out, they'd say! In the way of northerners, he was quick to judge if a man was being a fool, quick to strike the first blow, which often was the last. Sam Gainer was sitting in the tap; he'd sold his coble in Whitby but had pined, not having access to the sea living in Middlesbrough running the shop his aunt had left him. A year later, he sold the business and reinvested the money in a small motor coble, which he brought back to Ravenswyke. The day he arrived from Whitby, they'd gathered at the top of the landing and had given him a hero's cheer as the tractor they'd bought jointly to replace the horses dragged him over the scaurs on the cradle. Bill Brawnham was sitting by the fire, talking with Walter Clegg; their two lads were having a game of dominoes in the corner. Reuben knew the two lads were both waiting for their papers to come through, their seamen's papers for the jobs they'd got with Turnbull's. They were already talking round the village about the far-flung places they'd be visiting, the exotic foreign women they'd be enjoying. Bill Clewson had added a word of warning. 'Aye, and all them foreign diseases you'll be bringing back. Well, don't come to me for a lick of pitch when it drops off.'

'I can't understand why tha didn't stop in Middlesbrough,' Walter Clegg was saying across the table and the beer pots to Sam. 'Warm comfortable billet, nowt strenuous to do except push packets of baccy across the counter....'

Sam shook his head. 'My big mistake,' he said, 'was to take a place where I couldn't see the ocean. I ought to have sold that business and bought another one where I could have heard the sea from my bedroom window!'

'There's nowt worth looking at on t'ocean,' Bill Brawnham said lugubriously. 'Lot o' water, heaving up and down. Us sees enough of it from one low tide to the next. When I retire, mark my words, I'm going to get out a map of England, and a compass, and pick myself a little cottage that's at the furthest point inland from any ocean. The way the wind laps round my roof, and the watter thunders agin the rocks, is enough to drive a sane man out of his mind!'

'Just goes to show how daft we are, the lot of us,' Reuben said. 'To get out on the top of it and try to make a living.'

Reuben leaned forward. 'I've got summat I want to talk to you

257

about!' he said. Everyone listened. When Reuben wanted to talk, it usually meant something important, since he wasn't a man to waste words. 'You know it's this Friday as Dr Gilchrist is handing over to that young fellow Suddaby. Well, I think we all ought to chip summat in, and buy him a going-away present. Look at the years he's looked after us, and turned out in all weathers for us wives and babbies. Remember that time, Bill, when he came out to your coble to set your broken leg, and the waves was that heavy we had to tie both you and him into the boat. Every one of us, without exception, owes him summat. I think this'd be the time to show him.'

Not a single man in the room dissented. 'What about that lot in t'Falcon, aye, and t'Laurel? It's not just us as uses this pub as owes the doctor,' Bill Clewson said. But Reuben shook his head. 'This is from us,' he said. 'What other folks does is their own affair. What I think we ought to do is get Walter Brackley, when he's going round with t'letters, to mention it on every doorstep in Old Quaytown. Then whatever we got could be engraved, like, from the residents of Old Quaytown, know what I mean?'

'It'd be a grand gesture,' Walter Clegg said. 'I'm right glad you thought of that, Reuben. You can put me in for ten bob!'

'Nay,' Reuben said, 'there's no need to overdo it. Half a crown would be more than handsome!'

They were all silent for a moment, each one thinking his own thoughts, remembering the reasons they had for being grateful to Dr Gilchrist. Suddaby, all agreed, couldn't hold a candle to the old doctor. He was young and fresh out of medical school, or hospital, or wherever these young lads trained. He'd already caused a few ructions by changing people's medication. When you've been taking a pink pill for years, to hold back your rheumatism, you don't suddenly take kindly to being asked to swallow a green one, even though the doctor says it might actually cure you whereas the pink one was just keeping you going!

'I don't like the idea of that young lad handling t'babbies in t'future!' Bill Brawnham said. 'Apart from Amy Benson's, t'doctor has never brought forth a dud un!'

Amy Benson had conceived late in life. The baby, an unmistakable mongoloid, had lived, mercifully they all thought, only three months. Mongoloid children, it was reported by some of the newer tenants of Newquay Town, were commonplace in the slums of

Leeds and Bradford. Babies in Ravenswyke were born healthy with the minimum of fuss and bother! 'He'll have to pull up his socks,' Bill Clewson said. 'Esther Blakey won't last for ever. . . .'

'Nor will Alicia Pentyford!' Sam Gainer said. 'I reckon she's cured more ailments around here than any doctor!'

They nodded and looked at each other and Sam had the grace to smile. It was an open secret that Sam had been a hell-raiser as a young lad, and several of the village lasses had recourse to Alicia Pentyford, when they 'missed'. They well remembered when Amos Shingler had taken a rope's end to Sam and given him a right lathering. Thereafter, Sam had confined his attentions to lasses from the nearby villages. 'Aye,' Sam said, admitting his past misdeeds in public for the first time, 'we were very foolish in them days! I remember I'd walk ten miles for a lass. Now, I don't have the strength to walk ten yards! Not for that, any road!'

There was a generous and companionable laugh, then each drank his beer. It was time to go home, each his separate way, but all into Old Quaytown. They'd meet on the morrow, as sure as the tides would turn, but then the talk would be of the weather, the winds, the waves and fishing, not the remembrances of past deeds and misdeeds. 'Aye,' Reuben said as he drained his pint and got up to go. 'I'll be on my way. My lass will be waiting for me.'

He came out of the taproom, looked up at the bulk of the hotel above him, seeing the oceanwards window of the suite where Emma had taught him a thing or two. It seemed like a century ago but talk of the lasses had stirred his loins again.

He walked slowly up the hill through the moonlight, seeing the great flocculent scudding clouds alternately blacken and lighten his way ahead. The night had a clean cold to it, and the ocean smelled more salty than usual because of it. The kelp, the slate of the scaurs, all gave off that odour he'd never forget as long as he lived. The odour of Old Quaytown, Ravenswyke.

The light was on in the front bedroom as he went in over the step. Hannah was still sitting by the fire, but she'd put on her flannelette nightie and the slippers he'd brought her for Christmas. She was wearing her old cloth coat that now she used only as a dressing gown. She'd made him a pot of cocoa, and a thick cheese sandwich with pickled onions sliced on it, the way she knew he liked it.

259

He sat by her side, staring with her into the last of the flames, not needing to say anything. After a few minutes, she turned to him. 'I reckon as you can lig abed in the morning,' she said. 'You'll not be going out!'

'Here, who says I won't?' he said, resenting the suggestion of interference with his own decision. A fisherman decides for himself if he's going out or not, not has his womenfolk tell him! But, he had to admit, Hannah had a fine eye for the weather and usually knew what she was saying. Especially when she made a prediction.

'The weather'll say you won't,' she said sagely, as if the weather had given her a confidential tip-off!

'Then I shall decide that on t'landing,' he said, 'not ligging in bed! When did a Godson decide whether or no to go out with the blankets round his lug-holes!'

'You're a stubborn young tyke,' she said. 'I reckon you always was and always will be. You could lig abed next to that wife of yours,' she said. 'She could use a bit of comforting, it seems to me!'

'Comforting! Why, you interfering old crone,' he said, smiling at her to take any malice from his words. He knew it was her way of tipping him off about Emily's medical recovery. After the birth of each child, he'd always tried to be considerate and patient, not like some of 'em. That Harry Townsend, insisting on having his wife right there in the cottage hospital when she still carried the stitches from her caesarean! Apparently, so the story went, the ward sister had broken a bedpan on his arse! Reuben had made a practice of waiting until either Emily had made the approach to him, or Hannah had tipped him off in her blunt, but indirect way.

He stood in front of the fire when Hannah had gone up to bed, and stripped to the skin. Then he went through to the back and sluiced cold water over his body, rubbing himself vigorously with the block of olive oil soap. He came back to the fire, opened the fire oven, and from it took the nightshirt he knew Hannah would have placed in there to sop up the last of the warmth. There was also a plate, already wrapped in a scrap of blanket, and he tucked it under his arm when he went upstairs. Emily was lying in bed, wearing her pink flannelette nightie with the flowers embroidered around the neckline. He'd commented often about that embroidery and the garment. He slid the iron plate into the bottom of the bed and she moved her feet across to place them on it. 'Ah, that's nice,' she said. 'I wondered if you'd remember! Though my chilblains'll give me gyp!'

He stood for a moment at the foot of the bed, looking at her. She was sitting up on the pillow, her arms folded under her breasts. She was a good-looking woman, he thought. Even though she'd had six kids there was still something girlish about her. At that moment, he knew he loved her more than he could ever possibly tell her. 'I'm glad you're feeling a bit better,' he said as he slipped in beneath the blankets. She slithered down the bed until she was level with him; he put out his arm and she snuggled on it, her head resting in the hollow of his shoulder. 'Aye, I'm all right again now,' she said. 'I'll be getting up tomorrow. I've felt that idle lying in bed when you've been working.'

'Did the doctor come this evening?'

'This evening? I didn't know he was due. He doesn't like coming out in the evenings except for emergencies. He never has. . . .'

'I don't mean Gilchrist. I meant Suddaby, the new lad.'

'Him? What's he supposed to come for?'

'I met him in the street this afternoon. We were talking about Eleanor, and he said that if he had the time and Mrs Farthing wasn't taken this evening, he'd come down and have a chat with her. I guess Mrs Farthing must have been took bad.'

'Your mam heard she passed away.'

'Did she? That's another one gone. All the old families. Soon there'll be none left. I could remember when the Farthings had two boats here. One belonged to Mrs Farthing's family by her first husband, the other by her second. I can remember the way the six lads were all daggers drawn with each other. Many's the fight I watched as a young lad, right there on the landing. And now the lads are either dead or working out of Hull, and old Mrs Farthing, who buried three husbands in her time, has gone! It's all changing, Emily,' he said, his voice troubled. 'It seems to me harder and harder to keep it all together.'

'It's nowt to do with you,' she said. 'You don't have to keep it together!'

'Ah, lass, that's where you're wrong. Somebody's got to do it. Somebody's got to hold on to what we've got, else what'll be left to hand on to Wilfred, Arthur and Amos? Aye, and John in his time! I can't see four lads of mine working in an inland factory, breaking the line that stretches back all them years.'

She reached up and nuzzled his chin. 'One thing I've wanted to ask you, Reuben,' she said mischievously. 'What would you have done if all I'd given you were lasses? Like Hester Gramond and Mark Adam Tockett. . . . They say James Henry is going out of his mind, as if fate has taken its revenge on him for what he did to Mark Adam. . . .'

'Nay, Emily, that's nobbut a servant's spite,' he said, remembering the rumour and gossip that had been put about, claiming that James Henry had horsewhipped Mark Adam and forced him to marry Hester Gramond, as she then was. Shortly afterwards, the Irishman McCloy had been discharged without a reference and, some said, had gone back to his own country. Now Tockett House was staffed by the young widow of a clergyman who'd died early, and four girls from Hester Gramond's village, who lived in. The garden was tended by Wally Lockridge, also from Hester Gramond's village, an antisocial, teetotal Wesleyan who never came into Ravenswyke, and four lads from Dr Barnardo's, who lived in a hut in the grounds and were never allowed in the house. A fifth lad had been discharged and couldn't even get back into Barnardo's, when he'd been discovered in the bushes with one the housemaids by Wally Lockridge and given a thrashing that had made him black and blue for a month.

'Aye, happen, but what *would* you have done, Reuben Godson, if we'd had six lasses, one after t'other?'

'I think I'd have chopped it off!' Reuben said smiling. 'If all it could make were lasses!'

He felt her hand tugging the hem of his nightshirt, and lifted his buttocks from the bed so that she could pull it up. He could feel her hand, warm and companionable, on him. He put his own hand down inside the neck of her nightie so that he could hold her breast, feeling the nipple large with child-suckling.

They lay there, still, both content, both feeling the nearness of the other as a tangible force that ruled their lives. 'I'll tell thee this much, lass,' he said, and his voice was husky. 'I don't know what I'd 'a done if I'd lost thee, this last time!'

'Don't talk about losing me, Reuben,' she said, shivering, as if someone had walked over her grave.

'Happen, I'll lig abed in the morning,' he said, sleep quickly overcoming him.

'Aye, why don't you do that!' she said. 'Why don't we both!'

When John Fothergill had been taken on as the agent for the Tocketts, James Henry had briefed him about his job. 'You mun spend every penny as though it were coming out of your own pocket!' he'd said. Administering that principle had made Fothergill the most unpopular man in Newquay Town. He was standing by Bank Cottages when the lorry arrived from Whitby, carrying the roof tiles and the bags of cement, the load of fine sand and the timber.

Mrs Tockett rode behind the lorry in the Rolls, her three daughters sitting on the front seat next to Wallis, the new chauffeur, eyes looking everywhere. A crowd had gathered round the end of Bank Cottages and there were murmurings when they saw the Rolls, which had come more frequently since Hester Tockett had become Lady of Tockett House than any vehicle the Tocketts had ever owned. Hester had become a champion of the people's causes, and now it was she who conducted the afternoon meetings at which they were able to present their grievances, and not the old man, James Henry.

She came from the back of the Rolls and walked across to the lorry. The driver leaped from the cab to stand deferentially by Hester Tockett. He held out the bill of lading.

'Give us that here,' Fothergill said, not at all pleased by the present turn of events. For over a year the tenants of the three end cottages had been complaining that the tiles had blown loose on the roof, and several had been cracked by the recent winter gales. Fothergill had a programme of expenditures for the repair of the cottages, and as yet the tiles were not considered an early priority. He'd considered resigning when, a few weeks before, Mrs Tockett had come up with the idea, revolutionary to his ears, that the estate supply the materials, but that the cottagers supply their own labour. 'After all,' she'd said, 'those houses are a partnership. Between the estate and the tenants. We give them a lifetime economic rent, and we can surely expect them to do a little something for themselves in return?'

'With respect, ma'am,' he'd said, 'it'll never work. You don't know that lot down there, yet. Bone idle, that's what they are, bone idle when it comes to doing anything to them houses!'

'Nonsense, Mr Fothergill, stuff and nonsense. All they need is a bit of encouragement!'

And now the encouragement had arrived in the form of building materials. From time to time the men had worked on buildings locally. They had a sufficient reservoir of skill to be able to manage the simple job. A wall ladder, and one for the roof, had been brought from the estate yard and now stood against the wall of the first cottage. Fothergill was shaking his head as he put the bill of lading in his inside pocket and went to stand at a distance, indicating his disapproval of the entire affair. Hester knew that this occasion was, in a sense, a test of her beliefs, a baptism. Had she estimated correctly? Would these people respond? Could they be led to understand that these houses, these dwellings, represented a partnership between the formerly aloof House and them? Could she, Hester, bridge the gap that had been struck between them by hundreds of years of autocratic, feudal misuse? And could she do it and still maintain their respect? She was certainly not a socialist and didn't like many of the new ideas that were being put about. She believed in an ordered society that had clearly marked positions within it. For want of a better principle, money and position had to be the deciding factors, since that decided how everything else was divided. The employees and the employed, the leaders and the led, the lenders and the borrowers. Hester was quite satisfied that society contained its own survival instincts. It was possible for a young man to better his station in life. There were scholarships for the intelligent and compulsory education now meant universal opportunity for those who wanted to take advantage of it. She could not believe, with Fothergill, that these people were inferior and lazy. Many of them had been born, of course, when there was no universal education, when it was tantamount to impossible for a man to better himself except by slow means through several generations.

Would they take the opportunity she was offering? To help themselves? To join in the partnership?

'What's this, then, missis?' Walter Cole called out from the middle of the group standing outside the first cottage.

'What does it look like, Mr Cole?' she asked. 'It's roofing

264

material for the cottages!' She turned to the driver and walked to the lorry. 'Is this cement fresh?' she asked, pulling off her glove and placing her hand on the cement bag. That was a trick her father-in-law had told her. 'If the bag is cold, don't take it. The cement'll not be fresh!'

A ripple of surprise ran through the cottagers as they saw her handle the cement bag and heard her question. 'Yes, that's warm enough,' she said. The driver himself looked bemused. 'None of the tiles is cracked, I hope?' she asked, as imperious as if she were selecting material for her own table.

'No, ma'am, none of 'em is. I loaded 'em myself, most careful.'

Walter Cole seemed to have lost his initiative. 'Us isn't roofers, missis,' he called out from the security of the crowd.

She looked across at him. Know your enemy, eh? Well, this was one man she'd have to tackle, sooner or later. 'No, *Mr* Cole, you aren't a roofer. You aren't even a good donkey-engine man at the potash mine, either, to judge from the length of time the men have to stay down there, waiting for you to stop talking and get the steam up to pressure. Mind you, they say you're good at talking. I think they used to call you "the barrack-room lawyer" in the Yorks and Lancs Regiment, didn't they? At least, you talked yourself out of going to France when your battalion left, so I hear.'

Battle was joined and the cottagers loved it.

'Roofing is a skilled craftsman's job, and us isn't getting paid for it!'

Hester knew that any mention of money would lead to difficulties. These people wouldn't be able to understand the economics of running an estate, year after year, without losing money. They'd look at her, look at the Rolls and the children, and make comparisons with what it would cost to send a skilled man up on to the roof. They wouldn't realize that if such cost was repeated a hundred, a thousand times, then there wouldn't even be enough in the kitty to buy the materials. She walked to the car, and the chauffeur opened the back door. She beckoned to the front door, and he opened that. The girls came out, looking shy, standing in line. She led them by the hand to the side of the lorry. 'Take your gloves off,' she said. 'Come along, Felicity, help Elizabeth to take off her gloves. I'll help you, Netta.'

She lifted a tile from the back of the lorry and handed it to

Elizabeth. 'There, take the tile and put it near the bottom of the ladder, there's a good girl. But take care not to drop it!'

She looked at the cottagers, her eyes fixing on Walter Cole. 'If tha's too fancy, Walter Cole, to get thy hands mucky, us'll have to show thee how to set about it,' she said in a thick North Yorkshire voice.

Her imitation of Walter Cole's accent pulled a chuckle of approval from the crowd. They watched as each of the girls took a tile from her mother's hands and started to walk across to where the ladder had been propped. Elizabeth Jane, a tiny mite of four, staggered beneath the weight of hers. Then there came a roar from the cottagers and James Scannell rushed out. 'Nay, missis, nay!' he said. He rushed up to Elizabeth Jane. 'Come on, love,' he said, 'give us hold o' that!'

When he'd put the tile by the ladder he came back to the lorry, which the rest of the cottagers were already unloading. Two of the women were dusting down the fronts of the little girls' dresses and wiping their hands.

'Nay, Mrs Tockett,' James Scannell said, though with a twinkle in his eye, 'tha didn't need to shame us! Well, not all of us, any road!'

By the time that dusk came, the three girls were sitting in the back of the Rolls asleep, Hester Tockett was standing with John Fothergill, and the four end cottages were snug and watertight, with every loose or cracked tile replaced by the cottagers' own labour. Even Walter Cole had been bullied into mixing the cement that would hold the tiles securely in position.

The taproom of the Raven was crowded, but everybody fell silent when the door opened and Reuben came in with Dr Gilchrist, who was carrying his worn brown leather bag. The doctor looked around the room. 'Where is Sam Gainer?' he said. 'What have you done with him? Taken him upstairs? You ought not to have moved him, you know, if he has broken bones. . . .' The rest of what he said was lost in coughing.

The crowd parted and revealed Sam Gainer lying on his back across two table tops.

'There's too many of you in here,' Dr Gilchrist said, as he pushed his way through the crowd, which closed in and re-formed behind him. He brought a chair forward and put his bag on it. As he opened his bag, Sam slowly started to get up.

'No, stay still!' Dr Gilchrist said, still trying to stem the tide of his cough.

Sam continued to rise, a huge smile on his face. And then they all started to hum, and then to sing, and the strains of 'For he's a jolly good fellow' echoed round the room as they sang and banged their beer pots in time with the music.

Dr Gilchrist looked about him, uncomprehending at first, but then, when Reuben stepped forward with a case in his hand and headed towards him, he got the message.

They stopped singing. Reuben was standing in front of Dr Gilchrist, the case extended. The doctor opened it and gulped. It was a set of brand-new nickel-plated surgical instruments, all set in purple plush, each nestling in its own space. It had everything – scalpels, forceps, retractors, hypodermics.

'Take it,' Reuben said. 'They've asked me to make a speech but I'm not one much for words. We've all collected in Old Quaytown and we're grateful to Dr Suddaby for telling us what we should buy. It's, like, a going-away present. From each and every one of us. Like, happen, many of us wouldn't be here if it hadn't been for the way you've looked after us over the years. We know, like, that it's a doctor's duty to look after t'patients, that hypocritic oath and all that, but all of us reckons that you've always done more than your duty, and bugger t'hypocritic oath. . . .'

'Hippocratic!' Dr Gilchrist said hesitantly.

'Aye, well, whatever it is. We feel you've done more. And we'd like you to take this with you wherever you go as, like, a token of us gratitude, us respect, aye, and us love!'

The doctor couldn't remain standing; he reached behind himself, pulled his bag from the chair and sat down. Tears were running from his eyes. He held out his hand and Sam Gainer took it, holding it tight. When he'd regained partial control of himself he looked up at Reuben and at the grinning faces around him.

'For somebody who can't make a speech, Reuben lad,' he said, 'you've got the right gift of the gab!' There were wild cheers and shouts, and the men crowded in to slap his back or just touch him to show their involvement. A large whisky was handed overhead, and Reuben took it and placed it on the table where Sam Gainer had been lying, a victim – or so they'd told Dr Gilchrist to get him down to the pub – of an accident that appeared to have broken several bones!

Young Dr Suddaby came from his temporary concealment at the back of the crowd, reached and shook Dr Gilchrist's hand. 'It's a privilege, doctor,' he said owlishly, since he'd obviously had a few, 'to be associated with you! But, if I were you, I'd see a doctor about that cough of yours!' He turned round and the crowd roared approval of his joke.

'Now, don't you start making speeches, too,' Dr Gilchrist said. 'No wonder we couldn't find you to come out on this "emergency" – you were already down here, supping ale!'

Claude Cecil Gilchrist died a month later of consumption. They buried him in the cemetery at the top of the bank in the presence of everybody in Ravenswkye who could walk or find someone to push or carry them up the bank.

In his will, he left a sum of money to be used for the modernization of the Ravenswyke lifeboat.

He left his old leather bag, his case of new surgical instruments and his practice to Dr Suddaby – 'in certain conviction, though I have known him but a short time, that he will use this bequest wisely for the benefit of all the inhabitants of what I have come to regard as my village, my home.'

He left his library of non-technical books, his novels, his biographies, his travel books, his books of poetry, to form the basis of a free lending library for all the inhabitants of Ravenswyke, with a capital sum of 500 guineas, the interest on which would pay the wages of a librarian and the rent of a room in the Village Institute. 'It is my dear wish,' his will said, 'that the post of librarian be offered to Eleanor Godson, who, I feel sure, will carry out all its duties and responsibilities with exemplary dedication and devotion.'

Higgins took the fish in his hand and threw it against the wall. It bounced back and fell on the wet marble floor. Higgins bent down and picked it up, opening its gills to look inside, studying its eyes. 'Aye, I'll grant you it's a nice bit o' fish!'

Reuben opened the canvas bag he'd carried on his shoulder and took out a lobster that must have had a body weight of two pounds. Higgins examined that, too, with an experienced eye.

'That were pulled out of t'water this morning,' he said, like a wine-taster after his second sip.

'I should know,' Reuben said. 'It was me as pulled it out!'

'Ravenswyke, is that where you said you come from?'

'Yes. I've fished there all my life. And my family before me. I've four lads as'll take over when I'm gone.'

'And you're saying as you can keep us supplied, day by day, with fresh fish of that quality. You've obviously done your homework or you wouldn't have come to me, but you know we supply the biggest hotels in Leeds. And it's only the best as is good enough for them!'

'It's a long time, I'll be bound, since you saw fish of that quality,' Reuben said. The man from Newquay Town had given him the idea. If there was such a yearning throughout the West Riding for good fresh fish, why should they bother sending it to Whitby? Even if they moved swiftly there, the fish was bound to be at least a day old when it arrived in the West Riding. Sometimes, even two days old. But if he was taking his stuff up to the top of the bank and putting it on the train for Whitby, why shouldn't he send it the other way? He'd already inquired, and there were two trains a day that made the connection straight through to Leeds, one in the late morning, the other in the late afternoon. If they could get the morning train, they'd beat anybody on the Whitby connection by six hours at least. The first, with the best!

'What sort of price were you considering?' Higgins asked shrewdly.

'It'd be the same price you'd pay in Whitby.'

'Then there's no advantage. . . .'

'Yes, there is! You'd be getting your fish at least twenty-four hours sooner. It'd be that much fresher!' Reuben glanced slyly at the large sign over the large steel roll-up door: 'W. Higgins & Sons. Fresh Fish Daily'. 'Then, Mr Higgins,' he said, 'you could give that sign of yours some real meaning!'

Higgins looked up and laughed. 'Aye, well, signs above shops are like fishermen's boasts,' he said. 'A prudent man takes 'em both wi' a pinch of salt! Tell me, what happens when you have bad weather and can't get out? From what I remember, Ravenswyke is a hard port to fish from. You have to drag 'em out every night, eh?'

'We drag 'em out, we push 'em back in. We've been doing it

for four hundred years now, so we've got ourselves used to it!'

'You get out every day. Weather or no?'

It was a loaded question. From no port in the world could a fisherman guarantee to go out every day. 'It takes a hard blow to keep us in. . . !' Reuben said, knowing it was the weak point in his argument.

Higgins spread his arm wide. 'I've got commitments, Mr Godson, every day. They print the menus, you know. Somebody sees cod or haddock on the menu, or fancies a bit of fresh lobster, he expects to get it.'

It *was* the weak point of his argument. If *they* couldn't get out of Ravenswkye because of heavy seas, the chances were that a few boats would still be able to get off the Whitby pier, or out of Runswick Bay, Robin Hood's Bay or Staithes. It'd have to be a very special day, a really bad blow, before they'd all be kept ashore. And then, usually, the Whitby market would have kept a bit back from the previous day. It'd be a very rare day when the boxes arrived in Leeds empty.

'My business depends on *reliability*,' Higgins was saying. 'I've contracted to supply so much fish each day, and I daren't go under that. No, Mr Godson, good though your fish is, I don't see any way we can do business!'

Reuben wandered disconsolately out of the market, feeling ill at ease on a working day in his suit, feeling even more ill-at-ease trying to sell fish instead of catching it. On the *Hope* he was master, exercising skills he'd learned as a lad. But he felt he was no salesman! Too late he thought of arguments he could have used. When the weather started blowing up, Higgins could have held some of the fish Reuben sent him in his extensive ice and cold-storage facilities that Reuben had seen. Or, come to think of it, Reuben himself could have held some of the fish back. But his mind rebelled against the latter course. He'd come to Leeds on the basis of offering fresh-caught fish every day – he couldn't play false with the people he was trying to do business with!

That first meeting discouraged him. He walked round the streets of Leeds for an hour, hating the bustle, the people walking everywhere, pushing along the pavement. He hated the clank of the tramcars on their railings, the buses, the cars and lorries everywhere. The only horse he saw was by the Corn Exchange and that was tethered in a brewer's dray. He remembered a boyhood joke

– what's the difference between one of Kitchener's men and a brewer's horse? A Kitchener's man darts into the fray while a brewer's horse. . . . The joke did nothing to cheer him. He stood at a stall when he got back to the market and drank a pot of tea with a pie and some peas. Then he looked at the list he'd made and set off to see the next man, Josiah Featherby.

Even though he remembered his argument in time, Featherby made the same objection Higgins had made. 'If I've got to hold the fish over in my cold storage, it'll not be fresh that day and I'll have lost my advantage,' Featherby said. Reuben couldn't fault the logic. He wandered about all day, seeing every fish wholesaler, and was totally depressed when he made his way back to the station. It'd been a wasted day and, into the bargain, he'd lost the price of his train fare!

He was walking up the road beside the Queen's Hotel when he heard a car stop next to him. There was no mistaking the voice that called out 'Reuben? Reuben Godson?' He turned and saw Emma sitting in the back of a limousine that looked as long as a boat. The chauffeur sitting in isolation in the front was wearing a grey uniform, and a grey peaked hat. Reuben noticed the fancy bugger was even driving the car in white cotton gloves. As the car stopped, the chauffeur applied the brake and walked quickly but arrogantly round the bonnet. He opened the back door and Emma patted the seat beside her. 'Come on, Reuben,' she said, 'get in.' He climbed into the back of the car, the size of the cockpit of the new *Hope*, and squatted on the edge of the seat. His face creased in a smile. 'Emma,' he said, 'it is good to see you!'

She was eyeing him quizzically. 'You've grown,' she said, 'you've matured!'

He laughed. 'I'd better have,' he said. 'I've six bairns to feed now!'

'Six!' she said, laughing. Her voice still held that bell-like tinkle that had so attracted him all those years ago.

'And you,' he said, 'you're still a beautiful woman. Probably the most beautiful I've ever clapped eyes on!'

'I have two children, now, Reuben,' she said quietly. 'I'm married.'

'With Stan Baxter?'

'Who else? I told you. . . .'

Reuben looked at the back of the chauffeur's neck behind the glass panel that separated the front from the back of the car. 'Can he hear what we're talking about?' he asked nervously.

'No, the glass panel is soundproof. Oh, Reuben, I am delighted to see you. Stan is arriving on the train. We've come to meet him. He'll be so pleased to see you. . . .'

'I'm not so sure about that,' Reuben said with a smile hovering on his mouth. 'I seem to remember the last time we met, we didn't part too well. In fact, the boom of the *Hope* knocked him into the water.'

'I was watching,' she said, 'from the bedroom window! It was all I could do to stop laughing by the time he got back, soaking wet through. He doesn't hold any malice,' she said. 'That's one of the many nice things about him. He's quick up and quick down, but he doesn't hold malice or grudges. I tell you, he'll be pleased to see you.'

'I was getting a train myself,' he said, taking the half-hunter out of his waistcoat pocket. 'I mustn't miss it else I shan't get home tonight.'

'Oh, you'll stay with us, won't you, Reuben? Take a bite of supper with us, and then stay over.'

He was tempted; it had been a lousy day, especially for a man who'd never grown accustomed to being turned down. The issue was settled as soon as Stan saw him. He bounded off the platform wearing an alpaca coat, saw Emma and hugged her uninhibitedly, then noticed Reuben. 'Reuben Godson,' he said, 'by all that's holy!'

'I have to get a train,' Reuben said. 'I just thought I'd stay to say hello, but now I must dash. . . .'

'Catch a train? Never! We're going here in the Queen's to have supper and something to drink, and then you're coming home with us, isn't he, Emma?'

Reuben had no alternative; he was swept along on Baxter's tide of obvious pleasure at their meeting again, his camaraderie, his enthusiasm for any detail Reuben could give him about Ravenswyke. They marched into the Queen's Hotel, a somewhat incongruous trio since Reuben was still carrying the canvas bag in which he'd brought the fish to Leeds. Stan Baxter dumped that in the hands of a startled waiter. 'Get rid of that for the moment, lad,' Baxter said, with the confidence bred of money. They marched into the cocktail lounge on a sea of greetings – 'Hello,

Harry,' 'Hello, Mr Baxter.' 'Hello, Mavis, how's your boyfriend?' 'Hello, Mr Baxter, you know I haven't got one.' 'Ah, you would have, if I weren't already wed!'

'What'll you have to drink, Reuben?' Stan asked. 'I seem to remember you favour brandy.'

'Yes, that'd be all right!' Reuben didn't know what else to ask for. He was bewildered by the number of bottles behind the counter, by the waiter dressed in his uniform waiting for their order. He chafed as Stan and Emma seemed to take ages deciding what to have. Many people, though Reuben couldn't know it, were experimenting with American cocktails, and the contents of each one had to be explained. The waiter didn't seem to mind the delay.

When they moved into the dining room for an early supper, they were the only ones in there. Reuben eyed the ocean of white-clothed tables, the waiters again standing about, with dismay. It was as if Emma could sense what was going on inside him. She dropped back as Stan marched forward, demanding, though in a friendly way, what he called 'my favourite table, and Pete to look after us'. 'He's always like this when we go out,' she said, 'but you mustn't mind. It's not that he means to put on a show, but he's a man who knows what he wants and can pay enough to get it. You'd never believe it but the waiters all know him, and all like him! I think because they know instinctively he was one of their kind but he made it – they're not without hope that they might make it too when they see him.'

As they ate, Stan pumped Reuben about the recent events in Ravenswyke, without once referring to the aborted land sale, or the way Reuben's boom had tipped him into the ocean. He obviously had a prodigious memory for names and places and could ask direct questions about the people Reuben had grown up with. 'Sam Gainer,' he said, 'has he got rid of that business in Middlesbrough and come back to Ravenswyke?' Reuben was astounded Stan Baxter could remember Sam Gainer, but he went one step further. 'I said to myself, when I heard about that in-heritance, that Sam Gainer would never last behind the counter of any shop. I gave him two years before he was pining once again for the ocean.'

The car, which Reuben discovered was a Bentley, from Stan Baxter's instructions to the head waiter – 'Have them get my

Bentley for me, Charles, there's a good lad!' – whirled them quietly through the streets of Leeds to Stan's house, which was set in ten acres of ground; a double-fronted structure, it also had an L-shape jutting out at the back and was on three storeys. 'We only use the first two floors at the front,' Stan said casually. 'The rest is for the servants.'

Once again Reuben marvelled at the way Stan Baxter said these things, which could have been outrageous had they not come out with such a simple sincerity. While Emma went upstairs to change, Stan showed Reuben the guest bedroom, which had a bathroom beyond it big enough to contain the whole of Reuben's cottage in Ravenswyke, and a bath that must have been seven feet long and three feet wide. By now, Reuben was immune to superlatives. He washed his face and hands, combed his hair and went back downstairs. A servant was just coming out of the room to the right of the front door; she gave a bit of a stiff bob and said, 'The Master's in there, sir.'

Reuben couldn't remember the last time anybody had called him 'sir'. He would have had to admit to himself that there was something about it he enjoyed! Wait till he told Hannah and Emily about his adventure tomorrow!

Stan Baxter was sitting in an enormous leather-covered chair by a roaring fire, and motioned Reuben to sit opposite him. 'Emma sends her apologies,' he said, 'but she's got a bit of a headache and will see you at breakfast in the morning, if that's all right?' He didn't tell Reuben he'd instructed her not to come down.

Reuben nodded. After all, what else could he do?

Stan Baxter looked at him for a moment, then stirred himself, reached out to the table set between the two chairs and poured two glasses of brandy from a cut crystal decanter. 'Now, Reuben,' he said. 'You've listened to my braying long enough. Tell me, what brings you to Leeds?'

The first thing he'd noticed back in the railway station had been Reuben's worried and disappointed expression. Here, he told himself, was a man who'd suffered, or was suffering, some kind of reverse. Age changes all men, developing traits dormant in youth, extinguishing foolish fires kindled by inexperience. Stan Baxter had become less aggressive, more in tune with the thoughts of other people. Over the years, he'd developed a sensitivity that no one who knew him during his Ravenswyke days would have believed possible. And he'd found it profitable! Nowadays he didn't make enemies, didn't have to fight people to get what he wanted. Nowadays he made friends, and friends let him in on opportunities or gave him advance warnings of difficulties ahead so that he could get out of losing situations in time. Emma clearly understood what was happening to her husband. All his life, she realized, he'd sought wealth only because, in his eyes, it would bring respectability. Unlike most people, he didn't want the *power* that wealth could bring. He wanted to have so much money that everything in his life – his wife, the education of his children, his dress, his home, his whole style of living – would be beyond reproach. Slowly he was getting there. Now when they went to new places he didn't cultivate the staff as assiduously as in the past, insisting on memorizing all their first names and pressing large tips on them. Now he was content to lower his voice and behave himself, and still got the service he wanted.

Reuben found it easy to talk to him, and poured out his problems about the direct sale of the fish. Stan heard him out, obviously recognizing the names Reuben gave him of men like Higgins and Featherby. 'Aye, they're a cautious, tight-fisted lot,' he said at one stage. 'They'd be looking more to a financial advantage than to get fresher fish. Let's face it, so long as they can sell it, they don't care what the fish is like – you can bet they never eat it.' He took a small bound notebook from his inside pocket and a thin gold pencil. He jotted down a few figures, added them up, crossed them out again. 'That was your error, Reuben,' he said, 'if you don't mind me saying so. When you're selling, you've got to understand the lad you're selling to. You've got to get inside his mind to find out just what he's looking for. Is he looking for guaranteed quality, or a bigger profit? Is he looking for reliability of deliveries, or what? You've got to tailor your approach accordingly. Higgins and Featherby'll both be looking for reliability and a bigger profit. You'll have to guarantee deliveries every day, and knock at least three per cent off the Whitby price. I've worked it out that you could still afford to do that and pay the cartage and you yourself would still finish up twenty per cent above the price *you're* now getting. But your approach is wrong. They don't know you, they can't see beyond their noses; they won't trust you.'

'So you think the scheme is hopeless?'

Stan thought for a moment. 'In business, Reuben,' he said finally, 'I've always believed, cobblers should stick to their lasts. You're a fisherman, representing fishermen. You're neither a salesman nor an agent. Salesmen and agents are a very special breed of men, Reuben. They're like ferrets – they can go down a dark hole where you and I would see nowt, and they bring out a rabbit! What you need is an agent.'

'Like Fearon?'

'No. You need somebody a bit more than that. An agent who has access to a bit of cold storage on the quiet. Somebody who'll be in a postion to guarantee the wholesalers will have the supplies they need *every* day.'

'Even if it isn't fresh. . . ?'

'That's not your concern, Reuben. It'll be fresh enough to satisfy your conscience when it leaves you, I'll be bound.'

'But won't employing an agent mop up the extra we'll be getting?' Reuben asked.

Stan smiled. 'Ah, you don't know too much about business, Reuben,' he said. 'The agent will pay you the same price, day in and out, that you'd be getting from the wholesalers, three per cent below their usual Whitby prices. But he'll be selling on a guarantee. He'll get the same as the Whitby prices because of that guarantee. But – and here's where he'll make his brass – when there's a shortage in Whitby, when there're storms so bad that nobody can land any fish, he'll get his out of the storage, right here in Leeds, and he'll deliver it. At a price, of course. The way to make money in business, Reuben, is to put yourself in a position where you're the only one who has, here and now, what people want, here and now. I'll give you an example. When the last war came, I was ready. Everybody was crying out for cloth for uniforms, weren't they? I was sitting on a mountain of it I'd bought dirt cheap a few years before because nobody had wanted it. But I had a little dicky-bird tell me that war was inevitable. The politicians knew war was coming long before that nonsense at Sarajevo! That was only an excuse for a planned situation to take fire! I know just the man for you. Tommy Tomlinson has a small fish business. Right now I believe he specializes in wholesaling smoked. He'd be glad to get into the fresh stuff. And there's a point I hadn't thought of. He can mop up your surplus, for smoking!'

Reuben looked at him admiringly. 'Is there anyone, Mr Baxter, you don't know? Anything you don't know about?'

'I shan't want to know anything about you if you don't stop calling me Mr Baxter.'

The following morning Stan Baxter was up and about as early as Reuben himself, who had a fisherman's restlessness once dawn had broken. When Reuben caught the midday train to York, where he'd change for the North Yorkshire coast, the arrangements had been made. They would put their catch on the train each day; Tommy Tomlinson would take it off in Leeds. He'd already made a tentative contract with both Higgins and Featherby, on the strength of guaranteed freshness, an unbroken daily delivery *and* a three per cent price reduction! Reuben would see twenty per cent more for his fish, selling it this way, avoiding price fluctuations.

He was sitting in Stan Baxter's study; the telephone seemed to have been in use all morning as Stan phoned first one man and then the other, negotiating with the one against the other, telling what Reuben understood were monstrous white lies, no doubt the bait of business negotiations. When the last call had been made, the last arrangement had been clinched, he rang the bell and asked the parlourmaid who answered it to bring them coffee. He sat back in his chair while they waited for it to arrive, at rest for the first time since Reuben had met him at the railway station the previous evening. 'Now you see how the world of big business revolves, Reuben,' he said. 'Now you'll understand why I said a cobbler should stick to his last? This is my world; buying and selling, doing deals, making arrangements, is all in my blood! Just as going out every day after fish is in yours!'

'This morning has been an education,' Reuben said admiringly. 'All that, and you never even showed 'em a bit of fish!'

Stan Baxter laughed. 'Reuben, we sell and buy millions of pounds' worth of stuff every day and never see it. In some cases, we don't even know what it is! But so long as we know one man who wants to sell something, and another man who wants to buy something, we're in business. However, forget about that. There's something I've been meaning to say to you since I clapped eyes on you last evening. I owe you an apology!'

'*You* owe *me* an apology? What about?'

'The last time we saw each other!'

Reuben coloured when he remembered that boom swinging round and hitting Stan Baxter in the belly, knocking him arse over tip into the water. 'Nay, I reckon as it's *me* who owes *you* an apology.'

Stan was smiling and shaking his head. 'I can put it another way,' he said. 'As well as owing you an apology, I owe you my thanks. If you hadn't knocked me in the water, I wouldn't have got that chill and had to lay up in bed when I got back to Leeds. Aye, and while I was in bed, I put my thinking cap on. You know, the only reason I asked if I could come out on your boat was because I wanted to get to know you a bit better. I was a tactless, gormless devil in those days and hadn't learned there's a right and wrong way to go about anything. That's a lesson I've picked up slowly over the years. That business with the land purchase would have been good for everybody eventually, though I should have seen I'd never persuade you, because you have fixed ideas about Ravenswyke. Look, I'm not criticizing; don't get me wrong. I ought to have started in quietly, bought up a few bits of land, spent a bit of time among the folks to let them see there was no malice in me, that I wasn't just interested in gobbling everything in sight for my own profit!' He glanced at his watch, for once embarrassed by what he was saying. 'By gow, is that the time? I'd better tell Emma. She wants to ride to the station with you.' He rang the bell again and when the parlourmaid came in he told her to tell Mrs Baxter their guest was leaving, and to get the chauffeur to come round to the front door with the car. They both stood, looking out of the window. Stan seemed a bit awkward at first but, when he began to speak, Reuben understood why. 'Emma and me, Reuben, have *no* secrets from each other,' he said. 'What's past is past, that's my philosophy. But, once again, I'm grateful to you. You know, sometimes we don't know how much we value something until it looks as if somebody might be going to take it away from us!'

When Emma came into the room, dressed to go to the station, she realized at once that Stan had told Reuben he knew of their brief liaison. She linked her arm through an arm of each one of them. 'Friends are we, then?' she asked.

Stan laughed first, and then Reuben followed him. 'Aye, I reckon we are,' he said, 'I reckon we are!'

The arrangements Stan Baxter had set up so quickly were good ones; Tommy Tomlinson turned out to be a no-nonsense kind of businessman, scrupulously honest and meticulous. Soon he was pleading with Reuben to let him have more fish as he opened more outlets. Reuben signed up Sam Gainer, the Bredford boys, the Brawnhams and Cleggs. One day Bill Clewson came to see him. 'I've been having a word with Dr Suddaby,' he said, 'and he says the new medicine he's been giving me has worked a treat.'

'I'm right glad to hear that, Bill,' Reuben said. 'I'd noticed you weren't coughing as much these days.'

'Aye, well, the doctor also thinks it's all right for me to go back to sea. I've missed it that much, you know, Reuben, I've been aching to get back out there. I'm not a man for doing gardens and mending chimney pots. Or for taking folks for a quick run round.'

'That's grand news,' Reuben said, truly happy. None of them had enjoyed seeing Bill wandering around the place, a shadow of his former self and a figure of fun.

'There's nobbut one problem,' Bill said.

'You'll need a boat?' Bill's coble was old by now, and, though it was all right for rowing round the harbour, it could hardly face up to the heavy seas beyond the bay. And it had no form of propulsion except Bill's sturdy arms and the long sweeps the fishermen had used as oars. With a boat like that, a fisherman used two-thirds of his energies getting to and from the fishing grounds.

'I've got a bit saved,' Bill said tentatively, 'but not enough.'

Reuben didn't have to think for long. Bill Clewson had been known to Reuben all his life. He was born of a Ravenswyke fishing family, in Old Quaytown. 'Us'll have to find you a boat,' Reuben said. 'And you can pay it back from what you catch.'

Bill reached out his hand and they shook. 'Tha's like thee dad,' Bill said, 'a chip of t'owd block!' There was no finer compliment he could pay.

They found Bill a boat the first time of looking, in Whitby. It had belonged to a fisherman called Matthiessen whose family had originally come from Scandinavia somewhere. Matthiessen had grown tired of fishing and had gone to work in the yards, unloading the timber vessels of the Baltic trade. Jacoby the engineer had it lifted from the water on the gantry winch and probed the hull and the stern with his chisel. 'Sound as a bell,' he said. 'I can put you a diesel in that for fifty guineas! Secondhand, mind, but it'll be a goer. It's off a slurry pump they were using in the mine. The pump is buggered, but the engine's as sound as a bell!' Everybody knew and trusted Jacoby, and Bill Clewson set him to work.

When Bill motored the *Esperanza* round from Whitby, they all gathered at the landing to see him come in. No sooner had the hull touched the scaurs than they scrambled round it, tapping it, knocking it, looking at the engine. Then, in a moment of rare emotion – for fishermen tend to be a phlegmatic lot – they lifted Bill out of it and carried him across the scaurs and the sand spit, up the dock into the tap of the Raven. Most of them went home to their wives and beds the worse for drink that night. Why not? A fisherman saved from the land is a rare occasion, a time for celebration!

Emily was sitting by the fire when Reuben came in. They'd bought a sofa that occupied the left side of the hearth since the two chairs had cut off the warmth, Emily said, from the rest of the room. Now, on a cold evening, all the kids could sit with Emily and even leave room for Hannah to tuck herself in with her knitting, while Reuben had his grand and solitary chair, as was his right.

Eleanor had accepted the post of librarian; it paid her six pounds ten a quarter and gave her that much independence. Most of her time in the evenings was spent in the room of the Institute where shelves had been erected to house all Dr Gilchrist's collection of books. Eleanor, in the business of cataloguing the works under title and author, had opened one or two and had started reading the contents. Now she was like any new addict and every second she spent away from the library was a second lost to her. 'Mun as well take your bed up there,' Hannah had protested but not very sincerely. Frankly, any activity that got the gloomy widow out of the house was to be welcomed; though she was her only daughter, Hannah had long since ceased to feel any real affection for her. In Hannah's opinion, formed by a lifetime of habit, a woman kept herself right, found herself a man, and looked after him and gave him comfort and a family. That, Hannah was quite firmly convinced, was why women were born. She'd smiled wryly when she'd read accounts of women chaining themselves to railings so that they could get the vote, but what use was the vote to her? Whoever was in power in Scarborough made precious little difference to their lives in Ravenswkye. They had a parish council but the Godsons had never had anything to do with that. Anyway, the councillors, no matter which party was in power, were always the schoolteacher, one or other of the clerical gentlemen, and somebody recommended by the Tocketts, somebody 'county'. By her conduct, Eleanor had gone against, and still was going against, everything that Hannah had been brought up to believe in! Why, even Elsie Milner, for all her harum scarum ways, had finally settled down and got herself a man to look after! Eleanor's unmarried state was a constant reproach to Hannah. Now that she went out to the library and had to deal with the curious people who came to see this treasure Dr Gilchrist had bequeathed to them, at least she'd started washing her face and combing her hair. And she didn't smell any more. Reuben had insisted she fulfil certain household tasks in return for her bed and board. She still had the responsibility for the children, though Emily had wanted to end that when she'd fully recovered from John's difficult birth and insisted on tending the baby herself. But Eleanor looked after the rest of them and could only sneak off to the library when the kids were home for their tea.

Now that they were shipping regularly to Leeds, Reuben had bought a secondhand van which was used mainly to carry the fish up to the top of the bank and to bring down the empty boxes. Sometimes he'd use it on a Saturday to go into Whitby to look round the markets.

When Emily saw Reuben stagger in, she put down her knitting. She knew that look on his face. 'What've you been celebrating tonight?' she asked without rancour as she started to mash him a pot of fresh tea.

'Bill Clewson brought his boat from Whitby. We had to wet his head, hadn't we?'

'Aye, I reckon you had.'

She poured his tea into a mug and sat on the sofa. He had shrugged off his jacket, not without some difficulty, and now was having a problem getting the hanger over the peg behind the door. 'Chuck it on t'chair,' she said. 'I'll look after it for you!'

He did as she bid, came and sat down. She held his tea out to him and he took a long drink of it. 'You know, so long as I live I'll remember those words coming from you. *I'll look after it for you!* Aye, Emily, you've been a grand looker-after!'

She flushed with pleasure. It wasn't often he spoke his compliments to her! He was essentially a practical man, shy of words. When he'd go into Whitby he always came back with something for her, some little inexpensive gift but one she'd know he'd picked out with care, because it was something she needed, something she'd said at some time she could do with, something the right shade and colour. That way she'd learned that nothing she ever said was wasted, though he may not have seemed to hear it at the time. She was glad to remind herself of that, because there was something she wanted to say.

'Bill Clewson will be in your Leeds affair, will he?' she asked.

'Aye, that he will. I'll be down in t'morning, giving him his boxes!' They'd had a number of fish boxes made that could be tied with rope. The fish went to Leeds in them, and Tommy Tomlinson returned them empty. He'd done a deal with the railway company, and the cost of the return journey was absorbed in the payment for the full boxes. The boxes had been hot-metal stamped on the sides and the lid 'Godson of Ravenswyke'. It always gave Reuben a kick when he saw the piles of them bearing the family name!

'You don't think it would be worthwhile letting him send his stuff to Whitby?' There; it was out! Reuben looked surprised at her. A few years ago he'd have been angry if Emily had ever expressed an opinion on anything to do with the fishing side of their lives; it was a mark of the strength of their relationship that he no longer felt put out.

'How do you mean?'

'Like, I'm not trying to interfere. . . .'

He smiled. 'Emily, love, you *are* interfering, and you know it! You're putting your oar where it doesn't properly belong. But I'm listening. . . .'

'It just seemed to me, it has seemed to me since you got back from Leeds, that you're going against the tradition, the custom. And you're putting all your eggs in one basket. Oh, it's hard to explain what I mean. Folks hereabouts have always sent the fish they caught to market in Whitby. Look what happened the first time that pattern was broken. Two folks dead, and a lot of time wasted until you could square it right with Fearon again. Then the co-operative. That hasn't worked, has it? It's just dragged on and on, hasn't it? Tom Schofield is still sending his stuff to

Whitby, isn't he, like he's always done? Now there's *another* scheme going. This time to send the fish to Leeds. It goes against the *tradition*, Reuben. I don't know what your dad would have thought about it, honest I don't.'

Reuben sat upright, his head cleared after the drink he'd consumed. Anything to do with fishing, and his mind always concentrated like crystal. 'He'd have approved of it, Emily,' he said. 'Positive action! He was never a man for hanging about and letting others do things for him. That co-operative was a good idea while it lasted; tomorrow it's my intention to go see Tockett again, and bring it formally to an end. The climate's changing, Emily. A man's got to look out for himself more and more these days. Tradition was all right in its time, but now we've got to break new ground. We've got to start thinking for ourselves, not just doing what we do because it's what we've always done! Look at the tremendous advances in the modern world. Who'd have believed, when I were a lad, that we'd have fishing boats with engines in 'em, trains running to and from Ravenswyke? Who'd have ever thought I'd have owned a van? It's all changing, Emily, and we've got to change with it! Else we'll be dropped by the wayside. You mark my words!'

His head fell back against the seat. 'Don't fall asleep in that chair,' Emily said. 'Come up to bed. Else you'll wake up tomorrow morning with a crick in your neck and a temper like a bear. You mark *my* words!'

The new scheme filled Emily with a strange foreboding. The last time they'd changed the pattern, her brother Arthur had been one of the victims. With Sam Pitt. Well, Sam Pitt was due to go anyway, but not her Arthur. The death of her brother had nearly killed her mother. Now they were breaking tradition again and Emily wondered who the victim might be this time. Might it be her Reuben this time? 'You men,' she said, exasperated, 'always wanting things to change. You can never let a thing be without changing it, or trying to!'

She could see he wasn't listening to her any more. She pulled, pushed, cajoled, threatened, promised, tickled, slapped and finally half-carried him up the stairs to the bedroom. She worked quickly to undress him, then pushed him into the bed, flinging the blankets over him up to his chin. 'Get your clothes off, lass, and be quick about it! I've a mind to make a happy woman of you!' He tried a lewd leer, which twisted his face into a comic grimace. She stroked his forehead and closed his eyes with her work-hardened fingers. 'You do make a happy woman of me, most of the time,' she said. 'If only you wouldn't want to change the world every five minutes. . . .'

He was already snoring.

She went back downstairs and sat for a long time watching the fire, a gloom settling on her like morning sea-wrack on dawn's cold waters.

Reuben had a head that felt the size of a football the next morning and, as Emily had predicted, the temper of a bear. She'd laid out clean clothes for him before she'd gone to bed; remembering he'd said he was going up to see Tockett to bring the co-operative formally to an end, she'd put out one of his shirts with a collar attached, thinking he'd wear a tie to the big house. 'I told you,' he said with asperity. 'I have to get Bill Clewson's boxes ready for him!' He was damned if he'd wear good clothes to handle fish boxes. Emily knew how to deal with him in this mood and condition and gave him no argument, no resistance on which his hang-over anger could feed. She knew her Reuben wasn't a big drinker like some of them and, mercifully, a few drinks would usually be enough to make him too drunk to continue. She contented herself making him a big breakfast, with two big pots of tea, and sending him out of the way before it was time for the kids to get up and the rest of the household to stir. Reuben was already sorry for his snappiness by the time he reached the dock; he knew he'd no right to treat Emily that way just because of his own act of self-indulgence!

Bill Clewson was waiting for him like a boy about to start his summer holiday. Reuben had rented the large storeroom under the Institute for storing the new boxes. He took half a dozen out and a large sheet of the blue cartridge paper from which sugar bags are made. He'd remembered to bring one of the wax crayons the children used, and drew a large B and C as a monogram. 'That'll be your mark,' he said. 'Remember it. C is for Clegg, B is for Brawnham, G is for me, SG is Sam Gainer, and BC is you. It'll be up to you to make sure one of them papers is in every box; that way Tomlinson in Leeds will know who to credit. All the money comes to me, and I divide it out the way he tells me, based on these pieces of paper. But it's your responsibility to make sure one goes in every box. We've all agreed that in the event of a dispute, a paper getting lost or anything like that, the money for that box is shared evenly. If you take my tip, you'll get yourself a little notebook and keep a list in there as well.'

Bill was like an eager young puppy. 'Now, Reuben,' he asked, 'who decides when we go for what? You know, we've always left it a bit late round here to go for lobsters. In Whitby, they start with the lobsters at the back end of January. Aye, and they get a packet for them. . . .'

Reuben held up his hand to stem the flow. 'Bill, tha's too old to be taught how to suck eggs. How you do your fishing, when and where, and for what, is your business and nowt to do wi' me, or anybody else. If you want to drop your pots in January, you do it. Though, I warn you, the pots out here take a damn sight heavier pounding than they do off the mouth of Whitby. There's a lot more movement on the bed of the ocean out here, a lot more rolling and scouring. Drop your pots too early out here and you could lose the lot. Nay, but what am *I* telling *thee* that for? Tha' knows it better than I do!'

The talk with Bill Clewson had restored his good humour; he looked out over the ocean as the tide started to recede; it'd be a few hours before they could go out. He messed about with the *Hope*, killing time for a half-hour. A boat needs constant care, constant maintenance. He uncoiled one of the lines; he thought he'd seen a portion of it that appeared frayed when he was out yesterday; he ran it slowly through his fingers, seeking the first fluffiness, the first swelling, that would tell him faster than eyes that the rope was losing its nature. The gulls were heavy this morning, screaming from the rooftops at each other, dropping almost vertically off the tops of the roofs higher up the hill, to swoop down and soar in that miraculously easy glide path that has always excited men's envy. A group of them must have sighted a shoal of sprats out on the water; they went in formation, each one peeling off and diving sheer at the water, all at varying angles but not one of them colliding with any other. Though Reuben was too superstitious to say so out loud, it augured well for fishing that day.

He found the place in the rope that had caught his attention the previous day; sure enough it was the start of swelling, with the fibres beginning to separate. He checked the rope each side for a yard or two; the bad place lasted about a foot and a half. He took the ball of whipping twine he carried always in his pocket and his knife, whipped the rope either side of the bad place and then severed it. It was the work of a few minutes to separate the strands and whip each individually, then, sitting crosslegged on the stern thwart, he spliced one cut end into the other, pulling each segment of the rope tight before hammering it flat with an old oak belaying pin he kept for that purpose. Around him the other fishermen found something to occupy themselves as they came from their cottages in the early morning, when the rest of the world was lig-abed asleep and only the gulls screeching overhead kept them company. The lighted fires gave out a heavy morning coal-slack smoke, which quickly dispersed on the wind that whipped gently across the ocean, lifting up and high over the rooftops of Old Quaytown. Without realizing it, they were silent actors in a play that had been going on since the fifteenth century, with very little evidence of change; the boats were still shaped the same way, they still wore similar clothes and had similar features to those of their ancestors, stretching back into history. They didn't talk much after the initial morning greeting; each had a list of things to be done, and all welcomed a late tide as giving them the time in which to work peaceably before setting out over the ocean. Perhaps the tidiness of their boats, as compared with boats moored in a twenty-four-hours harbour, reflected this enforced waiting period; it would have been foolish to launch a boat down the slip with the tide battering the stones every fifth, sixth or seventh wave. In the old days, of course, the Cut had been usable for most of the day, with the bottom showing only at extreme low tide. It had been 150 years since the Cut had silted so that they could no longer use it except at high tide. It had become the haunt of young lads in rowboats, and the launching ground for such boats as they managed to complete in the Yard. The fishermen used their dock at the extreme north-east entrance, and left the Cut to the amateurs!

When he'd finished splicing the rope, Reuben coiled it neatly and stowed it beneath the thwart before going back up Chapel Street to the Institute and opening the big door. Mark Brawnham followed him up. He'd failed his test for his seaman's ticket on medical grounds – apparently he was colour blind or so they said;

though he could tell green from red he had some difficulty between green and blue, and red and orange. He could have gone in, if he'd been prepared to resign himself to being a deckie all his life, but he'd had his hopes set on a mate's and eventually a skipper's ticket! 'Are you going for the boxes, then?' he asked. Mark loved riding the truck up and down the hill.

'Aye, but I'm going to see Tockett as well.'

'Shall I come up and stack the overnight boxes, ready for loading?'

'Doesn't your dad have a job for you, then?'

'Nay, he told me to ask if you wanted a hand.'

'Right, you'd better come up with us, then.' Reuben primed the engine, set the spark and the choke, then swung the handle. It took only three swings before he knew that next time it would fire. He advanced the throttle slightly, and swung again; the engine fired and ran sweet. Reuben had spent a lot of time with Jacoby, on and off, and had learned a thing or two about engines. He did most of the maintenance on the *Hope*'s engine, a Perkins diesel, himself. The truck pulled slowly but surely up the one-in-four bank in bottom gear. Reuben was in no hurry. He kept his hand on the hand-brake ready, should the engine stop, to jam it on fast. The last thing he wanted was to career down that hill backwards. Harry Horse-and-Cart must have heard him coming; he had pulled his cart into the side of the bank just after the Laurel and its dog-leg bend; he was shielding his horse's eyes and holding its nostrils against the fearsome noise Reuben's truck made; he shook his hand in mock anger and Reuben shouted his usual quip – 'I thought tha were off to Ameriky?'

When they had passed the horse and cart safely, he shot a look at the lad sitting next to him. Why, Mark Brawnham must be going on for twenty now and Reuben realized with a shock the age difference that lay between them. He hardly knew what to say to the younger lad. 'Started courting then, have you?' he asked. 'I saw you in Whitby last Saturday!'

'Nay, that was a pal of my sister's,' Mark said, obviously embarrassed.

'Gerraway! Your Mollie has nice-looking pals! If I'd 'a' been a bit younger I'd have taken her away from thee!'

'You'd 'a' been lucky!' Mark said, grinning. 'She doesn't go much on older men!'

287

'Why, you cheeky monkey. . . . So, you've settled down to t'fishing then, have you?'

'For the time being.'

'What does than mean?'

'Till I can find summat better.'

'Summat better. . . ? You are a cheeky monkey, an' all! What can be better than fishing, tell me that?'

'Anything!' Mark said. 'Anything would be better than fishing!'

It had started as a bit of light conversation, but Reuben could hear the note of desperation in the young man's voice. 'I do believe you mean it, Mark,' Reuben said. He applied the brake and the truck stopped in the railway yard, beside the concrete-and-brick platform on which the boxes were stacked.

'It's not just me, you know,' Mark said defensively. 'It's *all* the young uns. None of us wants fishing any more. Aye, and none of us wants Ravenswyke – a right dead-and-alive hole this is. Why do you think we're all away to Whitby as soon as we've had our suppers and a bit of a wash? If it wasn't for the unemployment everywhere, believe me, you wouldn't see our backsides for dust. We'd be away into the West Riding, else down in t'Midlands, where we could earn a copper or two and not be sopping wet through half our lives, with our finger-ends chapped and frozen. . . .' As if conscious he'd said too much, he opened the side door of the truck and jumped out. 'I'll get 'em all stacked and ready for when you come back from Tockett's,' he said. 'Happen there's a few more ligging about on t'platform.'

Reuben said nothing, engaged the gear and the clutch, and drove out of the station yard and along the top road to Tockett's. Mark had surprised him, really surprised him. Of course, he'd noticed that the young ones didn't come into the tap of the Raven, hadn't hung about outside the way he had, seeing the tap as paradise. Now it cost only a few coppers to get into Whitby on the train, a few more to return home when the Whitby pubs and entertainments were over. Times were changing, certainly. He'd even seen Ravenswyke girls – admittedly from Newquay Town – going together into Whitby for an evening out, without escorts. That would have been unthinkable when he was a lad – why, they'd practically tarred and feathered Elsie Milner for nothing worse than such conduct.

He looked at Tockett House, looming in front of him, so different from the gloomy days when old James Henry lived alone. Hester Tockett had made a big difference up here; the gardens were neatly laid out with many flowering shrubs. In the summer the place was a blaze of colours. He used the gardens of Tockett House to dispel the mood that had come on him since he'd heard Mark Brawnham's words. He dismissed him with one thought – 'What does he know, he's nobbut a young lad.'

James Henry was sitting in his study, perched behind his desk, when Hester and Mark Adam came in. Hester had brought him his cup of coffee; it was a pleasing family ritual he had come more and more to enjoy. Like the tea times these days when, instead of his sitting in gloomy solitude, the three girls were brought in for him to play with, while they all took tea. Felicity Mildred was all of ten, Netta Lucinda a grand eight, and very forward, and Elizabeth Jane, seven, and already able to pick out several tunes on the piano and the recorder. No doubt who'd have the brains of the three of them. Aye, and looking at the picture of the three of them on his desk, no doubt who had the beauty. Felicity took after her mother. James Henry had realized long ago that fate had dealt a hand in the game. No matter how much we huff and puff, there are larger forces in command of our destiny than we know. Mark Adam had done everything James Henry could have expected after the horsewhipping had brought him to his senses. He'd married and had provided a family, show-ing the county gossips that there was nothing unmanly about *him*! But none of the progeny had been a son! James Henry could take it all philosophically. He'd have liked a grandson, but he'd learned to accept life as it was. And, bless 'em, the girls were such a joy.

'Here's your coffee then, Mr Tockett,' Hester said. She'd always called him Mr Tockett despite his many requests she call him Father. She put the coffee cup on the table, and he moved from behind the desk. The plate of biscuits stood next to the cup; he noticed the ginger-nuts he so liked. 'Now, if you don't mind, I have to go and see the doctor. Both Netta and Elizabeth are a bit off-colour this morning, so I think I'll take them for a run in the fresh air. We can call on Dr Suddaby while we're out, and he can check them over for me.'

'Make sure as they wrap up well,' he said, as she left the room.

289

'And wrap yourself up well, too. We can't have anything happening to thee!'

When she'd gone, Mark Adam sat by the fire, his coffee cup on the table beside his chair, companionable though silent.

'Reuben Godson is coming up this morning,' James Henry said. 'I suppose he's stopping the co-operative, finally.'

'It'll be no skin off our nose,' Mark Adam said absently. 'It's only been a low-interest financing operation, so far as we're concerned. We're better shot of it.'

James Henry never failed to be surprised by Mark Adam's coldness in some matters.

'I did it for the good of the fishermen, Mark Adam,' he said, mild reproach in his voice.

'Like you've kept the Yard open for the good of Newquay Town. Dad, I'd wish you'd let me close that white elephant. Tomorrow. It's a millstone round my neck.'

'It's not your brass yet, lad.'

'I know that! But it drains off income from other sources, income that could be put to better use increasing our capital. Just think what I could do with that income, in London. On the 'Change!'

Mark Adam meant the Baltic Exchange, in which the Tocketts had become very active. A week of every month of Mark Adam's time was spent in London these days, and always profitably. One thing only irked him. James Henry had an old-fashioned idea of capital. Capital was something you hung on to at all costs. Capital was meant to be hoarded and preserved. All speculation came out of income. You could pledge income and future income; capital was sacred and couldn't be either touched or pledged. It was like driving a powerful engine with the brakes on!

James Henry was chuckling. 'Aye,' he said, 'you've made a big difference to us these days on t'Change. People down there has started to respect you for yourself and not just for your family name or connection. Why you couldn't have started out like that, instead of mullarking about as you did when you were a lad, beats me! And, you understand, I'm not referring to t'other – I'm talking about you as a businessman!'

Since the day of the horsewhipping 't'other' had never been referred to by either one of them, though Mark Adam had always suspected his father would have given his eye-teeth to know exactly *why*. Since his marriage, a strong bond had developed between them. Each time Hester had given birth to a daughter, he'd sought in his father's eyes for the keen disappointment he himself felt at not producing a son and heir, but each time he'd been happy to see no trace of it. Mark Adam and Hester produced *children*; that had seemed enough for the old man.

'I'll tell you something I've never dared say before,' he said. 'When I was a lad I was frightened of you. Mortally scared. I can remember it as long as I've lived. It grew worse when Rupert Henry came along; it seemed to me you favoured him above me. Why, I used to think, Father's even given Rupert his own second name! I was jealous, I suppose. . . .'

'You'd no call to be,' James Henry said, looking into the fire but not consciously avoiding his son's eye. 'I didn't favour either of you, if the truth were known. Not until I started hearing tales about you. At first, I didn't believe them, but then I had to give some credence to them. Another thing, of course, was that I knew Rupert Henry had been smitten by the Tockett Curse, which mercifully now seems to have abated, bless the Lord for that. So, knowing he was doomed, I may have leaned towards him a bit in his lifetime.'

'And I went the other way. I rebelled against everything that smacked of our rough North-Country life. Including, if you like, the rough North-Country virility. And, what's more, I was so anxious to show you that I could make a go of it in London, on my own, that I never stopped to learn what London was all about. That's why I presented those deals as if they were my own; that's why you could expose me so easily with your little scheme. Well, now I've taken the time to learn, to know what goes on. . . .'

'You have that, lad,' James Henry said admiringly. 'And you've learned to beat them at their own game. There's only one thing that you haven't learned, however, since we're being so frank with each other – and about time. You've learned to be ruthless in business, but you haven't learned when to temper that ruthlessness with a bit of the milk of human understanding. Take the handling of this business of the Yard. I know we don't make any money there. Given the fact that it doesn't interest you – and I'm not criticizing you for that; I never thought it would, somehow – you could look upon it as a bit of self-indulgence. The Tocketts have to live in this place, Mark Adam. It's part and parcel of our blood. And living in it means we've got to make a bit of a contribution without necessarily counting the costs to ourselves. So, we drop a thousand or two on the Yard! What does it matter? We keep folks in work, and they know it. We've provided homes for them; we've been responsible members of the community. And that, I pray you'll learn some day, is worth a lot more than money. Anyway, we've no more time for talking. Godson's coming and, knowing him, he'll be on time. Is there anything you want to say about the co-operative?'

'Nothing, except we should bring it to an end as soon as possible.'

'Right. Do you want to handle it, or shall I?'

'You set it up, Father, you pull it down!'

The meeting with Reuben was a simple administrative matter in which no emotions were involved and no feelings were stirred. 'You doing well with this Leeds arrangement?' James Henry asked, but more from politeness than interest.

'Aye; it'll be better in the long run!'

'Everything's changing, Reuben, more quickly than I can follow at my age. I just hope you've studied carefully before cutting across the old traditional ways.'

'I think I have. We've merely cut out one or two of the middle men!'

James Henry chuckled. 'More bolshevism, eh, lad?' he said without malice. 'If you could only make up your mind to it, you'd be a good politician. Socialist, of course, but there's a lot of them about these days. People like Keir Hardie; he'd make a right one in Old Quaytown!'

'Just a name to me, Mr Tockett. I'm nobbut a simple fisherman!'

'Fisherman you most certainly are, but simple, never! Right, I've made the papers ready. I sign here, you sign there, on both copies, and then the co-operative is formally ended. The accounts have been drawn up, and the cheque for the balance is attached.'

'I hope it's been profitable for you, Mr Tockett?' Reuben asked solicitously.

'You don't hear me complaining, do you?' The profits from the handling of the co-operative hadn't even paid for Tockett's cigars but there was no point in going into that, Tockett thought.

Mark Adam came back into the room and greeted Reuben, who shook hands with him. 'How's your family, Mr Mark Adam?' Reuben asked, one father to another.

'Very well, considering. The two youngest girls aren't up to snuff today and Mrs Tockett's taken them to the doctor, but it's probably only a bit of a sniffle. The doctor will soon put them right again.'

James Henry came from behind his desk and Reuben was shocked to see how badly he walked across the room to the fireplace. It'd been so long since he'd seen the older Tockett standing up that he hadn't realized how emaciated and bent his frame had become. His face was lean and excessively cadaverous, as if the flesh had lost its juices. The collar he wore sat loosely round his throat, appearing to be at least three sizes too big for the scrawny neck. The old man must be over eighty, Reuben thought. Seen close to, he began to look it, though one couldn't doubt his mind was as sharp as ever. Reuben could also sense the changed atmosphere between father and son; there was a warmth and friendliness between them he'd never witnessed before. He saw the consideration with which Mark Adam settled his father in the chair by the fire and wrapped the travelling rug round his knees. James Henry's hands settled in his lap, part folded together. They looked like skeleton bones tight-wrapped in skin gloves.

'Aye, well, I'll be on my way,' Reuben said. 'There's no need to trouble you further.'

'Won't you stay and take a glass of sherry?' Mark Adam asked, surprising him. Reuben had never before been invited to a drink of anything in that house. Once again he sensed the feeling he'd had when Mark Adam had come down to the dock, that he would like to get to know Reuben better, to chat with him. It had taken a while for Reuben to separate what Mark Adam *was* and could be, from what he *did*. Reuben had only known him as a ruthless taskmaster, a business opportunist. He wasn't sophisticated enough to realize that a man's personality, like a coin of the realm, has two sides. In Reuben's simple world of fishermen, a man was so associated with what he did, how he thought and behaved, that for a man to have two aspects to his character was unthinkable. He would have liked to stay and drink sherry in this comfortable, warm room, to talk with Mark Adam and James Henry Tockett for a brief while as equals, but the lure of the tide was too strong for him. 'I don't have a lot of time,' he said. 'Perhaps you'll ask me another time, when I'm not going out fishing.'

James Henry cackled. 'You'll never find a fisherman supping sherry, Mark Adam,' he said, 'not if he's got the smell of salt spray in his nostrils!'

'Aye,' Reuben said, embarrassed, feeling that perhaps he had been uncouth but not knowing how to redeem himself, 'us as lives by the tide has got to respect it!'

'I quite understand,' Mark Adam said, thin-lipped. 'We shall have to make it another time, shan't we?'

Reuben left the house and drove back to the station, disquieted by his gaucheness. Why was it, he asked himself, that he who usually felt so confident in what he did, and what he knew he could do, should always feel at such a disadvantage in that household? It was the only chink in his armour of self-possession, and he wished he could find some way of overcoming it, but he couldn't.

Batty was waiting for him when he arrived at the dock with the boxes. 'By gow,' he said, 'I thought happen we weren't going out today.'

'Now don't you start!'

'The tide'll be full before we know it!'

'I told you, don't start! I've had a bit of business to attend to with the Tocketts!'

Whether it was to cancel the feelings of inadequacy that had assailed him up at the Tocketts', or just fortune smiling upon them, Reuben and Batty had a most successful day, with every line coming back up laden with cod, codling, pollack, many of such a size they'd had to use the gaff to bring them inboard. When high tide came at four o'clock, they'd already caught as many fish as normally they would have caught in an eight-hour session. They were sitting in the bay with the engine idling, drifting aimlessly for a few moments while they ate their snap. Reuben had lost all his early waspishness in the excitement and euphoria of a successful catch. 'What'll we do?' he asked Batty. 'Shall we go back in as soon as the tide has cleared the landing? Or shall we go further out and start all over again?'

Both of them had been examining the landing; the whitecaps were breaking over the slip, the waves running up the concrete and stone slope of it right across the foot of the roadway outside the Raven. Some of the waves were big, dashed against the landing by the wind, which had been blowing fresher all afternoon. Tockett Top was clear, but looking south they could see a nasty patch of scudding black rain cloud. If they were lucky, it would continue over the land; Scarborough would have a rough time of it but here they'd be outside the northern edge. Both knew instinctively it wasn't a day for venturing far, and this feeling was confirmed by the Cleggs and Sam Gainer, both of whose boats were working close inshore about a mile up the coast. Bill Clewson and the Brawnhams had gone further out and when he twisted round Reuben could see them hull down on the horizon. The sea picks up every mood of the weather in its strange reflections and refractions; that day the ocean had that heavy almost oily quality, a deep shade of green, like the complexion of a sickening child.

'We'll have a blow this night,' Batty said, reinforcing Reuben's view. Suddenly he reached inside the locker beneath the thwarts and brought out the brass-bound telescope they kept in there; he took the caps off each end and put it to his eye, extending it and focusing at something on the cliff top. 'Here, Reuben,' he said, 'there's summat up! There's two policemen up there – one of 'em looks like Sergeant Neckridge. They're fixing the tripod!' Reuben looked where Batty was pointing, midway between Tockett House and the edge of the Cut. That section of cliff contained three inlets, separated by towering walls of unclimbable shale. Many a picnicker had walked along the scaurs approaching high tide to find that if he didn't get a move on he'd be cut off by the waves. There had been one or two tragedies, and notices had been erected on posts, advising people to watch out. The shale cliffs were too steep, too slippery, to climb at that point and, when the water was full, no stretch of the shoreline remained for a person to stand on. The only way to rescue them was to mount a tripod on the top of the steep cliffs, and let down a rope up which the stranded person could climb. Reuben took the glass from Batty. Sure enough, the two policemen had erected the tripod and one of them appeared to be going over the edge on the end of the rope. Reuben instinctively moved the tiller over and kicked the engine into more life, heading the *Hope* towards the spot. The waves were high at that point, masking his view of the shoreline. He handed the glass back to Batty and concentrated his efforts on aiming the *Hope*, riding the top of each high wave, then running quickly when it hissed under the stern. As each wave hit the cliffs to each side of the cove where they'd erected the tripod, it bounced back boiling against the next incoming wave to create a maelstrom.

'Some bloody tourist,' Batty growled. He was trying to get a glimpse of the person on the shoreline but couldn't because of the boiling wave tops. He switched his attention to the top of the cliff in time to exclaim. 'Here, that's odd. They seem to be waving at us!'

Reuben had seen half a dozen people running along the cliff top, along the field path that had been run into the edge of the grassland by countless generations of grazing sheep. This was the land Mark Adam had marked and parcelled years ago. Already some of the parcels had been sold to provide building plots, though Reuben had heard the Tocketts were only giving the land as leasehold, not freehold. Several of the running people stopped, looking out over the ocean and sighting the *Hope*, and they too started to wave their arms at him, as if trying to pull him in. 'I reckon they want us to try to get the *Hope* as near as we can,' he said, though he couldn't think why for the moment. He guided the boat forward, throttling back, since the tidal movement of the waves was taking them in. He knew the tide would be full in about twenty minutes – anybody stranded at the cliff foot would be drowned by then, if they couldn't be lifted.

He knew from experience that where they'd mounted the tripod the descent and ascent were difficult, since the shale overhung and was loose. Anybody standing below could be buried by a sudden fall. It was in that part of the cliff that most of the fossils, the ammonites for which this part of the coast was world-famous, were found. The cove had been formed over the millennia by water draining off the top; constantly freezing to ice and melting back, the water had loosened the cliff face in many places. When Batty told him the policeman had gone back up the rope, Reuben instantly knew why. The cliff face must be weakened at that point; the policeman had been scared to go over it on the rope in case he launched a hundred or more tons on the head of the person stranded below. That would be why they'd be waving to Reuben. They'd want him to try to make the rescue from the sea – no mean feat of helm to get the *Hope* in through the maelstrom and back again, without ripping away its bottom on the teeth of the rocks.

Batty had understood what they must do. He turned to look gravely at Reuben. 'We going to try it?' he asked.

Reuben nodded. Both knew they had no alternative. 'Get out the long warp and both anchors,' Reuben said. 'We'll go in as close as we dare, but we'll drop an anchor, two anchors. You can take a couple of turns round the warp, and let us in, bit by bit. I'll have the engine on idle, ready to pull us out again if we look like getting in trouble.'

With both anchors down and holding, and with a couple of turns round the sternpost, Batty should be able to hold the *Hope* against the thrust of the waves trying to slam them in much more effectively than the revolving screw of the engine. It was the only way they would keep complete control of the *Hope*. As they drew nearer, Reuben kept his eyes on the strip of shoreline; suddenly his mouth dried as he recognised the figure he could see crouched on a rock that jutted out of the water, but which was flooded by each wave that came in.

'That's our Eleanor,' he said grimly.

Batty was using the telescope again. 'Nay, you'll see better with your eyes,' Reuben growled at him. 'That's our Amos she's holding in her arms.'

Amos was five years old, a tough little lad, born, it seemed, without the slightest fear of water. He took after his dad in everything, had the same features, the same tall but stocky build for his years.

Reuben ran his eyes up the cliff and saw the reason the policeman couldn't, daren't come down on the rope. A slab of shale fifteen feet tall and ten feet across had cracked out of the cliff face. Part of it had already fallen. If that lot were disturbed in the slightest way, it could all break out and come down. Eleanor and Amos would both be buried by it.

Now the wind, as so often happened just before high tide, was getting up, whipping the tops off the waves, driving a marrow-chilling spray across the top of the ocean. 'Get them anchors down,' Reuben said grimly. 'We'll try to go straight in!'

Batty had been waiting. He threw one to port, one to starboard, with the chain connecting them. He'd tied the anchor warp round the approximate centre of the chain and took a couple of turns on it round the sternpost on the port side. He jammed his feet against the gunwale, taking the strain on the warp as the motion of the

297

sea pushed the boat in. Reuben took the engine out of gear but left it running on fast tick-over, ready to slam the gear lever into reverse if they needed it. He moved forward quickly as the anchors bit, swinging the *Hope* bows on to the cliffs. Both knew it would be hell for Batty to hold; each wave ran up behind the *Hope* and rammed into the stern, swirling angrily round the edges and over the gunwale. Slowly, Batty let the anchor warp slip through his hands and the *Hope* crept forward. Reuben was in the bows looking at Eleanor, but also down into the water for hidden obstacles. With its stern fixed by anchors that way, the boat would rip its bottom out against any sharp-edged rock.

Eleanor had turned and had seen him. He saw the look of horror on her face, of total terror, and could tell she was shouting to him; the wind snatched the words from her throat in derision. Amos looked as if he, mercifully, were asleep; he wasn't moving in her arms and his hand was lying against her chest, in the nest of her lapels. She was finding it difficult to keep her feet on the rock and he saw her stagger as each wave hit. He looked back; the waves were increasing and soon one must come that would dash her from the top of that rock into the ocean. He walked back quickly, grabbed Batty's shoulder, and shouted in his ear. 'Run thirty feet out as fast as you can! Then check it there, and come up into the bows to give me a hand.'

Reuben grabbed the other line, deftly tied a loop in it, and wound it round his body beneath his armpits under his jacket.

'You're never going over the side?' Batty shouted.

'Aye, there's no other way!'

He walked to the bows of the *Hope*, carrying the line in his hand, then made the end of it secure round the bowpost, holding the loop tight in his right hand. The bows rose as Batty caught a wave and let the *Hope* run, as Reuben had instructed, the full extent of thirty feet before the anchor warp held it tight again. Eleanor and Amos were still fifty feet away. Reuben bent down and took off his boots. He stripped off his jacket, sat on the gunwale with his feet over the side for a moment, then dropped into the water. Ice-cold, the impact drove the breath from his body and he submerged beneath the surface, knowing that only his own movement-generated heat would keep him alive. He struck forward, letting the tide carry him, paying out the line as he went. He'd gone forty feet before he felt his feet touch the top of one of the scaurs, but the tidal race undercut him and sent him sprawling. He swam a few more strokes under the water, not wanting to risk trying to stand up again. The underwater pull dragged him, then thrust him sideways as it raced round a submerged rock, smashing the side of his forearm against the abrasive shells of limpets, stripping away skin and flesh. He recovered his balance desperately, turning his face away from those knifelike shards that could take his flesh down to the bone. Now he could find his feet and stand up; the water swirled round his body as he forged forward, trudging with the water at waist height one second, gasping for breath as the next wave dashed him forward and submerged him with its violent force, sprawling him across the limpet-infested surfaces, his skin rent as if by a hundred slivers of broken glass. Each time his head cleared the water he looked intently forward, saw his son cradled against Eleanor's breast, and that gave him the strength to push on ever closer to the rock on which she now cowered on one knee, fighting to maintain her balance. The ice-cold water had worked its mercy on him, numbing his flesh so that he no longer felt the pain of those rasping limpets and unyielding rock edges. He slipped and slithered forward, gasping for breath, fighting the waves racing in tumult about him until he was ten feet from the rock. Then one wave, one king wave mightier and more savage than all the rest, hit him solidly in his back and sprawled him inconsequentially, contemptuously, in its path, and his head went under as he slid; when he fought his way back up, the rock on which Eleanor had crouched with Amos was bare. She had been swept away. He raced forward as best he could, catching a glimpse of the blue material of her coat in the water. He was like a wild man thrusting his way through the maelstrom, gulping for breath, fighting the solid water movement, ignoring the thrust of the waves on his back. Now he saw the flash of colour again, twelve feet or so to the side, and he struck out in that direction. Here, beneath that towering cliff, the water was in total confusion, spray rising angrily ten feet in the air as the gigantic force of the ocean spent itself against the unmovable rock face and was dashed back upon its own confusion. He felt the small rocks and stones from the shoreline smashing around his legs and feet, sucked by the undertow. A wave caught him side on, spun him round and threw him sprawling on his back across the top of a flat rock. He felt his ankle catch in a crevice of the rock and tried to twist himself round to pull himself free, knowing that if he were caught and inundated he'd drown in a horrible spluttering death. He freed himself as the next wave came, and used it to ride sideways behind the scaur that had trapped him, following the blue of Eleanor's coat as she, powerless to prevent herself, was rolled this way and that by the force of the water. Finally, he was near enough to reach out and grasp the hem of her coat. He dragged her towards him, catching her leg, yanking her coat savagely through the water until he could turn her to face him. Amos was still, miraculously, cradled in her stiffened arm, and Reuben prised her grip loose to grab hold of the lad. He pulled the cord to which he was still attached, ran it round Eleanor's body, and knotted it in front of her. She was screaming hysterically, but there was nothing he could do about that. Amos's eyes were closed but Reuben had no time. He waved his hand in the air and felt the slack taken up in the rope, walking out to sea with Eleanor half-dragged, half-walking beside him, still screaming though the wind took away her voice in his ears. He followed the rope, walking for as long as he could, and then he was immersed as a seventh wave, more powerful, more arched than all the rest, hit him on the chest, knocking him sprawling in a whirling foam in which the force of the wave on the surface and the pull of the undertow fought for supremacy, with his body the ultimate prize. He'd lost his hold on the rope but had kept Amos in a locking grip nothing could have forced apart. He struggled to get his head partly above water and saw Eleanor being pulled nearer to the boat. The undertow caught his legs again and sucked him down, rasping him over the scaurs, carrying him out to sea deep below the surface. His lungs pounded and his senses reeled, but still he clenched his grip on his son. He had no fear for himself, no anger, no rage, only a fierce resolution to survive, to bring his son to dry land. And when he managed to kick and fight his way to the top, to gulp air into his lungs again, his terrible voice flung defiance back to the wind and the waves. 'Tha'll not have him. Tha'll not!' he yelled.

He was twisting and spinning as the undertow fought to control his legs again, striving to push the arm cradling the lad up above the waters. He knew this moment was touch-and-go for both of them, that this ice-cold immersion was the price he had to pay for a life spent conquering the ever-present dangers of his calling.

The sea, like the mountains, demands sacrificial victims, but Reuben wasn't ready yet to yield either himself or his lad.

He went down again and this time found it harder to fight his way back to the surface since he was tiring; further from the coastline the undertow dragged him deeper and deeper and his sodden clothing impeded his struggling strokes.

'Tha'll . . . not . . . have . . . us!' his mind said, drawing on his last reserves of energy, the spirit of survival he knew was his only hope. This time, when he burst from the maw of the sea, he knew he'd be a goner if he went down again. He flipped over on his back, Amos still cradled in his arm, and used the other arm in a crude stroke to pull him along, kicking out with his feet the way a frog will. The undertow was well beneath him – at least he'd escaped from its malevolent dragging force. Out here the waves hadn't yet broken. He was lifted and dropped with each successive swell and trough, but he *was* making progress, nearer to the boat. His legs felt heavy as lead in the waterlogged trousers and his heavy fisherman's sweater flogged round him like a sodden sack. His flailing arm was fit to be torn from its socket with every stroke, every pull. As he rose each time, he took a raw lungful of salt-laden air which left him gasping; in the troughs his head was submerged and he came up again each time spluttering. Now he knew his pulling arm lacked force; he glanced over his shoulder and could see the boat, and Batty steadily towing Eleanor. Batty belayed that rope, and threw another to Reuben, who caught it, then turned and trudged, half-swimming, half-dragged, until he reached the *Hope*. Batty used the gaff under the rope wrapped round Eleanor to draw her alongside. As he pulled her inboard, Reuben grabbed the gunwale with his right hand, holding on to Amos with his left. Once Eleanor was half over the gunwale, Batty reached down and Reuben passed Amos up into his hands, then hauled himself laboriously over the gunwale into the boat, where he lay face down, gulping for breath. Batty yanked Eleanor over the side and Reuben and she lay like two gasping fish. Batty went to the stern of the boat, kicked the gear into reverse, and slowly pulled the boat backwards away from the cliff, using the two anchor warps to assist the engine, making sure the warps would not catch around the prop shaft. When he'd reached the end of the warps, he found Reuben beside him; he broke the anchors free on the starboard side, then Batty pressed the throttle handle. As soon as the *Hope* had pulled itself away from danger, Batty watched the waves, then, immediately behind the crest of a big one, he threw the tiller hard over, smashed the throttle all the way down, and had swung round far enough by the time the next wave came to meet it head on.

Reuben went amidships; Amos was lying under his coat, jammed between two of the fish boxes. Reuben peeled the coat off him tenderly, but one look at his son's face told him all he needed to know. He'd seen death too often to mistake it now. He put the lad back down between the fish boxes and covered him again with the coat. He walked forward; Eleanor was squatting on the fore thwart like a whipped animal, shivering uncontrollably with the cold. There was nothing he could, nothing he wanted to do for her.

He went back to the stern. Batty knew Amos was dead. 'Are we going in?' he asked. Reuben nodded, and took over the tiller. Batty went forward with a tarpaulin and wound it round Eleanor's shoulders, dragging the sopping hair away from her face, and laying his hand tenderly alongside her jaw. Reuben brought the *Hope* in a wide circle, then aimed it for the landing, not knowing, not caring how he would get in. He studied the water as he went and his seaman's instinct gradually took over in his numbed mind, easing the bows over, telling him how it must be done. Waves pounded into the mouth of the Cut, bouncing back from the sides before streaming back out again, frustrated, to face the incoming tide. A Yorkshire coble is designed to be beached backwards. Reuben drove forward until he reached the only place of flat water in the bay, where the bulge of the bend in the face of Old Quaytown separated the maelstrom. There he drove the *Hope* round in a tight circle, clipping the gear into reverse three-quarters of the way round and bringing the *Hope* neatly stern on to the bottom of the slip. He drove it backwards up the slip, knowing that eventually it would beach itself on the two fins that were an integral part of its construction. The danger, of course, was that, if he didn't ram up the slip dead true, the force of a wave could spew the bows round bringing the *Hope* beam on; the next wave could hit under it and capsize them right there on the bottom of the slip. The undertow would take the capsized boat back out and round and smash it, plank by plank, on the rocks. Batty had coiled a rope and, as they drew nearer the foot of the slip, he threw it with all his force to the waiting crowd. All of Old Quay-town seemed to have turned out to watch them land. They ran the end of the rope to the heavier warp of the tractor, and bent the two together. Batty pulled his thinner rope in quickly, hand over hand, and soon had the tractor line. He made it fast round the sternpost on the port side. Sergeant Neckridge, who'd raced down from the cliff when he saw they intended to land, swung the tractor's starting handle, then climbed up on the seat. The crowd parted for him, and he drove the tractor forward, keeping the rope connecting him with the *Hope* taut. As soon as the fins hit, Batty waved his arm and the tractor moved forward rapidly, dragging the *Hope* clear of the waterline. A wave did have a last futile attempt to upset them, smashing under the bows, but by then the stern was too firmly ashore for the boat to slew. The tractor pulled forward, now slowly, until the *Hope* was beached on the hard, safe from the waves.

The crowd pressed round the *Hope*. Reuben saw Hannah among them; she looked at his face seeking confirmation and he nodded, tears blinking suddenly in his eyes though no one could see them for the water that still ran out of his hair. Willing hands helped Eleanor out of the boat and without a backward glance she set off in a crowd of them up towards their cottage. Reuben went amidships and picked up Amos's body, still covered by the coat. Hannah was standing by the gunwale. He reached out and placed Amos's body in her outstretched arms. Tears running down her face unbidden could not have been mistaken for ocean water; grief froze her features, driving the blood from her cheeks. She was looking at Reuben, her son, sharing the moment with him, knowing because of the sons she'd lost and mourned exactly how he must be feeling.

'Get on home,' Batty said. 'I'll see to it all, here.'

Reuben shook his head. 'Take him home, Mam,' he said. 'Tell Emily I'll be along presently.'

She nodded; many would think him unfeeling, not to rush up to the cottage to be with his wife, but she knew he understood that each of them would grieve separately, each in their own way. For Reuben his grief wouldn't show, he wouldn't indulge it, until he'd seen the *Hope* cleared away and shipshape again for the morrow.

'I'll take him home,' she said. 'Tha can leave him safely to me, now.'

They'd laid Amos Godson out on a board in the big bedroom when Reuben arrived home; both Esther Blakey and Molly Neckridge were drinking the traditional cups of tea by the fire in the living room. There was no sign of Emily, or Eleanor, but Amelia Duckett had come down from the top and her pink face was wet with tears. She laid her hand on Reuben's arm but he shook it off gently, despising her for her self-indulgence but trying to hide the fact. 'Go on, Ma,' he said, his flat voice neutral, 'have a good cry!' Hannah, dry-eyed, handed him a pot of tea without speaking. He nodded his thanks, then left the room to climb the stairs to the bedroom. Amos could have been asleep, lying there, dressed in his short knickers and stockings, wearing a newly ironed shirt open at the neck.

Dr Suddaby had been and gone; the cause of death would be 'by drowning', and the coroner's court, which would meet informally, would add its legal mumbo-jumbo of 'accidental death'.

Emily was sitting on the side of the bed; he seated himself beside her and put his arm around her waist. 'Well, lass?' he said.

She shook her head, not yet ready to speak.

After a couple of minutes of just sitting there, looking at the bairn, he got up to leave the room. Emily looked up. 'Be kind with her,' she said. 'I hold no malice!'

'Did Suddaby look at her?'

'Yes. He says she's had a bad fright. He's given her some pills to calm her down. She was practically hysterical when she got home. She'll be lucky if she escapes without pneumonia!'

He walked across the upstairs corridor and opened the door of the bedroom Eleanor shared with the two girls. She was alone in the room, lying in her bed alongside the far wall, the covers pulled up to her chin, a wild look still in her eyes.

He grabbed a chair, turned it so that the back was facing the bed, and sat on it, looking hard at her. 'All right, tell us what happened,' he said. The story came out disjointed, with many accompanying sobs and tears, but he persisted until she'd told it all to him. She'd taken the two older boys and the two girls up to school. Amos hadn't been feeling well, so they'd decided to give him the day off school. She'd taken him for a walk, hoping the sea air might perk him up a bit. They'd been caught by the tide.

'How could the tide catch *you*?' he asked, puzzled. Eleanor by
now ought to know as much about the coming and going of the
tide as anybody in Old Quaytown. It was a clock built in to all of
them, high tide, low tide, a permanent ticking pendulum that
never stopped.

She was silent, her head turned away from him. 'Look at me!'
he said, his voice hard, but she didn't move. He put his hand
forward and grasped her chin, forcing her face around so that he
could look into her eyes. 'You were reading!' he said. 'You were
sitting on a rock reading, and the lad was playing about in the
rock pools without you paying him the slightest bit of attention.
What happened, Eleanor? Did Amos get himself trapped, and go
under? Did he fall into a pool somewhere, while you had your
nose stuck in a book and were supposed to be minding him, is that
what happened?' His voice was low, but she could sense the controlled fury within him. It had happened the way Reuben had
guessed. She'd been reading, absorbed by the Brontë book. The
first she'd known about the tide was when it had lapped up against
the rock and wet her foot. She'd looked round and suddenly had
seen she was surrounded by water, isolated on the rock. The water
was already at ankle height, and she'd looked round for Amos,
dismayed and panicking when she couldn't immediately see him.
When they'd first arrived, he'd found a starfish and had brought
it to her, then a pretty-coloured stone. 'Don't bother me, Amos,'
she'd said. 'Can't you see I'm trying to read?' And he'd wandered
away somewhere. She'd shouted, but there'd been no reply. The
scaurs were deserted – it was no weather for a quiet stroll. Only
crazy Eleanor would be on the scaurs a day like that! She'd run
about, calling Amos's name, and she remembered the shock of
panic when she'd found him, floating face down in one of the
hundreds of pools of the scaurs. She'd snatched him up, held him
to her chest, but already his limbs were cold in death, his lips blue,
his eyes closed. She'd run back, splashing through the water, towards the cove. The waves were already too high for her to get
round the headland on either side. And then Sergeant Neckridge
had seen her. He'd been walking along the track at the top and
had seen her. He'd run to get the tripod and the constable, and
the constable had tried to climb down, until he'd come to the
crack in the overhanging shale, and had realized that, if he tried
to cross it, he'd have fetched the whole lot down on her head.

Then, only then, had she seen Reuben coming in on the *Hope* and had dared pray she might be rescued.

Reuben was talking again. 'I'm going to get hold of Dr Suddaby, Eleanor, and I'm going to have you committed to a Home, that's what I'm going to do!' he said. He stood up, grief lining his features with iron. '*I'm going to have you put away in a bloody Home!*' he shouted. '*Out of here and in a Home!* And so far as I'm concerned, you can stay in there until you bloody rot!' He took a step towards the bed, as if he would seize her by the throat to strangle her, but then he thought better of it, turned, and stomped out of the room, his hands thrust deep in his trousers pockets.

The rumour ran round Old Quaytown like wildfire. Elsie Milner is back; she's taken the same cottage, the one that used to belong to the Pitts. The winter that had seemed so long had slowly disappeared, and spring flowers had burst across the countryside. Emily was walking back from the top of the bank, surrounded by the children, pushing John, who was now five, going on six, in the pram that was laden with bluebells, late crocuses, even a few wild daffodils. She'd taken the pram to fetch back a load of the loam from the heather moors. Rich in peat, it was champion for potted plants. John had grown tired of walking, and was now perched on the top of the sack of peat-loam, happy. The others were taking it in turns to help mam to push, though it was a lot easier if she did it herself. Wilfred, ten, was big for his age; Arthur at nine more stocky, with wider shoulders. Already the two girls, Eliza and Anne, who could have been twins so alike did they look, were showing signs of what Emily knew would be a great and troublesome beauty.

Old Mrs Farnham came towards them up the one-in-four of the bank. Now ninety years old, she was beginning to 'lose her buttons', as the saying had it. Every day she walked up the bank to the cottages at the top but once there she'd forget whom she'd come to see, which one of the housewives she'd come to take a cup of tea and gossip with. Everyone accepted old Mrs Farnham as a village oddity. At her advanced age she ought to have been sitting by the fire with a shawl round her shoulders, but every day she'd put on the long raincoat that practically reached to the ground and, usually wearing carpet slippers, she'd set out walking.

She stopped as she drew near Emily and her brood, absent-mindedly patted the tops of the two girls' heads. 'Ah, Emily,' she said, 'your rival's back.'

'My rival?'

'That painted Jezebel, Elsie Milner's, back!'

Emily laughed out loud. 'My rival? Painted Jezebel? What are you talking about, Mrs Farnham? I'm a happily married woman, with five children! What does Elsie Milner have to do with me?'

'She's not wearing a wedding ring!'

'What do I care?'

'She'll be after your man!'

Emily laughed again. The kids had shuffled their feet when Mrs Farnham had stopped them, but now had carried on down the hill, impatient to get home where they knew Grannie Godson would have tea ready. Even John had jumped out of the push-chair to run with them. 'After my man? I heard tell she'd got a man of her own!'

'You'll have to watch 'em both, you mark my words!' old Mrs Farnham said, then carried on up the hill, while Emily followed her family downwards towards the cottage. When she neared home, she walked faster; she'd had a lovely afternoon with the children, up on the top of the bank, walking the field paths and re-exploring the woods and copses she'd known all her life, seeing the profusion of spring life bursting everywhere. What did it *matter* if Elsie Milner was back? She and Reuben were tied together with bonds of companionship – aye, and love, even after this long time – that no Elsie Milner, she told herself defiantly, could break. The smell of new baking assailed her nostrils as she went in through the back door, leaving the pram of loam in the yard. Grannie Godson had made a cake, and she'd also have baked some of the thin flat jam pasty they all liked. Reuben should be back now – it'd been low tide at half-past two today and she'd watched him, a speck on the ocean as seen from the top of the bank, making his way back into harbour.

He was sitting in his chair and had obviously been dozing when the children burst in. His mam had given him a pot of tea and a piece of her pasty; he was laughing and joking, trying to stop the two girls perched on his knee from pinching bits of it. 'Nay, this bit's mine!' he was protesting. 'You've had yours and gulped it down!'

She walked across the room and kissed him on the mouth. 'Had a nice sleep?' she asked. He looked up at her, puzzled. They didn't usually kiss each other during the day or when the kids were about!

'Aye, I've had a grand sleep. What was it like at t'top?'

'Beautiful. There's more flowers than ever this spring. I've never seen owt like it.'

'Aye, it's going to be a grand summer; I can feel it in my bones!'

The kids were crowding the sofa. 'Come on, hodge up,' she said, 'make a bit of room for me!' She sat down and Hannah gave her a cup of tea with a piece of pasty perched in the saucer. He looked across the space between them and saw the colour the walk had brought into her cheeks, the shine in her eyes. 'You like it up there, don't you?' he said.

'Well, you know me. I'm daft about flowers and things. I'd be in seventh heaven if we could have a bit of a garden. . . .'

'A garden? There's so many pots and tubs out there that I can hardly find space to mend the fishing gear! Tell you what. When I retire from the sea, when Wilfred and Arthur take over, and John here, you and me will leave this lot to it, and I'll buy you a little cottage on t'top, with a garden of your own. And I'll grow the taties and the vegetables. . . .'

She laughed at him. 'Reuben Godson, tha's a great dreamer!' she said. 'You'll be down here, sniffing the ocean, for as long as you can draw a breath in your body. So don't let's waste our time wi' talk about cottages on t'top! Have you heard? They say Elsie Milner's come back, moved back into Alf Pitt's old cottage!'

'Time somebody was living in there,' he said. 'Place was going to rack and ruin with nobody taking care of it.'

She looked at him for a moment. Was he pretending a lack of interest in Elsie Milner? Or was he truly indifferent? She felt she had to know. 'Why don't you pop up there,' she said, 'when you've had your tea? See if she wants for owt?'

He laughed. 'And have every tongue in Old Quaytown wagging?' he said.

'Don't flatter yourself,' she said. 'They'll know there's nowt to fear from you going up there.'

He pretended to be offended. 'You saying I'm past it, then?' He was going to carry on speaking in that vein but suddenly realized the kids were listening to the conversation, ears agog. 'Why don't you lot go out and play?' he said.

'Past *what*, Dad?' Wilfred asked, his face serious.

'Nowt to do wi' thee!' Reuben said in mock anger. 'Can't your mam and me talk together without all your ears twitching like Harry's donkey?'

The children got up, never reluctant to run out and play.

'I could always come up with you,' Emily said smiling, 'if you don't feel safe on your own! I'd hate owt to happen to you!'

'Gerraway!'

A younger generation of curtain twitchers were at work as he knocked on the door of Alf Pitt's old cottage and waited. It was an older, more settled Elsie who opened the door to him. 'I wondered if and when I'd see *you*,' she said as she stepped aside to let him in. He waited until she'd lit the gas and then sat down at the table. She sat opposite him, a smile on her face he couldn't yet decipher. 'Emily told me you were back,' he said, 'and she suggested I come up to see if you wanted for owt?'

Now her smile deepened and took on the mischievous look he'd known so well. 'Oh, Emily sent you up, did she? Are you doing everything Emily tells you to, these days?'

He looked at her across the table. She was older, of course, but her face hadn't changed much. He could see she'd matured; there were fine wrinkles beside her eyes, and her skin had the soft glow of frequent sunburn. She'd also lost a lot of the internal puppy fat and now was a distinguished-looking woman. She'd be what, thirty-five, -six, -seven? He could never work people's ages out.

'Emily and me, we agree on most things,' he said. 'You can't raise a family together without coming to think the same way. Even if she hadn't mentioned it, I'd have come up here to see you, if only to find out how you were, and if you needed anything. For old times' sake! We were good pals, once. I hope we still are?'

She reached out and touched the back of his hand with her fingers. 'Of course we are, Reuben,' she said. 'You'll have to forgive me if I'm a bit prickly, a bit sharp. It wasn't easy to come back here with my tail between my legs.'

'It didn't go too well, then? I heard you got married. Some rich fellow from the West Riding.'

She got up from the table and went to sit beside the small fire she'd lighted more for company than for the warmth it gave.

'Why've you come, Reuben?' she asked.

'To see if there's any way I can help you,' he said.

'To find out what's happened to bring me back?'

'That, too, but only if you want somebody to talk to who won't say, I told you so. How are you for money?'

'I've got enough to get by for a month or two, until I get on my feet. I was careful about that. Putting a bit aside, and not having a family, those were the two things that, thank God, I took care of!'

He left the table and came to sit opposite her by the fire. 'Do you want to tell me about him?' he asked. 'I'll hold my peace if you don't.'

'There's not much to tell,' she said. 'He was a good fellow, and nice with me. He took me everywhere, gave me everything I wanted. We travelled about all over Europe – Paris, Rome, Venice, Germany. It wasn't until later that I realized he was a man who'd never settle down anywhere. He had restless feet.'

'So you left him because you wanted to settle down?'

She shook her head and her bitter laugh hovered on the edge of hysterical. 'You could say, he left me,' she said. 'I thought he had a lot of money from his businesses, which he always said were doing very well. I didn't realize, and neither did anybody else, that he was a dreamer, a wanderer. His businesses were built on a house of cards and he was living off them. The accountants explained to me, afterwards, that it'd been hopeless from the start. He owed over a million pounds when he died!'

'When he *died*?' Reuben said.

'Oh, didn't you know? It was in all the papers. When he found out how much in debt he was, he put a gun in his mouth and pulled the trigger. I found him in the bathroom. . . .'

'Poor Elsie!' Reuben's voice was full of compassion. 'You must have been through hell. For your husband to kill himself like that. . . .'

'Thank God for small mercies,' Elsie said. 'He never married me! He always said we'd get married in the autumn, in the spring, this year, next year. You know, I think he had a premonition of how his life was going to end, and did me the one kindness of not involving me to that extent. They took everything, of course. All the jewellery he'd bought me, the house we lived in for about three months of the year, the flat we had in London. They even asked to see my bank book. Luckily, I had two, one for what you might call joint expenses, the other personal. I never let on about the personal one. That was my nest egg!'

'Why did you come back to Ravenswyke? To Old Quaytown? Surely, after all the smart places you've been to. . . ? This must seem very dull to you. . . ?'

'It's home, Reuben, that's why,' she said sincerely. 'It's home, real and stable. After all the wandering, after all the eating what I liked from the menus in all the smart places he took me to, I wanted to come back to peace and stability. I never want to walk into another hotel, never want to read another menu or pack and unpack a suitcase as long as I live!'

Two months later, the elderly twin sisters who had a tobacco, cigar and cigarette kiosk next door to the lifeboat station, by the side of the dock, both died within a week of each other. Minnie and Mollie had been together for the seventy-five years of their lives, always fractious with each other, always quarrelling, neither ever marrying, neither ever conceding an inch to the other. Minnie died first, of pleurisy. The locals said that Mollie went with her, just as a woman will often follow her lifetime husband into the grave, or a man his wife. Elsie Milner applied for, and was given, the renting of the kiosk, and she invested £100 of her capital in stock, including jars of boiled sweets and lollipops. Most of the fishermen who'd been buying their tobacco in the post office switched their custom to the kiosk. For one thing, Elsie Milner was a damned sight more cheerful and better looking than grumpy old Amos Linham. The kids all went there because she sold a smashing line of gob-stoppers, half as big again as Linham's.

They were all sitting round the room, washed and polished, when Reuben brought Eleanor home. Suddaby had pleaded with Reuben to let him treat Eleanor in the cottage hospital just out-side Towsker, rather than sending her to the asylum. 'Anyway,' he said, 'I can't agree to ask for a committal simply because she was careless and neglected your Amos. I know the loss of the little lad was a great shock to you all, but we mustn't let ourselves be vindictive. There's no profit in taking your revenge.' Reuben had agreed to try the experiment, and Dr Suddaby had arranged a room for Eleanor, without telling Reuben his sister would actually be employed part-time at the cottage hospital and that

311

way earn her keep. She was responsible for keeping all the hospital records straight, all the documents of the patients, sending out the accounts. Gradually, the doctors from the neighbourhood who used the hospital's facilities for their own operations began to trust her, to rely on her more and more to act as unofficial secretary to them. She even taught herself to use the typewriter in the hospital office, the first she'd ever seen, and did much of their correspondence on it.

Dr Suddaby was not content to be an average general practitioner. He'd always hoped to become a specialist, though there hadn't been enough money available when he'd qualified. Finding Dr Gilchrist had been a remarkable stroke of luck; Dr Gilchrist had known he was dying, and was less concerned about money than about finding a suitable successor. The price he'd asked for the practice had been derisory, and even then he'd left an equivalent sum in his will. As an undergraduate, whenever John Suddaby could spare time from his more formal studies of anatomy and physiology, he'd read the works of Freud and Jung and had been fascinated by the new psychology methods. Gradually over the years the conviction had come upon him that here was a branch of experimental medicine he would like very much to try. Eleanor Godson had been his first what one might call 'psychological' patient. Over the many months she'd been living in the cottage hospital, isolated from family pressures, he'd encouraged her to talk about her life, her early desires, her intentions, her fantasies. At the same time as they had been talking, he had treated her with the new drugs that were becoming more and more available to calm people's nervous tensions, to help them to sleep and generally to relax. He'd fed her with tonic material, put her on a high-protein diet. The effect on her of all this had been remarkable. For years, he realized, she must have picked at her food and hadn't been eating enough to give herself physical or mental energy to tackle life. Her early ambitions had been the normal ones of a pretty young girl. She'd wanted a husband who would love her and give her babies. She'd wanted a home of her own that was not her parents' home. She'd wanted the authority that would have gone with being the mistress of her own establishment. And yet, when Terrie and his brother had died, when she'd lost her baby, she'd had nothing. Not even her own domain. She'd been condemned to living in harness with the rest of the family.

When Reuben had brought Emily to the house, without realizing it Eleanor had resented her, especially when she started producing babies every year and demonstrating the sovereignty that Eleanor herself craved.

John Suddaby didn't realize exactly how large a part he himself had played in Eleanor's recovery. Quite simply, Eleanor had fallen in love with the handsome forty-year-old doctor and that, more than anything else, had speeded her recovery. The matron of the cottage hospital, however, was a wise woman; she saw quite plainly what was happening. If Dr Suddaby were not careful, his patient would merely exchange one dependency for another. She'd taken the doctor into her private quarters one day when he'd arrived at the hospital and had poured him a glass of sherry.

What she quietly, but authoritatively, told him that day convinced him he'd read his Freud and Jung manuals with only one eye open. The next day, he went to see Reuben to tell him that his sister Eleanor was cured and could, if Reuben so desired, come back home to live. He'd added one rider. It was important, he'd said, for Eleanor to continue with some kind of career. Since she'd taught herself to use the typewriter, and so many people were employing young ladies in their offices, and since there was a regular service to Whitby, didn't Reuben agree that Eleanor should be encouraged to take a position in an office there as a typist or secretary. That would give her her own salary, her independence.

Reuben had agreed to the proposal, and Eleanor's return home had been arranged. They'd given her one of the new rooms Reuben had built at the back. It even had its own bathroom and could be reached by a door from the back, so that anyone entering or leaving did not need to come through the yard and the living room. It would give Eleanor that much more independence.

Dr Suddaby had brought Eleanor down from the cottage hospital in his new car. He stopped by the dock, since the car couldn't go up the narrow streets between the old houses. He held the door open for Eleanor, held out his hand gravely, and she took it, and pressed it gently. 'I'll never forget you, Dr Suddaby,' she said, 'or what you've done for me!'

'You've been a model patient, my dear,' he said gallantly.

She smiled at him. Secretly she'd hoped she'd become more than that, but his treatment had been so successful that she was

313

able to overcome the disappointment of realizing that his interest in her was solely professional. Wilfred, impatient as ever, had been waiting by the dock with Arthur. The two fought for a while before deciding that both should carry Eleanor's bag up the slope. Eleanor followed behind them, strangely composed but realizing that that, too, was part of Dr Suddaby's miracle cure. The rest of the family were sitting round the room when she arrived, the two girls wearing print dresses, with their hair combed and ribboned, Hannah and Emily both without aprons, even John sitting up at the table with his boots on and stockings for once not down round his ankles. Reuben was wearing his best blue cotton fishing smock over his heavy-knit fisherman's sweater and dark tweed trousers. He got up and put his arms round her, hugging her to him. She saw, with a shock, that he had a few silver lines already in his black thick hair; Silas had been grey long before his time. She wondered if she herself had undetected grey hairs...?

'It's good to see you fit again, Eleanor,' Reuben said. He'd never been to see her in the hospital, but then she'd never wanted him to. Emily had been several times and brought all the family, and Hannah had been regularly. But never Reuben.

'It's good to be back again, Reuben,' she said simply.

She took off her hat, laying it with its pins on the sideboard. He noticed she was wearing a coat he'd never seen before and he helped her off with it. There was a label in the back, but he couldn't read it upside down. Coats with labels in came from Whitby – most of the women had their coats made in the village. 'I see you've bought yourself a new coat?' he said awkwardly.

She smiled without speaking and hung it behind the door. It was a symbol of her new independence, and both recognised it as such. She sat down, took a cup of tea and a piece of cake, looking round the room, noting the small changes. 'You've moved the ornaments,' she said, 'and got a new cover for the sofa!'

Emily, for once, was at a loss for words. 'Aye, we've done a few things,' she said. 'Wait till you see your new room. Your mam's fixed it up a treat!'

Eleanor smiled. 'Yes, well, I meant to talk to you about that. I went with one of the doctors to a house sale over at Mulaby Manor. There was some very nice furniture in one of the rooms, and I made a bid for it. For the whole room, just as it stood – bed, chest of drawers, chairs, curtains, carpet, bedspread, everything. Mine was the only bid, and I got it. Old Harry's bringing it down for me this afternoon on the horse and cart!'

'Nay, you've not been wasting your brass, have you?' Reuben said, embarrassed. 'We've plenty of stuff you could have.'

Hannah had been quick to see the determination on Eleanor's face. 'If you want your own stuff about you, lass, stuff as you've bought with your own earnings, then who's to deny you. It'll not take but a few minutes to clear the room out!'

Eleanor was looking at Reuben. 'You don't mind, then?' she asked.

'It's nowt to do wi' me,' he said, 'though Mam and Emily has worked like blacks today, getting the room ready for you. You should have said summat a bit earlier on. But it's nowt to do wi' me.'

'Well, while we're talking, I'd better tell you I've got a job,' Eleanor said. 'I'm going to work for Thrummell and Slade, in the office, as a typist. They're going to pay me a pound a week to start with, then see how I get on.'

'A pound a week?' Reuben said. 'My, you will be grand!'

It wasn't that he meant to be a curmudgeon. The idea of Eleanor buying her own clothes, having her own furniture, going every day to Whitby to do her own job for her own wages, was new to him, and totally outside his experience. No Godson had ever done it before! The Godson household had always lived on what it made from fishing, men, women and children. The women had always supported the men in their job of fishing. They'd always baited the lines, come down to the dock for the launch and to help bring the vessel back in again. They'd made their men's snap, and meals, had kept their clothes mended. In some vague way he couldn't understand, the idea of Eleanor going out to earn her own living, just like any other person, seemed to break the special relationship the Godsons had always known as a family, from generation to generation.

'Times are changing,' Hannah said. She understood what was going through his mind and didn't enjoy seeing the family traditions broken any more than he did. They'd lived by them all their lives, had drawn comfort and strength from them.

'I'll pay you rent for my room,' Eleanor said quickly, 'if that's what's bothering you?'

'You won't,' he said, his anger showing. 'No Godson has ever paid rent for a room in a Godson house, and I'm not going to be the one to start. You're a Godson, the room is yours by right. You'll not be paying rent, like this was a boarding-house!'

He got up, and grabbed his coat from behind the door. 'I've got to go and look at the *Hope*,' he said. It was the traditional way a Godson man ended a conversation.

He left the house and they heard the clatter of his boots on the cobblestones of the lane. 'You'll have to give him time, Eleanor,' Emily said. 'Time to get used to things. But he'll come round, you'll see. He'll come round!'

'He's not still holding it against me. . . ?' Eleanor asked.

'Nay, Eleanor. Amos is buried and forgotten. You know, Reuben's never even been to look at his grave! I'm not criticizing; Reuben's a man who thinks about the living, not the dead. I go up there, once every so often, and take a few flowers, but I don't tell Reuben.'

'Could I come up with you, sometime?' Eleanor asked. 'Could I?'

'If you want to. . . .'

The rest of the kids were starting to be restless. 'What time is Harry coming with his horse and cart, Eleanor?' Wilfred asked.

'He should be here soon.'

'Can we go and look for him, Mam? Can we?'

'I don't see why not,' she said. 'But don't get your best clothes mucky!'

Reuben was sitting in the *Hope* on the dock, a piece of rope in his hand, splicing an eye. He was looking out over the scaurs. Already the tide was coming back in, and he could see the black cap moving towards Tockett Top. With luck, it'd all blow over by the time they went fishing tomorrow, if the wind didn't veer to the north as it so often did in the spring. A spring storm could be every bit as bad, if not worse, than a winter blow. Once the land started to warm up, there could be some strange weather about, harsh and unpredictable. At least in the winter you got a steady predictable blow on most occasions and knew where you were.

He didn't see the man who'd walked down the bank and now stood watching him, until the man came close and spoke to him. 'Good evening,' he said. 'Been a nice day, hasn't it?'

'Aye, that it has,' Reuben said, feeling sociable for once.

'Bit out of the way here?' the man said.

'Aye, I reckon as you could say that. . . ! '

'The world passes you by, eh?'

'Some of it! The bit we do very well without!'

The man laughed. 'You're right there,' he said. 'The news is all so bad these days, so discouraging. All this talk about war, and this fellow Hitler.'

'Hitler? Can't say as I've heard of him,' Reuben said.

'Nasty doings in Germany and Austria.'

'Again? I thought they'd sorted that lot out in nineteen-eighteen.'

'Well, they haven't. You mark my words. There's going to be trouble again. My name's Dobbin, by the way, Frederick Dobbin.'

'Pleased to meet you, Mr Dobbin. Mine's Reuben Godson.'

'Yes, I know. This is the *Hope of Ravenswyke*, isn't it?'

'The selfsame. You from these parts, then? Since you know my name.'

'I shall be. I've bought a piece of land at the top of Cliff, I believe they call it. They're starting building me a house tomorrow. We're going to be neighbours!'

The wind came up as the sun went down, howling over the roofs of Old Quaytown under the pantiles, sending the gulls screaming inland for shelter. The sea was whipped to an angry foam that boiled off the landing, piling upon itself. Reuben walked down to the dock at half-past ten after he'd drunk his cup of cocoa and stood on the flat dock by the Raven Hotel watching the sea rush up the slip, boiling around the foot of the houses, the lifeboat station, Elsie Milner's kiosk, before spending itself in the alley-ways. Luckily the buildings in this part of Old Quaytown had all been constructed to resist the flooding tidal waters with large stone steps and doors that fitted snugly against them, but if the blow was sustained they'd all be sweeping the water out in the morning. Reuben couldn't remember when he'd seen the water as disturbed as it was now; out in the bay the waves were being lashed by the direct down-draught to a height of twenty feet or more, boiling wild with white showers of spray off every wave top, iridescent in the faint light of the late evening. Even the clouds in the sky seemed confused, broken at separate levels, each level being forced in different ways from the others. The fishermen

317

had all come down after supper when they'd heard the wind picking up, and all the boats had been dragged higher up the bank to the parking they normally only used in the worst winter weather. Several of the fishermen came down, and a small knot of them gathered around Reuben, not speaking, looking out over the troubled ocean, feeling a sympathy with the tortured waters like a man watching the woman he loves in labour, contorting herself with the pain of it. The ocean is always at its most troubled along a shoreline, when the incoming flood meets the solid mass bouncing back from the cliffs, two enemies hurling themselves upon each other in combat. Now some of the wave tops were being thrown forty or fifty feet in the air and even the phlegmatic fishermen, who'd seen it all before, would exclaim quietly, 'By gow, did you see that one!' The whole bay was in turmoil, the air full of a menacing ozone seaweed smell as if the undisturbed sea bottom on which the detritus of the ocean had piled high were being scooped clean, its fetid slime brought up to the surface to poison the atmosphere. Many of the gulls hadn't the sense to go inland, and flew over the fishermen's heads, cawking with frustrated rage, as if commanding the men to do something about this monstrous disturbance. The night was warm with an oily sweatiness in the air that made the skin prickle; the wind, despite its force and vigour, did nothing to clear the night, merely serving to swirl the heavy atmosphere more clammily, more sickeningly, about their nostrils.

'I'm away to bed,' Sam Gainer said. 'I reckon at this rate it'll blow itself out before morn! Damn it, nothing could last at this pace.'

Most of them agreed with him, but were not optimistic about getting any sleep, even if they did go home to bed. Throughout the village the clattering shutters, the rapping of the tiles and the squawk of the gulls added an obligato to the roar and slap of the waves that would puncture sleep with constant wakefulness.

Reuben sat on the stone wall beside the Raven, unable to take his eyes off the ocean which not even he had ever seen so turbulent, so defiant, so deranged!

He stayed there until midnight when suddenly he detected a changed note in the wind-song, as if the blast were finally blowing itself out, weakening under the strain of that perpetual motion. 'Aye, it's starting to go down now,' he said. He walked back up

318

the lanes and by ten-past he was in bed, asleep, with only the one
sheet and one blanket to cover him and Emily.

He walked down to the dock next day through an atmosphere
of restless heavy calm, as if the elements were shamed by their
previous night's outburst. The sea was still well up and full, oily
and heavy. Already the folks of Newquay Town were walking
along the few exposed scaurs, starting the daily search for flotsam
and jetsam, beachcombing for wood for fires, planks off cargo
steamers, crates of booze, though you didn't find such valuables
every day. While they witnessed the damage of the storm, many
of them were looking for the black shiny jet they could sell to the
Whitby jewellers, or fossils. The fishermen traditionally held the
beachcombers in contempt and dubbed them parasites. 'What do
you think, Reuben?' Sam Gainer asked.

'The blow is over. We could launch without waiting for the
tide to go all the way down.'

That way they'd save time. Sam started the tractor and one by
one they dragged the boats down the street to the top of the slip.
The usual crowd gathered, willing hands to help. One by one they
climbed aboard their vessels, and the tractor, which had a forked
planking mounted on the front, pushed from behind until they
were floating free. The men would grab their sweeps, give the
boats a bit of a pull to clear the bottom, and then start the engine.
Reuben was the last to go, with old Captain Walham himself
driving the tractor to push him off. He'd started the engine as soon
as the tailpost was immersed, kept it idling with the gear in
neutral; as soon as the *Hope* floated free of the tractor's yoke, he
slipped the gear into forward, and the *Hope* took off, aimed down
the long channel that ran between the scaurs.

Not one of them believed the fishing would be any good; most
of them had pulled out their pots the previous day when they'd
seen the weather was going to blow but now they'd wait a day or
two before putting them down again. Meanwhile they could try
their hand at lining. They spread across the face of the ocean,
some staying in the bay, some moving out of it. The sky was still
muddy from the storm, and the limpid water rose and fell in long
disturbing swells that rocked the boats fore and aft and from side
to side, a motion more sickening than any normal roll. With no
breath of wind left, the ocean had a rancid feel that all knew and
none liked. As Reuben and Batty worked, they were soon bathed

in a clammy sweat that stuck their clothes to them. Reuben pulled off his cotton smock and the shirt beneath it, working the boat in his vest and trousers. His body, like Batty's, looked as if it had been made in two pieces, with parts normally exposed being tanned a permanent deep brown, the parts normally covered a startling white. They toiled along a bearing across the mouth of the bay, about half a mile out, but each line came up with only a few stones of fish on it. The previous week, they'd made a total of £100, a fabulous sum. This week, if the present weather continued, they'd be lucky to gross £20, with wages, fuel, bait, insurance and tackle replacements to come out of that.

It was coming up to low tide when they went back in again, bone-tired from the hauling, dispirited with the smallness of the catch. They didn't imagine the others would have done any better – 'We'd have been better ligging abed!' Reuben growled as they stowed away the last of the gear and headed for home.

Sam Gainer was about a quarter of a mile in front of them as they went in; the tide was not yet fully down but he'd fetch up on the end of the sand pit between the scaurs, from where the tractor would haul him up the slip. They watched Sam position himself for the run between the walls of rock, knowing he'd be lining himself and taking his bearing for the entrance on the bit of a spire on the top of the chapel roof and the lightning conductor on the top of the Raven Hotel, their traditional navigation marks for coming in. Sam was going at quite a lick, no doubt frustrated with the failed day; Reuben was sitting in the stern, looking past the stub-mast and the forepost, when suddenly he saw the bow of Sam's boat rear. Both of them heard the shocking rasp and crack of wood they knew so well.

'He's hit summat!' Batty shouted. 'Summat in t'water!'

Reuben made for Sam's boat, which was obviously jammed on some obstacle, tilted at a crazy angle. Sam had rushed forward into the bows of his boat after he'd killed the engine, and Reuben could see the water pouring in. Batty had gone forward and was intent on the water in front of the *Hope*. 'Starboard,' he yelled quickly, and instinctively Reuben banged the tiller over and throttled back the engine. As the bow of the boat slewed round he saw why Batty had shouted. Where there should be clear channel for them, and at least six feet of water, he could see the jagged teeth of broken rock sticking out. If Batty hadn't seen it and they'd hit it, they'd be in the same condition as Sam Gainer, marooned on a rocky grave. They crept forward, with Batty crouched in the bows looking deep into the water before him, the engine pulling them forward at a snail's pace, turning port and starboard every time Batty shouted and jabbed in the appropriate direction with his arm. It was a tortuous slow progress along the channel where normally they could steam in without a thought, confident that only a smooth sandy bottom lay beneath them.

By now Sam Gainer's plight had been seen and a score of people had rushed across the scaurs. He'd fastened a line on the bowpost of his boat, and Horse-and-Cart Harry was driving the tractor, which had taken the other end of the line. The boat seemed to have freed itself from the side of the rock but it listed in the water, rapidly filling. They were dragging it as best they could towards the low-water line so that they could save it as the tide went out, holding it firm with the tractor. Reuben could see the many rocks that littered the shoreline, rocks that hadn't been there before last night's horrendous storm. Many of them were boulders at least three feet in diameter; a whole section of the face of the cliff had broken out, scattering hundreds of tons of rock and stone and soil along the shoreline. The rocks through which they were making their precarious way would, he knew, have been torn from the scaurs by the undersea force generated by those waves. People never realized what power the water had; a thousand-ton steamer, with plates made of iron, had been picked up by waves one time and had been thrown almost contemptuously fifty yards inshore, landing with its broken back on what was normally dry ground! The underwater scouring force of that storm must have broken the very seabed loose, had piled these enormous rocks along the channel they normally used for landing. Once that happened, the sand and gravel of the shoreline would gradually lodge itself between the crevices of the larger boulders, filling the spaces between the rocks inexorably, silting and blocking the channel on which the fishermen depended for their livelihood. It had happened inside the Cut 150 years ago; it could very well be about to happen here, now.

They drew level with Sam Gainer's boat; Sam was standing chest deep in the water beside it, walking along with it as the tractor slowly dragged it towards the shore. The boat was already waterlogged and the strain on the line made it taut as a piano wire. Thank God Harry was experienced in haulage, and kept the tractor moving at the same steady pace, maintaining the same steady pull. He'd cleared all the people away from the line; if it broke, the ends could whip around and sever somebody's head. Reuben kept the *Hope* behind Sam's boat; he looked over the stern and saw the rest of the fishing fleet coming in. They had seen what was happening and all the boats had a man in the bow, sounding the water in front of them. They were drawn out behind the *Hope* in a half-mile-long game of follow-my-leader. As they saw the rocks, just beneath the water surface, they'd started tagging them with weighted buoys normally used for identifying the location of lobster pots. The marked channel that was being created would be too sharply bent for them to negotiate with any safety in a high-running sea.

Slowly they dragged Sam Gainer's boat above what normally would be the low-water mark, and there it lay, a ruptured duck of a vessel. Reuben ran the *Hope* along the hard beside it before he cut the engine. A jagged hole had been torn in the bottom of Sam's boat, big enough for a man to crawl into. It looked, too, as if the keel plate had been fractured, and a couple of the ribs. The boat would be damned near a write-off. Luckily Sam was insured – they all were – but the repair would take time, and the boat would never be the same again, never totally trustworthy in a blow. Not many fishermen like to man a boat that's had its keel plate damaged.

One by one, the boats reached the landing, but it took hours to get them all in, whereas normally the job would have been completed in minutes. As the tide went lower, Reuben walked the waterline and saw the extent of the damage to the shore. Some of the displaced rocks were ten feet square, six feet high, and already he could see a score more of them. God alone knew how many more were in the deeper water, a hazard waiting for the unsuspecting fisherman coming home. He knew that one by one they could tag the rocks; they could drill them, let an iron post in them that would stick above the water surface even at high tide. That would be all right, coming in during the bright daytime, with a quiet sea running, but it'd be a hellish game of follow-my-leader at night, or in any kind of rough weather, when the posts themselves would be hidden by the spray. So far as he could see, there was no direct line where they could draw a channel with a light on one end to guide them in – the rocks had been thrown higgledy-piggledy by a frivolously malevolent force. There wasn't even a straight pull for the tractor to haul them out of the low-water beaching.

His mind active but bemused, he walked back up the landing to the slip. Batty had taken what fish they'd caught up to the station to catch the train and all the boats were now safely parked beside the dock; the door of the tap was open, and Reuben could see them all inside, obviously waiting. He went into the room through the thick atmosphere of gloom, accepted half a pint of mild beer, and sat down by the grate in which the fire had not yet been lighted. They'd want him to suggest something, to offer some leadership, but what could he say? Sam came and sat beside him. 'That boat of mine's buggered!' he said flatly. 'I'll get it fixed up but I'll never take the bugger out to sea again!'

'Well, Reuben, what do you think?' Bill Clewson asked. Clegg, Brawnham, all the fishermen were looking to him, giving him the chance to speak first. Each had his own opinions, but they'd hold their tongues until Reuben had spoken.

'We shall have to start coming in on high tide,' Reuben said. 'We shall never have enough water under us if we try to come in when the tide's low. And that shoreline, well, that's a mess. The time we spend tractoring over that lot will cost us a market. We shall have to put in a winch, bolted to the roadway at the top of the slip. We'll come in stern first, on a jury-line port and starboard. We can either chuck a line over the stern, for the winchman to catch, or he can chuck one to us, and then it'll be a straight drag up the slip. What we'll do is get some railway sleepers and let 'em into the concrete slip, so that we'll be sliding up wood instead of concrete. That way, we'll protect our fins!'

They considered what he was saying. It would work, of course. 'It'll take time, Reuben,' Clegg said.

'Aye, at first, but we'll develop a method for it. The key is the winchman.'

'What's wrong with the tractor?' Bill Clewson said, bewildered.

Brawnham told him. 'What holds the tractor in position, Bill? Four tyres and four brakes. You imagine the pull of a boat on that slip in the high tide. It could pull that tractor straight off the slip into t'water!'

'Not if the engine was running, pulling forward.'

Brawnham looked at him, pityingly. 'And what happens if you

323

get a big 'un, that swamps the engine? And stalls it? No. Reuben is right. We need a winch that's bolted down to t'roadway. Happen, Reuben, we could get a donkey-engine, and install it in a shed next to the kiosk. That way it'd be protected from the water, and give us a faster pull?'

Reuben was worried by that suggestion. 'Think of the length of wire rope you'd have, all across the roadway. It'd be impossible to keep the kids away from it. That rope breaking could do a lot of damage. . . .'

They all knew that the longer the rope, the greater was the risk of a break.

'It'd be a bugger to haul back off the donkey-engine, down the slip for the next one in,' Walter Clegg said. 'Nay, I don't reckon that'd work!'

They talked about the possibilities for an hour before Sam remembered he was still wearing his wet things. 'I'd better be getting home,' he said, 'else my missis'll kill me, sitting round here catching my death!'

The next day, as if to prove it could be done, Reuben went off at high tide and came back in when it was high again. He'd wasted a long time on the water when he came back with only six boxes to show for his labours. The others stayed behind and worked on the site for the winch, digging three feet down into the dock to provide a strong foundation for it. They used Reuben's truck to fetch a winch from the boatyard in Whitby, where it was for sale, cheap. They installed it and poured wet concrete around it; it'd take four days at least to set before they'd be safe to use it. When Reuben returned, after motoring slowly across the suspect landing with Batty probing in front of the bows with a long pole, they pulled him in with the tractor.

He'd missed the train to Leeds; the fish would be a day old when Tommy Tomlinson received it.

Reuben was first out again the next day, at high tide. A wave caught him, swung him side on, and threatened to get under his beam and tip it. Only by a superb bit of seamanship was Reuben able to slip the *Hope* over the crest of the wave, side on, and ride it safely out off the slip into the deeper water. Even then, he felt the bottom bump on some underwater obstruction.

Clegg came after him; he managed to get out all right.

Reuben came in safe, catching the tractor line first time. He'd rigged a jury from his port to his starboard sternposts; the line dragged him evenly straight up the centre of the slip.

When Walter Clegg came in, he missed the line they threw to him; the next wave caught his bows, smashed them over on the cross, and rammed him up against the stone footings on which the Raven Hotel had been built. Two of the ribs and three feet of the gunwale were smashed like firewood by the heavy impact.

One by one in the weeks that followed, they all had some adverse experience as they learned the new techniques, but gradually their experience as fishermen won out and they solved the small problems. Once they had mastered it, the winch worked well though it was slow. At least it was safe; once they had the winch hook on the jury-line they all now used, they knew they'd be taken up the slip no matter what sea was running. If the waves were running in, following the boat, often they would be picked up and carried up the slip in an enormous rush that would deposit them with an almighty thump on the concrete. They'd let the timber studs into the roadway and that helped, but the boats still took a wallop sometimes that seemed to jar every plank, every post, every nail.

They were sitting in the tap of the Raven one evening about three weeks later when the door opened and a figure only Reuben recognized came in. Reuben rose and greeted him, taking him round the tap and introducing him to everybody. 'This is our man in Leeds,' he said, 'our Tommy Tomlinson!' It was the first time, so far as they were aware, that the agent had been to Ravenswyke; they all clamoured to buy him a drink, happy as schoolboys.

He accepted a couple, to be sociable, then said to Reuben, 'They've given me a room upstairs. I wonder if you'd care to come up and have a bit of a chat while I wash myself and get myself ready?'

'Nay, I thought you'd be stopping with me at our place,' Reuben said. 'We can make room for you quite easy.'

'I'm better upstairs,' Tommy said. 'But thanks all the same!'

They went out of the tap and back into the hotel by the outside staircase. Tommy led the way and they sat down in the corner of the lounge. Tommy ordered a whisky for himself, and Reuben, remembering the previous times he'd been in this room, had a brandy. 'What have you got on your mind, Tommy?' he asked.

He knew the agent hadn't brought him up here merely to change his drink.

'I'm worried about the fish you're sending, Reuben,' he said. 'Our agreement was based – as was the agreement I've made with the buyers – on fresh fish. Fresher than they could get from Whitby or Scarborough. Well, I don't need to tell you, Reuben, it isn't fresh. The stuff I see coming from Whitby is often fresher than yours. I go for the evening train, and there's nowt for me from you, but plenty for the other folks from Whitby market. I have to wait for mine until the next day. Aye, and sometimes the morning train is missed again. What's happening up here, Reuben? I thought I'd better come up and find out for myself. I thought we had an agreement. . . ?'

Reuben didn't like being put on the defensive, though he could see the justification in what Tommy Tomlinson was saying. He explained to him the details of the damage to the landing, the way they'd had to solve their problem, the way they could no longer fish from and to low tide, but had to wait for high tide before they could come in.

'Which means that, like as not, you miss the trains?' Tommy asked. Though he was interested in the details, they weren't his concern. His business had been built on a promise which was no longer being kept.

'It isn't the high tide that makes us miss the trains,' Reuben said, explaining that the incoming and outgoing tides varied by one hour each day. 'It's the time it actually takes us to get back up the slip. That winch is good, but it's nowhere near as fast as the tractor was. That's where we lose the time, and often miss the trains.'

Tommy Tomlinson was standing on the dock the next morning to watch them go out; he had a curious birdlike interest in everything, looking at all the details of the arrangements. He saw the way they'd arranged matters as best they could; nothing immediately suggested itself to him as a possible improvement. He was on the dock again when they came back in, having, in the meantime, travelled to and from Whitby. He caught the late train to Leeds that night, the train on which the fish travelled. They'd missed the earlier train. When he got to his office the next morning, he found a formal notification from Featherby's solicitors, advising him that for 'reasons of breach of the spirit of the con-

tract of which he [Tomlinson] must be perfectly aware', Featherby
had decided to bring their arrangement to an end.

They say bad luck comes in threes. The destruction of the Ravenswyke landing ground by the storm was number one, closely followed by number two, the loss of the Leeds markets. Reuben, of
course, went back to the Whitby wholesalers in the fishmarket
with his cap in his hand. They bore no animosity and were
pleased to welcome him back to the fold, a sinner repented! But,
they warned him, times had changed. He soon saw how much
they'd changed when he started to get his daily fish receipts. Many
people were now using Whitby, people from overseas, fishermen
from the far grounds. The amount of fish landed each day far
exceeded anything they'd known and the market was booming.
The trawlers were bringing heavy catches from as far away as
Icelandic and Norwegian waters, having been out for as much as
three weeks with their fish stowed in ice in the holds. Some of the
new breed of trawler skippers, younger lads, were using newly
invented instruments to roam further afield and were receiving as
much as £1500 a year for their share of the catch; £30 a week, for
being a trawler skipper! To get that much money previously,
you'd have to be a doctor or a dentist! Most of the boats were
owned by companies, and the crews including the skipper worked
for wages and a percentage of the catch. The boats were bigger
and designed for all weathers, with comfortable quarters for the
crew below decks, even a cabin for the skipper. It was inevitable
that the sheer volume of fish being landed should depress the
price; fish had become a truly inexpensive commodity, a rich
source of cheap food. In the fish-and-chip shops of the towns of
the West Riding, you could buy the traditional Yorkshire meal
for twopence for the fish and a penny for the chips, and even at
those low prices the shops were profitable.

The effect on Ravenswyke's fishing industry was instantaneous.
Sam Gainer had his boat repaired but sold it immediately, without
ever putting to sea in it. He and his missis sold their cottage to a
holidaymaker from Leeds – the first to get a foot into Old Quaytown – and emigrated to Canada.

Bill Clewson found that his receipts from fishing just about
covered his repayments to Reuben. Reuben offered to waive the

repayments until times were better, but Bill's sense of honour wouldn't permit him to accept what he thought of as charity. He sold his boat to a fisherman from Whitby, and went back to his jobbing builder-cum-caretaker-gardener business.

Reuben was sitting in the tap of the Raven one evening when young Mark Brawnham and Billy Clegg came in. They ordered half a pint of mild each, then sat at Reuben's table. He could sense an air of excitement and expectancy about them.

'What-o, then! You two going out courting?' Both were wearing what might be called their best, tweed suits with chequered shirts and ties. They'd polished their boots, slicked down their hair. 'A right couple of mashers you are!'

'No, Reuben, we're catching the five-to-eight. We're off!'

'The five-to-eight? Off where?' He knew quite well the last train to York went at five-to-eight. York and all points south. Or north.

'We're going to Leeds. We've been accepted,' Mark Brawnham said.

'Accepted for what?'

'For the navy. We report in Leeds. Then they send us down to a place called Gosport for three months. After that, we may go to Portsmouth, or Chatham, depending on where they put us.'

'Got it all worked out, have you?'

'Yes,' Billy Clegg said. 'You know, Reuben, it's what we've always wanted!'

'We want to get out of this dead-and-alive hole and see a bit of the world,' Mark added.

'What about your dads. What do they think about it?'

'They don't know,' Billy said quickly. 'That's why we've come to see you. They think we're off out for the evening. With a couple of lasses! We've hid our bags round the back of the station, ready to go. But we wanted to come and see you to ask you to do something for us. When they find out we've gone, will you have a word with 'em for us? Tell 'em how it is with both of us!'

'How did you go about it?' Reuben asked, mystified. 'Surely, they must have sent some papers to you, all that sort of thing?'

'Aye, well, we had them sent to the post office.'

'And your dads' signatures? You're both under twenty-one!'
They both looked uncomfortable.

'You signed 'em yourselves . . .', Reuben said. 'That's forgery!'

'Aye, well, I signed his, and he signed mine. It's only a formality, Reuben. It isn't as if we were trying to twist 'em out of anything.'

Reuben drank his beer, went to the counter, and got another one for himself, one each for the two lads. When he came back he set the pots on the table top and sat down. 'Look, lads,' he said. 'You're starting off on the wrong foot! Your parents have brought you up; they've looked after you as best they could. It's not their fault if you've got itchy feet and want to see the rest of the world. But you do owe them something. Something a bit better than stealing out of the house without a word of thanks and good-bye. . . .'

'We mean to write to them, as soon as we get settled,' Billy said fervently.

Reuben shook his head. 'Writing to them is not the same thing. Believe me, if you do it this way, you'll have cause to regret it all your lives. Why don't you both go back home, and face your dads and mams? Tell 'em straight out what you've got in mind to do. I imagine it's too late to back down now, so it won't really matter what they say. But, like, face them, man to man. Not sneaking away like this, as if you've done something to be ashamed about. You'll both learn, in time, that we've got to face our responsibilities in life, no matter how much we may want to avoid them! So, do us a favour, eh? Go to your dads, tell 'em straight out, "Dad, I've joined the navy." And say goodbye to your mams in the right way. Remember this; they've brought you up, they've looked after you as best they can. You've got nowt to complain about on that score. So, sup your beer, go back home, and say your goodbyes in the right way, eh?'

The two lads were looking at each other. 'They'll try to talk us out of it,' Billy Clegg said, 'like they've always done.'

'My old man'll bray me,' Mark Brawnham said.

'Look at it this way,' Reuben said, smiling. 'If anybody can talk you out of it, then it's not right you should be going in the first place. When I've made my mind to do summat, then there's no power on earth that could talk *me* out of it. And, as regards the braying, I don't somehow think your dad'll lift his hand to you, when he sees you mean to go make a life for yourself. Knowing your dad as I do, he'll be looking in t'cupboard to find a few shillings to put in your hand. Aye, and both your mams will be that busy, making up some sandwiches to take with you, so's you won't go hungry!'

Reluctantly, the two lads got up, looking at each other.

'Give me your word,' Reuben said sternly. 'You'll not go sloping off to the station the minute you get outside. You'll go home, say goodbye to your mams and dads.'

'Aye, Reuben, we'll do it,' Billy Clegg said. He held out his hand. 'So us'll say goodbye, then, Reuben. I hope the weather keeps fine for you. And you catch a lot of fish!'

He shook hands with both the boys, and sat down at the table again, not wanting to leave now to make them think he was following them. Maybe they'd stick with their word and go back home to say goodbye. Maybe they wouldn't.

Sergeant Neckridge, out of uniform, had been sitting at the table by the bar. He came across the room and sat at Reuben's table, a half-pint for Reuben in his hand. 'That was a good thing you just did,' he said. 'I couldn't help overhearing. Brawnham and Clegg both know the lads are going tonight. They must both be daft if they think they could keep a thing like that secret in this place. But their dads haven't mentioned it. They hoped the lads would go to them, straightforward-like, and make a clean breast of it. Funny thing is, their dads have both bought 'em going-away presents, a cig case and lighter! The lads'll get a surprise if they do as you suggested and go home to say their goodbyes in a proper manner!'

'I'd heard the talk,' Reuben said. 'In fact, it was my idea to get them a cig case and lighter. Their mothers have knitted them scarves, to keep their chests warm. Bill Brawnham and Walter Clegg wanted to give 'em a box of them french letters, to keep 'em out of trouble!'

Both Reuben and the police sergeant roared with laughter. 'Trust Bill Brawnham and Walter Clegg to look on the practical side,' Neckridge said as he wiped the laughter tears from his eyes.

When Reuben arrived home, he found Wilfred and Arthur both sitting at the living-room table doing their homework. Wilfred was sixteen; he'd always been a bright lad at school and Reuben had made him stick at it. Now he attended the school in Whitby with his brother Arthur, both of them having won scholarships. Arthur, at fifteen, was taking his School Certificate. Wilfred was trying for his Higher School Certificate. Both were doing mathematics, biology and chemistry, and both had announced their interest in marine biology. He ruffled their hair with pride as he sat down at the table corner, where Emily had laid his supper. 'What're you working at tonight?' he asked.

'Maths,' Wilfred said. 'Calculus.'

'You'd have to explain that to me,' Reuben said. 'I'm nobbut an ignorant fisherman!'

Arthur was drawing, his coloured pencils littering his side of the table.

'And what's *tha* doing?' Reuben asked. Although the two boys were very much alike facially, and could never be mistaken for anything but brothers, their temperaments were quite different. Wilfred took after Reuben, was more outgoing, more ready to speak his mind. Arthur in so many ways was like Emily had been before her 'accident', before she'd learned to be bold and direct. Arthur appeared to be more compliant, to go along with whatever Wilfred might suggest. He did, however, have a hidden stubborn streak; once Arthur had set his mind against something – and that took a lot of doing – nothing would move him.

'I'm drawing the digestive system of a frog!' he said.

'Bloody hell! Is that what they're teaching you now?'

Education had never ceased to be a wonder to Reuben. Though he himself had been limited to what they taught at the local school, with no nonsense about digestive systems of frogs, calculus, School Certificate or Higher, he had an enormous respect for what the boys were doing. They had both wanted, earlier, to leave school and come fishing in the *Hope*, and Reuben had been sorely tempted. It had been his life's ambition to sail out of Ravenswyke in the *Hope*, with his two sons aboard, teaching them, just as Silas had taught him, all the details of the life of a fisherman, giving them all the lore, all the tall tales. Certainly, from the youngest age when they'd ridden in the *Hope* with him, they'd demonstrated that the sea was in their blood by the way they'd handled the lines. Why, Wilfred had even made the same mistake Reuben had made all those years ago, when he'd cast the anchor overboard without making sure the end of the line was made fast to the post. And Reuben had been just as angry as Silas had been, though he hadn't made the lad take down his trousers to leather his arse until it bled! Weekends and school holidays he'd been unable to keep the two boys out of the boat, and John, too, once he came of an age where he didn't want to crawl over the gunwales all the time. Taking them out on the ocean had taught Reuben something new. The first time was when they'd been fishing off Neb Point, a run of about three miles, and a storm had blown up while they were on their way back in. Suddenly he'd realized that he had the responsibility not only for his own life and the safety of his boat but also for the lives of his three sons. He knew now the anxiety his own father, Silas, must have felt when they were all coming home in a big blow. Lewis and Martyn, John, Alan and Reuben, all in the boat, all dependent on their father's skill to get them safely ashore. And now he, Reuben, with Wilfred, Arthur and John on board, had known the fear his father must have known, that the whole family, the line of succession, could be wiped out in one go. As the Framhams had been wiped out, the Coulsons, the Smiths, the Pentyford men, the Farnhams, the Helliwell men. All names from his own childhood, all gone, drowned at sea in the murderous freak storms for which this angry ocean was famous, and feared.

Ever after that, he was reluctant to take them out together, preferring usually to leave one ashore.

Linham's son, Peter, had come back to the village after studying away and getting a Teacher's Certificate. He'd taken over the village school as headmaster, a lazy sort of chap who seemed to be content to mark time for the rest of his life. He'd married a teacher from Whitby and they'd gone to live at the top of the bank. Wilfred had been ten when Peter Linham had sent a note down to the Godson cottage, asking Reuben to come up to the school to see him. 'What's tha been doing wrong then?' Reuben asked, immediately suspicious.

'Nowt, Dad,' the frightened youngster had said. He himself didn't know, couldn't understand, why Mr Linham should have sent a note. Reuben went up the following day and Linham took him into the tearoom that also functioned as a headmaster's study. It wasn't very grand accommodation, but the school had been built as a charity in early Victorian times and, as Linham explained, he was lucky to have anywhere to sit. 'You're going to have to take a difficult decision about your two lads,' he said. It was as good a way as any to open the conversation.

'In what way? What have they been doing wrong?'

Linham had smiled. 'Nowt wrong!' he said. 'They've been doing things right. You've got a couple of bright boys there, Mr Godson. We haven't had a couple like that in Ravenswyke for as long as I've been back!'

Reuben was chuffed, of course, dead chuffed that his two boys could earn such praise!

'Well, we've always made them get the books out, you know. When you started giving them homework, we guessed they were dropping back a bit. . . .'

'Dropping back. . . ? You're quite mistaken. I gave them homework, and nobody else, because I knew they were the only two capable of profiting by it. As it turned out, I was right. I didn't tell you, but I submitted some of the scholarship papers I'd had Wilfred do without telling him what they were. He can have a scholarship to Whitby Grammar School. If he wants one. I've talked with him several times and all he wants to do is leave school when the times comes, and become a fisherman with you. I asked him why he was bothering to learn, if all he was going to be was a fisherman – sorry, Mr Godson, it's a bit tactless of me to put it that way –'

'I know what you mean. You don't need a lot of book learning to catch fish.'

'Quite so. . . .'

'What did he tell you? About why he was bothering to learn. . . ?'

'Well, that's what's so surprising, Mr Godson. He's a remarkably mature young man, your son Wilfred. He said that it didn't matter what you did – a man could do any job and still win respect for the way he did it, even the most simple and humble of jobs. But what a man did with himself, what he was inside his mind, needed a bit of education. Now that's a very mature thought for a young person, Mr Godson. . . .'

'It is, to be sure. I'm not even certain I know what it means myself, but that's no matter. You want him to take this scholarship, right?'

'Yes, that's right. I have to warn you, however, that once he gets a glimpse of the bigger world outside Ravenswyke, once he gets an idea of what a man can do with educational qualifications, it's unlikely he'll be satisfied to spend his time catching fish for the markets. He may want to catch fish, but as a source of study

– I see he's very interested in biology and botany. I think your Wilfred will have his eyes on the stars, once he's acquired the education to do it. And here's another thing. It's early days yet, because he's one year younger than Wilfred, but I suspect your son Arthur is going to go exactly the same way. There's a very close bond between those two boys, Mr Godson, and it's enhanced by the fact that Wilfred seems, as yet, to be a leader, while Arthur, as yet, seems to be content to be a follower, with Wilfred as his inspiration and his guide.'

Reuben thought about what Linham had said all the time he was out fishing. When he was lying in bed that night, with his arm round Emily's warm shoulder, he told her, as best he could, what he'd learned about the boys. 'It'd seem we've made a couple of bright lads,' he said deprecatingly. 'Must be a throwback to our ancestors!'

'That's not very complimentary,' she protested, though she knew what he meant. Neither she nor Reuben had much time for book learning. There had been a time Reuben had read a few Walter Scott novels, but as he'd grown more and more involved with the children and the affairs of Old Quaytown, even that bit of reading had ended.

'Aye, maybe not. But what are we going to do?' he asked. She could hear the worried note in his voice. All his life, she knew, he'd had this dream of fishing with his sons, of carrying on the tradition and the line. He'd shown Wilfred the place on the beam where his name would go one day; he'd told the boys several times about how surprised he'd been to find his own name up there, after Lewis had died. 'Of course, there's no question of that with you lot,' he'd said. 'There aren't going to be any more wars, so you'll never know the death and destruction we knew then, with over half the lads of the village going under. Aye, and since we've the new engines, the fishing's a lot safer. Half the trouble we had when I were a lad were caused either with the sails going wrong, or the rower not having enough strength left to get the coble back in over the waves. Now we've got diesels we can run home with our tails between our legs whenever we see a bit of a blow coming up!' This conversation usually deteriorated into a 'Life's a lot easier for you young 'uns than it was for me', and Emily would make it her job to come to the table with a pot of tea and a few buns, effectively shutting Reuben off.

She shifted her position in the bed, getting comfortable again in his arm. 'Well, we either let them take their chances with the scholarship, or we don't,' she said. 'I think you'll have to accept, though, that if they're as bright as Linham says – and I think he knows what he's talking about – and if they go away to grammar school, it'll be the end of any plans you might have for them as fishermen. I can't see them going to school like that, and mixing with all the people they'll meet there, and then being content to go out fishing to earn a living!'

'There's nowt wrong wi' fishing,' he growled. 'It's a better way of making a living than some I could mention. A man can hold his head up, which is more than you can say for some of them and the jobs they do. At least you've got to be a man to be a fisherman!'

'You're very physical, Reuben,' she said, sighing. 'You'll never give credit to any man who works with his brains, not his brawn. You always seem to despise any man who can do his job sitting down. You're really going to have to think; it's no good putting the two lads into a way of education, a way of life, that means you're constantly going to be sneering at them because they work with their brains instead of with their hands. They're Godsons, Reuben, just like you. They'll have the right to be respected for what they do. Unless you could understand that, you'd make life hell for both of them. Unless you can see what I'm talking about, you'd do better to pull 'em both out of school when they get to school-leaving age, and set 'em on full time in the boat with you. . . .'

'I've got to think about it,' he said, with some asperity. Reuben, if the truth were known, didn't like having to think about new things and lately it seemed to be happening more and more often. The old traditions, the old ways, were changing so fast that a man no longer knew what to think. It was easy to cling to the past, to say 'What was good enough for my father is good enough for me', but more and more a man couldn't do that. Reuben knew Silas would have despised the diesel engine he now depended on so much. His father would have thought he was foolish shooting his lobster pots in January. He wouldn't have approved of sending the fish direct to Leeds. Aye, and he wouldn't have liked the way some of the lads and the lasses of the village were behaving these days, and some of the married men who ought to have known better. When Liggett had gone to fish out of Hull, they said he'd set up with a woman there, living openly with her, coming back every three months to Old Quaytown to see his wife and kids, often to make another baby before he went again. They said he already had three bairns in Hull with the other woman. Samuels had gone up to Middlesbrough; he was going to send for his wife and kids as soon as he was settled, but he never had. They said he, too, was living with another woman, though he did send his missis something every week, and she made up the rest by taking in the heavy washing and ironing. If he let his two lads off the leash, if they went to Whitby every day, they'd change. He knew that was inevitable. They'd be talking like Dr Suddaby before you knew where you were. He'd seen the lads from the grammar school come down to Ravenswyke for a day's nature study on the scaurs; he'd heard the sound of their voices and had cringed at the way they talked. Take a man like James Henry Tockett; he talked the same way Reuben did, more or less, though he occasionally used words Reuben hadn't heard of. But he didn't talk like that bloody soft lot from the grammar school. It wasn't Suddaby's fault he talked posh; he'd been born and bred in the South, where the folks were weak any way! Reuben had a North-Countryman's lack of respect for anyone from the South. But Wilfred and Arthur had been born here, in the North, and the thought of their behaving and talking in that effeminate, posh way was too much for him.

'What do you think, love?' he asked.

'We've got to give them the chance,' she said. 'We *ought* to, Reuben. We owe them that!'

'Nay, love, we don't *owe* them owt. We've done our best for them; thanks to you they've never lacked for a hot dinner, a clean shirt on their backs, a warm bed to sleep in. We've never been ones to leave 'em on their own. Nay, we don't *owe* them owt!'

Emily sat up, exasperated with him. 'They didn't ask to come into this world, Reuben,' she said. 'They have a *right*! That we'll do the best we can for them. And if it so happens they're bright enough to go to the grammar school, then we must give them the chance, it seems to me. And if you lose them as fishermen because of that, well, that's a pity in one way, and a blessing in the other!'

'A *blessing*! How do you mean, a blessing?'

She turned and looked into his face from a distance of about six inches, as if putting him under a microscope. 'Reuben, love,' she said tenderly. 'There's so many things you know! You have so much strength! And yet, there are so many things you don't see, because you have so many weaknesses! It shouldn't be for me to say this, but surely you can understand that fishing, coble fishing the way you do it, can't last much longer. If it wasn't that you were so good at it, we'd be on the breadline! Have you thought how much money the Cleggs, and the Brawnhams, are making? You haven't talked to their wives, have you? And, don't forget, both of them are paying off the loans on the cobles and the engines. Just think, they've been fishing all their lives and they're still paying off the engines! That shows you how much money they've been making over the years. You've been lucky; your father left you a good boat, a good house and a bit of capital. You've never had to pay off rent, or the loan of a boat. If you'd had to carry that burden, Reuben, as well as the rest, we wouldn't be in the position we're in now. What kind of a future would that be for the lads?'

She could see the stubborn set of his jaw. 'I know,' she said hurriedly. 'Once a Godson always a Godson, and always a fisher-man! I've never spoken about this before. It was never my inten-tion to interfere. You do what you want to do, and you'll always find me at your shoulder, helping the best road I can. But give the lads a *chance*, Reuben, to make something a bit *better* for themselves. Give them the chance, Reuben. They have a right to it! Really they have.'

'I don't agree with what you say about inshore fishing,' he said. 'We're going through a bad patch right now. We're having our ups and downs. But we always have bad patches, always have ups and downs. We'll pull through this time as we always have. But, lass, we're talking about the lads, not basically about fishing!'

'I don't agree, Reuben,' she said firmly. 'We can't talk about one without the other. What happens to fishing is what happens to the lads, if you put them into it as a way of life. If you give them an education, they can be their own masters. They can make up their own minds. They can go anywhere, do anything!'

He remembered that conversation. He remembered that night. It was the first time anyone had ever put a doubt into his mind about the essential correctness, the absolute unassailability, of being a Godson and an inshore fisherman. It was the first time anyone had ever made him take a step back from himself, and see himself as an *individual*, and not merely one link of a chain that went from generation to generation, fixed in time like the names were fixed on the living-room beam. Once he'd done that, the decision to send them to grammar school had not been a difficult one to take.

Now, as he looked across the table at both of them doing their homework, he was glad he'd made the decision the way he had. Every moment they could spare from schooling, they spent out in the boat with him, if they didn't have homework. Now that they weren't *committed* to becoming fishermen, they seemed to have developed a far greater enthusiasm for it. He could even see the effects of their education; when he talked to them about things, about the way of doing even simple things, they'd work out the reasons why, on mathematical and other principles. They'd tell him something he hadn't known, that a fisherman's instinctive knowledge of his craft is often based on a scientific reality which they, bless them, could understand. He'd never known *why*, for example, a pulley works. He'd known you get an easier pull if you take two loops round a wheel instead of one, but it had taken Wilfred, dammit, whose voice hadn't even broken at the time, to explain to him why you could lift a heavier weight, drag a heavier boat using a pulley than you could with a bare rope. The lads came with him every Saturday and Sunday when he went out. At first Emily had banned their coming out on a Sunday morning, but that was because Captain Walham had been having a go at her about sending them to Sunday school at the chapel. She and Reuben had never been either chapel or church-goers; one day, when the kids had asked her why *they* all had to go, if Reuben, Emily, Grannie Godson, Grannie Duckett and Auntie Eleanor didn't go, Emily had not been able to find a satisfactory answer. They'd never gone again.

Wilfred finished the work he was doing, closed his books, and rubbed his eyes.

'Tired, love?' Emily asked him, putting her arm round his shoulder.

'A bit!'

Arthur finished work and he too closed his books. Reuben finished his supper and Emily cleared the corner of the table and took away the white cloth, smoothing the chenille table spread before she went into the scullery to wash the few pots Reuben had used.

'Do *you* think there's going to be a war, Dad?' Wilfred asked.

Reuben liked these few minutes they sat round the table together in the evenings, before the lads went off to bed. Eliza and Anne would be sitting, either with Eleanor or with Hannah, probably both. John would already be in bed. Emily would finish the pots, then she too would come and sit with them, rarely speaking, content to listen to the 'men' talking.

'A war, lad? Whatever put that thought in your head?'

'Mr Brooks, our history master, has been telling us about the growth of National Socialism in Germany. The persecution of the Jews. According to him, this man Hitler is mad, but he seems to have a very big following.'

'It's not something I know anything about. Mr Brooks reckons there'll be a war, does he?'

'Yes. It seems we have treaties with various countries. If the Germans attack these countries, we'll have to help them. . . .'

'Seems wrong, somehow, doesn't it? That we have to go to war because of something that's none of our business happening thousands of miles away. I just don't understand it!'

'We can't be chauvinistic, Dad, not any more!'

'That's a new word. What does that mean?'

'I know that!' Arthur said, bursting with enthusiasm. 'It comes from a man called Chauvin. A leader of the French Revolution! He was very narrow-minded. . . .'

'So,' Reuben said with mock offence, 'you're saying I take after this Chauvin fellah, eh? That I'm very narrow-minded!'

'No, Dad, that's not what I'm saying. It means that we can't take a narrow view of politics. That what happens to one country can affect what happens to another. In a way, it's like fishing. When the Russians bring their catch into Britain, it depresses the price of fish here. The reason they bring it in here is because they've got too much where they live. . . .'

'The world's getting to be a very small place, Wilfred. By the time you and Arthur are my age, it'll have shrunk down to the size of Yorkshire! Folks are already going by aeroplane to America, they tell me. Not that you'd ever get me up in the air in one of them things! I like to have my feet planted on the ground. . . .'

'Else in a boat,' Wilfred said smiling. 'I reckon an aeroplane is probably about as safe, or as dangerous, as a boat, when you come to think about it!'

Emily had finished in the scullery. 'Look at that clock, the pair of you,' she said. 'You won't want to get up in the morning. Off you go and have your wash and get yourselves up to bed! And put them books in your satchel, ready for the morning!'

She sat on the sofa by the fire when they'd gone. Reuben sat in his chair, thinking about the Clegg and Brawnham boys. 'They're going away from us, Emily,' he said with ill-disguised regret in his voice. 'All the young 'uns are going away!'

He told her about the Brawnham and the Clegg boys coming into the pub, and how he'd sent them to say a proper goodbye to their parents. Emily, in common with every other adult in Old Quaytown, had known about the boys enlisting in the navy, though until Wilfred had spoken that evening Reuben hadn't realized there was an actual danger of war breaking out again.

'Our lads would never do that,' Emily said to reassure him. 'Our two would never enlist and walk out of the house without saying goodbye!'

He was silent for a long moment, looking into the flames. 'They've already left,' he said, 'or as good as! You've got to realize that all this learning they're getting is putting a distance between them and us, a distance that'll never be covered. They've gone too far already. Had you ever heard of this fellah Chauvin? I never had! And the digestive system of a frog?'

'Aye, I'm already proud of them,' she said. 'Fancy a lad of ours getting his matriculation. And now going on for his Higher! Who'd ever have believed it? Happen he'll go on, to the University?'

'He's got to get his Higher first!'

'According to his reports, he'll have no difficulty about that. Nor our Arthur neither! If I could only get the lasses to put their minds to it, the way the lads are doing!'

Reuben came and sat on the sofa beside her and put his arm round her waist. At thirty-seven, her figure had thickened with the childbearing, but she was still a handsome woman, still capable of stirring him, though at this moment his mind was on other things. 'Emily,' he said. 'There's one thing you're going to have to put your mind to. If what Wilfred was saying is right, there'll be no talk about university for either one of them. Wilfred will be seventeen next year, eighteen the year after. If there's a war, the way he was saying tonight, they'll be looking for him to go. . . .'

'Nay, he'll be able to stay out, as a fisherman. . . !'

'He's *not* a fisherman, Emily. He's a student, not a fisherman. They'll be looking for all the men they can get, you mark my words. One year they'll have him, the next year it'll be Arthur. Aye, and if they get short, they'll be taking me. . . .'

'You!' She turned her panicked face towards him. 'Nay, they won't have you, Reuben. *You're* a fisherman! And you're too old, surely, you're too old!'

He shook his head. 'We mustn't kid ourselves, lass,' he said gravely. 'I'm just the age my dad was, when they started that last lot. You remember, the war to end all wars, that one was. . . .'

'I could stay, Hester, if you'd like me to,' Ellie Dowsett said, but Hester shook her head. The last thing she wanted was to be bothered by a socialite chatterer at a moment like this.

'No, really, Ellie, I'll be all right!' she said. 'You'd better get along, or Walter will be wondering where you are.'

Ellie pouted. 'He won't know I've gone out,' she said. 'He'll be in the billiard room with Thomas and Chauncy. If he's not already been put to bed by the butler, blind drunk!' Ellie paused, pulling on her gloves. Only daughter of the ship-building Lundholmes of Middlesbrough, Ellie had been born into the North-Country world of privilege. Everyone thought it a perfect match when she married Walter Dowsett, the son of the largest coal-importing-exporting family, and they settled in the Manor at Towkser with its 250 acres. No one had known at the time that Walter, a heavy drinker since his late teens, was already impotent.

'You know, I envy you so much,' Ellie said. 'You have such a wonderful life here with your Mark Adam, and the girls!'

Hester saw the sorrow in Ellie's eyes. No wonder the woman chattered so and was active on every committee in the district! She put her hand on Ellie's arm, her sympathy aroused. 'It'll get better,' she said. 'Perhaps your Walter will settle down. . . .'

'It's already too late,' she said. 'I've been to see a gynaecologist in London. He tells me there's nothing wrong with *me*! Apparently, *I'm* ready and able to have a child at any time! And God, how I'm *willing*! Perhaps I ought to ask the butler to put *me* to bed one night!'

After Ellie had gone, Hester sat by the fire with the room lit only by one lamp. She preferred the soft light to the harsher glow of the electric. She picked up her sewing, but couldn't settle to it in the dim light. She couldn't get the image of Ellie, and her bitter words, out of her mind. She couldn't forget Ellie saying how much she envied Hester. It *was* strange how few of her young contemporaries, all of whom seemed to have made good marriages, were happy and at peace with the world, whereas she and Mark Adam seemed to have found a very suitable way together. She'd been shocked to realize a few months before that the ardour of their love seemed to have disappeared. Now that they had the children, they had settled into a steady way of being together, more like two friends than lovers. Hester had devoted her married life to running Tockett House correctly, to bringing up the girls and providing a stable home background for Mark Adam and his father. Deep down she still harboured a resentment of the old man and the way he had manipulated Mark Adam's and her life. When her own father had died she'd attended the funeral dry-eyed, remembering the way he'd sold her out.

There was a tap on the door and she called, 'Come in.' Binny entered, carrying the coal scuttle. 'I've come to make up the fire, ma'am,' she said.

'Binny! It's way past your time for stopping work!' Hester said.

'I've been doing a bit of sewing for Miss Felicity, ma'am,' Binny said.

'You should have finished and been up in your room an hour ago!' Hester said. She didn't hold with the practice of treating one's servants as if they were sub-human. Though she maintained an iron discipline in Tockett House, she recognized that each of the servants was a human being, each with individual rights and feelings.

'It's no trouble, ma'am,' Binny said. She crossed to the fire and used the tongs to place a few more pieces of coal among the flames. She set the full scuttle by the side of the hearth, swept the grate into the ashpan, and picked up the old scuttle, which still held a few lumps of coal. She stood upright with the old scuttle in

342

her hand. 'Can I make you a hot drink, ma'am?' she asked.

Hester shook her head, smiling.

'A drink perhaps? Glass of brandy's nice, they tell me, in the evenings.'

Again, Hester shook her head. 'Now you've very kindly mended the fire, you can go up to bed!' she said firmly. 'I shan't be wanting anything else.'

'Happen the doctor might need something, ma'am?' Binny said.

Hester rose, took Binny's arm and gently, but firmly, propelled her towards the door. 'I'm perfectly capable of pouring a glass of something for the doctor, if he needs anything,' she said. 'Now off you go to bed, this minute, and no arguments!'

But Binny hadn't yet finished. 'Oh, ma'am!' she said, tears forming in her eyes. 'We're all that *sorry*, really we are! How God . . . in His Heaven above. . . !' Choking with emotion, she turned and bolted for the door. 'How such a thing could happen to *you*, ma'am, of all people. . . .' The door closed behind her and Hester was left alone, at last, with her grief.

She'd tried, hadn't she, she asked herself, to do the best she could, always the best she could for her husband and her family. For the house and the servants. She'd been to church every Sunday and had prayed, had prayed so hard. She'd shepherded the girls with her and had taught them to pray for a long and *devoted* life. She'd gone down into Newquay Town, helping the old people, the sick. She'd ended the reign of separateness that had existed since the cottages had been built. Whenever anyone had a problem down there, she'd encouraged them to come to her, rather than go to the agent who interpreted his tasks with a curmudgeonly tight-fistedness he thought was a translation of the Tockett intention. She'd even clashed with Mark Adam – he'd shown her how uneconomic it would be to install inside lavatories and bathrooms with the small amount they received each week in rent. She'd argued passionately with him. 'You can't reduce people's lives to a question of *economics*, Mark Adam!' she'd declared.

She'd even enlisted Suddaby to add to her case. He'd pointed to the number of people who suffered from bronchitis because of the dampness of some of the cottages in that cold sea-misted climate, the incidence of pneumonia caused by people having to go out to the back during a cold night, and the haemorrhoids caused by sitting on ice-cold lavatory seats.

343

The old man, James Henry, had laughed coarsely at that. 'They ought to use a pot, the way any civilized person does!' he said. He was constantly amused by the fierce arguments of Hester, this firebrand he'd brought into Ravenswyke, this angel of mercy who'd taken over what had become the chore of his afternoon meetings. Her solutions were always pragmatic; if the villager could prove a case, he usually got what he wanted, though often, without Hester realizing it, the fancier trimmings of some of her wilder ideas were quietly pared away by her husband and the agent. When Hester had discovered that fact, she and Mark Adam had come close to having their biggest argument ever. 'Economics,' she'd said, raising her voice for the first time since he'd known her, 'is that *all* you can think about?' The old man had come to her in the sewing room where she was furiously working a treadle of one of the machines. 'You've got a wild streak in you, lass,' he'd said. 'I reckon you're going to have to learn to control it afore it does a mischief for you!'

She was not to be placated and treated him and Mark Adam with icy disdain for a couple of days, spending more and more time down in Newquay Town.

Now that some of the cottagers were more involved in the maintenance of their dwellings, Newquay Town had taken on a new aspect. The gardens were being planted, the surrounds of the houses were being cleaned. Now it was difficult to judge between those cottages that were estate-owned and rented, and those that Mark Adam had sold off to buyers from the West Riding. The whole place was losing its former surly aspect as if somebody, at last, cared.

Had it all been in vain? She was sick with worry and couldn't recall when she'd last had a good night's sleep. More and more her mind seemed to be occupied by demons that wouldn't give her any peace. Suddaby had prescribed medicine but it hadn't done any good. He'd given her iron and sulphur tonics, had warned her constantly she'd have to learn how to relax to get some rest, or she'd surely crack. But she couldn't rest, she couldn't relax.

Not when she had such gloomy forebodings about the future.

'It's good of you to come so late, Dr Suddaby,' Hester Tockett said as he was shown into the sitting room. He put his bag on the runner across the table, and opened it, taking out his stethoscope and clipping the ends round his neck.

'There's been no change?' he asked.

'None!'

'That new medicine hasn't brought up their temperatures?'

'No. The nurse took their temperatures about half an hour ago. They're still one degree below where you said they should be.'

'Is it all right for me to go up to see them?' he asked.

'Yes, of course.'

She led the way up the stairs, turning right on the first landing into what was grandly called the West Wing. Netta Lucinda and Elizabeth Jane, fourteen and thirteen years old respectively, each had bedrooms of their own, but Elizabeth Jane had been moved into Netta Lucinda's room to facilitate the nursing. The night nurse was sitting on a chair between the two beds, a piece of knitting in her hands, when they came in. She set the knitting down and stood up. Dr Suddaby took the wooden boards clipped to the foot of each bed and held them side by side. The temperatures matched; both were one degree lower than they should be. Damn, he thought. That new stuff he'd obtained from Switzerland was reported to have worked several times, as reported in *Lancet*. The cases had seemed identical to these. Why the devil hadn't it worked for these girls? He looked down at each of the girls in turn, noting the waxen complexions, the complete lack of colour. He was completely baffled as were Professor McIvry and Mr Taistow, the two consultants from whom he'd sought second and third opinions. He checked the heartbeat rate, the pulse flow. Both low, very low.

'You don't think they should go to hospital, Dr Suddaby?' Hester asked.

He could understand her question; of course she was worried. And, being worried, she would wonder if he were capable of doing the best for the two girls. He'd not waited before suggesting the two specialists come to give a second opinion; though he hadn't told Mrs Tockett, he personally was convinced the girls were dying – of what had historically been called the Tockett Curse. Pathologically he knew exactly what was happening within the girls, or rather, what was *not* happening. The girls were simply not making enough red corpuscles in their blood to replace the normal attrition of corpuscles that takes place in all of us all the time. As soon as he'd realized what was happening, he'd taken the girls into hospital and had given them a massive replacement blood transfusion, seeking to replace *all* their existing blood with new blood. It was the same treatment they tried for haemophiliacs, with varying success. Sometimes the infusion of new blood seemed to help or stimulate the production of healthy corpuscles which would clot adequately. At other times, the new blood made no difference; it would clot for a while, but when it became diluted by the haemophiliac's own produced blood, the clotting ability would gradually fade away. He had hoped that the massive transfusion would stimulate the production of additional red corpuscles, but that hadn't proved to be the case. Both the specialists had suggested methods of stimulating red corpuscle production – the professor by chemical means, the surgeon by surgical, replacing part of the thyroid gland. But, though they'd tried both over the six months since the girls had developed these symptoms, neither had worked.

He'd run parallel checks on their elder sister, Felicity Mildred, and had even used her as a source of blood for the transfusion. He'd taken blood from Hester Tockett herself and her female relations on the Gramond side.

And now he was baffled.

It seemed that the disease had come to both girls in their puberty. Netta Lucinda had been late starting periods, and Elizabeth Jane had been early. Both girls had started at approximately the same time. This often happened where two sisters were close together, almost as if the onset of periods could be controlled by psychological factors. In their case, the onset of periods had also brought about this attrition of the red corpuscle count. That wasn't totally surprising; when a young girl begins her periods, her whole body chemistry changes to prepare her for childbearing.

'We could try the transfusions, Mrs Tockett,' he suggested.

'With any hope of success?'

He drew the sheets back over the two girls' shoulders and turned from the bed. Mrs Tockett followed him from the sickroom and they went downstairs. She offered him a chair in the sitting room, and poured him a drink from the whisky decanter that had been placed on a side table. 'I won't lie to you, Mrs Tockett,' he said gravely when he'd taken a sip of his drink. 'I am completely baffled by this disease. Professor McIvry and Mr Taistow are the two leading experts in this country on diseases of the blood. One specializes, as you know, in surgery and is concerned with the flow of blood through the heart, the lungs, the liver and kidneys. The other, Professor McIvry, is the leading homoeopathic specialist. His field is the actual chemistry of the blood, the way it produces itself, its composition, its function as a solvent of the materials it carries round the body to nourish us. Both men are known in the widest possible field, both here and abroad. Both of them are as baffled as I am. I've shown them the notes Dr Gilchrist made in the past. Now, we could take the two girls down to hospital in London. We could try them in Switzerland. . . .'

'Then let's do that, Dr Suddaby. I need hardly say that money is no object!'

'I wasn't even thinking of money, Mrs Tockett. I was thinking of the girls. My own feeling is that we shouldn't do things just for the sake of it. We should try everything that has the slightest chance of succeeding, certainly, but only if it does have a chance. I would suggest that, for the moment, we restrict ourselves to trying transfusions again, though, this time, I'd like to suggest a change of method and source. Both Mr Mark Adam and Mr James Henry have survived this illness. They must have created an immunity within themselves. I suggest we try their blood. Perhaps we can pass that immunity to the two girls.'

'Oh yes, try it,' Hester said eagerly. 'Try it, by all means try it! And then, if it doesn't work, we'll send the girls to that place you were talking about in Germany, or Switzerland!'

He shook his head, looking graver than ever. 'I'm afraid that sending them to Germany, Mrs Tockett, would be out of the question. . . .'

'Why not? I'll go with them, put up somewhere locally, and visit them every day!'

'That wouldn't be possible, Mrs Tockett. We could hardly put the girls in hospital in Germany if we were fighting a war over there, could we?'

The snow that fell thick on the tops, cutting off the villages of the North Yorkshire moors, had come as no surprise. All January, the temperature had been dropping after a bitter Christmas and New Year. Folks had taken extra food and fire fuel into the farmhouses and when they woke to a thick white blanket one morning they settled back to sit it out. Farmers put extra wrappings round their leggings and walked out to look after their flocks of sheep, huddled against the snow breaks, waiting for the bales of hay that would keep them going for fodder until they could nibble the ground again.

The farmers' wives cleared paths from the house to the barns where the cattle lived, knowing they'd never get out the milk, but would have to churn it to butter, set some down for winter cheese.

The gentle breeze off the ocean had blown inshore and up the narrow streets of Old Quaytown, preventing the flakes from settling. No matter how heavy the fall might be on the tops, the streets of Ravenswyke, swept by that winter inshore wind, were always clear. The one-in-four was slippery and could be nego-tiated only with care. Gulls perched on the edges of the red pantile roofs, their beady eyes looking round constantly, surprised by the white snowflake flurries that penetrated everywhere. The sea itself was flattened, the swells long and oily with no wave tops, no cat's-paws in the breakers, just that long uneasy roll hated by all mariners but in particular those in small boats in intimate contact with the water. Like fishermen!

Reuben and Batty were sitting in the stern of the *Hope* eating thick jam sandwiches, drinking tea from the Thermos bottle Emily had given Reuben for his Christmas present. 'Lobster pots next week?' Batty said idly.

'If the weather keeps up like this, we may as well.'

'I'll come down tonight and work on 'em a bit, if you like?'

Reuben chuckled. 'Too late,' he said. 'The lads have done 'em. Can't keep their hands off 'em. Honest, I'm thinking of retiring!'

Batty stuffed the last of his sandwich into his mouth and then tried to speak with his mouth full. Reuben could just make out his words – 'The day you retire I'll. . . .' The rest of the sentence was lost in the splutter of jam and crumbs.

He was looking at the shoreline by the landing. 'I reckon it's high enough for us to go in,' he said. They'd taken twelve boxes of good fish; this cold weather tended to fetch a few of the bigger ones inshore and they'd had good luck. At the four shillings a stone they could expect, since not too many people were out, they'd do all right. Walter Clegg and Bill Brawnham were already heading back in; when their lads had left, the two of them had talked it out, then sold Bill Brawnham's more unwieldy boat, put a better engine in Walter's coble, the *Mathilda*, and had joined forces. Now, with less overhead to pay off, they both seemed to be prospering, though they had constant arguments. Two fishermen in one coble can be like two housewives in one kitchen!

Sam Foster hadn't come out today, Reuben noted. Sam was a lazy fisherman, always had been, and he didn't like coming out in the cold. Reuben was wearing three guernseys, two pairs of trousers, three pairs of socks. He had gloves and mittens, hanging on strings round his neck; from time to time, he'd shove his hands in them but no fisherman born can work in gloves.

'Batty,' he said, 'there's something I want to ask you.'

'Yes, Reuben?' Batty was putting away the remains of the snap; he'd taken a swig of the tea and was tucking the Thermos bottle into the canvas bag.

'You got any stones in the pocket of that overcoat of yours?'

'Stones?'

'You know what I mean. . . .'

'Aye, I reckon I do.'

'Well, you got any?'

Batty turned away from him, his ruddy face darkening. 'I reckon that's my business, Reuben,' he said gruffly. 'Are you going to take the *Hope* in, or shall I?'

'I will. You can catch t'line!'

They went in using the well-practised manoeuvre. Bill Clewson was waiting for them, as usual. They gave him a fish every day to work the winch for them when they came in on the high tide. As Reuben brought the *Hope* backwards towards the slip, Batty coiled the line ready to chuck it, standing beside Reuben at the stern. Reuben knew he could have reached out his hand and tapped Batty's overcoat pocket to see if he had any stones there; it was impossible to see anything in the bulky shapeless garment. But he couldn't bring himself to do that; it would have been an unwonted intrusion into Batty's privacy.

'Right,' he said, 'you can chuck it.'

The line flew high and true, and Bill Clewson caught it first time, bending it quickly through the loop on the towing hawser. Batty pulled the rope hand over hand, bringing the steel-wire hawser on board, and dropping the loop over the hook in the centre of the two stern lines. Bill had run back up the slip to the winch, winding the handle rapidly. When the towline was taut, Reuben cut the engine, unshipped the rudder, and the *Hope* went

349

smoothly over the sleepers, riding on the two fin-skids they'd reinforced with a copper strip.

There were half a dozen folk standing on the landing, despite the weather and the flurry of snowflakes; it was the work of a few minutes to manhandle the *Hope* sideways to park it on the flat bit of the dock beside the Raven.

Batty went up the road behind the dock to bring down the truck; they loaded the fish boxes, stacking them up at the front. Reuben had wrapped a fat sole in a piece of newspaper, and handed it to Bill Clewson. 'You'll wait for Cleggy?' he asked Batty.

'Aye. You going on home?'

'No, my blood's that cold. I'm going in the tap to get a rum.'

A man wearing a navy-blue pea-jacket had detached himself from the crowd of spectators and was hovering near them as they spoke. Neither took any heed of him; lots of people, finding fishermen colourful, love to eavesdrop on them. As Batty turned back to the *Hope*, the man came forward. 'Reuben Godson?' he asked.

'Aye, that's me?'

'Do you have a minute?'

Reuben looked at the man, assessing him. Clean-shaven, military bearing. Stiff collar, striped tie, the florid features of an outdoor man. Nearly as tall as Reuben himself, but something there, in the bearing. . . . 'Aye, I was just going in the Raven here, for a drink. Come on in if it's owt important!'

The man followed him in. Reuben ordered his rum, which Alf made for him with hot water, lemon and sugar, the way he liked it. The man ordered a half-pint of beer and tried to pay for Reuben's drink. 'We buy our own here!' Reuben said, though not unkindly, merely indicating quite clearly that he would retain his independence.

'As you wish,' the man said. Educated voice, but not county. A man used to giving orders and taking charge, Reuben would guess. When they were seated at the marble-topped cast-iron table near the fire, the man introduced himself.

'Liversedge, my name,' he said. Obviously not a man to waste words.

'You know mine is Godson.'

'Yes!' Liversedge took a long pull of his beer, watching Reuben take a gulp of his rum, obviously not wanting to start the con-

350

versation until Reuben had refreshed himself. He waited while Reuben held his hands out to the fire, then rubbed them together.

'Right!' What did you want to talk to me about?' Reuben asked, settling back in the carver chair.

'Chief Petty Officer Liversedge, Royal Navy, retired. . . .'

'I see. I had you down as a navy man!'

'Well, I was retired. Now they've brought me back.'

'And that's why you're here?'

'Yes. How closely do you keep in touch with what's going on in Europe, Mr Godson?' Liversedge asked conversationally.

'My lad's studying history at school. He tells me what I need to know. He says there's going to be a war, but the last paper I saw said that it'll all blow over. The paper seemed to indicate this Hitler is all wind and piss, if you'll pardon the expression.'

'Winston Churchill doesn't think so. . . .'

'Ah, yes, and who might he be? It's not a name I've ever heard. . . .'

'Some of us think he's a man to be listened to.'

'And he thinks there's going to be a war?'

'Yes, and a few more like him. That's why the Royal Navy is calling a few chaps like me back. To start a recruitment drive. I'd like to see you in the Royal Naval Voluntary Reserve. You're a sailor with a vast experience of handling small boats. We might need a lot of chaps like you in a hurry. If you were in the Voluntary Reserve, it'd be that much easier to mobilize you in the event of war!'

Reuben finished his rum. Liversedge beckoned towards the glass, offering to buy another one, but Reuben shook his head. 'I'm not a drinking man, Mr Liversedge,' he said, smiling. 'That one has warmed me up nicely! The fact that you're here in civilian clothes would mean you're not doing this exactly officially, would that be right?'

Now it was Liversedge's turn to smile. 'I can see not much gets past you, Mr Godson. No, as yet, it isn't official. But the man I work for . . .'

'. . . no names, no pack drill, eh?'

'Something like that. The man I work for, and the man *he* works for who is a rear admiral, is convinced that it will be made official, eventually. He wants to sort out a few people who'll *volunteer* for the Naval Reserve, know what I mean?'

'He's jumping the gun a bit, eh?'

'Call it looking beyond his nose. Being a bit more far-sighted than the chaps down in the Admiralty and the Government.'

'What is it you see me doing, if I join this *Voluntary* Reserve?'

'It'd take you one or two days a week, no more. We'd pay all your travel expenses, of course, for you to come to Middlesbrough. We have a school up there in a converted destroyer. The first thing the Germans will do in the event of war will be to sow mines in the North Sea and the Channel. You'd be learning how to sweep them, how to get rid of them. It'd be a vital job in the event of war.'

Reuben remembered being a boy of sixteen, sailing the *Hope* on his own. He could remember the daily terror he'd had, fishing off the coast, knowing there were mines about. So many fishermen had been blown out of the water that the authorities had tried to ban the fishermen going out. He remembered the submarines, and the way they'd destroyed the boat called the *Edith Cavell*.

'They'd mobilize the trawlers again, to sweep the mines?'

'They'd have to. But they'd need a few men on board who knew what they were doing. We've reason to believe the mines the Germans would lay this time would be a lot improved on the ones they used before. The new mines would be so sensitive you wouldn't need to *hit* them! Just to drift near them would be enough!'

'My dad was a fisherman,' Reuben said. 'But he joined the army.'

'That'd be a waste. You have a vast experience of the sea.'

'I have an experience of fishing, that's all you can say!'

'You know the tides, you know these coastal waters. And, I'm told, you're a natural leader of men....'

'Somebody's been pulling your leg....'

'I don't think so. I'd hope that if you joined the Voluntary Reserve you would help us by getting the rest of the fishermen to join it, too. I can't see you staying as an able seaman for long. If you could get the rest of the fishermen to join, we'd be making you a petty officer before you knew it!'

Reuben laughed. 'You're trying to bribe me,' he said. 'Offering me a carrot! But where's the stick? A carrot always has a stick behind it....'

Liversedge spread his hands on the side of the table. 'This time, when the war starts – and, believe me, it's not just wardroom talk; some of us truly believe we'll be at war with Germany this year – the Government will have to vote for some kind of compulsory service. They won't be able to rely on volunteers. There'll be conscription. If that happens, they'll be able to draft you into whatever service they like. You could wind up being an infantryman, carrying a pack into the front line. If you join the Royal Naval Voluntary Reserve, you'll be sure of a place in the navy, doing what you know best, sailing a boat! Think about it, Mr Godson, I urge you. I'm not going to try to put any pressure on you. I'm not going to make any false promises, either.' He reached inside his top pocket and took out a pasteboard card. 'That's where you'll find me,' he said. 'I'd like you to think about what I've said, and either drop me a line or give me a ring on the telephone. Now, are you sure you won't have another drink, to warm your bones?'

Reuben shook his head. 'If I ring you on the telephone, or drop you a card, you can buy me a drink then,' he said.

Wilfred Godson took his examinations for Higher School Certificate in the late spring of 1939. He passed in biology, chemistry, mathematics and English. He was seventeen and a half years of age. He applied for, and was granted, a place at Leeds University to study for a Bachelor of Science Honours Degree in biology. The West Riding County Council offered him a scholarship for the four-year degree course, and the University accepted him in the Devonshire Hall of Residence. He was six feet tall, weighed thirteen stones, had black hair, just like his father. Reuben took him into Whitby and ordered a tailor-made suit from the same firm which had sold Reuben his only suit, all those years ago. The same man was still in the shop and remembered Reuben.

Arthur Godson was sixteen and a half years of age. He'd passed his Matriculation, with two distinctions and six credits, and now was halfway through his Higher course. He also was studying biology. His hair was as black as Wilfred's.

Eliza Godson was fifteen and a half, and had left school the previous summer. She had taken over from Eleanor as librarian of the Ravenswyke Free Lending Library, to which, since the bequest of Dr Gilchrist, over a thousand volumes had been added by various benefactors in the village. She had blond hair, and a temper!

Anne Godson was fourteen and praying for the summer to arrive so that she, too, could leave school. Her principal interest was in knitting, and already she had developed a bit of a local name for her guernseys, which she knitted in the traditional Ravenswyke pattern. Mrs Humble had sold a couple of the guernseys in her shop, and had offered to take Anne as an apprentice when she left school. Anne had black hair, like her father, and a sweet equable temperament. Nothing ever seemed to ruffle her placid nature, not even the tantrums of her more volatile sister.

John, the baby of the family, was eager, but no amount of teaching was any help to him. He was consistently bottom of his class at the village school, though he tried very hard and often wept in tears of utter frustration when he couldn't learn something simple. Ever since the two older boys had proved to be so brilliant at school, John had felt himself overshadowed by them. He spent every spare moment of his time out on the boat with Reuben and had become a wonderful companion, the seagoing son Reuben had always wanted. Now Reuben had an ear for all the sea-lore he'd inherited from Silas and his brothers. There could be no doubt, Reuben often thought, looking at John, that the Godson line had skipped a few, throwing up the two oldest brothers and then settling down again with John. John was the link in the chain Reuben had always believed himself to be, a natural successor to his father, his grandfather and all the Godsons whose names had been inscribed on the beam for hundreds of years. More than anything else, John had the nose. They could be out on the water on a quiet day, ready to shoot the lines. Batty would be sitting on the thwart waiting for Reuben to decide. Reuben would keep an eye on John, sitting on the stern thwart, seemingly gazing aimlessly about. And then, suddenly, he'd see the look of interest on John's face, see him point himself, almost like a gundog, in one direction or the other. If Reuben followed John's nose, they very rarely came home with empty baskets! Batty had no sea-nose. They used to joke and say that Batty wouldn't know where there was a fish if it jumped out of the ocean and landed on his lap.

Eleanor had blossomed with her job at Thrummell and Slade, and now ran an office for them that included four typists. She wore very severe clothing, usually a black woollen suit over a white blouse, and a hat. She'd become a member of the Whitby

Philosophical Society, eventually taking on the job of Secretary. Now she spent two evenings a week in the Philosophical Hall conducting meetings, arranging for important speakers, or even musical performers. She'd become the centre of the cultural life of the district and, Reuben used to boast, probably the only person in the district who'd read *all* the volumes in the Ravenswyke Free Lending Library. Somehow, he believed, Eleanor and his two boys came from the same rogue Godson strain.

'I shan't be home tonight, Reuben,' Eleanor said one morning in May, as she set out for the train that would take her to the office.

'Night on the tiles, Eleanor?' Reuben said, joking as was his way, the only way in fact that he could communicate with his intellectual sister. She coloured as she always did; Eleanor went infrequently to listen to musical concerts given by groups in the towns of the West Riding, deciding whether or not to recommend to the committee of the Philosophical Society that they be invited to Whitby. It was a huge responsibility she took very seriously; so far, she had never picked wrongly and the people who'd come to perform had always maintained a high standard.

'Hardly! I'm going to Bradford to hear the Massenier Quartet. They're playing Vivaldi; we haven't had much Vivaldi and it would make such a change. But I shan't be able to get back tonight. I'll travel on the first train in the morning; I needn't go into the office until midday.'

'Tha knows thy own road best,' Reuben said, lapsing into the coarseness she so often provoked in him these days when she talked about her 'programme'. Who the hell was this Vivaldi? And the – what did she call them? – Massenier Quartet? He didn't ask her for an explanation, knowing he wouldn't understand what she said. 'You all right for brass?' he asked her, his standard question.

'Oh yes. The Philosophical Society always pays for me and Mr Clipstow.'

'Oh, tha's taking a fellah wi' thee, then?'

Really Eleanor coloured so easily. 'Not a *fellah*!' she said. 'Mr Clipstow is the Programme Secretary. He does all the negotiations. We feel it's better if a man, especially a trained accountant, discusses these matters of contracts, fees, travelling expenses with our artistes!'

355

'Well, tha watch thi'self,' Reuben said, his protective brotherly authority asserting itself, despite his complete trust of Eleanor.

The Massenier Quartet played in the Trade Hall in Bradford to a capacity audience. A programme consisting entirely of Vivaldi was daring, Eleanor felt, but there were so many opportunities for each member of the quartet to show his abilities, so many occasions when the musical verve of the players expressed itself so clearly to the audience, that the evening was a triumphal success. Eleanor was determined they should bring the quartet to Whitby.

'Oh, Mr Clipstow,' she said as they ate their sandwiches in the lounge of the Royal Hotel after the performance, 'we must have them. We simply must!'

He beckoned to the night waiter, who came slowly to their table. A man of at least sixty, to judge by appearances, he didn't appreciate too many people using the lounge last thing at night when he should have been sitting comfortably in the kitchen. 'We've had such a lovely evening,' Mr Clipstow said to him. 'We've been to listen to the Massenier Quartet!'

'Oh yes,' the waiter said, disguising as best he could the fact that he hadn't the faintest idea what the customer was talking about.

'Yes! Simply splendid. And I was wondering . . . it being such a lovely evening . . . a little something to celebrate . . . perhaps a half bottle of claret. . . .'

'Oh, Mr Clipstow,' Eleanor said. 'I'm not sure the Philosophical Society . . .'

'Nothing to do with the society, my dear!' Clipstow said in the full tide of enthusiasm. 'If I might be permitted. . . . It's been such a splendid evening. . . . I just thought . . . claret is such a celebratory wine. . . .'

'If you want wine,' the waiter said ponderously, 'it'll have to be in your room. I can't be serving wine here at this time of night. We'll have the whole town in here, asking for wine. . . .'

Eleanor's eyes sparkled; she thrived on overcoming opposition. As Secretary of the Philosophical Society, she'd triumphed many times over the stick-in-the-muds who'd thought that all music began and ended with the *Messiah* and brass bands, or a tenor singing to a piano accompaniment. 'Very well,' she said with determination. 'If the only way we can have claret is to drink it in your room, I suggest we go there *immediately*! Then our *friend* here can have the pleasure of climbing the stairs with it!'

Eleanor, though Clipstow would never have guessed it from her confident demeanor, was trembling with a fearful anticipation. It had not been by accident that she had suggested coming to the Massenier performance, and that he accompany her. She had come to enjoy her new, emancipated life enormously; she welcomed the freedom it gave to indulge herself in the pleasures of the mind and the senses. Often, when she heard an orchestra or a chamber music group playing, she derived a feeling from the sound so intense it was almost sexual. Of course, she couldn't speak about such things to *anyone*; no well-brought-up lady was supposed to have such feelings or, if she did have them, to *talk* about them. And she would so like to know someone sufficiently intimately to be able, at least, to hint about the way she felt, the way music affected her.

When she'd first met Mr Clipstow, she'd sensed the same sort of reaction emanating from him. They'd sat together several times, and often she'd wanted to take his hand and hold it during these moments of such extreme joy, especially since she felt he was responding to the beauty of the playing in the same way. But, of course, they couldn't sit in the concerts of the Philosophical Society actually *holding hands*. That would never do.

But perhaps away from Whitby, alone together in a hotel, might they not, perhaps, share something of that feeling? Might they not share an intimacy that was denied them in Whitby? Might they not, in fact, perhaps explore other areas of the senses? Find some deep spiritual and sensual communion with each other? The last time she'd known a man she'd been an immature girl. Terrie Pitt had appealed to her young romantic heart. She'd wanted to give him everything, to take anything he had to offer. His death, and the death of his brother, had so affected her she'd not wanted even to look at another man in that way. She knew now that as a young girl she'd been hopelessly immature, romantic. Now, she felt, she was *mature*. Now she had a mind to offer as well.

As well as what? she'd asked, trying to be honest with herself.

As well as her body!

But not coarsely, as when she was a young girl and she and

Terrie Pitt had made a crude fumbling love anywhere they could be alone. She remembered always the smell of the tarred ropes she'd lain on in the fish-shed behind the Pitt cottage, the evening she'd given Terrie her virginity.

Now she had the intellect and had acquired the good taste to make everything much more *refined*; yes, that was the word for it. *Refined*. With the properly delicate approach and sensitivity, who could know what heights of sensuality, and yes, perhaps, *passion*, she could explore with a man who felt as she did!

She had become convinced that, given the right opportunity and encouragement, perhaps Mr Clipstow, *dear* Mr Clipstow, could be that man!

With anticipation flooding her, she got up, clasped her bag, went up the stairs, turned right along the corridor. Clipstow fumbled the key into the lock, threw open the door. 'I'll leave it open,' he said, thinking of the proprieties. It took the waiter five minutes to arrive upstairs with a tray, two glasses and a full bottle of a Château Pontet-Canet 1934. He removed the cork from the bottle, poured two half-glasses without bothering to ask Mr Clipstow to taste it, and left the room, closing the door firmly behind him.

Clipstow raised his glass. 'To the Philosophical Society,' he said, 'and the most wonderful Secretary we've ever been privileged to have.'

Eleanor stopped her wine at her lips. 'Oh, Mr Clipstow,' she said, 'you mustn't say things like that. You really mustn't!' She was blushing again, and knew it, but somehow she didn't mind. She was in a state of euphoria. Who would have believed that she, Eleanor Godson, was standing in this hotel in Bradford, after loving every moment of a magical musical evening, being toasted in a French claret?

Who would have believed it of a Godson of Ravenswyke?

She drained her glass. It tasted like vinegar, but she knew that all wine, all alcohol, is an acquired taste and she wasn't going to spoil Mr Clipstow's, dear Mr Clipstow's, enjoyment by grimacing. Very well, if her new status in life demanded that she learn to taste and appreciate wine, she'd do that. Nobody was going to hold her back. She was quite determined that the finer things of a life of the mind and the newly awoken senses would be hers. New fields to conquer. New avenues to explore. New realms. 'Yes,' she said, when Mr Clipstow, dear Mr Clipstow, held the bottle to the rim of her glass. The second taste of the claret was much less tart, much less bitter.

'Oh, what a wonderful evening,' she said. She put her glass on the table, reaching into her handbag to take out the handkerchief with which to dab her lips.

Clipstow put his glass on the table next to hers. 'Oh, Eleanor!' he said. She looked at him, and saw that he appeared to be having difficulty breathing.

'Are you all right?' she asked.

She was quite unprepared, and in fact off balance, when he launched himself across the intervening space between them, his arms held wide apart, his face working as if he were about to have an epileptic fit. The momentum of his forward dash drove him into her and she felt herself falling backwards. She clutched his jacket to prevent herself falling, but it was too late. The side of his bed caught behind her knees and she felt herself falling spread-eagled across his counterpane. The weight of his body was on her; his mouth appeared to be seeking hers, wet with spittle. Where was the delicacy? The refinement she'd anticipated? Suddenly, all those memories of a man's embrace, the coarse crude nature of a man's sexual desires, the fumbling importuntings, returned to her. She twisted on the bed quick as an eel, swung her weight forward so that her shoulders were lifted. She regained her feet and staggered two paces across the room while he was trying to turn himself over. Terrified, she looked over her shoulder, saw him begin to approach her again, and seized the first thing that came to hand, the claret bottle, and crashed it down on his forehead. He stopped as if playing the game of statues; his eyes rolled upwards and then slowly he dropped like a felled tree on to the carpet at her feet.

She looked at the bottle, still held in her hand like an Indian club, the wine glugging out of it and running down the front of her skirt.

'Oh, Mr Clipstow,' she wailed, 'why couldn't you be *gentle*?'

She bent down and turned his shoulders round so that she could see his face. The bruise was already beginning to swell along his forehead, but the skin hadn't been broken. 'You beast,' she said, 'you drunken filthy beast!' She let his head fall back on to the carpet, picked herself up, stood the claret bottle back on the table and went out of the room, down the corridor, to her own bedroom.

She slept beneath the counterpane, still fully dressed, until the maid knocked on the door with the early morning tea she had ordered.

Mr Clipstow resigned from the Philosophical Society and his place as Programme Secretary was taken by Mrs Hapgood, head-mistress of the local girls' school.

The bedside lights had been dimmed so low that the night nurse couldn't see to knit. She sat between the two beds, alternately looking one way or the other, to make certain her two charges were still breathing. She looked at the watch she kept pinned to her uniform on a chain; two minutes to ten o'clock. Mrs Tockett would be here in a moment to relieve her while she went down to the kitchen for her supper, a welcome half-hour in the light. Nurses know when a job is coming to an end; she didn't think this one, pleasant though it had been, would last much longer. She stood up and tidied the two beds, drawing the sheet tightly and tucking it in, smoothing the girls' hair on the pillows. Really, they had been two ideal patients; she'd be sorry to leave them.

The door opened and a shaft of light from the landing fell softly across the room. She went to the door where Mrs Tockett was standing, her eyes adjusting to the gloom.

'They're fast asleep, ma'am,' she said. 'I've taken their tem-peratures and pulse rate; there's nothing to be done. I'll be back at half-past ten.'

'Thank you, nurse,' Hester Tockett said.

The nurse looked at her. 'If you don't mind me saying so, ma'am, it's time you had a bit of rest yourself. . . .'

Hester passed her hand wearily across her forehead. 'I'll be all right,' she said. 'When my husband gets back, I'll be able to rest.'

The nurse nodded and left the room. Really, she thought, as she walked along the West Wing corridor, Mrs Tockett was killing herself with work and worry. All the time the girls had been in hospital having their transfusions, she'd been in and out of Whitby, running the house, supervising the servants, trotting off to the hospital. If she didn't get some rest soon, she'd crack up. Already her eyes, the nurse had noticed, had a wild look, as if thoughts pressed heavily behind them, refusing her peace.

360

Hester stood between the two beds, looking down at her daughters. She could hardly tell they were breathing, so immobile were they. Dr Suddaby had said they'd have to wait, to see if the immunity had developed from the blood Mark Adam had given the two girls. It hadn't been possible to take any from James Henry at his advanced age, though he'd offered. Now Mark Adam had had to go away to London on pressing business matters, and Hester had never felt so alone in her life, so hemmed in by events, so helpless.

She turned and sat on the chair, but almost immediately got up again, unable to remain seated. She walked to the window and drew the curtain back so that she could see out over the bay to where the water gleamed like silver. The weather during this summer of 1939 had been wonderful but she had seen so little of it. All summer long she seemed to have been hastening from one place to the other, seeing all the specialists and consultants they had asked Dr Suddaby to find, exploring every avenue. All had the same negative answer – no one knew why the girls were not making red blood corpuscles, why their bodies were slowly fading. Now the two girls' skin was almost transparent, like the covering of a pale pink pearl. They were rarely conscious but, in their few moments, they looked at Hester in complete listless apathy, as if surprised to find themselves still alive. A sob broke from her. What would she do, oh what would she do, if her two beloved daughters should die? Hester had loved all her children with a fierce passion. To be married to someone like Mark Adam, who'd been a wonderful husband to her, and to produce a family, had been her sole ambition for as long as she could remember. Since she'd had the children she'd devoted herself to them absolutely, a fierce tigress in their defence, a proud doting mother in their praise, a strict disciplinarian in their interests.

She thought she heard a slight movement from one of the beds, turned, and went quickly across the room. Yes, Netta Lucinda had moved, had turned partly on her side and had arched her back, exposing the long length of her throat. Her eyes were open but sightless. Hester bent low, her ear next to Netta Lucinda's mouth, trying to hear the sound of breathing. She reached her hand into the bed down the neckline of Netta Lucinda's nightgown, laying her fingers gently on the girl's chest. She could feel no heartbeat, none whatsoever.

She reached in panic for the girl's wrist, and tried to find a pulse. The girl's arm felt lifeless, without any mobility or resistance of its own.

Hester knew suddenly, in a fierce blinding flash of despair, that Netta Lucinda had died.

Her first instinct was to rush from the room and call for the night nurse; she realized that she could pull the cord beside the bed and the night nurse would hear the bell jangle in the kitchen. She did neither. She reached into the bed and straightened her daughter's lifeless body, pulling the sheets up round her throat, arranging her hair on each side of the bed on her pillow.

Ten minutes later, Elizabeth Jane made the same sounds, and then she died, in the same manner as her sister.

When the nurse reappeared after her supper and entered the bedroom, she saw the two girls lying peacefully in bed, but there was no sign of Mrs Tockett. She rushed across to the beds and looked down at her two patients. They looked the same as they had for the past two days since they'd returned home from the hospital. Then, suspicious, she put her hand beneath the sheets and reached for Netta Lucinda's wrist. The body temperature told her all she needed to know, even before she started to search in vain for the girl's pulse.

Hester Tockett was out of her mind with grief. She stalked along the West Wing past the principal staircase. Her hair flowed grey-brown behind her head; her eyes gleamed with a fierce light. At the end of the East Wing, she opened the large mahogany door and went into the principal bedroom. The first room was an annexe to the dressing room and bathroom; she turned right into the bedroom itself. James Henry Tockett slept with the curtains wide and a gentle breeze blew in through an opened window. She stood by the side of his large bed, looking down at him. He was fast asleep and the breath bubbled out through his lips. In sleep his features had relaxed and the skin covered his face like a skull. He slept without his teeth in, and his cheeks were sunken.

Hester's mind blazed with an incandescent anger. 'You,' she thought, 'you carried this Curse, this disease. You gave it to my girls, you poisoned their bodies and killed them.' She stood there, trembling with the force of her passionate rage, pulsing with anger. At that moment, Hester Tockett was possessed by her hatred for this man and the dreadful disease he carried in his body and had transmitted through the blood of his son to her darling daughters.

She crossed rapidly to the desk beneath the window where he sometimes sat to do his correspondence in the mornings. A brass-handled letter opener with a fine Solingen steel blade lay on the top of his blotter. She grabbed it and went back to the bed, then without hesitation slashed it again and again across the old man's throat. He opened his eyes and started to scream but only bubbles came from his throat where the blood gushed freely. He tried to lift his arms but had no strength in them. She was still slashing at his scrawny throat when his eyes glazed over. She turned purposefully from the bed, her blood lust not yet satisfied, her dreadful hunger for revenge not yet assuaged. The night-light on the far side of the bed was a large glass lamp, filled with methylated spirit, with a glass body through which the alcohol could be seen, and a large glass globe. She picked it up, holding it at shoulder height.

'You,' she shrieked, 'you! You did it!'

Then she threw the lamp across the bed full in his face. The fine cotton of the bed sheets caught alight, setting fire to the hanging drapes, and in an instant the whole top of the bed and the corpse within it were a mass of flames.

She stood there as the fire mounted, her mind already unhinged by the sorrow of the deaths of her daughters, feeling a pressure which, like the boiling interior of a volcano, had to erupt. She fell, inert, across the bed into the fury of the raging fire.

It was a bright clear day when they laid James Henry Tockett, Hester Tockett (née Gramond), Netta Lucinda and Elizabeth Jane Tockett to rest in the Tockett plot of the Ravenswyke Parish Church. It seemed that all the inhabitants of Old Quaytown, and all the original inhabitants of Newquay Town, had turned out to attend the funeral. Certainly there hadn't been a crowd in the church like it in living memory.

A tea had been arranged in the church hall, consisting of ham sandwiches with lettuce and cress, cheese sandwiches with chutney and pickle, and bakehouse buns. Mark Adam Tockett stood just inside the door as people arrived, with Felicity Mildred beside him. Felicity Mildred was wearing a pure white dress, with a black armband and a black ribbon in her hair. She hadn't cried once, not during the reception in the church hall. Her grandmother, Mrs

Gramond, aged eighty-six, sat in a chair clutching her ebony cane and, remarking the gleam in the young girl's eye, put it down to the fever of sorrow.

The bodies had been discovered by the nurse; she'd kept her head and had sent for the butler, knowing she could do nothing to put out the fire and realizing intuitively that the flames could, perhaps, perform a useful function.

Sergeant Neckridge had been the first 'official' into the partly burned-out room. Dr Suddaby had been the second. 'It would seem to me, doctor,' Sergeant Neckridge had said slowly and deliberately, 'that Mrs Tockett had the misfortune to knock over the lamp, accidental-like, and then, in trying to rescue the old man, was herself overcome by the smoke and fumes and gave her life in a brave attempt to save that of her father-in-law.'

'I can see nothing that conflicts with that opinion, sergeant,' Dr Suddaby had said. 'Is that the way you'll be writing your report?'

'Yes, I think so, doctor.'

'Good; then I'll write mine accordingly,' Dr Suddaby had said.

The coroner's inquest, held the following day, had found nothing to refute that 'eye-witness' evidence, and a verdict of accidental death had closed the matter so far as anyone but the nurse, the policeman and the doctor was concerned. Not even Mark Adam Tockett had been told the truth.

The crowd by the door had dissipated itself, and Mark Adam was standing upright and alone when Elsie Milner came in. She was wearing a black cloth coat over a black dress trimmed with white lace at the neckline and wrists.

When he saw her, the memories of his youth in Tockett House flooded back to him. She was a fine-looking woman at forty-three. In her shy smile was a recognition, a remembrance of things past. He recalled instantly the time he'd gone into his father's study and had found her bent over his father's desk with her skirts round her waist, his father's hand in her drawers. It had been his first sight of adult sexuality. Often in the intervening years he'd wondered if that sight had affected him, had made his flirtation with homosexuality inevitable.

'My father wronged you, Elsie Milner,' he said simply. 'I take it as a great act of kindness that you could forgive him to come to his funeral.'

She knew instantly what he was talking about. She glanced round; no one was within earshot. Felicity Mildred was standing next to her maternal grandmother's chair, being fed the corner of a sandwich. Most other people were helping themselves from the laden trays, plates and cake-stands. A funeral is a good excuse for a feast, the food acting as a safety valve to relieve tension.

She smiled sadly at him. 'Aye, it was a pity we were both so young, then,' she said, 'or I could have explained something that would have eased your mind. Instead, I reckon you must have been carrying all sorts of grievances in your mind for years after. There was no malice in your father,' she said, 'and he never wronged me, in my estimation! He was never sly, never false. He never made any threats, never held out any promises. He asked for what he wanted and, when there were no objections, he took it! Without greed, without *dirtiness*. I wish you and him could have been friends; I wish you could have seen the side of him that I saw. You might have respected him, the way I always have!'

He stood there, thinking deeply. 'Thank you for that, Elsie,' he finally said. 'Like you said, I wish we could have had this conversation a few years ago. It would have made a big difference. . . .'

Reuben Godson had dragged his old suit out of the back of the cupboard and Emily had done a fine job of sponging and pressing it for the funeral. Eleanor, Hannah, Emily and the children, stood beside him as he stepped forward to say goodbye to Mark Adam, who reached out his hand for Reuben to shake. 'It's you and me, now,' Mark Adam said, accepting the sovereignty of both of them. 'I shall be closing the Yard.'

'I thought you might be,' Reuben said. 'Happen it's time.'

'Perhaps you'd like to come up in a few days, and have that drink we didn't have time for?'

'I'd like that. Shall we say Tuesday? It'll be high tide at three; if I come at eleven?'

'I shall look forward to that.'

The first of August 1939 was a hot day in Ravenswyke, with the sun shining from a cloudless sky. Low tide was at eleven o'clock; by then the scaurs were covered with holidaymakers, many of whom had brought deck chairs with them and had spread blankets for picnics. Elsie Milner had added iced lollipops to her stock and all the morning she'd been run off her feet. Her takings that day were the highest they'd ever been.

Captain Walham came down at midday for a bag of mints. He was wearing grey Oxford bags, a shirt open at the neck and a linen coat. He'd made a cap by knotting the four corners of his handkerchief; she laughed happily when she saw it. 'Been in the garden,' he said. 'Forgot to take it off!' At ninety, she felt he was entitled to a little forgetfulness.

Wilfred Godson came in just after twelve. 'Can I have a packet of Players?' he asked.

She replied with her standard joke. 'Your dad know you're smoking, yet?'

He gave her his standard answer. 'They're not for me; they're for our John!'

She watched him go; he was a good-looking lad. Somebody would be having him, and soon enough at that. He looked just as Reuben had looked at his age, with a devilish self-confident twinkle to his eyes.

She'd added a tiny storeroom at the back of the kiosk and was in there, bringing out another box of chocolate bars, when the bell went again. She went back into the shop and saw Mark Adam Tockett. 'Felicity Mildred would like some more of those cinnamon toffees,' he said deferentially.

She reached for the jar, took it down, and weighed out a quarter-pound. A quarter-pound was what he'd bought the six times he'd been in recently. She screwed the neck of the bag into a twist, took a sheet of brown paper, wrapped the bag in it, and tied it with the blue-and-white-coloured string, the end of which hung from the tin on the wall. The first time she'd wrapped the toffees this way, she'd done it without realizing it, to delay his departure, sensing that he was shy but would like to engage her in conversation. She'd been right. He paid her for the toffees from the waistcoat pocket of his light grey suit, which bore black velvet cuffs and a black velvet collar as a sign, a token of mourning.

She gave him the change, carefully placing it on the counter next to the parcel. He took up both, then leaned forward and whispered conspiratorially. 'Same time this evening?'

She nodded without speaking, though the smile on her face told him all he wanted to know. For the first time in her life, Elsie Milner was in love.

366

Hannah was sixty-two years old on the first of August 1939, but they held no party. She was lying in bed, having difficulty breathing. Dr Suddaby came in to see her each day; after the second day he'd taken Reuben on one side. 'Do you want me to speak bluntly, Reuben?' he asked.

The two men had become friends since Dr Suddaby had taken over the practice, and Reuben had even learned to play chess. Sometimes they'd sit in the tap of the Raven for an hour or two of an evening, and recently Reuben had even started winning occasionally. 'Aye, I reckon that's t'best way,' he said.

'It's Hannah's heart. It's quite literally worn out. She's been having a flutter in it for a year or two now. . . .'

'She never said owt!'

'I know. She forbade me to mention it. If you asked, she told me to tell you she had indigestion. There are all sorts of new techniques in surgery these days. A lot of it is experimental, but they have had *some* successes. . . .'

'Have you mentioned it to her?'

'Yes.'

'And what does she say?'

Dr Suddaby gave a little mirthless laugh. 'I need hardly tell you what her reaction was. She said she didn't want to interfere with nature. If her body was worn out, so be it.'

'I can't go against her wishes,' Reuben said.

'I thought that's what you'd say. But I have to tell you, I don't think she'll last out the month!'

'Shall you tell our Eleanor? It'll be a blow to her. She and Mam have been very close this last couple of years.'

'Yes, I'll tell her!' He put out his hand, seeing the look on Reuben's face. 'Don't worry about Eleanor,' he said. 'In some ways, she's the strongest of the lot of you! She's certainly the most independent. She's managed to lock herself inside herself, if you see what I mean, so that nobody and nothing can get in there to hurt her. She'll take the death of her mother in her stride, more's the pity. It would do your sister a bit of good to learn how to cry!'

The crowds streamed off the beach that first of August as the tide started to come in and flood the scaurs. One by one the sandcastles were inundated, their paper flags on sticks the only trace of their existence, until they too were swept away. The café that Bill Clewson's wife had opened, in the ground floor of the house at the foot of the one-in-four, was soon choked with people wanting a pot of tea, sandwiches and buns. The old bakehouse, which had extended itself across the river that ran down into the Cut, by the old post-bridge, was full; Dobby's cream cakes were the best in the district.

Reuben, with Wilfred and Arthur, had to push his way through the crowds to get to the dock. 'Look, Mam, the fishermen!' children exclaimed, seeing them dressed in their guernseys with their working smocks on top. The day might still be warm, but the night would be cold before the next high tide. Reuben hated coming down to the dock when the trippers were about – more and more charabancs were bringing people to the top of the bank of Ravenswyke and discharging them like a stream of ants down the road. Bill Brawnham was waiting at the dock, with Batty. Now that Walter Clegg was practically crippled with rheumatism, which some called 'the fisherman's complaint', and Reuben had his own lads to help him, Batty had gone with Bill Brawnham, who'd given him a share in the boat. Sam Foster was standing there; trust him to come out on a warm day like this. Tom Schofield was loading his baited line baskets into his boat. Reuben looked around. Four of them, the most they could muster these days! When he was a lad, there'd have been at least fifteen of them waiting to go off. The horses would have been champing at the bits, waiting for the pull. The womenfolk would all have been down, and the kids, to see the fleet away. Now a multitude of tourists and trippers clogged the streets, making it hard for them to get through with their baskets, and the comments would make them feel like men from Mars. 'Right, you lot, get back,' Reuben shouted, pushing a group of them away from the *Hope*. He ran his eye quickly round the boat. If you didn't watch out the buggers would climb aboard and mess about with the rigging. They'd even started losing things from boats as people from inland stole 'souvenirs'. 'Where the hell is Bill?' he asked angrily, as they heaved the *Hope* in line with the slip.

There was no sign of their erstwhile winchman. 'Missing again,' Reuben growled. 'Right, Arthur, into t'boat and stand by the engine. You, Wilfred, take the pole up in t'bow.' They set the *Hope* in line with the slip, then Reuben climbed aboard, put the winding handle into the diesel engine, fixed the rudder on the stern and the tiller handle into it. 'Right,' he said, 'give us a shove!'

The other fishermen pushed; the water was lapping limpidly at the top of the slip; the bows went in and lifted, the stern rumbled down the railway sleepers on the coppered skids. Bill Clewson was so often missing these days, too busy with his missis's shop, they'd stopped relying on him and often brought the boats in and took them out without the winch's help. The bow of the *Hope* slewed round but Wilfred was ready with the long pole, fending them off the wall of the Raven Hotel. As soon as the screw was submerged, Reuben wound the diesel handle vigorously and nodded to Arthur, who dropped the valve lifter. The engine started first thump, the rhythm steadily increasing as Reuben opened the throttle and the screw started to bite.

Arthur had the line ready coiled across his arm; Reuben took the *Hope* out of gear and they drifted slowly while the *Celeste* was readied on the slip. Arthur cast the line, Sam Foster's son caught it, and the *Hope* dragged the *Celeste* down the slipway. Thus the fleet was launched, one boat pulling the next one into the water, then casting off.

'Pity our John couldn't be out today,' Arthur said as they motored across the water of the bay.

'Somebody's got to stay at home, in case your Gran goes. . . .' Reuben growled, the bad humour caused by the presence of the trippers and the absence of Bill Clewson still not dissipated.

'The girls are all at home. . . .'

'Don't argue with me, lad! They need a man at home, a time like this! Just count your blessings it wasn't your turn! And go and give Wilfred a hand – I think he's taken up knitting!'

Wilfred was standing in the centre of the *Hope*, coiling the line that had been used to tow the *Celeste*. Arthur went to stand beside him. 'He's in a rotten temper,' he said softly. 'We can't tell him today!'

'We'll have to!' Wilfred said. 'But we can wait, see what the catch is like.'

It was one of those endless warm evenings; they worked steadily in the *Hope*, about a mile offshore, dropping the lines, waiting, picking them up again, in a pattern set before any of them was born, a timeless economic rhythm of minimum movement, minimum effort. Gradually, as the boys had anticipated, Reuben's good humour was restored. He was a man never totally at peace with himself on dry land; his natural habitat was the ocean, the ebb and flow of tidal water, the constant surging swell of waves and troughs following each other in inevitable motion. As the sun went down over the horizon, framing Tockett House in an aureole of blood-red light, the air was sharpened, and the houses of both sides of Ravenswyke were picked out with an astonishing clarity. The gulls wheeling overhead, high above the pantiled roofs, caught the last flickers of light, reflecting its glitter from their poised feathered wings in sparkling flashes of diamond. The grey and brown stone of the houses seemed to take on an inner luminosity, setting the jewels of each of the windows reflecting the sunset in silver and jade mountings of a natural, undesigned but incomparable beauty.

'Aye, it's a grand evening,' Reuben said, at peace with the world of his choice, knowing that the evenings of such contentment could come but rarely, sensing the disquiet that daily seemed to grow more tangible as the summer of 1939 drew on.

They hauled the last length of line; it carried a fish on every hook – cod and codling, pollack, a couple of chubby soles. They took the fish from the hooks, dropped them into the boxes laid ready, pre-sorting them. Reuben grunted with satisfaction, seeing the way Arthur dragged in the line, standing with his foot in the scuppers the way Reuben once had stood and now had taught his son, flicking the line deftly so that it lay ready coiled for baiting again without the unnecessary labour of uncoiling it to tease the hooks apart. Wilfred stood face to face with his brother, each part of a team. Wilfred held the gaff ready and didn't need telling when to dip it down, hook it into the gills of a big 'un, to help Arthur with the haul. More often than not, the gaff went down; the fish were a good size and they'd do well with them.

With the last fathom inboard, the lads came to the stern and sat down. Wilfred took out the snap bag, and handed round the sandwiches Emily had prepared. Now they had two Thermos bottles of tea, and even a wide-necked Thermos jar into which Emily had ladled hot soup. They'd save that for later during the cold night.

'I can remember when we had cold tea!' Reuben said as he blew the steam off the top of the liquid in the tin mug.

'Unless you hurry up and drink it, Dad, we shall be having it cold again!' Arthur said.

Reuben could sense something different about the lads, a mood of anticipation, a feeling of something to come. He thought he knew what it was, thought he had explained it to himself, when Wilfred took a crumpled packet of cigarettes from his pocket, and a box of matches. 'Here, would you like to try one of these, Dad?' Wilfred said, trying to appear nonchalant. Reuben took the packet and examined it as if he'd never seen a packet of cigarettes before. In truth his mind was scudding along the various paths of thought. All right, the lad wanted to show his dad he was grown up. Wanted to smoke a cigarette. What should Reuben say? He'd never smoked – never wanted to. He'd tried a pipe a couple of times but it had only made him feel sick. But Wilfred was growing up, and did Reuben, he asked himself, have the right to hold him back? Should he let go the parental line, give the boy a bit of slack to play with? Or should Reuben bring down a heavy fatherly hand? 'Players,' he said. 'What are they like?'

'Not bad,' Wilfred said. Reuben gave the packet back to him, and saw him hold it out to Arthur. Arthur took one and put it into the centre of his mouth.

'Tha smokes an' all?' Reuben asked, smiling. 'Next we know, tha'll be going out wi' t'lasses!'

'You're too late, Dad,' Wilfred said, sticking a cigarette into his face with a more practised movement. 'He's already doing a bit of courting!'

'Courting, eh? You young bugger! Well, I'll tell thee t'same thing my dad allus told me. Don't get t'lass into trouble, whoever she may be!'

They lit the cigarettes and the acrid smoke drifted across the boat. Reuben didn't mind; the three of them sat there in companionable silence, the two lads puffing away, Arthur obviously having difficulty preventing himself from coughing, blowing the smoke out of his mouth in an obviously unpractised way.

Soon, however, the companionable silence became oppressive. There was something, Reuben could sense, the lads wanted to say. And they were having trouble deciding how to say it. Well, let them stew over it; he was in no hurry and wasn't going to prompt them.

'Dad!' Wilfred said finally, after looking despairingly at Arthur

371

for a lead and not getting one, 'Arthur and me, we want to join up!'

There, it was out.

'Join up?'

'Yes. There's this scheme. If we get in now, we can go in as cadets. We'll have to go before various selection committees, but if they take us – if we pass – they'll train us as officers. The army *and* the navy have schemes. Even Arthur can do it on the strength of his Matriculation.'

'Officers, eh? All la-di-dah!'

Reuben, though he had never admitted it to himself, had been fearing this moment ever since he'd heard about the Clegg and Brawnham boys. How many times had he lain awake in bed next to Emily, unable to sleep for the thoughts pressing in on him? He could remember each of his brothers as if it were yesterday they had left home to 'join up'. And he could remember Hannah's face every time a telegram had come. He could remember Lewis, sitting in the stern of the *Hope* – the other boat – with him, and seeing the pain on Lewis's face, remembering what he'd said about Elsie Milner. 'You got any stones in your pockets, Wilfred?' he asked.

Wilfred shook his head, puzzled. Then he suddenly remembered the old tales. 'Oh, stones in my pockets. No. But I can swim, you see. I learned to swim in the baths.'

Arthur was looking at Reuben, the question still on his face. 'Can we go then, Dad?' he asked. 'If we're going to do it, we have to take the forms in tomorrow. They'll give us a first interview next week. We could be *in* the week after, if they accept us.'

'And what about your Higher? You'd chuck all that away?'

'No, Dad, I could start again when I came out.'

'And what about your degree, Wilfred?'

'I could take that again, Dad, when I came out.'

'I see you've thought it all out, eh? Made up your minds? Your mam has her heart set on you both getting a degree! Have you thought about that?'

'Yes, Dad, we have. But don't you see, if we go in under this scheme, we get a better chance of becoming officers. Surely Mam would be happier if we were *officers* than if we waited, and were taken in as soldiers or able seamen. You know there's going to be conscription. We'll all have to go.'

'You're so damned certain there's going to be a war, then?'

Wilfred looked thoughtful. 'I don't see how you can doubt it, Dad,' he said. 'Surely, we can't stand by and watch this man Hitler growing in strength from day to day. Somebody's got to stop him.'

'But why you? Surely, your place is here? Why volunteer? Why rush into something you know nothing about? If there is a war, there'll be a need for food, a need for fishermen. Even if they have this conscription you talk about, they won't take the fishermen. Somebody will have to stay behind to keep things going. . . ?' Wilfred couldn't answer him; of the two boys, he was the pragmatist, the logical practical realist.

Arthur looked at his father, saw the puzzled concern on his father's face. He reached out and put his hand on his father's knee. 'Whenever has a Godson waited to be told what to do, Dad?' he asked quietly. 'You made us, we are what you made us, Godsons. We've got to do it, because we are Godsons. You can understand that, Dad. Everything you've ever told us, everything you've ever said, about being a Godson of Ravenswyke, means that we have to go and do it as best we can. It means that we can't hang around and dodge our responsibilities!'

'It'll break your mother's heart,' Reuben said.

'Does that mean we can go?'

Reuben had already thought about what he'd say when the lads asked him this question; he'd puzzled over what answer he could give them. 'It means that Wilfred can go, with my blessing. So long as he makes me a promise that he'll finish his education when he comes back home again. . . .'

'And me, Dad? What about me?'

'You stay at home until you've taken your Higher. And then, you can go!'

He could see the disappointment on Arthur's face, but knew the lad would accept what he said. 'We'll do it one at a time,' Arthur said.

'Yes, lad, one at a time. That way, it'll soften the blow for your mam. And it'll mean, I hope, that you won't be caught like my brothers were caught, serving in the same unit, both being killed at the same time by the same mine!'

'We're not going to be daft enough to get ourselves killed, Dad,' Wilfred said.

Reuben put out his hand and ruffled Wilfred's hair. 'If you could know that, lad, know it for sure, you'd have the power in your hand to make your mam the happiest woman in the world!'

He reached down and picked up the starting handle. 'Look how far we've drifted,' he said. The two lads knew it was the end of the conversation. Wilfred gathered the remains of the snap and put it away. 'Right,' he said to Arthur, 'back to work. It's your turn to bait the lines.'

On 1 September 1939 the German army invaded Poland and a new word, *Blitzkrieg*, was born.

Elsie Milner locked her shop at five o'clock and walked up the bank to the top road, a heavy burden of decision and responsibility lying on her shoulders, though one could never have told it by the lightness of her step, the sparkle in her eye, the bloom of youth revisited on her cheeks. Elsie Milner was forty-three years of age, but she felt as if she were about to be born again.

Mark Adam had watched for her coming from the window of the room that had been his father's study. No messenger was ever awaited with such eager anticipation, such a mixture of hope and dread. He walked to the door and flung it open when he judged she would have come into the drive from the line of trees that had hid her for the last fifty yards of her approach. He clasped both her hands and drew her into the hall, closing the door behind her with a kick of his foot. She disengaged her hands, took off her coat, and placed it on the box of the hall-stand. Without vanity she patted her deep brown, lustrous hair into place, and they walked holding hands across the hall she had so often swept with a broom and into his study. A timid fire crackled in the hearth but the room still held the warmth of the day. He offered her a chair beside the fire; she sat down, her knees primly together, her skirt drawn down over them. Emma had done her work well all those years ago, and Elsie's travels in foreign lands were now paying dividends in her relaxed poise.

'Well,' he said. He was nervous; the decanter clanked against the glass on the tray and would have pushed it over had Elsie not quickly reached out her hand to steady it. He poured sherry for her and for himself. 'Well?'

'We should wait a year,' she said. 'They'll talk.'

'Damn them, let them talk!'

'You'll be dropped by local society!'

'Damn local society. Elsie, I want you. Now. Desperately!'

'I know you do, Mark Adam,' she said.

He fell clumsily on his knees beside her chair. 'What about it? Will you? I've been in agony all day!'

'So have I. What about Felicity Mildred? How would she take it?'

'She'll be going away, Elsie. I'm sending her to her mother's second cousins. They have a large house outside Philadelphia in America. They're quite prepared to look after her while the war is on.'

'And you, Mark Adam?'

'I heard this morning from my old company commander. He's colonel of the regiment now and happy to have me back. I was never dismissed, you know, never asked to resign officially. They just put me on the unpaid reserve. They can call me up any time. They will, too, when Chamberlain makes up his dithering mind to declare war. That's why I want us to be married right away. I don't care what anybody says or thinks. I don't want to leave until I'm married to you, and you're installed here in Tockett House. Look, Elsie, we've been over this ground before. I've held nothing back. You know my father picked Hester for me and we got on very well together. We were very close together, Elsie, and we had children together. I *thought* I was in love. I *thought* that what Hester and I knew together was perfection. Well, when she died and I met you again, I realized it was nothing of the kind. Hester and I were very good friends. We were compatible. We lived together, we slept together, we even made love and produced children together. But now I've met you, and I *love* you, and I simply can't find the words to tell you how different is this love from the feelings I had for Hester. It's as if I'm another man, starting out on a new life with a whole new set of feelings and emotions. Look at me this afternoon, actually counting the hours and the minutes until you would come, standing in the window looking for the first glimpse of you as you came along the road. I was always happy to see Hester when she came back from being away, but I can truthfully say I never stood in a window with my heart beating faster, because I knew she was coming. Oh, Elsie,' he said, 'can't you realize? I've been a man of business, a sophisticated man of affairs. I've taught myself to read balance sheets, to buy and sell, to invest. I've tried to be a good husband, a good son, a good father. But, suddenly, I read a poem and I say to myself, it's right, it's right, it's absolutely right! Oh, I know I'm a beginner in these things but suddenly I am beginning to feel again with my mind and my heart. Can you understand that, Elsie? And, Elsie, I want to go on exploring this new ground, these new feelings, because I love you, and I want you to marry me, just as soon as we can find someone to marry us. Now, please say, you will?'

'I will, Mark Adam,' she said, the joy shining unmistakably from her eyes. 'I will. And let's make it soon!'

Reuben was sitting by Hannah's bed, holding her pale wasted hand in his, when the boys came up the stairs and into the room.

'You're off, then?' Reuben asked quietly.

'Yes, Dad.'

'You said goodbye to your mam?'

'Yes!'

'Well, that's it, then. Just don't you forget, we've given you an education, so that means you'll have no excuses not to write. I want to see a letter drop through that letter box for your mam every week, understand?'

'Yes, Dad. There'll be a letter every week, we promise.'

'Just one more thing. If they make officers out of you, and they'll want their brains examining if they do, then remember where you come from, and don't go getting stuck up! If they give you other people under you to boss about, well, just remember they're human beings as well as you!'

'Yes, Dad. We'll remember!'

'Now come and say goodbye to your gran.'

Reuben stood up, then bent over the bed. 'They've come to say goodbye, Mam,' he said quietly, his mouth near her ear. He reached his arm behind her emaciated shoulders and raised her slightly on the pillow. She turned her head when the boys came forward to stand awkwardly by the bedside.

'Is that you, Lewis?' she said. 'Martyn? Off, are you? Well, be good lads!'

'It's Wilfred and Arthur, Mam,' Reuben said, knowing her mind was wandering again.

'Aye, Lewis and Martyn. Be good lads, else your dad'll skelp the pair of you,' she said, her voice quavering.

Arthur reached across, the tears in his eyes, and kissed her bony forehead. 'Goodbye, Gran,' he said. 'We'll write to you!'

'We'll write to you, Gran,' Wilfred said as he kissed her forehead.

'Aye, mek sure you write!' she said. 'Write a letter to your mam.'

Her head fell back on the pillow, exhausted by the effort of looking at them. Reuben and the two lads walked over to the door. 'They've said they'll give us leave,' Arthur said, 'so we can come back if anything happens.'

'Aye, well, Dr Suddaby says it could be any time. Apparently she's got the strength of a carthorse locked somewhere inside her. I'll send you a wire when it happens. Now, you all right for brass?'

'Yes, Dad, we're all right.'

Reuben put his arms round the shoulders of both his sons. 'Remember what your mam said,' he said, hugging them hard. 'The reason we're letting you both go together, well, that's your mam's idea. So that you'll both be together, to look after each other. Well, make sure you do, the pair of you.'

Their arms were round his waist; they stood together for a moment, too full of emotion to speak. Then Reuben disengaged his arms. 'You'd better be off,' he said briskly, 'else you'll be missing the train.'

He turned back to the bed, not wanting to see them go. He sat down and held Hannah's hand. 'You done your pots, Silas?' Hannah said sharply.

'Yes, Mam, they're all done.'

'I'll get up in a minute or two, go up to Fewster's, get us some brawn for tea.'

'Right, Mam, you do that,' he said.

He heard the outside door shut and then the soft footfall of the two pairs of shoes on the cobbles of the street. 'Oh, bloody hell!' he said quietly.

Hannah's eyes were closed. He drew the sheet up under her chin, smoothed her iron-grey hair on the pillow, thin and wispy but still soft as a girl's. She had fallen instantly asleep when the boys had gone, her mind doubtless roaming in the green pastures of her youth.

He got up quietly and walked across the bedroom. He looked back when he got to the door, then went outside, leaving the door partly open. The two girls were sitting in their room across the hall with the door open, a crayoning book open on their knees. Eliza at fifteen, Anne at fourteen, both lovely girls, Reuben knew. His mind flicked back – which one of them, he wondered, had Hannah looked like at that age? Which one shared the same temperament? Eliza with her quick up-and-down temper or the more placid Anne?

'How's Gran?' Eliza asked.

'Just the same. Listen out for me, will you?'

'Yes, we will, Dad,' Anne said. She would, too. Eliza, harumscarum, might let her attention be distracted, but not Anne.

Emily was washing pots when he went into the scullery. He came up behind her, seeing in the mirror behind the sink the tears that stained her face. He put his arms round her, his chin on her shoulder. 'You'll have John, and the girls, to keep you company,' he said softly.

'Aye, I suppose I will have to be grateful for that,' she said. He turned her round. 'Nay,' she said, 'my hands are all mucky.' He put his arms round her waist and his cheek alongside hers. 'I'll not see thee cry,' he said, 'even if thy hands is mucky!' He smiled at her, trying desperately to cheer her. He put out his tongue and licked it up her cheeks, saying 'miaeowww'. She managed a smile beneath the tears, and muttered, 'Tha's a clown, tha is. A right clown.'

He hugged her close. 'Happen I am,' he said. 'Tha ought to know. Tha married me!'

They both heard the outside door open and the clack of Eleanor's fast footsteps on the strip of wood before the carpet. Eleanor had taken to wearing high-heeled shoes, lipstick and powder. 'She doesn't want to admit it to herself,' Emily had said, with rare understanding. 'She doesn't want to admit to herself that she's put the world on one side. Even though she was married she's turned into an old maid, but she's not ready to admit it yet.' The words had not been meant unkindly.

'How's Mam?' Eleanor asked.

'The same. The lads have gone.'

'I know. I met them at the station. They got on the train I got off. I'd bought them each a present. A brush-and-comb set in a nice leather case. At least it will encourage them to comb their hair!'

Emily bit her lip and turned back into the scullery.

Eleanor poured herself a cup of tea from the pot that was always warm on the hob. She poured it into the cup she'd bought for herself when she bought her room furniture. It was high and had a fluted edge of gold, with panels on the side painted with scenes. Eleanor's cup! Tea, with lemon. No sugar. Reuben eyed it; the mixture, he thought, summed up his sister's attitude to life, to everything about her.

'I heard today,' he said, 'they were asking for ladies to learn to drive ambulances.'

'Oh, yes?' She didn't seem interested.

'Aye. They reckon they'll need volunteers.'

'Thrummell and Slade are going to be very busy. They're taking on a lot of legacy work just now. You know, you ought to think about drawing up a will. . . .'

'Nay, Eleanor, I'm not ready for t'grave yet,' he said.

'Mr Thrummell says you never can predict where lightning can strike next!'

'A right cheerful lad he is.'

'I saw Dr Suddaby in Whitby this lunchtime,' she said.

'Oh aye, and what did he have to say?'

Reuben knew the answer. He had seen Dr Suddaby on the dock that day.

'He says Mam can't last the night out.'

'Aye, well, that was what he told me. You didn't mention it to t'lads, I hope?'

'No, of course not.'

'If they'd missed the start of this course, it'd have held 'em back by three months. We shall write and tell them. I'll not send for them to come to t'funeral.'

'That's wisest, Reuben,' Eleanor said. 'Now I'll go up and sit with her.'

'Let me know if you want a bit of a rest. I'll come up and spell you.'

Eleanor looked across the room at him, her eyes colder than he'd ever seen them. 'I shall stay with her,' she said, 'until it's all over.' She came across the room and as she approached he watched the transformation that came over her face, saw her

379

features relax from the bitter old-maidish expression she seemed so often to wear these days, as if there was an unpleasant smell under her nose. For some time he'd suspected that his sister despised the world and everyone in it. 'Reuben,' she said, putting her arm round his waist. 'You've got to let me do this. You've got to let me stay with Mam now. Oh, Reuben, how can I explain it to you? You've always been so strong. You've always been the successor to our father, so reliable, dependable, strong. Emily has always been a successor to our mam. She's carried the Godson name properly, faithfully. She's given you, given the Godsons, a family, a continuation. And look at me. I've done nothing; I've been nothing. For years I wrapped myself in my own selfish misery; I even killed your son. . . .'

'That's all done and forgotten, Eleanor,' he said softly, 'all forgotten.'

'I've never forgotten it,' she said. 'I've never forgotten it for the simple reason that it shocked me into doing something with *myself*, by *myself*. I can't be a Godson, Reuben. I never could be. But, you know, though a man would never admit it, I do have my strength. It's not a strength you or Emily would understand. Because you're Godsons. You're carrying the Godson responsibility. Mam knew what I'm saying. It's been a link between us since I came out of hospital. She knows I can only be myself. Because she made me that way to be myself. She made the boys, she made you, Reuben, for the Godsons. She made me for myself. And now she's going and I'm strong enough that I want to be there with her to watch over her as she goes, to let her see me if she has any lucid moments, to let her know, in whatever life she's going into, that I've succeeded because she gave me the strength, these last few years, to succeed!'

Reuben couldn't understand exactly what Eleanor meant, but he could absorb the intensity of her purpose. 'Right, lass,' he said. 'If that's what you want. Just give us a call, will you, when it's all over. We shall be within earshot, all of us.'

She squeezed his hand, then took her filled teacup and went through the door to the bedroom stairs.

Reuben heard the knock on the door. He went across to the scullery. 'I think that's him,' he said. Emily quickly took off her pinny and dried her hands. Reuben went to the door and opened it. 'Come in, Mr Liversedge,' he said.

'Thanks for calling me on the phone,' Chief Petty Officer Liversedge said. He was wearing his full naval uniform. 'I've brought all the forms, Mr Godson,' he said, 'and your travel warrant to Middlesbrough.'

'You'll have a cup of tea?' Emily said. 'I've got one ready, on t'hob.'

The cawking gulls wheeled high overhead, swooping aimlessly but with great intention over the red pantiled roofs. It'd be light in ten minutes, another warm day. The dock was deserted, then slowly they assembled, one by one, sleep in their eyes, but a feeling of inevitability about them. They carried down their baited lines, making a roll call of the names of Old Quaytown whose echoes stretched back as far as the fifteenth century. Godson. Brawnham. Clegg, limping from rheumatism in the early morning but drawn irresistibly to the ocean at high tide. Foster. Schofield. Batty came down last, smoking a thick shag pipe.

They put their lines in their boats without speaking, stood a moment in contemplation of the sea, the morning clouds. They turned as one man to look at Tockett Top. No sign of a black cap, nor would be for a week or two.

They bent their backs beneath the *Hope of Ravenswyke*, practised heaves moving the boat smoothly across the railway sleepers at the top of the slip, where the high-tide waters lapped and spumed.

The *Celeste* came second.

One by one, the cobles took off, until Walter Clegg was the only man left on the dock side, shading his eyes against the dawn light as he watched them make for their chosen fishing grounds. Wars may come, wars may go, but men's bellies must be filled with food. And what better food than fish?

John Godson sat with his hand on the tiller, feeling six feet tall, but also frightened. It was the first time, the very first time, he'd taken out the *Hope* on his own. But, with his dad away to war, and his two brothers, somebody had to carry on the tradition, hadn't they. That was the Godson way, wasn't it?

OUTSTANDING WOMEN'S FICTION IN GRANADA PAPERBACKS

Mary E Pearce

Apple Tree Lean Down	85p	☐
Jack Mercybright	85p	☐
The Land Endures	85p	☐

Kathleen Winsor

Wanderers Eastward, Wanderers West *(Volume 1)*	95p	☐
Wanderers Eastward, Wanderers West *(Volume 2)*	95p	☐

Charlotte Paul

Phoenix Island	75p	☐
A Child is Missing	£1.25	☐
Wild Valley	£1.25	☐

M3481

OUTSTANDING WOMEN'S FICTION IN GRANADA PAPERBACKS

C L Skelton

Hardacre	£1.95	☐
The Maclarens	£1.25	☐
Sweethearts and Wives	£1.25	☐

Christina Savage

Love's Wildest Fires	£1.25	☐

Nicola Thorne

The Girls	85p	☐
In Love	95p	☐
A Woman Like Us	95p	☐

All these books are available to your local bookshop or newsagent, or can be ordered direct from the publisher. Just tick the titles you want and fill in the form below.

Name ....

Address ....

....

Write to Granada Cash Sales, PO Box 11, Falmouth, Cornwall TR10 9EN

Please enclose remittance to the value of the cover price plus:

UK : 40p for the first book, 18p for the second book plus 13p per copy for each additional book ordered to a maximum charge of £1.49.

BFPO and EIRE : 40p for the first book, 18p for the second book plus 13p per copy for the next 7 books, thereafter 7p per book.

OVERSEAS : 60p for the first book and 18p for each additional book.

Granada Publishing reserve the right to show new retail prices on covers, which may differ from those previously advertised in the text or elsewhere.

M5481